BALTIMORE
BLUES

BALTIMORE BLUES

Lee Moler

St. Martin's Press New York

Production Editor: David Stanford Burr

Design by Judy Dannecker

Library of Congress Cataloging-in-Publication Data

Moler, Lee.
    Baltimore blues / Lee Moler.
        p. cm.
    ISBN 0-312-05819-5
    I. Title.
    PS3563.O396B35   1991
    813'.54—dc20   90-28092
                                     CIP

First Edition: May 1991

10 9 8 7 6 5 4 3 2 1

Special thanks to:

Charlotte, a woman of seasons, a wife for all reasons.

Connie and Gordon Moler. My own children should have it so
good.

BALTIMORE
BLUES

1

I recommend summer as the best time to remake your life. The long humid days develop a slow river-rhythm which carries you along when your will runs dry. Night winds whisper past your ears in slow heartbeats out of the late-coming cobalt clouds. Summer is a personal kind of season that eases loneliness and softens danger. And remaking your life is both lonely and dangerous. It's like jumping into a new dimension where desire is the only light and determination the only rule. I know, because during a hot summer at the end of the decade I jumped, and almost hit the wall.

The morning it started I was feeling tired and a little mean from the Jack Daniels I'd drunk while sitting up all night in my car. I'd been following a working stiff named Walter Samski whose wife, a pile of mashed potatoes named Doris, suspected he was doing some horizontal moonlighting. I thought so too, but we were both wrong. When I followed him I found he was going to work, at night, at an electronics company called Armco where he was employed on the day shift. He would meet two other guys at midnight and they'd let themselves into the plant with a key and stay there until dawn.

I sat outside in my aging Toyota listening to the tape player drinking bourbon to cut the boredom, waiting. Usually, about 6:30 in the morning, the men would come out and Samski would go to a bar called The Point.

It was a joint on North Point Road, a four-lane highway built to carry traffic between Baltimore and the Bethlehem steel plant at Sparrow's point. Beth steel was running a night shift, and when steelworkers get off work they want beer. On North Point they get it, even at 5:00 A.M. Closer in toward the city are the topless joints where high-breasted, pale-skinned Polish girls shake the hell out of it at an hour when most people are punching the snooze buttons on their alarm clocks.

It was a Wednesday in August and The Point was packed with big-armed guys wearing tractor hats and drinking Buds with shots of bourbon or schnapps on the side. I had on jeans, a black T-shirt, and a tan windbreaker. Add to that ensemble the Caterpillar hat I'd bought in Ocean City the previous summer, and you have instant camouflage. I ordered a Bud and a shot of Jack black, then stared vacantly in Samski's direction.

He was putting a quarter in the juke box beside the shuffleboard machine. Bruce Springsteen came on singing "Born in the USA." I heard once that the Reagan people wanted to use the song in a campaign commercial, which only proves that old people are not able to understand the words to rock and roll. Bruce's lyric is about a vet with a brother who disappeared in Nam and a job that disappeared at home. None of that worries me though because vets are in style lately. Pretty soon we'll all be in beer commercials just like old jocks. Watching Samski nod his head to the beat, I was suddenly sure he was a Nam boy himself.

As he bent over the shuffleboard with an aimless liquidity, I could see he was about six feet tall with long legs and the whipcord body of someone used to making steady time over rough ground. Samski looked like any number of hillbilly coon hunters I'd seen in West Virginia; mountain men with hollow death mask faces and a scary way of replying "yeah" with a rising inflection to anything you might say to them, as though they're keeping score of a series of offenses.

Maybe it was just the whiskey glow of the place, but I was beginning to feel a certain camaraderie with the guy. There was a chance that we were not only veterans of the same psychotic episode in American history but were both West Virginians. After my second shot of Jack I was sure of it. He left the shuffleboard and sat alone at a table that had just been vacated by two bare-bellied schnapps drunks who said they were going to a topless place to see some "shaky pudding." Samski exhaled a blue plume of Marlboro smoke and tapped his beer can in time to the Willie Nelson tune now playing. I heard him mumbling the words to "On the Road Again" with a wistful air as I approached his table.

"Mr. Samski?"

"Yeah," he said with a rising inflection.

Definitely a West Virginian. "I bet you were in the Nam, weren't you?"

"Yeah." He looked at me with his hollow face like he was sighting a raccoon down the barrel of a shotgun.

"So was I."

"Yeah," he repeated. "That make us relatives or somethin'?"

"No, I don't think so. My name's Ransom, Lowell Ransom." I stuck out my hand. He looked at it like it was a fish he was thinking of throwing back, then took it listlessly.

"My name's Samski," he muttered. "I was just leavin'. You can have the table. Nice meetin' ya."

"I know."

"You know what?"

"I know your name's Samski."

He gave me the shotgun look again. "Yeah, how come you know that?"

"Your wife told me."

"You been talkin' to my wife?"

"Why don't you sit down a minute? You're going to be interested in this." He glanced toward the door, wondering if anything interested him more than going home and giving the wife a quick left hook. "I promise you," I said, holding up my right hand like I was being sworn in court. "You should hear what I have to say."

Samski turned into his chair and sat in one motion. I'd have to be a little careful with this guy, he could be quick. I sat across from him and pulled my chair back six inches to allow escape room if he came over the table for me.

"The reason I've been talking to your wife is that I'm a private detective and she hired me to follow you." His mouth dropped open as if he'd just swallowed a cue ball.

"Wha'?" he drawled, "she what?"

"She thinks you're shacking up with another woman."

"Doris? You're talkin' about Doris, my wife?"

"Yeah, Doris. She hired me to find out where you've been going three nights a week for the past six weeks."

His careful hunting-dog eyes took a frightened jump from my face to the bar and back again. "Didja tell her?"

It was the right question but the wrong voice. He meant to sound curious but he broke the *t* in the word tell like the hiccup in a country song. He was scared. "No," I answered after a pause, "I haven't told her anything yet. I wanted to talk to you first."

"Where in the hell did she get the money for that?" he wondered, more to himself than me. Then he said he needed another drink and I told him I'd buy. I skipped the whiskey this time because I wanted to be in control.

I made my way back through the crowd in front of the men's room with two Buds and a double shot of Seagrams. I plunked one of the Buds and the shot in front of him and slid into the seat. He downed half the whiskey, then followed it with a big pull of the beer. "Now, tell me this shit again," he said, lighting a cowboy, trying to get it to tell him what to think.

"Well, she couldn't help but notice that you were staying out all night three times a week; she hired me to find out who you were with. I've been following you the last five times you went out. I know you go to Armco with two other guys and stay inside until the morning, and then you come here before you go home. That's pretty much it, until now."

"That's pretty much it period," he said. Smoke came out his mouth as he spoke and made little mushroom clouds around his eyebrows.

"I don't know," I said carefully.

"What don't you know?"

"I don't know what you do in there all night."

"An' you ain't likely to find out any time soon."

"What am I supposed to tell your wife?"

"Tell her the damn truth, that's what the bitch paid you for." He popped the word bitch out with real pleasure. I could see the whiskey was starting to fire him up so I decided to just run with the wind for a few minutes. "Who were you with in Nam?" I asked.

"One seventy-third airborne brigade."

I gave a low whistle. "You all took a lot of casualties."

"Most fucked-up, hard-luck outfit in the whole goddamned war," he said bitterly. After downing the rest of his whiskey he said it again. "We couldn't fuckin' buy a break." His eyes drifted about twenty years and half a world away. It was a look I'd seen often in the mirror. "What the fuck," he said finally.

"What the fuck," I responded; the only fitting epitaph for a place that changed a generation of men from who they were to whoever they are. "I was with the Fifth Infantry division, up on the D," I said, establishing my credentials.

"Yeah," Samski replied flatly, his eyes returning to the present. "What'd you do?"

"LRRP."

"Lurp huh?" He got that wary look I'd seen so often from people who knew what it meant.

"Lurp huh?" he said again. "I ate lunch once in a lurp compound. It was high noon in that mess hall. About thirty of you guys sittin' around eatin', but there wasn't a sound in the place. Couldn't even hear the knives and forks clankin'. It was weird."

I thought back to all the lunches I'd eaten in LRRP compounds, and how they'd all seemed noisy to me. "That's the thing," I said. "You already know what everyone's thinking. You don't have to talk."

"No shit?"

"No shit."

"Well I'll be damned. That's somethin'. Why you even bother ta ask me what I do at the factory then? I mean you can probably just read my mind, can't you?"

"Now you're fucking with me," I said.

"Naw, just wonderin'."

Maybe he was sincere. His hollow mountain face had sunk so far into itself that it was all fissures and crevices. The real face was buried somewhere inside. "All right," I said, "let's try a little mind reading. I bet you're from West Virginia—somewhere around the Ohio or Kentucky border."

He got the cue ball expression again but recovered his coondog cool more quickly this time.

"Jeezus," he coughed through a Marlboro cloud. "I wouldn'a believed it."

"I'd like to let you believe it," I said. "But the reason I know you're from West Virginia is that I'm from there myself. There's something about the way a West-by-God Virginian talks that I can always tell." I thought that might draw him out; West Virginians have a kind of resentful togetherness. People assume you're a hillbilly and we're always at pains to show them that, one, we're not hillbillies or, two, we are hillbillies but to be a hillbilly is to know the secret of Gary Cooper's appeal.

"Where you from?" he asked.

"Elkins."

"College town," he said as if I'd told him I was wearing panty hose. "I'm from coal minin' country myself. Welch, right on the Kentucky border."

"Just like I said."

"Yep, just like you said."

He was a tiny bit impressed. I might be from a college town but I was a LRRP and I could read minds.

"Yeah, it's beginning to come back to me now."

"What is?" Samski asked.

"The way to read minds. I can tell something else about your mind."

"Yeah, what's that?"

He was trying to sound casual again.

"You're scared. When I asked you what you were doing in that factory you were scared. Isn't that right?" He leaned slowly back in his chair and took a big pull on his beer, then stretched his long legs out from the table and took his John Deere hat off and inspected it.

"Yeah, I'm scared," he said, pulling the hat back over his eyes.

"What of?" I asked, and he went through the hat routine again.

"I need me another drink."

"Man, you are scared."

"Everybody's scared," he said.

"Of what?"

The hound eyes flicked up at me for a second and then went back to the bottom of his glass. "Same things," he said with more care than I'd heard him use yet. "Bills, taxes, the unemployment line . . . dyin'."

"What about divorce?" I asked.

"What about it?" he said, tensing his shoulders over his drink.

"I'm on my second wife and I can tell you divorce is some heavy dues on your mind, and alimony . . . very heavy dues."

"That's one reason I ain't gettin' divorced," Samski said.

We were now about to get into dangerous territory.

Samski was working man lanky but had big forearms and powerful hands. I'd spent part of the last two years beating on the heavy bag in my basement so my five-foot-nine weighed a boxerly one-seventy, all ropey arms and sheet metal back. Still, Samski was tall. I pushed my chair back a couple more inches, put my hand casually into the pocket of my windbreaker, then gave him the bad news. "I got the idea that depends on whether she thinks you're hanging with another woman or not."

He repositioned his hat so his eyes were level with the brim and hissed a slow stream of smoke in my direction, not near enough to be a challenge but close enough to let me know he was serious. "Now just where," he said deliberately, "would she get an idea like that?"

"She already has the idea. That's why she hired me."

Samski stubbed out his Marlboro in a tin ashtray and leaned forward on his elbows; one elbow slipped in a puddle of beer. I was glad I'd left the whiskey to him. "But you're gonna tell her the truth . . . aren't ya?" He sounded part hopeful, part threatening.

"I don't know the truth, do I?" I said.

"You know all my wife or you needs to know."

"I've never been inside there. For all I know you guys are in there having orgies with the secretaries."

Samski was getting hot but staying under control which surprised me. He impressed me as someone with a temper. I could see perpetual anger in the hard line of his jaw.

"You know goddamn good and well there ain't no secretaries in there," he said between his teeth.

I decided to push it some more. "Now how do I know that?"

"Ever see any fuckin' secretaries?"

"I've never seen Alaska either but I believe it's there."

Samski leaned back in his chair. "So that's the way it is, huh?" he said almost to himself. Then he lifted the hat and looked me in the eye. "You'd do that shit?" he asked. "You'd say that shit even when you know it ain't true?"

I intended to say yes. I was now a PI with a new license and an old problem with my wife. I needed money. I smelled money and I was going to get it. I was going to say yes. I knew I was going to say yes.

"I don't know," I said. "I was going to tell you yes but I don't know. Like you said, we're all scared. We've all got problems. You and I have some of the same ones. I don't know if I can tell that big a lie. Probably not. I'm sure going to think about it, though."

"Suppose I told you I'd kick your ass right up between your ears?"

"Suppose I told you I had a blackjack in my pocket."

"I'd say I got a shotgun out in my car."

"I couldn't let you get that far then, could I?"

We were staring into each other's eyes like two guys arm-wrestling in a Stallone movie, except neither one of us thought we were Stallone. "I'll be a son of a bitch," Samski said wonderingly.

"Ain't life a bitch," I commiserated.

"Why?" he asked after lighting another smoke. "Why you wanna know so bad?"

I answered him with the truth. "I smell money."

A new look came over Samski's face, a pinched, calculating

look that seemed to make his nose longer and his eyes even narrower. It was the look of a West Virginia bookie setting the line on high school basketball as he stands behind the bar of his saloon. "Money, huh?" he said. "You ain't the only one who likes money."

"Is that right?"

"Yeah, how much money you talkin' about?"

"I don't know, but I can smell it."

"Lemme tell ya somethin'," he said. "I am scared. I'm scared of losin' my job an' I'm scared of somethin' else."

"What else?"

"I don't know. But them guys don't want it found out what they're doin' or they wouldn't be havin' it done in the middle of the night, now would they?"

I had thought until now that anyone dumb enough to marry Doris would be dumb about everything, but he wasn't. "You have to take chances to make money," I said.

"Mister, I take a chance on goin' crazy ever time I go in to that fuckin' job."

"So what are you saying to me?"

He fooled with the hat, getting the sweat band adjusted just right. "Well, I'll tell ya," he said. "If, like you say, we both got some of the same problems . . . seems like maybe we could work somethin' out, a kind of a, uh, trade, ya might say. About the money, I mean."

"Look," I said, "I've only been doing the investigator thing a little while. I'm kind of short, cash wise. I mean I might be able to get up a couple hundred, or maybe . . ."

"Fuck that," he cut in. "I ain't talkin' about no couple hunnerd. I mean a piece, a piece of whatever you get outta what Armco's doin'."

This guy was even more like a West Virginia bookie than I'd thought. "I don't even know for sure anything's there," I said.

"Just supposin' there is?"

That's when inspiration hit. "Well," I said, "that depends on if you were willing to do a couple things for your end."

"Just what would my end be?"

"That depends on what you have to do."

"No it don't."

If I said it did we were back where we started, and I was tired.

"All right, twenty percent."

"Fifty."

"Zero, and have a nice rest of your life in the factory."

"Thirty then."

"Twenty-five."

"How do I know you're gonna come through on your end?"

"I'll count it out for you."

"How'm I gonna know you ain't skimmed some off the top?"

"I don't know," I said honestly. "I'll make sure you're there when I get it, if I can. But I don't know how it's going to happen yet."

Samski crossed his legs, jiggled a foot, traced his initials on the wet tabletop, and then sucked happily on his cigarette. "How 'bout this?" he said, examining the Marlboro's ash. "If I ain't there when you get it, my piece goes up to forty percent. That'll give you a good reason ta make sure I'm there an' me a good reason not to care if I ain't." He looked at me with the satisfied squint of a man who's just made a two-rail bank shot to sink the eight ball.

What could I say? He was right. "No," I said.

"Fergit it then," he answered. "I'll take my chances with my problems. I do that every day anyhow."

"All right," I said, "it's a deal." We shook hands. "Now what is it you're doing?"

"Solderin'."

"So?"

"So that's it. I take two old circuits out of the boards and solder in two new ones, then I run a wire between the two new ones. They gotta be connected in exactly the same way as the old ones."

"That's it?"

"That's it. Borin' as hell, but they're payin' me thirty dollars an hour to do it."

I was beginning to believe I really could read minds. If they were willing to pay him thirty dollars an hour to solder circuit boards in the middle of the night there was definitely money involved, heavy money. "What kind of boards?"

"You know, circuit boards, like you got in your stereo and every other damn thing."

"What do they do, I mean, what are they for?"

"I don't know. Armco's just a sub-out business for Dynatron."

"Dynatron?"

"Yeah, it's a big outfit down around Washington that assembles systems for some other big outfit. That's the way it works. It all goes down the line. We just make circuit board assemblies. I put 'em together the way they tell me to. I don't give a shit what they're for."

"What do the other two guys do?"

"Same thing, only on different boards."

"Different boards?"

"Yeah, it's a fuckin' assembly. It fits together to make a box like."

"So what is it?"

"I tole you, I don't give a shit."

"Don't you read the plans?"

"Sure."

"Well what do they say?"

"They say circuit board number Z dash one double H dash T and shit like that is what they say."

I believed him. If Armco was going to pay people to solder through the night it stood to reason they were going to be pretty close to the vest about what they were soldering. But someone had to know. "Who's in charge?"

"Nobody, we all just go there and solder, ain't nobody in charge."

"No, I mean who gave you the job? Who told you to do it? Who pays you?"

"Art Fredericks. He's a wheel at Armco—the comptroller or somethin'. One day he asks me into his office at quittin' time, for a chat he calls it. That's the kind of shit them personnel weasels use when they're gettin' ready to slap your hands fer scratchin' your balls in front of the secretaries or somethin'. Except Fredericks ain't a personnel weasel, he's a wheel. So I don't know what the fuck's comin' off. He asks me would I like to make some easy money. I tell him that's my favorite kind. He tells me what I have to do and when, gives me a key, then he tells me if I say anything to anyone about it I'll get fired quicker'n an eagle can shit. That's it."

"How do you get paid?"

"That's the best part. I get paid cash. It don't show up on my pay stub and I don't pay no taxes."

"All right," I said, "that's it then. I'll be in touch."

"I 'spect you will since we got a deal."

"I will."

"One more thing," he said. "You're gonna take care of my wife, right? Even if we don't get no money."

"I'm gonna tell her you're as faithful as a hound dog but you have to take care of her yourself."

"Yeah," he said ruefully. "Don't I though?" and pulled the hat down over his eyes. "Would you of lied about me to her?" he asked from beneath the brim.

"I'd have thought about it," I said, and downed the last of my Bud. "Probably for years." As I walked toward the door the juke box was playing "Tumbling Dice" by the Rolling Stones. And they say modern life lacks irony.

2

The long night, the alcohol, and my tense conversation with Samski had induced a fatigue high that made me feel like a dream someone else was having. Driving blearily into the smog-red morning sun I could almost believe that the dreamer was my wife Arla. The day I told her about my new business she asked sarcastically what kind of detective drove a 1980 Toyota Corolla. I told her maybe Japanese detectives. She laughed and said I was insane. I disagreed and the argument repeated itself daily until she suggested it might be best if I left the house "until things work themselves out."

The trouble with Arla is that, like a lot of people from unhappy homes, she has a desperate belief in proper habits. . . . If you have the right habits things will be all right. My childhood was regular Norman Rockwell stuff and, like a lot of people from happy homes, I tend to believe that bad habits produce empathy with the less fortunate and promote the growth of individuality. Arla was sure I'd soon be getting my mail at a bus station toilet, but I loved her anyway. And she loved me. I knew because she kept finding excuses to see me, the latest being a request that I drop by and mow the lawn. I was going to ask her to pay me for it but then I got the case: a plump blonde named Doris Samski with a typical east Baltimore beehive hairdo. Doris complained that her husband had been disappearing three nights a week for the past six weeks.

"What do you mean disappearing?" I asked her.

"I mean he disappears," she said, stroking the Elvis tattoo on her upper arm and sucking a Marlboro like it was a Presley appendage.

"You don't mean he actually, uh, disappears?" I was sure she was going to tell me he was an alien from the planet Zircon.

"What the hell have I been sayin'?" she bawled. "He freakin' disappears. All night, a couple times a week. Get it? Jeez, you're as dense as a fuckin' car mechanic. A woman tells 'em the brakes are bad and they try an' sell her a set of tires."

"I'm sorry. I thought you were trying to tell me he, you know, disappeared."

"What're you, Captain Kirk? I wanna find out who my husband's shacking up with. Can you do it or not?"

"Sure, sure, I do it all the time. Where does he work?"

He worked at Armco, soldering secretly through the night, and now I had to decide what to do about it. I was desperate to show Arla that instinct can be practical. What she didn't understand was that there are things you can touch with your brain that your fingers will never know exist. But work long enough in a windowless fluorescent cubicle and your fingers will be all you have left. Still, the best way to show someone how practical you are is to make some cash, and there was no doubt about the pungent smell emanating from Walter Samski's secret job.

Money. It was a scent nurtured by nights in Nam spent looking at my rifle and speculating about how many were being made and how much each one cost. That led to thoughts of bullets and boots and the conclusion that a lot of people were making a lot of money on the war and I wasn't one of them. Since then I've tended to believe that the logical reason behind any illogical action is usually . . . almost always . . . money. For Armco to pay Samski for working a private night shift was highly illogical. It was an act that had the same smell as my rifle.

*   *   *

My office was a reassuring chrome and fake-fabric layout on the second story of the downtown building that housed the credit bureau. The place had been vacated by a bail bondsman whose murder-one client had been released on a two-hundred-thousand-dollar bite and then disappeared. Word had it that his former associates had treated the client to a skin diving vacation in the wet cement of the new USF&G building. The bail guy couldn't prove it though and had to pay the court the whole tab. Being a venture capitalist is a risky business.

I stumbled through the office door and collapsed on the convertible sofa, feeling even more depressed. The sofa was the only item of furniture I'd taken with me when I left my house. I missed that house and its family the way a dying fish misses water, but it was too early. Arla had given me an ultimatum when I told her about the detective business and she wasn't going to back down, not yet. Not until I showed her I could do it. And I was going to do it. I had to, because I could never go back to sitting in a cubicle under cancer lights like some mutating geranium. I couldn't live like that and I didn't want to live without Arla.

3

What the hell was Samski doing on his private night shifts? The question ran through my sleep like the thread of a dream. I rolled over and looked at my watch: one o'clock, A.M. or P.M.? Earth or Mars? The spot along my belly where Arla's curves used to sleep felt as empty as a piece of outer space. I bolted upright to escape the loneliness.

What the hell was he doing in there? That was the first thing I had to find out. Who knew? The comptroller. What did Samski say his name was? Fredericks, Art Fredericks. I made a cup of instant coffee and stared out the window. I wondered what Fredericks was assembling. Like history it was being made at night, which meant it was probably just as unethical, and the unethical only has one object: money. Illegal money is found money, isn't it? Sure it is.

I was starting to work up a healthy dislike for Art Fredericks and I hadn't even met him. A phrase from a song ran through my head: You can't get what you want unless you know what you want. Samski had said the thing fit together like a box. What kind of boxes did Armco make? If I knew what they made in the daytime it might give me a clue as to what they were unmaking at night. I spent the rest of the day in the library reading back issues of *Warfield* magazine. It was a slick paper rag that billed itself as "the best of Baltimore's business." Either Armco wasn't among that elite group or *Warfield's* hadn't gotten around to anointing them yet.

When I couldn't find out anything at the library I phoned the editorial offices and told an officious female voice that I was a grad student at Johns Hopkins doing my master's thesis on communications vectors as they relate to the calculus of trigonometric structure in the modern business matrix. She immediately handed me over to someone in a position of authority whom she probably hated. I made an appointment to see him the following morning.

I arrived at 8:50, wearing the one three-piece suit I owned. I'd had it made for me when Arla and I were married and it was expensive. Anything less and the *Warfield's* offices would have rejected it the way a body rejects transplanted organs.

Warfield's was like upstairs at Chase Manhattan: Carpeting that could be cut into coats and worn to the opera, air conditioning that could keep a salad fresh, secretaries as symmetrical and well painted as porcelain vases, and an air of hushed quiet as crisp and authoritative as newly printed currency.

The man I was to see was Miller Sorenson. He was a tall WASP type, about six-foot-four, with the swept-back blond hair and monument face of a guy who's going to be puffy and bald by the age of forty-five. At least I hoped so. I had a perpetually sunburned, triangular Irish face that had been described as foxlike, but only by people who liked me. If Sorenson didn't get puffy and bald there was no justice in the world. He wore a two-piece blue pinstripe with a white shirt, red braces, and a banana yellow tie with red ducks on it.

The monied in Maryland revere the duck the way insurance companies revere the eagle. You find the mallard imprinted on everything from bank checks to belt buckles. Everywhere you look rich people are wearing ducks. Maybe it's a secret society like the Masons. I bet the son of a bitch has yellow duck socks to match his tie, I thought as I slid into a Naugahyde chair across from Sorenson's real leather one.

He was assistant editor in charge of research, "among other things," he hastened to add. He spoke in the clipped nasal tones of central Maryland's Worthington Valley wealthy. It's thorough-bred country where even the horses look down their noses like they want a shoeshine and the people look like the horses.

Sorenson had gone to Hopkins and wanted to make chitchat about the lacrosse team and professors we might have in common. Since the only things I knew about Hopkins were that they had a great lacrosse team and the ugliest coeds in the world, I told him I thought the lacrosse team would do fine if they could get past North Carolina. I said I didn't want to discuss any professors because they were one of the vectors included in my study. I didn't mention the coeds because I thought there was a good chance he was married to one, even though most Worthington wives go to college just long enough to show off a year in the life of their wardrobe.

"Ah yes, your study," he said. "I'm afraid the title doesn't mean much to me."

"Ever take much math?" I asked, wondering what I'd say if he had.

"Just enough to get to the bottom line—accounting, economics and such. Finished Phi Beta Kappa in those, but nothing very advanced."

How lucky could I get? A Phi Beta Kappa. He was so smart he'd supply his own answers.

"Now then," he said, "about your thesis."

"Yes, well, my study," I said, lifting onto my lap the Naugahyde briefcase I'd gotten with my subscription to *Time* magazine. "What I'm attempting to do is build a three-dimensional model, the first one if I'm successful, of the American business structure. I'm attempting to do this by applying the vector analysis principles of calculus to the cubed trigonometric functions of solid geometry, substituting of course what I call economic nexus points for the usual graphed matrix points."

In the back of my mind I knew I was getting carried away but I was beginning to believe it could be done: a new economics, a complete explanation of the structure of American business using an indisputable mathematical proof. It was real Nobel prize stuff.

"Real Nobel prize stuff, huh?" Sorenson asked with a snide fluffing of duck feathers as he rearranged his tie.

"Well," I said cryptically. "Without the duck Peking is just a city, isn't it?"

Sorenson looked as though he'd been struck lightly between the eyes with a tiny mallet. His file of urbane rejoinders was thin in the area of nonsense. He squinted slightly, trying to see if I was serious. "Something my calculus professor used to say in reference to differential equations," I said offhandedly.

"Right," Sorenson said as though waking from a dream. "Originality versus conventional wisdom, that sort of thing."

"Certainly," he said.

"Mathematical philosophy."

"Certainly."

Sorenson shifted uncomfortably and reached into his shirt pocket for a pack of Winstons. "I'd like to hear more," he said with a pained expression that told me he'd rather spend the day having his teeth drilled. "Unfortunately we only have half an hour, so how can I help you?"

"Well," I said, unwinding a long accordion of computer paper from the briefcase, "let me see." What I saw was an interminable list of numbers and symbols which, since I'd found the printout in a dumpster in back of the First National Bank, probably represented large quantities of money. I pretended to study it. "I need to place Armco Industries Inc. in the matrix but I can't seem to find out much about them. In order to vector them accurately I need to know just a few simple things."

"Such as?"

"Nothing very complicated actually, no price-earnings ratios or management structure. I can get that later from other sources. All I really need is a little biographical profile, you know, ownership, recent history, product line."

"I think we can help you there," Sorenson said, reaching for a computer terminal. "One question, though, why didn't you go directly to the source? I mean why didn't you go to Armco with these questions?"

"Oh I've made it a policy never to do that when it can be avoided." Of course I had, but why? There's a good reason for everything, all you have to do is make it up. "To be meaningful, this study has to be as accurate as I can make it, and companies tend to put the best light on their own affairs, don't they?" I hoped devoutly that they did.

"Yes, yes they do." Sorenson puffed the Winston with a satisfied air as he punched buttons on his terminal. "Ah, here we are." He leaned back comfortably and placed his cigarette in the bill of a silver-plated duck which stood, eternally hungry, in the middle of a silver ashtray. "They're a small electronics firm, owned jointly by two brothers, Calvin and Stevenson Hobson. They're elderly gentlemen who live in Wilkes Barre, Pennsylvania, and leave the hand-on management to their plant manager, Howard Mills. The company employs one hundred twenty-five people. Until six months ago they manufactured small chip circuits for household appliances and stereo equipment. Then they suddenly began assembling the same type of thing for the Dynatron company."

"The same type of thing?"

"Yes, chip circuits for computerized electronics systems."

"I didn't think Dynatron made household appliances." Dynatron might have made duck ashtrays for all I knew but, if they were, it didn't seem likely they'd be making them at 3:00 A.M. for thirty dollars an hour.

Sorenson punched another button on his terminal. "Hmm," he said, raising one eyebrow. "They don't, actually. They make aircraft systems—radio components, radar, some fire control systems, fire detection systems, mostly for jet fighters."

My heart started to pound. Jet fighters, now there was something you might want to get into in the middle of the night.

"Hmm," I said, doing my best to imitate Sorenson. "Armco has, in effect, become a sub-out firm exclusively for Dynatron then?"

"It appears so." Sorenson was mildly interested himself. I wanted to leave before he got too interested.

"Well that about does it." I started tucking First National's printout back in my briefcase. "Thanks so much. If I win the Nobel prize I'll owe it partly to you."

His laugh was a short bullet aimed not only at my attempt at amiability but at the idea of me winning the Nobel. "In that case you can send me part of the check," he said. "Let's not hold our respective breaths." I turned to go, then turned back, taking a note pad and pen from my breast pocket. "Just one more quick question if you please?"

"In the interest of the Nobel, sure. What?"

"Ah, Dynatron. I'm not quite clear on their ownership and the distribution of their stock—limited or traded publicly?"

He turned toward the computer, placing another Winston in the duck's mouth. Checking his watch, he leaned toward the screen. "Traded publicly," he said. "But the controlling interest is held by Pecosa Diversified, a holding company out of Dallas."

"Dallas, huh? Well thanks for your time." I tucked the note pad back in my pocket, shot my cuffs, and shook hands with him. "If there's ever anything I can do for you. . . ."

"Yes," he answered, and I left before he could think of something.

Back in the office I locked the doors and dimmed the lights. I didn't want any other cases until I found out what was going on with this one. You can't get what you want unless you know what you want. I stripped off the suit and sat at my desk in my underwear, wishing I could talk to Arla about it. It was just the kind of thing she liked if only she'd admit it. She had a way of zeroing in on the opposite of what I was thinking that made everything clearer. I had an impulse to call her, but dialed Samski's number instead.

"Wha'?" Samski said groggily.

"It's Ransom."

"Ransom who?"

"Wake up. It's time to start earning whatever money you might make out of this deal."

When I told him what I wanted he came fully awake. "Fuck you," he said with conviction.

"It's the only way. We're not going to get anywhere unless I find out what the hell you're doing to those boards. Since you don't know I have to take one of them to someone who does."

"Fuck you," he said again. "I ain't about to steal no boards. Who do you think's the first person they'd come lookin' for?"

"You haven't been listening to me. I'm not asking you to steal it. I'm going to steal it. All you have to do is give me the key."

"I ain't givin' you shit. They'd sit on me so hard I'd hatch." He was right. Just the same, I had to get one of those boards. "Look," I said, pacing my office in my underwear, jacked up on instant coffee and the smell of doing something I was good at. "I'll break a window when I leave, that way it's just a break-in, no heat on you. I'm gonna do all the sneaking around. I'm good at it. I'm damn good at it. You may not know it, but what you're doing in there is making assemblies for jet fighters."

There was a pause on the other end while Samski made the jump from blenders to F-16's. "You know how much jet fighters cost? Twenty, thirty million apiece. We're talking something worth a lot of money, but first we've got to find out what the hell it is."

"I dunno," came the voice over the line. He sounded far away and unsure.

A slow burn worked its way up from my toes to my earlobes. "Listen, goddamnit," I screamed louder than I'd planned. "I want this. I don't know where you got so stupid that you think a lunch pail and a pat on the head from the man is all you need, but I'll tell you one thing. This is just what you need to quit feeling like you're walking around in a dead man's shoes. Get it up, motherfucker. You hear me? Get it up. This is opportunity knocking. You love your life so much you can't take a chance? You having such a great time you don't wanna see anything change? Don't give me any bullshit either, I know you. I've been walking around in a dead man's shoes myself and I'm sick of it. I'm going in there with or without your fuckin' key, and if they catch me I'm gonna tell 'em why, and then they're gonna know someone told me. Think about it. I've had it." I was holding the phone three inches from my mouth and shrieking into it at the top of my voice. My hands were shaking, my neck was pulsing along with my heart, and my eyes were focused with trigger concentration on one particular hole in the mouthpiece. I realized to my surprise and fright that I wasn't kidding.

There was a long pause on the other end but no click. I kept staring at the hole in the mouthpiece.

"I hear ya," he said in a weary voice. "An' I ain't givin' you no key. If you get caught it ain't going to be with my key in your pocket."

I pulled the trigger on the mouthpiece. "Fuck you then. I'm going in alone. If I get something, it's all mine. If they catch me, it's part yours."

"Shut the fuck up and listen," Samski said, and I knew he was staring at his phone the same way I was staring at mine. "I ain't givin' you the key, but Tuesday night I'll leave the door unlocked when I leave. An' one more thing . . ."

"Yeah?"

"The split. I get thirty-five percent or you go in cold and we both take our chances."

He meant it and he was right. He could be in for plenty of heat if things went totally gonzo. "All right," I said, "sure."

"Don't be shittin' me, I done some creepin' around myself ya know."

"I'm not shitting you. We're partners now, but don't make me have to talk you into everything. You're in for thirty-five or you're out, right?"

"Awright. I hope you got a good memory is all."

"Don't worry about it."

"Just see that you do," he said.

4

Four-thirty in the morning. I sat in my old Toyota, parked across the road from Armco Industries, which was located in corn country about twenty-five miles north of Baltimore. The liquid-stone light of a full moon dressed the Armco compound in iridescent silk, changing the clump of tin-roofed sheds to shadows and whispers, whispers I hadn't heard since 1969, the LRRP year.

Long Range Reconnaissance Patrol. They choppered you and your small team far out into the mist of the Laotian mountains, as far away as it was possible to get from your daddy's guidance or your mamma's love. All you had in the world were your weapons, your team, and the killer gleam burning in the base of your brain. You became so much a part of the night that you could smell, taste, and feel like an animal. Communication was a series of hand signals, hard taps, and glances you could feel but not see: LRRP telepathy.

But that was twenty years ago. Last night, I'd run two miles at a high school track, then done two hundred push-ups and a hundred sit-ups. Now that I was sore, cranky, and weightlessly nervous I had to remind myself that a little breaking and entering was just one more step on the road back to Arla. And, besides, in 1969 I'd been facing wired-up veterans. Now all I was facing was my own reluctance and a rent a cop guard.

Samski had said there was only one of them, a different one every week. They ranged from retired cops in their sixties to playground basketball stars picking up minimum wage while they waited for the NBA to call. I was more scared of the old cops. They'd know what they were doing and, what was worse, they'd care. No young black guy was going to risk his knees or his face for a bunch of circuit boards; not if he could help it and I intended to see that he could.

I'd brought a blackjack but no other weapon. It occurred to me that twenty years ago I had been equipped with every death-dealing device the mutants in the Pentagon basement could devise. Just as well; I was bound to be rusty. Give me anything stronger than a blackjack and I might use it prematurely and blow away someone who was only reaching for a sandwich. The point was moot anyway. I had the blackjack and a certain amount of experience and that was it.

It was 4:35 when they came out, about an hour until first light. Samski was last in line. He turned and made locking motions at the door. They got in their cars and were gone, leaving the factory a pale graveyard skeleton in the fading light of the morning moon. Time to go. I took a few minutes to clear twenty years of easy living out of my head, then peeled out of the car.

I went down to where the shadows of the tree line intersected with the shadow of the factory, crossed the road, moved to the dark side of the building, and stood flat against the iron wall, casting my hearing out beyond the sounds of my own breath. There was nothing but a small wind in the treetops. I pressed the palms of my hands and my ear against the wall. Nothing. No small vibrations in the window pane caused by footsteps; no small hum in the metal caused by diffused sound from inside. I looked down the building's moonlit side to the door and planned my exit route. If things went well I'd go back the way I'd come. If not, I'd sprint back down the wall and straight into the trees, away from my car. When they know your car they know you. It was only about twenty-five yards to the trees and once in there I could work my way around to the car while the watchman was inside phoning the police. Even an ex-cop wasn't going into the trees for minimum wage.

I took another listen, then loped through the moonlight in six strides, opened the door a crack, heard nothing, slipped in and crouched in the darkness. As my eyes began to adjust I could make out the shapes Samski had described. The production line was the long arm of an L. The short arm was a wing of administrative offices separated from the line by a set of double doors. That's where the watchman would be, probably in the middle of the late movie or sound asleep. Samski had said the guard wasn't allowed in the production section while they were working.

The line was set up as a series of work stations with all the attendant tools at each station. The product was passed down the line where each person did whatever small thing was his specialty and passed it on. What I had to do was get to the far end of the line where the boards were stacked neatly in color-coded bins according to project number. Samski had said the place had very strict inventory control so the plan was to steal one of the altered boards and four others so that it would look like I'd taken the special one by accident. An ordinary petty theft, a prank even, no special heat on Samski's crew and no special measures taken. That was the plan.

The spot where the boards were stacked was even with, and about twenty feet from, the administrative wing. I made my way down the line in a crouch, sweeping the floor in front of me with my hand, feeling for obstacles. When I got to the end of the line I located the bins, then looked for the light switch. The first thing the watchman would do if he came in would be to turn on the lights. I had to know how long that would take. Not long. The switch was only a step inside the double doors. I could hear a radio inside playing forties dance tunes. Shit! It was an old ex-cop. No young dude was going to be listening to Glenn Miller. If he came in he'd turn on the lights, look around, and then check the main door. He wouldn't find anything wrong there because I'd locked it when I entered. The peace of mind it would give the watchman was worth the time it would take me to open it.

I located the bins quickly, took the four ordinary boards, counted down three in the bin Samski had specified, felt the piece of tape with which he'd marked it, then took the altered board. The whole batch felt like it weighed less than two pounds. Things were moving right along. I was three steps up the line toward the door when I heard "In the Mood" getting progressively louder. The son of a bitch was coming down the hall with his radio, and no doubt his mace and gun. I'd never make it to my door before he got to his. I spun and went back to the end of the line. The work stations were little booths set across from each other with plywood separators between them. I was crouched behind the one nearest the approaching music. He couldn't see me unless he came to the line and looked over the top of the work station. If he did I was going to have to hit him. I laid the boards on the floor and took the blackjack out of my back pocket . . . my breathing slowed . . . my wrist was loose and flexible, and my weight balanced to allow for either a forehand or backhand. *Welcome back,* my past said silently to the watchman.

He paused at the doorway where I could sense him feeling the old cop mistrust of the dark. Then, humming a riff, he turned on the lights. The factory was an explosion of fluorescence. I looked reflexively at the floor, squinting blindly like a mole in the sunlight. If he came toward me now I'd be lucky if I didn't hit myself. But it took him a few seconds to adjust his own eyes then he moved down the line toward the door.

I felt ten pounds lighter as I heard the music moving away from me, but then I realized with a jolt of terror that he might not go back the way he came. He might take a stroll. I had to guess right or move . . . no choice. As he walked down the line I picked up the boards and, watching his back, edged around my end of the line. I made the door to the administrative wing in a fast glide and slipped through into a dead-end hall with office doors on each side. Drops of sweat from my face counted the seconds for me as I worked the doors to the offices and found them locked. The music was getting louder and the only open door was the one to the guard's office. I could hug the end wall like a frightened rat, charge the guard, or find a way to disappear. I was on my way toward the door hoping neither one of us made a mistake and killed the other when I noticed the restrooms and decided to disappear. Easing into the dark women's room I leaned against the wall and hoped the watchman was a traditionalist; a guy who would only enter a women's room to save a child stuck in the toilet. I kept my eyes on the light switch. If an arm came toward it someone was going to get hurt. The music rose in my ears like a jet taking off then turned left, into the guard's room. I slid down the wall to a sitting position and tried to start breathing again.

It was five o'clock, thirty minutes since Samski had left. Two hours until the day shift arrived. How long would the watchman stay? If I stepped out the door I'd be staring him right in the face. I had to think of a way to get out of the place unnoticed. At 6:50 I was still thinking. The day shift was due any time, and there would be plenty of women heading straight for me. But first they'd have to punch the time clock. There would be a crowd around the clock and it was the best place to get lost. Except they didn't know me. Who could I be? Who might walk right through a crowd saying howdy and carrying stolen items? I could feel my eyes bulging like a panicked horse as I looked wildly around the room and then saw the answer: the janitor. Sure, him. I was nobody, just the janitor, the one who just started. *Just the new janitor, boss.*

At seven I ripped the metal top off the garbage receptacle, pulled out the plastic bag, stuffed the boards in the bag, opened the door and looked into the hall: empty. The administrative people didn't come in until later. Thank God for the privileges of rank. I went into the men's room, stole its garbage, then went to the doors that opened onto the line. Through the windows I could see a crowd milling around a time clock located on the wall to the left of the main entrance. It was the usual workday crowd; half the people drinking coffee and jiving, the other half hoping it was all just a bad dream.

The watchman was nowhere in sight. I waited until they started sifting into their places before I untucked my T-shirt and moved with what I hoped was a fatigued slump through the doors, holding the bags in my arms so they would partially obscure my face. I stopped at a spot about halfway down the line where there was a pathway through the work stations to the entrance. There I pulled another trash bag from a wastebasket and made for the door.

"Hey," a woman's voice called, after I'd made it about twenty feet. I looked to my left and saw a young fat girl, her hair rolled onto about a hundred of those little curlers that make women look like defective electrical appliances. She adjusted her black square-rimmed glasses. "Hey you," she said, "what about mine?" She was pointing flirtatiously at a wastebasket by her feet.

"Be back in a minute," I said when my heart started again, and plowed steadily for the door. Outside, I went to the back of the building where I threw everything except the bag with the boards into a dumpster. I started to go but remembered what I'd promised Samski—that I'd make it look like an ordinary break-in.

Stripping off my T-shirt, I moved in a panic of quiet haste to a window located a few feet to the left of the fire exit. I wound the T-shirt around my hand, punched a hole in the window with a straight right, and then leapt into the woods as if I were running on crocodiles.

I worked my way around to a spot parallel to my car, crossed the road, jumped in with the bag and eased away. Three miles down the road I pulled to the side and screamed as loud and long as my throat would allow. Then I wheeled out, turned on the radio, and sang along with the atonal joy of a kid on his way home after his first time in bed with the love of his life.

5

"How are you?" The question had a little outward ripple around it that told me she wanted to know if I missed her.

"Fine, I guess." If she had to guess I was still in the ball game.

"How are the kids?"

"Great, they love having a father who can make himself disappear."

"Seriously, how are they?" I moved the receiver to my other ear.

"Confused. Katherine wants to know if you've gone up in the space shuttle."

"What'd you tell her?"

"I told her you didn't need the shuttle, you're already spaced."

"Very funny."

"Who's joking?"

"I miss them."

"They miss you."

"How about you?"

"I've got an extra space in the toothbrush holder. Now I can alternate. It's a whole new world."

"I don't even have a toothbrush holder."

"You always were a Bohemian."

"You've always been a sucker for Bohemians."

"Maybe I've just been a sucker."

"What's that supposed to mean?"

Arla didn't say anything. That meant she was crying. With some women, crying means you're getting through to them, melting the ice, but not with her. She hated crying. She was ashamed of it, and later she held it against you. "Don't cry, Arla," I said. "I don't want to make you cry."

There was a honking sound as she blew her nose then she returned to the phone, a little shaky but determined. "Then stop acting like you're ten years old," she said.

"You stop acting like you're my mother, goddamn it. I thought we were supposed to be a team."

"A team," she said with an icepick laugh. "Your idea of teamwork is remembering to yell, 'follow me,' when you jump off a cliff."

"And your idea is me pulling the sled while you scream, 'mush.' "

Her laugh was a little less dangerous this time. "The battle of the network metaphors," she said. "Why did you call Lowell?"

"To tell you I got a job."

"A real job?"

"Just as real as marching off to the petrified forest every day."

She tried to sound tired and succeeded, her voice flattening from its usual tropical trill to a kind of anchorwoman newsbleat. "We need the mortgage, Lowell, not promises," she said.

"You've got the mortgage. We had enough saved for three months worth, maybe four."

"That was supposed to be for new furniture, goddammit."

"There's some pretty nice furniture in my office, we could switch, and don't forget I've got a job. Things are going to work out Arla, believe me."

"It's easier to believe what you can see."

"That's what they said to Louis Pasteur when he told them about germs."

"You're crazy, Lowell. Besides, Lister discovered germs."

"I thought he discovered Listerine."

She laughed a little for real then but figured it was enough. "I have to go now," she said. "Are you going to come out soon . . . to mow the lawn?"

"Sure, soon. I just have to take care of a couple things first."

"Sure," she said, "when you get a chance." I thought I heard disappointment in her voice. Maybe she had the same lawn in mind I did. "Goodbye, Lowell," she said, and clicked the phone down without waiting for me to respond. Good sign or bad? Bureaucracy or coquetry? Hell, she didn't know either. I had to get to that lawn soon.

But first, *these things. These things* between my feet. I was lying on the sofa in my office with the phone at my side and my fourth beer in hand, gazing at the boards propped between my feet as though they were hieroglyphs. Hell, they were. They could tell my future. They could tell whether I was ever going to see the sea shining out of Arla's green eyes again or whether I was going to touch the model-perfect bones of her slim, sly face, or whether I was going to feel the taut, packed, palm-rounding slide of her thighs against my hands.

"Enough! Jesus! Enough," I said out loud. "What about the boards? That's your ticket home, baby, 'cause you're sure as hell never going back to desk city."

Now that I had the boards, what was I going to do with them? What was Armco doing with them? Who could tell me? I needed an engineer. Where did you find engineers? I downed the rest of the beer and reached for the yellow pages.

6

The certificates on Harry Armetrout's office wall testified to his life as an engineer. He was a short guy wearing a rumpled white shirt with a plastic quiver of pencils in its pocket. His hair was made up of wispy brown comb furrows leading back from a widow's peak in a wet arrowhead. His taffy-colored glasses and the nervous way he gnawed his pencil made him look like a big, friendly rabbit. He was charging me fifty dollars an hour and he had bad news.

"I'm afraid there's really nothing much I can tell you Mr. Francona," he said with an apologetic frown. I'd decided to be Frank Francona this time. It had the kind of consonant-heavy flatness I thought might have the same effect on his mind as a good solid transistor connection. In addition, Tito Francona had been one of the few early Baltimore Orioles to hit over .300; spray hitter, nice level swing. He'd been a favorite of mine when I was thirteen. This was my small homage.

I was discovering that my new occupation favored a kind of existential remaking of myself, much like acting, or being ten years old. Arla was probably right about me, but being right is easy. Being correct is what's hard, as Sartre or any .300 hitter might say.

"Uh, as I was saying Mr. Francona . . ." Armetrout said in a loud voice.

"Oh, I'm sorry." I looked up. "I guess I've been spending so much time the last few days wondering about these things that I've become preoccupied."

"Perfectly understandable," Armetrout said. "Were you and your uncle close?"

"My uncle was a little eccentric, like most inventors I guess. He wasn't really close to anyone. That's why I was so surprised when he told me he was leaving these boards to me. He acted like they were worth a fortune."

"But he didn't explain what they were for?"

"Well, he was very ill at the time. In and out of reality. You know."

Armetrout picked up the altered board again and compared it with the standard one I'd brought. "Hmm," he said, poking the pencil thoughtfully into his nasal passages. "It's certainly nice work. Your uncle knew his way around microchips alright. He's made a modification here." He took the pencil out of his nose and pointed to Samski's work. "But these are just parts of a whole. You're sure these two were all he had?"

"They were all he gave me anyway."

"As I explained, they're just parts of a whole. Without a schematic of the entire project, or at least some idea of what the project was, all I can tell you is that these are fairly complicated loop circuits designed to record and analyze information, and then to send that information to relevant gateways."

"Gateways?"

"Uh, let's see. . . ." Armetrout searched for an equivalent phrase from the pre-postliterate age. "It, uh, makes a decision, so to speak. Mathematically that is. It, uh, puts the sheep in the right pen, uh, so to speak."

"But you have no idea what type of sheep?"

His face brightened with the gratified flush of a missionary who'd just talked Ula the native into wearing shoes. "Exactly," he said, "exactly. I can tell you what it's supposed to do but I can't tell you what it's doing."

"So to speak."

"Exactly."

"Who could tell me?"

He squirmed and propped his shoe on the bottom drawer of his desk. He was wearing white socks. "Ah, in the absence of any plans, I'm afraid probably only your uncle." Armetrout colored a little and stuck the pencil in his mouth like it was a bone. He shrugged and removed the pencil. "Mind you," he said, "I'm not being flip."

"I understand."

"If it's any consolation, I don't see anything here that would lead me to believe he's discovered anything new. This modification is really the only innovative feature, and it looks to me like the most worthless part."

"Why is that?"

"Well, from what I can deduce, it essentially takes information it already has and simply repeats that information to itself. In English, it's sort of the equivalent of a, uh, paradox."

"A paradox?"

"Yes, it seems to consider information from two mutually exclusive points of view."

"And the only person who can tell me what they are . . ."

"Is the engineer who designed it or whoever he was designing it for. You're sure he wasn't working for someone?"

"Why would you think that?"

"The quality of the materials and construction is of the highest order. It's almost as if . . ."

It was time to go. Armetrout looked like he was trying to remember where he'd seen that kind of work before.

"Time to go," I said. "I suspected it was probably just a pipe dream. Uncle Samuel did nice work in everything. He was very particular but not very practical. Invented flea soap on a rope, things like that."

I locked the boards in the trunk of my car, bought some pizza at the 7-Eleven, and returned to the office. There was a woman of about seventy waiting for me in the hall who thought her cat had been kidnapped by her neighbor's pet monkey and wanted me to check into it. It was a little disconcerting to realize that, were it not for the thing with the circuit boards, I'd probably take the case. I told her I was busy and to go next door and check the monkey's credit rating to see if he needed the ransom money. She told me everyone knew that monkeys always used cash because they couldn't write, and that I was probably a lousy detective anyway.

After she left I went into the office to munch pizza while I pondered the words of that eminent philosopher Reggie Jackson: "Don't give me a hundred percent, give me whatever it takes." He'd said that once when he was broadcasting the American League playoffs and now I was up against the Reg's standard. I could throw the boards in the trash and forget the whole thing, or I could do what it took. I could start shaking Armco's tree and see what fell to the ground. Of course it was possible that it might be me who fell. Club Armco had taken great pains to keep what they were doing a secret. What pains would they be willing to give when they found out it wasn't? If I followed through I was going to create a situation far more complicated than simple breaking and entering. Another thing I was going to create was a new set of enemies, the most dangerous kind of enemies—unknown ones.

I consoled myself by remembering that old saying about a man without enemies being a man without character. On the other hand maybe someone had gotten that wrong. Maybe what it really meant was that having enemies made you a character. And we all know what happens to characters. They end up getting their mail at the bus station. Luckily, the phone rang and I didn't have time to think about it anymore.

I picked up the receiver and recognized Samski's drawl. "Well, the shit has hit the fan," he said.

"What?"

"They found out them boards was missin' today an' Fredericks is runnin' around like he's wearin' porcupine underwear."

"Already? It's only been one day."

"I told ya they kept strict count. Fredericks called the other two guys in the office an' asked 'em all about did they see anybody around an' did they have their keys, an' who locked the doors."

"Where are you now?"

"Home. They give me one day off durin' the week ta make up

for the night work. Today is mine, but Fredericks called me here an' said the other guys tole him I was the one that locked up."

"Didn't they notice the window in the back?"

"Yeah, but that looks kind of funny 'cause if it was broke at night the burglar alarm shoulda gone off."

"So, what else did Fredericks say?"

"Nothin', he wants ta talk to me tomorrow, see my key."

"So, no problem."

"I'm damn glad you ain't worried."

"Relax," I said. "If Fredericks doesn't mention it ask him if anybody could have come in with the morning shift. Ask him if anybody saw anyone they didn't know."

"Why?"

"Because somebody did. I had to wait all night in the place because of the watchman."

I could almost hear Samski gulp. "They saw ya?"

"Not so they could remember. I had a few trash bags in front of my face."

"Jesus, you're supposed to be good at this."

"I'm here aren't I? I'm not dead or in jail, and I have the boards don't I?"

"Who saw ya?"

"I don't know, a fat girl wearing Roy Orbison–style glasses."

"Penny Winkles, horny bitch. She won't remember your face, but you better hope they don't put your crotch in a lineup."

We talked a few more minutes about what I hadn't found out about the boards. Then I told him not to call me from his house.

"Why not," he asked in a higher voice than normal.

"It connects you to me, that's all."

"Fer who?"

"Anybody, probably nobody, but neither one of us ended up back in the world by sticking our heads up did we?"

"Chee-rist," was all he said before he hung up.

Then I called Armco's switchboard, got Art Fredericks on the line, and told him I was from the department of motor vehicles. He sounded angry when I asked him why he hadn't mailed in the plates to his car as requested. His outrage grew when I told him he'd failed to submit a certification that he had repaired his defective headlight, and that we were therefore requesting that he return his license plates. And he turned apoplectic when I said: yes, our records definitely showed he had failed to repair the right front headlight on his 1978 Ford. He told me in no uncertain terms that he drove a 1987 Cadillac Seville with tag number TSK 550 and that he had never been issued a repair order on that car and to check my records again because I was obviously another lazy, incompetent parasite just like the rest of the state workers. I apologized in an official tone as I told him that, indeed, I had the wrong Fredericks. The problem had been the similarity in license numbers. He said he was a busy man and told me to stuff it.

At five that afternoon I was in my Toyota following a 1987 Cadillac Seville with tag number TSK 550 into the parking lot of the Hunt Valley Hyatt. I parked three rows away from Fredericks and watched him walk into the Hunt Cup bar. He was a dark, overweight, clumsy-looking waddler. He wore a summer gray suit, tasseled loafers, and prescription shades. His hair was razor cut in some seventies kind of hair-helmet style that made him look from a distance as if he were wearing a winter hat. He emerged from the car in his shirt sleeves and hustled into his suit coat on his way to the bar. My car was three rows away but Fredericks looked like one of those nervous types whose faces are always covered with an oily mixture of sweat and lime aftershave. Even from a distance he depressed me. He reminded me of a more expensive version of my former boss at social services; another sweat-sheened chain-smoker whose butt was exactly the width of a state-issue office chair and whose heart was in his butt. "We institute policy, we don't make policy" is what he used to say whenever you wanted to cut a break to some starving well-digger who was twenty bucks a month over the max income for food stamps.

My ex-boss was right of course. The department of social services' mission is to see that no one gets social services who isn't entitled to them. It was the way he enjoyed it that got to me. Let's face it, if it wasn't for the unemployed well-diggers, the people who issued them food stamps would all be unemployed.

None of that mattered here in Hunt Valley. It was a sterling silver June twilight. The sun was falling low over the Irish green fields, giving the bordering black fences a smoky glow. The sight filled me with a kind of melancholy nostalgia. I felt a longing for a time past, when love was physically safe but emotionally dangerous and I was just an idea, a warm and romantic dream conjured by my parents on the same kind of evening.

But now the Hunt country was Hunt Valley Industrial Park, and past lovers had been replaced by white-shirted hard guys who played squash in the basement of the Pentagon as they discussed missile throw weights.

Jesus! It was five-fifteen. I'd been sitting in the Toyota thinking about what used to be for fifteen minutes. That's the trouble with nostalgia: It makes you cynical about the present and you miss your opportunities. To be a success you've gotta believe.

I did believe. What I believed was that Fredericks would have to talk to his engineer about the missing boards. I also believed that if the thing with the boards was a broadly based managerial decision, they wouldn't be doing it in the night with three workers. That made me believe the two of them would have to talk about it in private, and as soon as possible, at a convenient spot to which Fredericks would repair in his Cadillac, a spot like the Hunt Cup bar.

I covered the distance between my car and the bar at a dead run. The Cadillac hadn't moved. Inside, I sat down and ordered a beer. When my eyes were adjusted to the light I spotted the two of them at a table on the far side of the room. It would have been hard to pick Fredericks out of the guffawing herd of slicked-down wart hogs who were exposing the sweat marks on the underarms of their white shirts as they leaned back to cram handfuls of free popcorn into their mouths. They all seemed to be wearing identical gray summer worsteds and hair that didn't move as they milled around the bar baying their orders to the hostess. She was a bubbling young thing with bouncy blond curls and nice tits who accepted all the attention with the fey sprightliness of a kid tap dancing for her parents. A stab of pain made me realize she reminded me of my seven-year-old daughter Shana, who levitated like an angel when graced with approval. I had to get home soon.

Fredericks fit the crowd perfectly but his friend didn't. The other man's hair was a tennis ball burr and he was wearing tan slacks with a plaid sportshirt, complemented by three pens and a small screwdriver clipped to its pocket. He was fiddling with a draft beer and blinking frequently, as though the smoke bothered him. Raising the beer glass to his lips, he didn't notice the coaster stuck to its bottom until it slid by his eyes. Then he almost dumped the beer in his lap as he swatted at the coaster like it was a killer frisbee. This was a guy who didn't spend much time in bars, definitely not any kind of manager. Not the kind of guy Fredericks would be meeting unless they had urgent business.

As I watched them I could almost read the conversation through their gestures. Fredericks chopped the air a couple of times with the side of his hand and then pointed at the other guy, "You must have told someone." The guy shrugged and shook his head in the negative, "No, not me." Fredericks kept talking and then the other guy got a little hot. He pointed back at Fredericks, almost jabbing him with a finger, "Why does it have to be me? It was probably you. You've got a big mouth anyway." Fredericks spread his arms and then let them flop to his sides, "Well, who cares whose fault it is, what are we gonna do about it?" The other guy shrugged again, "Damned if I know." Fredericks shook his head disgustedly, "You're a big help. I gotta do everything around here."

Samski had said Armco's engineer's name was Mosby and I was sure he was Fredericks's burr-headed buddy. I left and waited in my car while they felt each other's heads for scapegoat horns. The plan was to ask Mosby what they were doing. I'd put the question to him in the same way I'd put it to Samski. If he refused to tell me, I'd make a trade with him: "Tell me or I'll phone Fredericks and tell him that the guy who stole the boards sold them to me, and I'm willing to sell them back along with the name. Guess whose name that will be?"

First though, I had to have proof he was Mosby. Samski knew his name from a memo announcing his recent arrival but couldn't recall having ever seen him. No problem, I'd just follow the guy home. If he left the door to his car unlocked I'd take a look in his glove compartment. People always seem to have something with their name on it in their glove compartment. I was soon going to find out if he was different because he was leaving the bar and heading into the parking lot.

Mosby had a Mazda sport pickup. I followed it to Cockeysville, a ghetto of singles apartments and franchised fun joints which sits on the northern perimeter of Baltimore city like a giant green room for "The Dating Game." The day had been hot and now the sky was turning rapidly dark as it readied itself for an evening thunderstorm. There was no wind yet. No drops. Just the sucking pull of dead air as it fell to the ground along with my stomach. The day was not only done, it was dying. I could smell decay as the lowering atmospheric pressure pulled the smells from the hamburger joints and dumpsters down to the hot asphalt where they lay in a blue psychic muck. A lone yellow Big Mac wrapper rocked hypnotically on the nonwind at the entrance to Cranberry Garth. It moved a few feet to the side as the Mazda pulled into the entrance.

Cranberries are only seen in Cockeysville on Thanksgiving so the place was probably named for the color of the developer's Mercedes. It was a typical luxury brickyard with a goldfish-sized swimming pool and a couple of tennis courts. The engineer parked the Mazda in space 210, which I assumed matched the number of his apartment. There was a small cold wind now curving out of the north in a downward arc. I slipped my Toyota into a spot opposite, and a few spaces away from the Mazda.

The wind was heavier now. A queasy chill dried the sweat on the back of my neck. "Come on," I said, as the guy sat in his truck fiddling with the radio. "Get the hell inside before it starts to rain." I was going to get soaked while checking out his glove compartment but that might be good. If it was raining it would increase the odds against him locking the doors. The sky, now midnight black, was shooting gusts of wind that rocked my small car as if it was sitting on water.

The engineer climbed out of the cab holding a vinyl bed cover and started to clip it to the pinions around the edge of the truck's bed. Hell, if he was that particular he'd be sure to lock the doors. The only tool I had for breaking into a car was a coat hanger, and the last time I'd tried using that method was a year earlier when

I'd locked the keys in my station wagon after slamming the door during a fight with Arla. It had taken me forty sweaty minutes to get in. The prospect of standing outside in a thunderstorm for forty minutes running a metal coat hanger against a metal car was enough to make me switch to plan B. I'd just call the plant and ask for him. He might know the call was bullshit but what the hell? He wouldn't see my face.

I was reaching forward to start the engine when I saw him slap the side of the truck in disgust. He was having trouble with one of the cleats. It seemed to be bent and he couldn't stretch the cover far enough to get it attached. What he needed was a pair of pliers. I saw him look hurriedly at the sky and then to the second floor of the building, making a quick calculation. Could he get inside and get the pliers before the rain started to come in sheets? "Yes, yes damnit," I said. "Sure you can. Run in there and get them, and don't waste time locking the pickup's doors." He was doing it! He headed toward his building in a graceful lope. Tall guy, probably played a little basketball at some point in his life.

As soon as Mosby disappeared inside the door I bolted for his truck. Crouching on the passenger side I riffled quickly through the glove box; it was nothing like mine. No bottles, pizza wrappers, or old parking tickets. He was a very neat person, had his registration attached neatly to his insurance verification with a large paper clip. Glenn Mosby was his name, apartment 210, Cranberry Garth Apartments, Cockeysville, Maryland. I made it back to my car just as the rain started, jumped behind the wheel, and was all set to leave when I saw two guys wearing suits come out of the building and look through Mosby's truck. It was now raining like hell and these two guys were taking a lot of time, in their suits, in the rain, to look through Mosby's truck. After a few seconds they went empty-handed to a beige Mercedes 450 SL and left. I sat very still. The last thing I wanted was for anyone to remember seeing my blue Toyota. As a matter of fact I was thinking of using a rental for any other expeditions in connection with the boards. I noticed as it went by that the Mercedes had DC plates.

I sat in the car listening to the rain beat against the windows wondering why two guys in suits would be rifling through Mosby's car. Maybe they were doing the same thing as me. Maybe Armco had already hired a security consultant. If that were true the only way I was going to make any money out of this deal was through out and out extortion: "Give me the money, I give you the boards." I wasn't sure I wanted to do that; the thought of it made me feel a little like a pimp. It had now been seven minutes since Mosby went inside. The unattached corner of his bed cover was flapping in the wind like a loose sail. Had he given up on it or what? Then a replay of the two suits flashed in front of my eyes and the certainty hit me with such force that a sharp pain ran up the back of my head, causing me to grunt out loud. Something about them sealed it for me; something about the way they went through Mosby's truck, they did it so slowly, so carelessly. They knew he wasn't going to catch them. They knew he wasn't coming back out.

The building was of standard garden apartment architecture; an entryway with a bank of mailboxes, two sets of four stairs leading up to the second floor, and one step leading down to a ground floor apartment. I took the stairs two at a time and pressed my ear to the door of 210. No sound, no TV, or stereo. I covered the doorknob with my shirttail and gently turned; it was locked. When I got back to the entryway I noticed another door across the hall from the ground floor apartment. At first I thought it was another apartment but then I saw that there was no name on it and no bell. The door was supposed to close automatically but the spring was apparently a little weak and hadn't latched. It probably led to a hallway with chicken wire stalls where the residents kept things like bicycles and the janitor kept his mops. He was going to need them.

As I watched, it came moving with surprising speed through the crack in the door. My breath stopped halfway out of my lungs. For a second I was in two different realities; one denying the other but knowing it was true. I knew. I knew because I'd seen it move before with the same infuriating languor. I'd never expected to see it again but there it was; a slow-trickling, ever-increasing, running river of blood, pooling and sliding into the ground floor landing. Just to confirm that I'd now been dropped on the surface of another world I took two steps down, nudged the door a bit wider with my elbow, and saw Mosby's body; his entire stock of blood was flowing obscenely out of a pool below the ear-to-ear gash in his throat.

7

"Hi, Arla," I said. "Is there any whiskey in the house?"

"Lowell?" Arla said, as though she were looking at someone who only resembled me. It was still raining. I'd been standing at the door trying to find my key but couldn't get my hands to work any better than my mind. I was encased in a gelatinous substance that seemed to make movement difficult and thought impossible. It's called terror—mortal fear, fear for the soul. When you're afraid for your soul you want the place that contains the balm of memory, the healing salve of self-reference and eye-to-eye validation. You want home, and that's where I'd gone after seeing Mosby's body. I didn't remember the drive. I didn't remember anything except the red smile in Mosby's neck.

I only knew that suddenly I was wet and shaking on my own doorstep, asking for comfort like a dog shoved out of a moving car.

"Lowell, what are you doing here, like this?"

At least she was sure it was me. If she was sure it must be true.

"I have to come in," I said. My teeth were chattering so hard I wasn't sure she could understand me.

"Well, come in then." She reached out a hand and grasped my upper arm. "Come on," she said as she pulled. I saw the warmth of the house's interior and went for it. I brushed by her in the narrow foyer, conscious even in my numbed state of the flower-earth smell at the nape of her neck, the smell that had always transformed my crotch into a heat seeking missile. Not this time though. What I wanted, and needed like a saint needs a vision, was whiskey.

I went to the pantry in the kitchen and looked on the top shelf. Arla liked Scotch and there it was, an almost full liter of Bell's. I took as much whiskey as I could force into my mouth and swallowed. The Scotch's liquid heat scorched its way through my system, trailing a hypnotic cloud of peat smoke. I took another drink and sank to the kitchen floor, leaning against the cabinets under the sink. I wished I could stay there.

"Lowell, are you drunk?" Arla stood over me, a familiar anger sending flint sparks from her eyes into a spot on my forehead. How did she always get me between the eyes?

"No," I said simply. "I'm scared."

The flint in her eyes spread and coalesced into an even glow. Intense, but not angry, a little afraid herself. "What of? What happened?" she asked. She was still standing over me. I took another drink, beginning to be able to put thoughts together, beginning to know why the sight of Mosby's body had frightened me to my backbone. I'd seen plenty of bodies, bleeding, broken, puffed, and bloated, any way at all. But with the whiskey I was beginning to understand why this one was different from the others. They'd known they were in a war. They'd rolled the dice and lost. Mosby hadn't even known he was in the game. And I'd started the game without telling him. Now he was dead and there was a crippling possibility it was my fault. I could feel him inside me asking why. I took another big drink of the Scotch.

"Lowell, stop that and tell me what's going on." Arla had squatted in front of me and was attempting to pull the bottle out of my hand. "Tell me," she said. I let her take the bottle because I was beginning to feel nauseous. Another big slug and I'd be crawling around trying to find the waste basket. I pulled myself off the floor by the edge of the sink and stumbled into the dining room where

I sat contemplating a return to social services. Maybe if I just went back and pretended none of this ever happened. . . .

"Tell me, goddamnit!" Arla slammed the bottle on the table. "You can't just come sloshing in here like some bum, get drunk on the kitchen floor, and not tell me what's going on. Is something wrong or is this just your way of saying hello?"

How was I going to tell her? I wanted to tell her but this wasn't the time. I had to wait until I knew what I was going to do about it, if I was going to do anything about it. Tell her now and it would just confirm her opinion that I was a gold-plated fuck-up.

"It's the job," I said. "The job I told you about on the phone. Something happened."

"What? What happened? Are you in trouble?"

That was an interesting question, one I hadn't considered in any depth. "You mean with the law?" I asked.

"Of course. What other kind would you be in?"

Another interesting question. "No, but something happened, that's all, something, ah, disturbing."

"What?"

"I don't want to talk about it."

"That's it? You come in here like this and you don't want to talk about it?"

"This is my home, Arla, remember? I felt like coming home, that's all? You hate me now? You hate me so much I can't come home for one night?"

"You know I don't hate you." Her voice was softer, more conversational. If I hadn't felt Mosby's body on my back I might have smiled at the thought that, after twenty years of women's liberation it's only fair that men get to use the guilt thing too.

"I don't hate you at all, Lowell," Arla said, pouring some of the whiskey into a glass for herself. "But this isn't fair. The reason we're in this . . . this situation, is your so-called job and now you come in here and tell me it's scaring you. Doesn't that tell you something?"

"It's not like that, not exactly."

She took a slug of the Scotch. "I'm waiting."

"I'm not going to tell you. Not right now."

"Why not?"

"I don't know enough about it myself yet."

"Are you going to go on with it?"

"I don't know." I thought I was just putting her off but I really didn't know. Home felt pretty good. And Arla looked great. Small, neatly compact dancer's body. Those legs, those dancer's legs. Athletic legs different from those of a gymnast or swimmer only in the way the curves were softer, more elongated, made by music rather than competition.

She was looking at me with an almost conspiratorial bemusement, as if she knew what I was thinking. She tilted her head a little to the side, an unconscious cover pose for *Vogue*. She had dark roan hair cut in an asymmetrical way that accented the sardonic French invitation of her face; a thin, sharply sculpted face that derived its beauty from geometric precision, but its sexiness from a secret wink lurking somewhere close to the surface. It was a face that knew its beauty was the bait, but its passion was the catch. That face, those legs, that straight, strong back, and small but interested breasts, she was quite a package. It would be nice to be home again. I was tired, discouraged, beaten with my own stick.

"You don't know?" Arla looked at me over the rim of her glass, trying to see if I was lying.

"I told you, I don't know."

"Does that mean you're thinking about giving it up?" The question in her eyes went deeper than the one from her mouth. She needed me to say yes; she needed me. We'd been married seven years. In that time we'd had some matches that made Ali-Frazier look like mild arguments but none of them had ever been about the bedroom. The matches we'd had there had been just as intense, and always gone the distance, but they'd always ended in a draw with both parties agreeing to a rematch, one that was now overdue. She took a little more of the whiskey and fidgeted with the glass.

It would have been easy to answer her question with a lie, to say I was going to give it up and come home. I knew that's all it would take to get her from the dining room to the bedroom but it had never been like that between us. If it happened, it had to be strictly because we wanted it to, no bargaining, just honest want. That way she'd know she needed a next time. I moved one chair closer to her. "Could I have just a little bit more of that whiskey?" I asked. "I'll use a glass this time." I didn't wait for an answer but went to the kitchen for the glass. When I came back she was pouring some more for herself.

"I don't hate you, Lowell," Arla said again as I poured myself a shot. "You know that, don't you?"

"Sure I do," I answered. "But what I want to know is if you love me?"

"We've been through this."

"I want to hear it from you, Arla. Believe me, if it's true I need to hear it from you. I need to hear it now, tonight."

She looked down into her glass, auburn highlighted hair falling gently forward, brushing her ear. "Why tonight?" she murmured.

"Because I need some grace, I'm out of it. When you've got no grace you're a straggler, and the stragglers are the ones that get eaten. Am I making any sense?"

"No, but I'm used to that." She raised her glass and I saw a crooked little smile float tartly across the Scotch like a twist of lemon. "I love you, Lowell," Arla said, "I'll always love you." I sat in the chair next to her, wanted to stroke her back, but she knew it and stiffened. "You're not in trouble?" she asked. "Because I swear, if you are and you don't tell me I'll never forgive you."

She was rigid. She'd forgive almost anything except a deliberate lie, something that had always caused problems since I seemed to be such a natural liar. "Only with myself," I said. It was the truth as I knew it. The law didn't know I existed, Armco didn't know I existed. Samski knew but couldn't say anything without putting the heat on himself. I was in big trouble with myself though. Was I the man I thought I was? Had I ever been? If I had been, had I lost it? I felt cut off by guilt from the person who might be able to break out of social services; I had to connect with him. I came around the table to Arla and placed a hand on the side of her face, hoping to see the man I was looking for reflected in her eyes. She looked up, searching for him too. I slid my hand gently to the spot I knew she liked, the spot where her spine joined her skull in a curve as graceful as poetry. I tried to speak with my hand and she bowed her head to accept what she knew was a prayer.

I dropped next to her on one knee and spoke into her ear.

"Everyone looks ugly to me," I said. "Since I haven't been with you everyone looks ugly—people in cars next to me at stoplights, girls, men, TV, everything looks ugly to me."

Arla turned her head to look in my eyes. We were only a breath apart. "Lowell," she said, and stroked the side of my face with her hand, a gesture that flowed through my nervous system like a series of small kisses. "Lowell, Lowell, what is it? What is it about you?"

"You're what it is. You're what it is about me. You're what it's always been about me."

Upstairs, in the soft peach tones of the low-level lamp by the side of the bed, she put both hands in my hair and groaned low and hungry as she threw the sheet aside and hooked me inside one of her shadow-channeled thighs. "Come here," she said, "c'mere, sweet thang." I did, and it was . . . sweet.

The next day I mowed the lawn; after the kids found me at seven-thirty and shrieked their delight, after I'd taken them in my arms and pulled the memory of them into me. Shana and Katherine, seven and five, aware and confused about what was happening to their parents and their lives. Both girls had the artistic prance and irritating intelligence of their mother. Shana was blond, and wise enough to start asking me a lot of questions about what we were going to do. She sensed instinctively that, for little girls, plans are the best perfume. Katherine was dark, plump, solid; muscular enough to ask the question and dare me to give the wrong answer: "Are you going to stay home now?"

"What do you want for breakfast?" I answered.

Later, after the lawn, and lunch, I sat in front of the TV watching the Giants play the Dodgers, thinking how much more orderly games were than life, Zen poems instead of traffic accidents. I hadn't told Arla what happened. To her it would be absolute divine proof that I should have stayed with my hated job and beloved family.

Maybe that was the truth. Should I have been able to see the violence waiting around the corner? Or it might have been just a coincidence. Suppose Mosby had been fooling around with someone's wife and the husband hadn't liked it? Maybe it didn't have anything to do with me at all. Maybe the next guy who hit a home run would run backward around the bases.

The Giants were batting in the bottom of the eighth and I was at the bottom of my sixth beer when Arla stopped making salad and came to sit beside me. "Thanks for mowing the lawn," she said.

"My pleasure," I answered, and then realized with a disturbing jolt of satisfaction that I meant it.

"Speaking of pleasure," Arla murmured as she stroked my arm, smoothing the hair as if it was her own.

"Yeah," I said, as I remembered last night. "Jesus, Arla, I feel human again."

She again stroked my arm. My toes started to get warm. "I needed it too," she said.

"So when am I coming home?"

"You don't have to go back to social services. There are other jobs."

"I know. I have one."

"You think you have one."

"I know I have one."

"How do you know?"

"Because I'm doing it."

"Very existential, but you forgot your beret and beat poetry when you fell in here on the floor last night."

"I didn't fall on the floor, I sat on it."

"Had a little trouble getting to a chair though, didn't you?" she said, and headed back to the kitchen to chop viciously at some carrots.

"All jobs have their problems," I said lamely.

"So what was the problem?" She slammed the knife onto the counter and lit a cigarette, nervous, talking through the exhale. "Tell me, Lowell. It's obvious from your glassy-eyed gaze that you need to tell someone. Why not tell me?"

I could think of about ten reasons without even trying very hard. The main one was that I knew she'd go completely gonzo, run around shrieking about the police and growing up. It was just the difference between us, the difference that couldn't even be communicated, let alone bridged. When she'd been dealing with Sister

Agnes Marie about the length of her hemline, I'd been dealing
with brother Charlie about the length of my life. I was grown up
all right. I was too grown up to sit in an office and be treated like
I was in the sixth grade. To Arla that was an immature attitude,
to me it was an attempt to protect what I'd won.

Arla was right about one thing. Before I could go any further
I needed to talk to someone. I had to find someone who could
help me read a map of the moral terrain. If I was in the wrong
I'd lose. The home court advantage in sports is that the crowd
makes the players feel they're the good guys, that they should win
because it's right. Fighting for your home gives you strength because you know you have a right to victory. Now I had to decide
where home was in the Armco affair. Had I invaded Mosby's
country and gotten him killed for no good reason or was there
something heading my way that ought to be stopped? No way Arla
could help me with a question like that. There was someone
though, someone whose name caused me to bolt upright in my
seat.

"What's the matter?" asked Arla as I lurched to my feet.

"Nothing, nothing. I have to go. We'll talk about this later."

"What're you going to do?"

I walked over to face her; she had to understand a little of it.
"Listen, Arla," I said, taking her hand in mine. "You may be
right. I really don't know but I have to find out. Understand? You
might be right and if you are I swear I'll admit it. But give me
some time to find out. All right? I'm in between now; I want to
find out for sure."

She squinted her eyes, looking hard for bullshit. "You're not
twenty anymore, Lowell," she said. "You're not even thirty. I
know you don't want to hear that but if I don't tell you who will?"

"Just a little more time."

Arla sighed and looked away. "I'm not talking about a time
limit," she said. "This thing seems like something you should have
gotten into when you were younger. I know you're in good shape
and all but . . . just make sure you're not kidding yourself, about
your . . . anything."

"A point well taken, I'll stop around and mow the lawn next
week and we'll talk, okay?"

"Sure, but one day soon the talk has to come to some conclusion."

Right again. I had to stop or move; questions had to be answered. I needed to talk to someone who'd helped me through another rough time: Retired Master Sergeant Daslow Michael Gervin III.

8

I got to Baltimore about seven-thirty that evening. The drive from my house in the suburbs had taken about forty-five minutes and the sun was sinking behind the left field stands as I passed Memorial Stadium. As I headed down Thirty-third Street, a broad, four-lane boulevard separated by a wide green median strip, I checked out the rotating thermometer in front of a bank. It said ninety-five degrees.

Baltimore's harbor is surrounded by a Tiffany ring of high-rise malls and tourist hotels but in summer the rest of the city is a study in fading brick gentility, crumbling under its own heat beneath a lacy veil of smog. The old oaks and sweating pastels of Thirty-third Street reminded me of Hue City. It also smelled like Hue, dead shrimp and live garlic.

Thirty-third Street was the main street of a neighborhood called Waverly, which was the center of Baltimore's Asian community. Within a four-block area you could get Thai, Korean, Filipino, Chinese, and Vietnamese food. Daslow Gervin liked to hang out there because he had fond memories of Asia. That was where he had suddenly, in the ninth month of his second tour in Nam, changed magically from Daslow to The Daz. He did it by becoming, as he puts it, "very extremely wealthy."

It happened to him on a typical August morning in Nam. The kind of a morning when the heat drove your head into your shoulders. Daz's company was moving on an area about twenty clicks west of Longh Binh that had been reported as an NVA headquarters. They were flanking a village, coming in careful as fog from two sides. When the company saw an NVA runner heading north in his pith helmet they smoked the place, mortared it, called in choppers, free-fire, the whole shot, killed every moving thing in sight.

Afterward there's always a few minutes of confusion, taking prisoners, guys yelling for medivac, officers yelling for order. It's a few minutes of every man for himself, and it was in those few minutes it happened.

Daz crashed into a hut, kicked aside a mat, found a trap door, dropped a percussion grenade down the hole, waited, jumped into the hole, and found what he was looking for. It was a five-by-eight cavern with an adjoining tunnel that served as an NVA command post. The grenade had whipped the shit out of the place, throwing chairs and maps all around, but it hadn't destroyed anything, which was lucky for Daz, because in a corner he found a metal box containing one million dollars in greenbacks.

He didn't know it was a million but he knew it was a hell of a lot of money. The NVA used greenbacks to bribe officials and buy black market equipment. Daz decided to take the box prisoner. He ran down the tunnel to where it made a sharp turn, stashed the money, and came out of the hole just in time to hand his lieutenant a batch of maps and code books.

Later, when everyone was hanging out bullshitting, Daz slipped back into the hut, emptied his pack, and stuffed it with money. He went through the rest of the day sweating blood over the possibility he'd get killed before he could get the cash out of country.

But get it out he did, brought it right into Fort Lewis, Washington, in his duffel bag. He'd been through the drill before and knew incoming customs was a bunch of fuck-off corporals who spot-checked about one in ten bags. To make sure, Daz milled around until he spotted a young black working one of the customs lines wearing a leather bracelet and blue shades. Daz waited until lunch, followed the kid into the mess hall, and offered him a thousand dollars to go light on his bags; five hundred before, five hundred after. The brother assumed it was about dope. He had a thousand to gain if he agreed, five hundred if he didn't. He went for the thousand.

Daz had been planning to stay in the army for the full thirty years but being rich soured him on eating government food and being shipped around the world like lost mail. He retired at the earliest opportunity and came home to Baltimore, where he bought a huge Tudor place in Brooklandville, an unincorporated money zone about ten miles north of the city, populated by pruned trees, doctors, and more limos than United Nations Plaza.

I'd stopped at a 7-Eleven after I left Arla and phoned Daz. I got his French-Vietnamese wife, Li Anh, who told me he was at the Dong Ha restaurant. It figured; he was probably conducting business. Daz had bankrolled a lot of the restaurants in Waverly in return for a percentage of their profits. "Always good business to invest in Asians," Daz told me. "Most relentless people in the world, but then I don't have to tell you, do I?"

He didn't. Anyone who went to Viet Nam knows that in his blood, whether he wants to admit it or not. Since I've known Daz I don't mind admitting it, and I've known him for ten years. We met when he counseled me and a group of other vets who were getting weird. I'd seen an ad one day:

VETS: THINK YOU MIGHT BE CRAZY?
I CAN HELP.
NO GOVERNMENT CONNECTIONS.
NO GOVERNMENT HASSLES.
CALL 899-9000

I'd been having a little problem with fantasy homicide; imagined killing everyone I didn't like, which was just about everyone. But

I knew I wouldn't and couldn't. My cells wouldn't accept it. Still, the ideas were there, so I drowned them in enough booze to fuel a career in country music.

Daz helped me. Basically, it came down to accepting the fact that, in being around Asians and Asia, we'd become different. We'd brought home a piece of it all and had to learn from it instead of eating our livers. "Live with the privacy of priests," was his advice. "Accept and wait. Get to be a little Eastern. If you think you're a loser then imitate the winners. Look what that did for Japan. You guys are just ahead of your time."

It was hard advice, but it helped. And Daz and I had become friends. Friends, but not bosom buddies. Nobody's that close to Daz because he's too many people. If he had less money you could probably call him schizoid but, since he's rich, he's just eccentric. I see him a couple times a month. Sometimes we have to go through a Zen tea ceremony while we talk; sometimes we just get drunk. Sometimes we look through a telescope on the roof of his house while smoking the joints he gets directly out of Thailand. Sometimes I meet him downtown at his office on the twentieth floor of the Mercantile Bank Building where he wears Italian suits and runs Dazco Inc., pretending he's a businessman.

I say pretending because a businessman's objective is always profit. Daz is trying to do good. Really. That's what he tells me. "I've got enough solid investments to last me," he says. "With the rest of it I'm just trying to do good. You know, it's stolen money in a way, so I have to pay moral interest."

That's what he says and I believe him. He did good for me. He did good for the people he set up in business. He did good for himself. I know that because, in addition to his place in Brooklandville, he's got one on Cape Cod and one on Aruba. What else he's doing I don't know, but I believe him.

I like Daz; I trust him. But I don't want to see any more of him than I do. I like to keep him a little apart so I can get hard advice.

The Dong Ha was a little Vietnamese place between a Greek pizza joint and a store that rented Chinese video tapes. The local food I tried in Nam looked and tasted like screamingly hot dishwater.

And most of this neighborhood apparently agreed with me. The place was about half full and all the customers were Vietnamese. I guess the great Nam chop vogue will have to wait until the black pajamas appear in Saks' window.

Daz was in an office located off the kitchen. The girl at the register waved me back when I asked for him. He was behind a desk eating noodles and going over a set of books. He'd put himself in the spirit of the occasion by donning a long robe of red silk brocade.

"Brother Lowell." He stood as I entered and bowed. "What do you think?" he asked, fanning a piece of the silk over one arm.

"Can't you hear it?" I answered.

"What?"

"The sound of one of my hands clapping."

"Zen stand-up, I love it," he said. "Fake my wife, pleasingly."

"Haiku," I said:

> *New adornment*
> *Red spring poppies*
> *Chinese embassy draperies.*

Daz laughed and bowed again. "Chinese draperies cover the entrance to the secret palace."

"Or Italian underwear."

He laughed again, a high-pitched cackle. "You gotta admit, it shows off the Mongol in me."

Daz claims he's one-eighth Mongol and, with his bald head and slightly upturned eyes, you could almost believe him. But with that wide receiver's build he's a little too rangy. Just the same, he's the type of black guy who suggests some exotic mixture. His thin face is the color of refrigerated chocolate, kind of a frost over the brown, the nose narrow and hooked like an Apache's, the lips thin as a banker's. With his big slanted headlight eyes he reminds me of those sketches people make under hypnosis of aliens who supposedly take them aboard spaceships for free urological exams.

He sat down and offered me some tea, which I declined in favor of a bourbon.

"I thought you quit bourbon," he said as he poured me a shot of Jim Beam.

"Sometimes you need to burn a few things off," I said through the whiskey's retroheat.

"Uh huh." He closed the books and waited for me to tell him. When I was finished telling my story, he pushed the tea aside and took a shot of the whiskey for himself. "Uhhhh-huh," he said emphatically. "I see your problem."

"Do you?"

"Yeah, you wanta jump into the shit and stay clean."

"That's about the size of it."

"No way to do that without stayin' in then, is there?"

"Meaning what?"

"You shoulda started checking out the science of chaos when I did."

"I'm trying to stay away from chaos."

"Can't be done. Chaos has a pattern, did you know that? Even events we think are random have a pattern. Water dripping from a spigot, beach erosion, probably even quantum changes in subatomic particles."

"You mind if I just read the book sometime?"

"Wait a minute now," he said, taking off the robe to reveal a white linen shirt and charcoal silk Italian suit pants. He put on the suit coat and came around the desk to stand in front of me.

"You're not going to do your professor thing, are you?" I asked. "You're not gonna get out that damned pointer like you did at your house that time, are you?"

"What time?"

"The time you were explaining that symbolic logic course you took at the University of Baltimore."

"I got an A in that course."

"It must have been the pointer."

"All things symbolic are logical but it wasn't the pointer. Now listen. . . ."

Daz took a pair of tortoise-shell glasses out of his suitcoat pocket and put them on.

"What the hell is that?" I yelled. "You don't wear glasses. Those are just plain glass."

"They're symbolic, and therefore logical," he said with aplomb. "Just because they're not convex or concave doesn't mean the light passes through unaffected does it? . . . Well, does it?"

"Probably some slight prismatic effect, depending on how you hold your head."

"Aha," said Daz triumphantly.

"Aha?"

"The way I see it, you're like plain glass in the lens of this affair. Your purpose wasn't to bend the light, so to speak, but you had some slight prismatic effect and wham, Mosby gets killed."

I sat back in my chair and had another whiskey. He was right, I think. "So," I said. "The question is, am I responsible?"

"Hell yes you're responsible. But are you culpable?"

"I feel culpable."

"Yeah?"

"Yeah," I said. "I feel he'd be alive if I hadn't got involved."

"So?"

"So, do I stay in or try to get out and forget about it?"

Daz sat on the edge of his desk. Taking his glasses off, he gestured with them. "Listen, you didn't let me finish telling you about chaos. I was saying that random events really have an underlying pattern. By keeping track of the intervals between apparently random events that pattern can be reproduced on a computer screen. That pattern is called a strange attractor."

"Is that like, scientifically occult or what?" I said.

"Don't stop me now, listen. These strange attractors are like similar, but never repeating figure eight ellipses. In other words, they wind themselves around related but moving poles."

"Jesus," I said, "if I get rich will I get like you?"

"No, you'll just have the time to get more like you."

"All right," I said. "What's the point?"

"The point is that you breaking into that factory was what seemed like a random act, but it was really part of a pattern. You are now one pole of a strange attractor my man. You're in the pattern. The way I see it you can try to get out but all that's gonna do is move the pole. The pattern might change but it's eventually gonna come around. See what I mean?"

I didn't know if it was the whiskey, the silk suit, the glasses, or the possibility I might be from the same planet as Daz, but I thought I did see. "Yeah, yeah," I agreed. "Let's say that's true. It doesn't answer the main question."

"No?"

"No. How do I get the weight of this guy's death off me? How do I get clean now that I'm in the shit?"

"That's a question, all right," Daz replied. He pulled a fat Thai joint out of the desk drawer and we smoked it in silence. I saw my life, as well as three or four others I'd never lived, flash before me while I sat staring at the brocade in the robe Daz had discarded. I was about to swear I could read his name woven into the thread of the fabric in Chinese figures when he rocked forward and slammed his hand on the desktop. "I've got it," he said, "goddamn, it's simple."

"What?"

"The answer to your question. You get clean by staying in, that's all. It's a strange attractor; it's a circulating pattern. You're one pole, it was the other pole that killed him. I mean, shit, you didn't stick in the knife, you're just part of the pattern. It was the other pole killed him. You've gotta unwind this thing, find the other pole and you change the pattern."

"You think?"

"Yeah, if you really care about your part in getting this man killed. Personally, I say fuck him. He knew what he was doing. You want to play, you gotta accept the odds. I mean who was he, little Mary Sunshine? Sometimes if you're a player, they take you out of the game."

He turned those big lamps on me from under upraised brows and waited. "Yeah," I said, "but I . . ."

Daz cut through what I was about to say with the taut-wire tone in his voice. "I'm not talkin' about you," he said. "I'm talkin' about them. Forget about you for a minute and think about them."

"Yeah, so?"

"Why do you think they killed the dude?"

"Probably because they thought he was the one who stole the boards."

Daz didn't say anything. He took out a Pall Mall and fired it up. Then he sat back in his chair and gave me the look again.

"You don't think so?" I asked.

"You're the detective," he said. "You go through it and tell me what you think."

What did I think? I felt responsible but what did I think? "I think they thought Mosby was the one who stole the boards," I answered.

Daz blew a long cloud of smoke into the air and watched it drift upward. "Why'd they think that?" he asked.

"Hell, because the things were gone. They're obviously worth something, he knew how much. As far as I can tell he might have been the only one besides Fredericks who did know."

"Uh huh," Daz said skeptically.

"What?"

"You tell me what."

It was all true. Mosby had met with Fredericks; they'd talked about the theft. Mosby had been killed. It was all so, so . . . what? So logical, so connected. So inevitable. "Jesus," I said.

"Right," said Daz. "How'd Mosby think he was gonna get away with it?"

"Right, right. He was the first one they would have suspected."

Daz leaned across the desk and pointed with the remains of the Pall Mall. "He was a player, so he must have known who he was playing with," he said, stubbing the cigarette out with finality.

"Christ," I said, sure of it. "They didn't think he stole anything. The motherfuckers killed him just because he knew what was going on."

"That's the way I see it," Daz said. "Kind of alters your perceptions a little doesn't it?"

It sure as hell did. Now it was scorched earth. It was serious. It was warfare. They didn't give a damn who did what. They were simply going to kill anyone they thought might know the details of what they were doing. "These people are seriously bad," I said, almost to myself.

"I think now might be a good time to ask yourself if you're gonna stay in," Daz said. "I mean, if they get wind of you . . ." He spread his hands and left the rest of it to my imagination.

He was right. They were going to snuff me like a bug if they even began to believe I was involved. My first impulse was to do just what Daz was suggesting and get the hell out, but then I remembered what he'd said about strange attractors. I was part of a pattern I couldn't even see. Suppose they came around to Samski? They already knew he had access to the factory, presumably they thought he was harmless because he didn't know what he was doing. Suppose that changed? Christ, suppose they were just waiting until the job was finished to kill him and the other two?

"I've gotta stay in," I said to Daz.

"Yeah?"

"Yeah, if I stop and they come after Samski . . ."

"Given certain methods of persuasion, he's gonna tell them it was you."

"Given the fact that I roped him into it in the first place, yeah, I'd say he would."

"Goddamn. Not to be pessimistic, but you are in the shit. . . . There's always the cops."

"Yeah, I'll just go in and tell 'em I broke into Armco's factory and ask 'em if they'll protect me. To back up my story I've got an assembly worker who won't be around by the time anything comes to court."

Daz gave a short, wicked laugh. "Court's for civilians."

"There it is," I answered.

"What about Arla and the kids?" he asked. The thought had been sitting in the back of my mind like a nasty virus but I hadn't wanted to face it. "These dudes don't sound to me like the kind of people who're gonna cut noncombatants any slack," Daz said softly.

That was it. He knew it. I knew it. There was no getting out until the other pole had been found. Even Samski didn't know anything about my family or where I lived, but if I got out now there would always be that chance. A chance that one day I'd come home to see that second smile on Arla and the kids. That couldn't happen; I'd willingly die first. "What the fuck have I done?" I said.

I didn't expect Daz to answer but he did. "Well, my friend, I'd say you just went to war again. But it ain't like you haven't done it before, is it? And it isn't like you don't have allies now, is it?"

"What?"

He came around the desk with a predator's economy of movement, shedding the suit coat on the way, did about ten stroboscopic
karate moves, then stood over me, relaxed and breathing easily.
"Do I look old and out of shape to you?" he asked.
"No man, hunh-unh. No way I'm gonna ask you to get into
this thing. I only came here for advice."
"Okay," he said, "here's my advice. You go on ahead, I don't
wanta get into it. Leave me back as backup. You get up against
it, you get in touch and I come in from behind, small unit tactics,
remember?"
"It's my problem."
Daz was suddenly talking fast, a mean whipcrack in his voice.
"Listen motherfucker, if I say it's my problem . . . it's my problem.
We got some bad motherfuckers going around offin' people and
thinkin' they're some kind of fast guns, thinkin' they got the cit-
izenry by the balls. Well, I am the motherfuckin' citizenry and
I'm sick of that shit. They don't know who they're fuckin' with.
The war was a losing proposition, existentially speaking, but the
motherfuckers who fought in it were the hippest bastards breathing.
We both know that. And for the last twenty years we been laying
down drinking or layin' back and gettin' fat while the fecal forces,
the brown berets, the bullshit brigade, took over the country.
Something's going on here, my friend. It obviously involves military hardware and slime; that's a bad combination. You get into
a problem you call on the old citizen here. I got the time, I got
the money. I damn sure got the knowhow. And," he said, pointing
a finger at me, "I got some connections."
Now he was the sergeant, pacing, pointing, his voice rising and
falling with practiced intent and operatic effect. He stopped in
front of me, placed his hands on his hips, and leaned over to get
in my face. "You hear me?" he asked in his drill sergeant bellow.
"Hear me now?"
"You mean it?"
"No, I don't mean it. I'm just running for public office on a
national defense platform. . . . Your fuckin' A I mean it."
"I'm not getting you into it unless I have to."
He stood up straight, relaxed, went back to the executive side
of the desk, and shrugged back into the red robe. "I certainly hope

you're not," he said. "We don't want three poles in this pattern. But just remember, a lot of reputable physicists now think the multiple universe theory is the most viable. Chaos theory even tends to support that viewpoint."

It was amazing. He'd gone from DI to oriental professor without a glitch. "Just think of me as an alternate universe from which help might arrive, unannounced. Dig?"

I believed him. What's more, I respected him. "Okay," I said, "you've got it."

"One more thing," he said, holding up a clenched fist.

"Yeah?"

"Get mad. Get the sonsabitches. Get 'em and get anything else you can. Get any fucking thing else you can. It's good to have money, Lowell, it's good to have money you've won. Makes you a better person. Makes you live like you're giving thanks. Go after it, bro, but be snaky. It drops from heaven, but like my man Bobby D says, it's a hard rain."

By nine o'clock, when I drove away from the Dong Ha restaurant, the night air was so humid it seemed to ooze around me. I looked at my hands on the wheel; they were thicker at the knuckles now, the veins beginning to come to the surface like the roots of aging trees. By God though, they had a power they'd never had when I was young. This battle was for my turf, my life, my family. I had the home court advantage. This time, goddamnit, I was right. I knew it, I felt it. I was carrying an extra five pounds around my waist but I was also carrying the venom of middle age; old enough to feel creeping decrepitude but young enough to take my anger about it out on someone else. I knew instinctively that Daz was right. If I was able to do this, do it to keep my family safe, any money I made out of it would be truly and usefully mine.

Then I thought of Arla. My home had come out of her body as surely as my children. How was I going to tell her I couldn't be anywhere near her until this thing was over? How was I going to tell her I couldn't even tell her, not over the phone. No direct contact. Get mad Daz had said. I was.

9

There was nothing in the evening paper about Mosby but the eleven o'clock news was full of it. If it bleeds, it leads, is the motto of TV news, and Mosby bled a lot. The beachboy type doing a stand-up in front of Mosby's apartment building hadn't even finished when my phone began to ring. I picked it up and could almost hear Samski sweating. He wasn't the quickest guy in the world but he knew who Mosby was and he could add two and two; he wanted out. He wanted nothing more to do with the whole deal. He was going to quit the night work, he was going to quit Armco. He was going to quit listening to me and, if it looked like they were going to give him any grief, he was going to tell them about me and let the devil take the hindmost.

It took me about a half hour of very tense conversation to make him see he was safe only as long as they thought he knew absolutely nothing. As long as they thought he was just a dumb schmo trying to earn a few extra bucks, but the minute they thought he knew something weird was going on he was dead.

"You've gotta stay there," I told him. "You quit now and they're gonna know something's up and come looking for you. What's their next move after you tell them about me?"

It finally sank in. There was no way they were going to put the screws to him and then let him walk away to talk about it. "What if'n they don't have to put the screws to me?" he asked. "What if I just walk in an' tell 'em straight out?"

"Well," I said, "in that case I'm sure they'll send Doris a nice thank-you note after they kill you. You're the one who let me in. I don't think they're gonna care too much that you had a change of heart and came back to the fold. They're gonna kill you. Think about it."

After he calmed down he did. Then he accused me of being romantically linked with several varieties of barnyard animal and suggested other members of my family might also be so inclined. I let him get it out of his system before I got to the point. "Listen," I said, trying to sound reasonable, "you're in. At this point no one's going to believe you're not. So it seems to me your best way out of this is to help me if you can. The faster we get this cleared up the better it's going to be for us both."

At first Samski suggested I try on myself what he'd accused me of doing with the animals, but he started to come around when I pointed out that, if they were really interested in him, he'd have heard from them by now. As long as he stayed normal, ignorant and quiet, he'd probably be all right. "Oh, one more thing," I said, trying to sound offhand, "no more calls from your house. I wouldn't be surprised if they decided to bug your phone." He started to melt down again but I told him it was no big deal. Armco was a high-tech firm; it would be surprising if they didn't try high-tech methods. Hell, they'd probably bug everybody's phone.

When I hung up I had the feeling he was beginning to see it my way. He even felt well enough to mention the money he might have coming. He was okay for now, but I knew that sooner or later they were going to call the three night guys in and really put the questions to them; not because they expected to get anywhere, but just as a fishing expedition. If Samski stayed calm he might stand up. I had to start moving, though, I had to show him we were getting somewhere. I was going to have to start putting the pressure on and hope something cracked.

Before going to sleep I decided there were three things I had to have before I started kicking out the jams: another location, another car, and some firepower.

At ten the following morning I hauled out the plastic and bought an answering machine I could access by beeper and installed it in my office. Then I called Daz and asked him if there was a spare room in one of the buildings he owned. He gave me an address and a name. It turned out to be a Chinese restaurant in Waverly run by an old guy with a face like a baked apple named Huan Lo. The room was above the restaurant and wasn't bad. It smelled like the inside of an egg roll but it had all the amenities to go with the TV I'd brought from the office: bed, table, telephone, a chair, a window, a bathroom down the hall, and several six-legged companions. But what the hell, pets are a comfort when you're lonely.

For the firepower I went to my bank and the safe-deposit box where I'd stashed an unregistered army forty-five pistol and an M-79 grenade launcher I'd mailed back from Nam inside some stereo equipment. From more than twenty yards the forty-five was less accurate than a rock but it hit like a bowling ball in a tornado.

The M-79 had once been my best friend. It's basically a little shoulder mortar which fires a forty-millimeter shell that looks like a bullet with a glandular condition. There were three kinds of ammo: high explosive for the big bang, white phosphorus if you wanted something that would stick and burn, and a shotgun round full of obscenely large pellets, in case you wanted to turn a knot of people into spaghetti. Of the three kinds, though, I had none.

Ammunition for the forty-five was no problem but not even the cops had M-79 rounds. Blowing up houses and burning down neighborhoods tends to create bad press. I did know someone though, someone who ran a sporting goods store along with one of the best sports books in town. If Miles Klyman didn't know where to get a commodity, you could stop looking.

After I'd put the weapons in a flight bag and taken them back to Huan Lo's, there was the matter of the car. I didn't know how connected the other side was. For all I knew they had access to DMV records. I needed something that couldn't be traced to me, or Arla. I could rent a car, but that meant presenting ID. If they were connected enough to search DMV they could probably check the car rental places. I didn't think rental companies kept centralized records but, in case they did, I stopped by the Avis lot at the airport and discreetly exchanged the tags on a K car I'd rented for ones off a blue Camaro. Then I drove the K car to Ace Sporting Goods in Pikesville.

Pikesville used to be known to everyone as the golden ghetto because it was home to Baltimore's Jewish population. That was, however, before civil rights and ethnic sensitivity. Now it's only called that by Jews.

Miles is a thin, wiry Jew who went to school at City College in the days when it was 90 percent black; he was one of only two white people in his graduating class. As a result he'd acquired a kind of rapid-fire effusiveness I think of as Jewish be-bop. He's got wire-rim prescription shades, the *bandido* mustache, a corona of black curls, and a joking glint in his eye that makes you feel he knows something you don't, a feeling which is usually accurate. One of the things he knows is that, when you have a personality like his, you can throw the book out the window. He's the kind of guy who didn't know dick about what they tried to teach him in school but did know who was screwing who and what it took to get someone to tell him about it.

He has the instant camaraderie and perpetual good humor of a born salesman. Even people who don't like him like being around him; he makes you feel better because he seems to feel so good. In all the time I've known him I've never seen him visibly depressed or openly contemplative, and I've known him for ten years.

Daz had introduced him to our counseling group to prove to us we could relate to someone who hadn't been to Nam. Miles had gone to Canada where he hustled pool, played cards, and repossessed cars until President Carter told him he could come home.

Daz didn't tell us all that. He just introduced Miles as a guy who'd paid his own dues in his own way. By the time we found out what his story was we all liked him so much it didn't matter to us that he'd come home with a big enough bankroll to start his own business.

Surprisingly, nobody tried to kill him or even punch him out. Maybe it was just because he had the guts to come in and talk to us. At first everyone just sat and stared at him like they were at the circus, but he grew on you; we've been friends ever since. I like to go to the track with Miles because it's the only time I ever win, and we don't even bet on the same horses. Some people are just lucky to be around. That was half the reason I went to see him. The other half was the M-79.

"My main man," he said, coming around a glass counter where he'd been arranging hunting knives. "My man Lowell. How've you been, buddy? Talk to me, tell me something good."

"I've been busy."

"Busy people are happy people."

"I could be happier."

Miles spread his arms. "Buddy, buddy, what can I do for you? I was talking to a jockey about Wild Hair in the fifth tomorrow at Pimlico."

"Okay, put me down for a hundred on your book."

"Yeah, my book, I got your book. The track'll take your action, and don't tell 'em who sent ya. So what else?"

"I'm in kind of a deal. I need to put my hands on some M-seventy-nine rounds."

He laughed like a king at a jester. "My main man," he said, shaking his head. "My man wants M-seventy-nine rounds. You having a little trouble with the neighbors or what?"

"You knew I was going into the detective business."

"Hey, I didn't know you were detecting tanks."

"Yeah, well, it is something like that."

"Talk to me," he said, and led me to his office in back of the store.

I didn't tell him the whole thing and he didn't want to know. I did tell him there were some people who already didn't like me even though they didn't know who I was, people who'd already greased one guy.

"You got a place to stay?" he asked me.

"Yeah."

"Daz?"

"Yeah."

"My man Daz. Took me down for two thousand on the Pistons and Celtics."

"You laid it off anyway."

"Didn't need to, lotta white guys bet their hearts instead of their heads when it comes to the Celtics."

"The rich get richer."

"Speaking of which, is there any money in this deal?"

"Not right now, maybe later."

"How're you doin'?"

"I'm a little thin right now."

"Need any cash?"

"I'm already gonna owe you for the ammunition."

"I didn't say I could do it."

"Can you do it?"

He popped a piece of gum in his mouth and chewed in rhythm to some drums in his head. "What'ya got now, anything?" he asked.

"A forty-five I sent home from Nam."

"Man, I hope you don't have to hit anything smaller than a garage."

"I hope I don't have to hit anything. Can you do the M-seventy-nine?"

"Yeah, I think so. It might take a few days, though. They're not exactly what people keep in stock."

"Only place I can think of is the army, or the National Guard."

Miles laughed. "Well, my main man, they are America's first line of defense."

"You know someone inside?"

"Busy people are happy people."

"What about the money?"

"I'll front you the money. Just don't forget me when the time comes. I might be able to get you a little something else too."

"What?"

"Wait and see," he said. "I don't want to make any promises I can't keep."

"I'll be waiting."

"How'm I gonna get in touch with you?"

"You're not. I'll call you."

"That's the gig, huh?"

"You don't want to know."

"You're right. Call me in a couple days. I'll be here."

"Thanks, Miles."

"Tell 'em where ya got it. On second thought, don't tell 'em."

I'd have liked to hang around Ace Sporting Goods talking trash with Miles but I needed to be at the Armco plant before quitting time.

I pulled into the lot and waited for the executives to leave. At about five Fredericks got into his Seville. I followed him, hoping I wouldn't have to spend two more hours listening to the haircuts talk deals at the Hunt Cup bar.

I was in luck. Fredericks drove past the Hyatt entrance and onto the northbound ramp of Interstate 83. He got off on Belfast Road and headed east, toward Sparks, more hunt country. Sparks was a gentleman farmer community in the upper reaches of the county; old money, newly restored farm houses, long winding lanes surrounded by wooded acreage. It was high-priced country for the comptroller of a small firm like Armco. Fredericks had to be making more than his salary.

The Seville turned onto Zylar Mill Road. I waited a few beats and followed. He stopped to check a mailbox on the corner, then rounded a bend and disappeared up an evergreen-lined lane. The number on the box was 1779. I drove back to Belfast Road where I found a Wa-Wa store, located a pay phone, and dialed information. I was in luck again. If Fredericks had had a nonlisted number I'd have had to write him a letter and killers probably don't write many letters.

I got back to Huan Lo's about seven, had the number two combination dinner, and went up to my room and its phone. First I checked the answering machine at my office; nothing from Samski. He'd either calmed down or he was dead; I'd check his house later. Next I called Arla and told her I'd be in touch but I wouldn't be mowing the lawn for a while; she didn't understand. There were a few rough moments until I made her realize it had nothing to do with who was mad at whom. But it did. I was mad at Fredericks. Now was the time to call him.

"Fredericks," I said when he answered.

"Yeah?"

"Mosby didn't have the boards."

"So?"

"So that only leaves you."

The sound on his end was distinctly like a gawk. "What! Me! What the hell do you mean, me?"

"I mean come up with the boards or you and your friend Mosby are going to be together again."

Indignation now. "Who is this?"

"What do you want Fredericks, references? try Mosby. I'm a consultant. And I'm either gonna get the boards back or make sure no one else gets them. Mosby didn't have them. That leaves you."

There was a ruffling silence while Fredericks tried to get his blood pressure under stroke proportions. "What," he gasped. "What the hell? Are you crazy? What'ya mean me? How could it be me for Chrissake? I'm the one who told you all about Mosby. Why the hell would I do that if I had the fuckin' things?"

"What else could you tell us Fredericks? That you had 'em, and did we mind?"

His voice started to grow a big panic blossom. "Listen," he said, "listen to me. I don't have 'em. What the hell would I do with 'em if I did. What could I do with 'em huh, huh?"

"Jesus," I said with as much disgust as I could muster. "You're pathetic, you know that? You'd fuckin' sell 'em back to us through a third party. There, are you convinced you're not dealing with morons?"

"But, but, listen to me, I . . ."

I decided now was the time to lay in the heavy guns. "No, you listen. Shut up and listen because I'm only going to say it once. This is your only chance. Come up with the boards and all you'll lose is your job. Keep this up and it won't be as nice as it was with Mosby. It'll be ugly. That's the deal. Now talk to me."

The indignation in Fredericks' voice was replaced by a little-boy whine. "Jesus, Jesus God, why? It's not me. I never wanted to get into it in the first place, really. It's not me. Talk to Rodman if you don't believe me. Talk to him. He forced me into it. Talk to him. I'm just a little guy. Talk to Rodman before you do anything. Please, just talk to him. He'll tell you I'm not up for anything like this. Talk to him."

Fredericks was obviously telling the truth. Rodman was the guy I should talk to, but who the hell was he and how did I get to him? "Shut up," I said, "don't do anything. Stay where you are. Don't call anyone, don't go anywhere. I have a man near your house with contingency instructions. I'll call you in forty-five minutes. Repeat it back to me."

After Fredericks repeated my message I hung up and checked the phone book. There were seven Rodmans. *Excuse me, are you the Mr. Rodman who had a man killed recently?* Nah, I didn't think so. I got in the rental car and drove back to the Wa-Wa on Belfast Road. It took me about forty minutes. I used the extra five to rehearse what I was going to say. I dropped a quarter in the pay phone and Fredericks answered halfway through the first ring. "I talked to Rodman," I said without preamble. "He says you're a gutbag who wouldn't have the balls for this, but he wants to see you. No calls, he's afraid the government's got a line on his phone. You're to go to his house, now. If you don't show, or if you call, you can refer to our previous conversation."

"Uh, what's he want?" he asked, like a schoolboy hauled out of class to see the principal.

"I'm a consultant," I said, "I don't deal in whys." It took me seven minutes to drive to Zylar Mill Road and find the entrance to Fredericks' lane. I swung the car into an area of shadow and waited. It was a gamble but what did I have to lose?

At ten o'clock I saw the Seville come to the end of the lane. When it got to the juncture of Zylar Mill and Belfast it swung left, heading west. It followed Belfast until it hit Falls Road, where it turned north through a section of houses priced in the high 290's and continued on to Butler Road, where it made a left and proceeded through the high 390's, 490's, 590's and finally, about ten miles west, achieved orbit in the million zone. These weren't houses, they were estates. Their acreage was so vast the houselights were hidden by small forests. The Seville slowed and went through a fieldstone arch bridging a blacktopped drive that led up and away into the distance. It was ten-thirty-five.

At eleven-forty the Seville reappeared and headed home. When it turned onto Zylar Mill, I headed back toward the Wa-Wa, lusting for a beer. It was an expensive tasting summer night, too dry to be balmy, light, but possessing a warm finish and a complex bouquet of wildflowers and alfalfa. I had the radio off, enjoying the sound of the liquid air as it rushed by my ears. That was the reason I was able to hear the shots, six or seven bursts of overlapping automatic weapons fire, distant but plain.

I braked and made a U-turn, heading back toward Zylar Mill Road. I knew what it must be; what else could it be? I knew, but I headed toward the sound anyway, wanting to be sure, wanting to be wrong. As I got to the intersection I was forced onto the shoulder of the road as a big car made a high-speed turn out of Zylar Mill onto Belfast. A big beige car. A big beige Mercedes 450 SL with DC plates.

My first instinct was to follow it until I remembered that it was probably loaded with men carrying automatic weapons. All I was carrying was the knowledge that I'd seen them before. My second instinct was to go to Fredericks' and make sure, maybe help him. But if the automatic weapons fire had been for him the only way I could help would be to hose him off his driveway. I didn't follow either instinct. What I did was get the hell away from there before someone called the cops and they showed up to take names and shine their flashlights in people's eyes.

I bought a six-pack at a 7-Eleven farther down the road and drank it on my way back to Huan Lo's. By the time I got there I knew one thing for sure: Either Rodman had made a call after Fredericks left and ordered him killed, or he hadn't.

10

The beachboy was on the news again: "Beverly, I'm standing in the driveway of 1779 Zylar Mill Road in northern Baltimore County. This is a section of expensive, executive-style homes, that, until last night, imagined itself far away from the violence which so often characterizes the inner city. This used to be the home of Arthur Fredericks, comptroller of the Armco Electronics Company, located in nearby Glen Arm. I say used to be, because some time late last night Mr. Fredericks was gunned down right where I'm standing. Mr. Fredericks was divorced and lived alone, there were no witnesses. Police say death was caused by multiple gunshot wounds, probably inflicted by one or more automatic weapons. Lab results are not yet available, so the exact type of weapon is still in question. As you can imagine, Beverly, residents of this area are asking themselves how it could happen here. Police think they may have come up with an answer. A large quantity of cocaine was found in the trunk of Mr. Fredericks' car. Police spokesman Donald Bromley told us just a few minutes ago that the cocaine, and the method of execution, indicate that the slaying was drug related. Yet there is one other interesting aspect to the case, Beverly. Armco Electronics was also the employer of Glenn Mosby, an engineer who was found murdered just a few days ago at his apartment in Cockeysville. Officer Bromley informs me that, even though the cause of death was different, the police think that Fredericks and Mosby may have been jointly involved in a cocaine distribution network. Whether other workers at Armco may also have been involved is a matter now under investigation. Back to you, Beverly."

Sure, I thought, that's it, drugs; the root of all evil. Just ask the cops, ask Geraldo. Ask anyone running for elective office. Ask whoever planted the cocaine in Fredericks' trunk.

It could have been a coincidence, of course. Maybe Fredericks was in the drug business and the coke in his trunk was just a lucky diversion for the killers, but I was willing to bet the only coke Fredericks ever pushed was in a shopping cart at the supermarket.

The cops would love the drug angle, though. They'd be all over Armco, probably actually uncover the guy in any workplace who's selling a few grams on the side. They'd bust the poor fucker, keep him in a room until he admitted killing Fredericks, Mosby, and John F. Kennedy. Then they'd close the book on the whole deal. Very convenient for whoever was coming up from DC to make war in Maryland. I'd seen the plates on the Mercedes that almost ran into me at Zylar Mill and it was the same car that passed me at Mosby's.

The news had ended, and I was staring blankly at the screen as Chef Tell whipped up some kind of rabbit dish with roquefort sauce. "Hour Magazine"'s Gary Collins stood by for the obligatory taste like a man waiting to be led to the gallows. Life goes on, except for Fredericks, and Mosby, and me.

I hated the room over Huan Lo's and I'd only been there for two days. I could hear the cooks screaming at each other in Chinese below my feet. I was right over the kitchen and every so often small jets of steam would shoot up from between the cracks in the bare wood floor. It was like living in an off-Broadway play about the entrance to hell, written by Rod Serling. Why doesn't anyone ever ask if Rod Serling is really alive, a guy like him, big with the mysterious shit. Maybe Stephen King is really Rod Serling. Maybe he's really dead and he's still Stephen King.

Those are the kinds of fractured ideas you get when your train of thought jumps the track. And I was completely derailed. It wasn't getting me anywhere. I'd been tracing my way upward, but every rung on my ladder was ending up dead.

Rodman. That was it. That's what was hanging me up. What was his place? If he hadn't ordered Fredericks killed then he was likely to be the next victim. If he had, it made him the man I had to squeeze. It also made him the man who could squeeze me into a grease spot on the highway. I had to find out which way it was before I could proceed. But this time a phone scam was no good.

I'd known how Fredericks was involved; I'd used that knowledge against him. If Rodman was the head man, and I called him with the same scam I'd used on Fredericks, he'd know there was a wild card in the game. His play then would be to sucker me into a situation that would force me to come out of hiding. I'd have to do that at some point but it had to be on my terms. Before I could start to set those terms I had to know whether Rodman was one of the big players or just another rung on the ladder.

By the time the beachboy started to repeat the story of the Fredericks killing on the noon news, I'd decided what I was going to do. I called the office of the Baltimore County Clerk and found out that land plats were public knowledge. You could look them up by development. If they weren't in a development you had to find them by name and date of purchase. I called around and got hold of Daz at the Dazco office downtown. Anyone into as much real estate as Daz could surely find out when an expensive plat like Rodman's had been purchased. Big sales like that one mean big commission and big talk at happy hour. He told me to call him back at five.

I got to Ace Sporting Goods at two, after stopping at Pimlico to put an advance hundred on Wild Hair in the fifth. Miles was on the phone about the M-79 when I got there. I let him work while I picked out some camouflage gear, a shelter half, a surplus entrenching tool, and a poncho.

When Miles came out of his office he held out his palm for me to slap. "My man," he said with a canary-eating grin. "You owe me but what's new?"

"You got it?"

"You're in."

"What'd you get?"

"How 'bout ten high explosive, ten shotgun, and three Willie Peter?"

He held out his palm again and this time I reddened it. "You are amazing," I said, "a-fucking-mazing. How much is it gonna be?"

"Don't worry about it," he said. "It'd only fuck up your head. I'll tell ya later."

"That much huh?"

"I said don't worry about it. We'll work something out."

"When can I get 'em?"

"Tomorrow, about this time."

"Good enough."

He gave me another one of the bird-eating grins. "C'mon back," he said, and led me toward his office. When we got there he sat behind his desk and opened a drawer. "I told ya I might have a little something else for ya," he said as he laid it gently on the desk.

"Is that what I think it is?" I asked as I reached for it.

"Nine-millimeter Beretta," Miles said like a proud parent. "Now the standard side arm of the U.S. military. It's just as powerful as that antique you've got but about three times as accurate and holds fifteen shots. Look at it."

I was looking at it, with undisguised affection. "Nice," I said, turning it over in my hand, feeling the balance.

"No," he said, "look at it close. Whaddya see? Or rather, what don't ya see?"

My heart skipped as I looked. He was right. It was clean as a newborn baby without a name. No serial numbers, none; they weren't filed or scratched out. It was smooth. There had never been any numbers on it. "Where in the hell did you get this?" I laughed.

"Where else?" he said, leaning back and putting his feet on the desk, feeling comfortable, prosperous, like he helped run the world.

"The factory," I said with awe.

He took the opportunity to give me a little education. "You're in the gun business for a while and you find out most factories have a few guys doing a little piece work on their own. They're supposed to turn out so many a week, they turn out so many plus a couple more, only the couple more are naked, like this one. Factories baby, most of 'em make a little more than they're supposed to . . . free enterprise." He shrugged.

"That's what it's all about."

"Whaddya mean?"

"Never mind."

"Gotcha."

I hung around Miles' store until three-thirty when the results of the fifth race were broadcast on WBAL. Wild Hair by two lengths, paid $22.20. I'd made $1,110. "That'll just about cover the cost of the Beretta," Miles said, "but you can get back to me when the detective business takes off."

"It might not take off for a while."

"Just don't forget about me."

As I was getting ready to leave Miles pulled me out the door and around the corner of the store. He kept it light but he was serious. "Listen," he said, "that Beretta makes you double-o-seven. Know what I mean? Untraceable, gives you a license to kill. Just remember this ain't the movies."

"Self-defense, Miles, nothing but self-defense."

"Well," he said, raising an eyebrow. "Try to make sure you're defending your butt instead of your mouth."

"I intend to keep my butt down and my mouth shut."

"Dig it," said Miles. We slapped hands again and I headed for Pimlico to pick up my winnings.

I got back to my room at five. Time to call Daz. He had the information I needed. Rodman had bought the property in December of '87 from an investor who'd been flattened by October's stock market crash. The exact date of the deed was December 10. The time frame was about right; Rodman moved in December. Armco had been purchased in January, and Samski had started his night work in June. Rodman could be the man, but he didn't work for Armco. If not Armco then who? Dynatron? Maybe. Probably. But I had to be sure. If it wasn't Dynatron then there was another wild card in the game.

I hated to waste a night but I had no choice. I couldn't move on Rodman without the exact layout of his property and that was now locked in the county clerk's office until the next morning.

I used the evening to check on Samski and Arla. Samski was comparatively calm. The cops had been around questioning people about cocaine but that only made him feel better. He hoped it was about coke. Maybe the killings didn't have anything to do with the boards at all. I told him to stop dreaming. It would make him careless. The coke thing was good, though. With the cops poking around Armco the boys at the top would probably try to go light on the killings this week. They'd also be likely to wait a while before they began quizzing Samski and the other guys on the production line.

Arla was another story. Her wife radar was beginning to pick up my scent around the fringes of the stories she'd been seeing on TV, but she didn't think my refusal to give her my phone number or tell her my location was coincidental to the timing of the news stories. Then she brought up the other likely possibility: I was staying with a woman. "Jesus, Arla," I said, "that's all I need, another woman. I can't handle one, let alone two." She didn't laugh so I tried again. "Besides, it's too expensive. You know our situation. How am I gonna afford another woman?"

She still didn't laugh, but I got the feeling it was because what I was saying made sense to her. Great woman, Arla, practical as well as beautiful. I told her it would all be over in a few days and then we'd talk. When I hung up the phone it occurred to me that I could afford another woman. I had eleven hundred dollars in cash on me. Only I remembered I didn't want another one. I had business, and that business was partly for Arla. If none of it worked out, then maybe it would be time to think about another woman. I started to watch Johnny Carson but fell asleep after the kid who held the world's record for knocking over dominoes was replaced on the couch by an actress talking about her face lift.

11

I was at the county clerk's office at eight-thirty. By nine-thirty I'd made a rough pencil sketch of Rodman's property and that of his surrounding neighbors. He lived on an approximate trapezoid comprising ten acres. The house was located in the right front corner of the trapezoid, and was connected to the road by the lane I'd watched Fredericks turn into. Behind the house there was a stream flowing roughly parallel to the front property line. The ground sloped gradually upward from the rear of the house, toward the stream. Once it reached the water it sloped more sharply. Based on what I'd been able to see from the road I was willing to bet that the area to the rear of the stream was heavily wooded.

Rodman's house was located at the extreme lower right of his property, with an entrance from Butler Road. A couple miles further on, at the intersection of Butler and Dover roads, there was a church. I'd leave the car there.

At noon I filled a gym bag with the camouflage gear and the rest of the stuff I'd picked up at Miles's store. I put the M-79 in the bottom of the bag. The Beretta and three full clips I stashed in a flannel Crown Royal whiskey bag in the trunk of my rental.

Then I headed for Ace Sporting Goods where I picked up the M-79 rounds, a high-powered set of Navy binoculars, which were convertible to infrared, and two pairs of rawhide shoelaces.

"Hey, buddy, buddy . . ." Miles said, "help yourself. What else ya want? My house? My wife? What?"

"You'll get 'em back."

"Where do I look for ya if I don't?"

"The news. And don't believe what you see."

"Hey," he said, spreading his arms, "who does?"

I drove directly from Miles's store to the church on Dover Road. It was Thursday, about noon. The church was a small country clapboard building that looked as if it would hold about a hundred people. A sign in front announced it as the First Church of the Holy Redeemer; a nonaffiliated little fundamentalist place. The pastor probably ordained himself after a midnight vision told him what would happen to him if he didn't stop drinking. The service would consist of a lot of wailing and screaming backed up by hard-stomping Baptist hymns. That kind of church was as out of place in this section of the county as I was. "Good," I said to myself, "if anyone sees me I'm just a deacon out for a little retreat."

Thursday is a slow day for churches and my car was the only one in the gravel parking lot. I put a clip in the Beretta and stuck it in my waistband under the loose brown sport shirt I was wearing. I left the camouflage stuff and the M-79 in the car and walked casually toward the estate to the left of Rodman's. When I got to a fence I turned uphill until I came to the spot where the fence turned right, the place where Rodman's property began. The terrain was uphill and forested with sixty-foot birch and chestnut trees. Stands of short white pines and firs had covered the ground with a soft brown snow of needles. They were wet and soaked up the sound of my footsteps.

I walked diagonally, crabbing my way uphill but staying close to the property line. I wanted to get to the top of the hill as far away from the house as possible. If there were bodyguards they were going to stay close to the body, and the body was usually going to be close to the house. Four steps from the crest of the hill I sat down and leaned against the base of a birch tree. I took out the Beretta and placed it next to my right thigh under a thin mound of pine needles. Then I leaned back against the tree and stared upward into its height, letting the afternoon sun catch my face, just a sensitive soul out quoting poetry to himself. If Rodman had lookouts on top of the hill they would come down to ask me what I was doing on private property.

After half an hour no one had showed up so I put the Beretta in my hip pocket and crabbed my way to the top of the hill; there was more forest sloping down to the stream and then a lawn as green and long as a fairway. I could barely make out the house through the trees. In order to see anything I'd have to set up shop close to the stream. I'd still have the high ground in relation to the house but would be below the crest of the hill. If there were bodyguards, they'd be able to flank me and fire at me from above. First though, they'd have to see me. I was going to need the camouflage gear and the entrenching tool.

It was two o'clock. The morning paper had said sunset was at 7:33. If they were going to increase their defenses it wouldn't be until then. I had plenty of time to backtrack to the church parking lot, scrawl a "won't start, be back soon" sign for the car window, get the gym bag out of the trunk, retrace my steps, and find a good place to dig in.

At three-thirty I was working my way along the crest of the hill looking for a sightline to the house. I'd only gone fifty yards downhill when I passed a hole in the trees that shone like a spotlight on the rear of the house; a little tube of vision through which I could see most of the house, the entire pool, and the driveway, which formed a cement moat around the place. This was it. The house's rear entrance was about 150 yards away but, with the binoculars, I'd be able to see the pattern on their china.

I took the entrenching tool out of the bag and dug a shallow hole six feet long, eighteen inches deep, and just wide enough to accommodate the length of my body. The ground was soft and sandy. Even though it had been twenty years since I'd dug a trench (and swore I'd never dig another), it only took me a half-hour. I changed into the camouflage jump suit. Then I cut four branches from a nearby pine, used the shelter-half, the rawhide shoelaces, and the branches to lash the whole thing into a roof for the depression I'd dug. Picking up a few dead pine branches, I stuck them in the remaining grommets. I laid the roof over the hole and stood back . . . not bad. You'd have to be pretty close to tell it from the rest of the forest floor. It was four-thirty. I sat in the hole using my arms to brace the binoculars against my eyes. I was as comfortable as a man reading in the bathtub.

The rear entrance to the house had a wide set of French doors that led out to a flagstone patio big enough to be a truck stop. To the right of the patio and down an asphalt path were three tennis courts; to the left, a swimming pool. The pool, which was big enough to float a cabin cruiser, was surrounded by an alien landing fleet of yellow tables with umbrellas growing out of their middles. I could see dining room furniture through the French doors and living room furniture through twenty-five square feet of plate glass on the side of the house. A row of casement windows ran the length of the upstairs wall before they turned the corner. I scanned upward with the binoculars and saw a stained glass skylight. There had to be an immense tub below that skylight, or a Jacuzzi, or a sauna, maybe another tennis court. The rich are different from you and me, at least from me. Daz has a handball court in his bathroom. It's true: so he doesn't lose his sweat between there and the sauna.

I saw no cars so I guessed the garage must be on the side away from me. There was no movement. No gardeners or servants, no shadows moving inside the windows. I assumed no one was home and was proved right at five-fifteen.

That's when the big beige Mercedes rounded a turn and came in a luxuriously slow crawl toward the turnaround in the front of the house. No one came out to meet it. No one objected when three short, swarthy, blue-bearded guys got out of the car and went toward the front door. I thought I recognized two of them as the ones I'd seen coming out of Mosby's apartment. One was carrying a black briefcase. He headed toward a power pole which was nearly hidden in a row of blue spruce that ran toward the road. Another carried a walkie-talkie and stood by the car listening to it. The third carried another black bag and a reptilian machine pistol; one of those things with the wire stock and viperlike sights. He headed uphill, toward me.

I ducked into the hole and pulled the roof over me, leaving a small slit through which I could watch. I made sure the Beretta was easy to reach and waited. The man heading up the hill wasn't used to country life, or water. He tried to skip daintily across the stream on some rocks but slipped ankle deep into the burbling muddiness. He swore in a language I didn't recognize and, holding his pant legs up like some school marm crossing a cow pasture, came up the hill for about fifty yards and stopped. He looked around in disgust, then sat down on a fallen limb and took off his wet shoes and socks. He wrung out the socks as he watched the guy near the pole put on a pair of climbing spikes and clump his way up to a junction box. The climber opened the box in a few quick movements, did something inside, then shouted to the man with the walkie-talkie.

With the power to the burglar alarm now disconnected, walkie-talkie had no qualms about picking the lock on the front door and going inside. In front of me, wet socks pulled a headset and a small tape recorder out of his black bag and nodded in affirmation while speaking into the microphone attached to the headset.

When they were finished bugging Rodman's phone, walkie-talkie came outside and spoke to the electrician on the pole, who then reconnected the power before climbing down to join him for a conference at the car. When the consultation was over the electrician came up the hill to join the third man, who was smoking a cigarette and trying to dry his socks with a lighter. When he heard what the electrician told him he shook his head disconsolately in the affirmative but pointed at his shoes. With a shrug the electrician called to walkie-talkie who was now standing just on the other side of the stream. Walkie-talkie made a command decision and then it was the electrician's turn to yell. He waved and gestured and made some kind of foreign fuck you gesture to the guy on the hill but in the end he came up and took off his shoes and socks. He threw them at the seated guy, then stepped into the wet shoes and made his way back down the hill, turning every now and then to make the fuck you gesture.

After the guy on the hill returned the gesture, he sat down, talking to himself. Walkie-talkie and the electrician got in the Mercedes and left. Shit rolls downhill doesn't it buddy? I thought to myself.

Now it was just the swarthy guy and me. Him watching the house and me watching him. He took a coat and blanket out of his bag and put them on the ground. He also had his own walkie-talkie which he tested in whatever language they spoke. I tried to place it but couldn't. It was some kind of rolling rhythm with la-las everywhere. It sounded like something sung by a dyslexic doo-wop group. After looking at him for a few minutes through the binoculars I was pretty sure I could place his locale. He had the perpetual five o'clock shadow, the dark curly hair, charcoal pock-eted eyes, big hooked nose. He was definitely Mediterranean or near East. Greek maybe. Jewish maybe. Arab maybe. Arab probably.

At six-fifteen a red 1987 Corvette came slowly up the lane in a sedate prowl and disappeared on the garage side of the house. There was still over an hour till sundown and I judged the temperature to be close to ninety when I saw her come out of the rear entrance and head toward the pool. When I put the binoculars to my eyes it was five seconds before I could breathe again.

She had long rolling chestnut hair that caught the evening light and reflected it against a body that only nature at its most sala-ciously benevolent could have produced. No amount of exercise, no amount of working out or dieting or surgery could have pro-duced legs so long, so symmetrically rounded, so exquisitely fitted into a perfectly matched set of absolutely circular, shining, spring-bounce buttocks. An infinity of sit-ups couldn't have created the great flat golden plane of that lush desert of skin which flowed from the three-cornered, fruit-swell, almost-goddamn-talking-to-you presence of her breathing crotch to the breasts just big enough to be slightly behind each of her movements, just small enough to catch up to the rest of her with their point-pout arrogance.

She had an ex-model's body; gone from elongated anorexia to all-night energy. She flowed, she bent, she rippled. She sluiced when she moved and juiced when she didn't. Hell, even her hair looked like it was ready to get fucked. I could see the body in all its magnificence because she was wearing a white bikini whose top covered her nipples like a narrow scarf she'd grabbed in an emergency. The bottom of the bikini was a handkerchief tucked into a shoelace. The back of the handkerchief had moved inexorably into the valley of the shadow of bittersweet sin, leaving nothing but the sin to the imagination.

And imagine it I did. So did the swarthy guy below me. If he wasn't careful his eyeballs were going to come out the other end of his binoculars. The woman eased into the water and floated around like a wet dream for about fifteen minutes while the two of us on the hill forgot the cares of the world. Then she was out and gone in a long white towel and it was just the two of us again. I tried not to look at him too often because I didn't want to activate the radar that tells humans at traffic lights everywhere when someone in the next car is looking at them.

Traffic light radar; it's real. They even had it on the Ho Chi Minh trail. The only way to deal with it is to use a sweep look that picks up whatever it can on the way past its object. I swept the guy a few times and was more sure of his origin with each pass. He had a hard set of eyes but was getting a little thick around the middle. He'd be quick laterally but wouldn't turn well. The machine pistol would do his turning for him. The machine pistol was the thing that puzzled me. If you're going to shoot someone from 150 or 200 yards you want something more accurate.

So what was he going to do, rush Rodman when he got out of his car, from this distance, in the dark, in someone else's shoes? These guys didn't work that way. They either hit you neat and quiet or loud and in force. No. The machine pistol was just to make the guy feel better about sitting in the dark by himself all night in a strange country.

I had a decision to make. Should I stay the night with the guy in the wrong shoes or wait until dark and slip out the way I'd come? My question about Rodman had already been answered. If they were tapping his phone and watching his house then he was just another player, not the main man. Still, there was the possibility, paranoid as it might be, that he was setting me up; anticipating that the wild card who had called Fredericks would get around to him. He could have tapped his own phone, for what . . . to prove to the ones above him that I existed? I was 90 percent sure the people watching his house were there for the same reason I was, but I wanted that other 10 percent. I decided to stay.

At eight o'clock a BMW 735 rounded the turn and headed to

the same side of the house as the Corvette. A light went on in a corner of the downstairs. I could see Rodman intermittently as he passed a small open space in the curtains. He was tall and thin, with steel gray hair and a nasty pair of wire-rim glasses that made him look like a colonel in the Gestapo. He was drinking whiskey as he talked on the phone. No sign of the wife. Believe me, I looked. She wasn't in the room with him, didn't come in. There was a light on upstairs. He didn't go up. They sure weren't a couple for sentimental homecomings. Trouble in paradise?

The swarthy guy down the hill from me was listening intently to Rodman's phone call and I could see that his state-of-the-art bugging apparatus gave an LED readout of any number Rodman called. He compared the number Rodman had dialed with a list of numbers he kept in a small notebook but didn't show any particular agitation and didn't call anybody on his walkie-talkie. Whatever they were listening for wasn't happening. Not surprising, since they were listening for me and didn't know it. It was fun watching them watch for me when they had no idea what I looked like, or even if I really existed. I felt a little like God, or Tom Sawyer going to his own funeral.

The cramped dampness of my hiding place was starting to re-mind me of why I'd been so ecstatic the day I was discharged from the army. I ate the sandwich I'd brought, drank a few hits of the Jim Beam, relieved myself of the Jim Beam in a paper cup, dumped the contents outside the hole, dozed, watched the lights go out in Rodman's house, dozed, watched my partner in voyeurism do the same, dozed some more, and then, in what seemed no more than a week, it was dawn. The guy below me was speaking animatedly into the walkie-talkie, probably demanding his replacement. It made me a little nervous to realize that any such replacement would have to walk in from the back using the same route I had. Now I had two directions to watch.

I also had a problem. How was I going to get out of my hole and leave without the swarthy guy seeing me. I'd already been there for eighteen hours. I hadn't found out for sure what Rodman's place in the scheme of things was, but I had a working hypothesis and I had the ace of knowing someone was bugging his phone. I didn't know how yet, but I was sure there was a way to use that information. I wanted to leave but couldn't unless swarthy went to sleep or was distracted in some way. I'd wait awhile and if neither one of those things happened I'd have to either supply a distraction or put him to sleep.

At nine sharp Rodman left in the BMW. At ten an older woman I took to be the maid arrived in a Ford Escort and let herself in through the French doors. At eleven-twenty a white van arrived and parked in the rear by the Escort. Aqua letters on the side of the van announced that it was from the Care-Full Pool Service. A guy got out who looked like his last job had been as an underwear model for Calvin Klein. He was as blond as California sand and had abdominal muscles on which you could grate cheese. I could tell because he was wearing cutoffs, shower thongs, and no shirt. His face looked a little like Meryl Streep's but he was prettier. I admit it, I hated the son of a bitch. He worked on the pool until noon. That's when she came out.

She was wearing a T-shirt and sweating just enough to make the white cotton stick slightly to her breasts each time she moved. Below the T-shirt were a pair of blue shorts cut high and loose enough to be nothing more than a pleasant rumor. The pool guy turned as she approached and didn't seem at all surprised when she bent and licked the sweat off his great abs. She didn't seem at all surprised either when he put one hand between her legs, one in her hair, lifted her, and threw her in the pool. I was a little surprised when, after she swam to the side where he was now sitting with his feet in the water, he lifted her half out of the water by her hair and stuck his tongue down her throat. He then dropped her back into the water and let her climb out on her own. As far as I was concerned the world could now call off all further wet T-shirt contests. She was the winner. Forget about it. Retire the cup. You could put out an eye on her nipples.

The two of them were just getting started. He bent her over one of the lawn tables and conducted a fairly thorough gynecological exam. Neither of them seemed to give a damn about the maid who had to be somewhere nearby. Either Mrs. Rodman was paying her extra or Mr. Rodman wasn't too popular with either one of them. The two lustbirds got into the front seat of the Care-Full van and Mrs. Rodman's head disappeared below the steering wheel. A fifteen-room house and she'd rather do it in a van? I was beginning to get the picture. I'd have loved to stay around for the finish but the guy down the hill from me was glued to his binoculars, bobbing and weaving with the action, inching uncontrollably down the hill toward the porno de mondo which definitely qualified as a distraction.

I stuffed my belongings in the gym bag, exited the hole, replaced the roof, and made my way up the hill, hoping the pool guy wouldn't go over the top until I did. Good man I said as I crested the hill and started down the other side.

12

As I was pulling out of the church parking lot I caught sight of my reflection in the rearview mirror. I looked like every police composite I'd ever seen in the newspapers—wild matted hair, mossy beard, and a gaunt thousand-yard stare. I looked like a guy who bowled with human heads.

I was a couple miles down Butler Road trying to decide the best time for my next move. I couldn't call Rodman or see him without the guy on the hill seeing me. There was someone who could help me, though; someone who probably knew more than she thought she did, Mrs. Rodman. I couldn't get in to see her either but I knew someone who could.

I pulled to the side and looked in the mirror again. There was dirt smeared on both sides of my face and across the bridge of my nose. The effort of lying semimotionless for all those hours had given my face a lean strain that made it look drawn but somehow younger. The man in the mirror was almost a stranger. Anyone who saw me would have a hard time recognizing me later. I was tired and sore but it had to be done now.

It was almost one o'clock. If the guy in the woods was using a walkie-talkie to communicate with the others they couldn't be too far away. I'd have to introduce myself to Mr. Care-Full at another location. I swung the rental back onto the road and headed for the entrance to Rodman's lane, hoping I hadn't missed the kid. I parked about a hundred yards from the lane and waited.

At one-fifteen I saw the top of a white van moving down the lane. When it turned left I followed it for about five miles until it swung into another lane guarded on either side by two tall blue spruces. The trees would limit to a few seconds the time anyone could see into the lane. The house, like all the others in this neighborhood, couldn't be seen from the road. The setup was good enough. I'd do it there.

After the van disappeared up the drive I turned the K car around and drove back along Falls Road, looking for a place to leave it. After I'd gone about three-quarters of a mile in the direction of Rodman's place I found a wide spot on the shoulder beside a salt drop used by the department of highways. I parked, put my sign back in the window, retrieved the gym bag, and started toward the lane where I'd last seen the Care-Full van.

When I got there I sat behind one of the spruce trees and hoped the pool boy would allow me a little time to rest by giving the lady of the house the same courteous service he'd bestowed on Mrs. Rodman. It was a dead quiet afternoon with a nasty haze in the air that made even the bees seem to labor as they lurched drunkenly from plant to plant. Only two vehicles passed, both of them delivery trucks. The rich were staying inside today. He wouldn't be able to count on anyone seeing us.

When I saw the van's top zigzagging its way toward me, I took the Beretta out of the gym bag, stuck it in my belt, under my shirt, and lay down across the entrance to the drive. There was a sharp turn not far from my position which I hoped would keep him from building up any speed. I figured it was a better bet than standing in the middle of the road with the gun pointed at him. That way he could hit the accelerator and call my bluff, and since that's all it was, I had to get him to stop.

Out of a slit in my right eye I saw him start to accelerate. In another half second it would have been time to roll out of the way and call it a day, but he hit the brakes and slowed to a crawl.

When he eased to within about ten feet of me he stopped and leaned out of the window.

"Hey," he said in a solid tenor. "Bud, hey, what are you doing? Hey, you alive?"

I groaned and rolled over, my back to him, my right hand under my shirt.

Jesus, he said to himself. What's a wino doing in this neighborhood?

He got out of the truck and came toward me. "Why me?" he said. "Probably got puke all over him."

When I heard the kaflip-kaflap of his shower thongs stop behind me I rolled over and came up with the Beretta about an inch from his nose. "You see this?" I asked him.

His tan drained away, leaving in its place the pasty gray of an uncooked turkey. He started to back away.

"Don't move a fuckin' inch kid, not an inch," I said. "I asked you a question."

"Whaat? A quest-ion," he said with a little hiccup of fear.

"Yeah, you got a good look at this?"

"Yeah, uh, I mean yes."

"You convinced it's real or do I have to prove it?"

"No, no. I mean yes. I mean no, you don't have to prove it."

"All right then, shut up, get in the truck, and drive where I tell you. Do that and I won't harm a hair on your head, understand? That's all you have to do to keep looking just as young and studly as you do right now. Otherwise I'm gonna hurt you, okay?"

Not surprisingly, he agreed. I had him drive a few miles north on Falls Road. After we exchanged clothes and I'd checked the name on his driver's license I put him out at the point where Falls intersects with Black Rock Road. He was out of the glitz zone, in farm country, houses few and far between. I felt kind of bad about it. The kid had never done anything to me but I had big things at stake. All he had at stake was a little pride and some shoe leather. Of course he'd eventually find a cop and they'd put a bulletin out on the van, but I didn't think they'd spend much time cruising Falls Road looking for it. After all, if I wanted to stay in the area why would I steal a car?

13

When I finally cruised slowly up the Rodmans' stately drive it was midafternoon. I'd used the water left in my canteen to wash my face and was now wearing the kid's thongs and cutoffs. They were a little tight around the waist so I left the top button loose and covered it with a Hawaiian shirt the kid had left hanging on a hook in the van. It also covered the Beretta. When I got to the house I pulled the van around to the garage side. If the swarthy guy was still in the same position he wouldn't be able to see me, and if he'd moved, I looked like a pool boy. Not the same one, but the most logical assumption on his part would be that Mrs. Rodman just happened to have an appetite for pool boys. Hell, the guy would probably be considering buying a Hawaiian shirt himself.

The entrance to the house on this side had another set of French doors facing out onto a flagstone patio which met an asphalt parking area where, in addition to the red Corvette, a Toyota 4-Runner and a Pontiac Fiero were parked.

I parked the van as close as possible to the entrance and took the binoculars out of the gym bag. I pressed the buzzer twice before the maid answered. She was a waspish, efficient-looking woman, trim, with nice silver-fox gray hair. If it hadn't been for the pinched eyes and vertical lines around her mouth she'd have looked more like someone's executive secretary than a maid. But then, what did I know about maids? The only maids I'd ever seen were wiseacre black women who matched repartee with Danny Thomas or Cary Grant. Today those women would be talk show hosts, so who knew?

"Yes?" she said, taking in the van.

"My name is John Huntington," I said deferentially. "I'm the manager of Care-Full pool maintenance service."

"Yes," she said, "I believe someone's already come today."

I thought I detected the slightest of hesitations before she used the word come but it was probably just my natural perversity.

"Well," I went on, shuffling my feet a little. "That's what I'm here about. Actually I need to talk to Mrs. Rodman about Aldon Harris, that's the name of your regular pool technician."

"She's in the shower right now."

The thought of Mrs. Rodman in the shower made me warm all over. I had an urge to say that was fine, I'd just go right on up. "Well, ah, I really need to speak with her," I said. "I'm afraid his job may depend on it. I'd hate to see the boy lose his job without being fair to him."

"There's some problem?"

"I'm afraid there may be. That's actually what I'm here to try and ascertain."

"If you tell me what it is I'll pass it along to Mrs. Rodman."

Jesus, the woman *was* an executive secretary.

"Look," I said, "this is a rather private matter. I'm sure you understand."

A sly, knowing look shot across her eyes like a news bulletin at the bottom of a television screen. "Yes," she said, "of course I do."

She invited me in and had me wait in an entry hall at the front of the house while she went up to get Mrs. Rodman. The hall was about the right size for a high school prom and ran between a living room on the right and what looked like a study/game room on the left. I could see bookshelves and the corner of a pool table in that one. The next thing I noticed were the phones. I read an article once about how high achievers like to be in touch at all times, about their almost compulsive need to eliminate down time by conducting business even while driving or sitting in their hot tubs. The Rodman house bore out this premise. I counted four phones in the hallway; one standard and three cordless, strewn about like after-dinner mints. Nothing like a refreshing little stock purchase to put the capper on a walk down your hall.

The maid had me sit on an antique settee that looked as if it had come off Cleopatra's barge, but as soon as her feet disappeared up the curving stairway I went into the living room to see if I could spot swarthy's location. Standing to the side of the curtain, I scanned the hillside. I was at the edge of the big plate glass window I'd seen the previous night. It was a disorienting sensation, like being outside the flow of time, outside the boundary of any rules but my own; a new place, but a place where it seemed I'd always lived.

I shook my head to bring it back to more practical matters. I could spot swarthy's location but couldn't see him or make out any movement. I heard the two women padding down the hall above my head so I hip-hopped back into the hall and sat on the barge, my eyes on the staircase.

There was a window on the landing where the stairs made a final turn and, as she passed it, the light fell on her taut but liquid thighs as they floated through the butterscotch light. I couldn't even see the maid anymore. All I could see was the honey-dripping form of Mrs. Rodman. She was wearing a white terry-cloth robe that reached only to the top of her thighs and was secured by a knotted sash of the same material. As she turned her back to the landing window, a shaft of light caught her from behind and I thought I saw a wisp of fine, red-gold hair between her legs. I felt like a kid peeping in a window and I liked it.

They came toward me, the invisible maid leading the way. "This is Mrs. Rodman," she said. "Mrs. Rodman, this is Mr., ah, what did you say your name was?"

My mind went blank for a second. Who had I said I was? She was wearing a towel wrapped around her head like a turban. With no hair to obscure it I could see the perfect arrowhead bone structure of her face. High, even cheekbones, tapering down to a chin just pointed enough to emphasize the full pout of her lips. The eyes were large and of an odd color; a kind of light, hot brown, with the color and fire of good Scotch whiskey. The lids drooped low over her eyes, half covering them. It gave them the tacky allure of a pair of half-drawn window shades on a summer night. She wore no makeup but the left eye seemed to have a touch of mascara around its socket. A bruise? I heard the maid's voice again. *Who the hell was I?*

"Ah, uh, Huntington," I said, "John Huntington. I'm Aldon Harris's supervisor . . . at Care-Full pool maintenance."

She held out her hand. She was barefoot and I noticed that her hands and feet matched exactly. They were both long, strong, and artfully defined; all twenty nails were polished the same soft blue magenta as the bruise at the corner of her eye. Accidental or mildly perverse?

As I shook the proffered hand I noticed it was surprisingly cool. I'd expected it might melt my shower shoes. "Elise," she said, "Elise Rodman. Mrs. Downey said you wanted to talk to me about Aldon."

Her voice was a shaded contralto which still dripped a bit with the melonlike residue of a Southern accent.

"Yes," I said, feeling the tips of her fingers slide across my palm as we ended the handshake. "Is there someplace private we could talk?"

She gave a one-sided little laugh that sounded to me like remembered sex. "I have very few secrets from Mrs. Downey." There it was again; that Southern cat's tail wrapping itself around the word Downey.

"I can appreciate that, but I'd feel better about it, and uh, in all frankness my, ah, liability position would be improved if we talked in private."

"My," she said, raising an eyebrow while toying with the sash to her robe. "You're going to say something slanderous? Sounds exciting."

I started to make uncomfortable motions with my neck and shoulders but as a flicker of disappointment crossed her eyes I remembered Aldon lifting her out of the water by her hair.

Straight on; that was the way to play it with her. "It's important," I said, lowering the pitch of my voice a notch. "Very important to him, potentially important to you. I'd appreciate it very much if you'd humor me for a few minutes."

"All right," she said without hesitation. "Let's go in the living room. I'm sure Mrs. Downey has things to do anyway, don't you?" She gave Mrs. Downey a slight get-lost nod but she was already turning her back to us and hurrying down the hall.

In the living room I stood as far away from the big window as I could, my back against a marble fireplace at the far end of the room. "Won't you sit down?" she asked, motioning toward a red brocade sofa that ran along the adjacent wall. I sat at one end, she took a seat at the other. I could smell her bath powder, some kind of honeysuckle. "Now then," she said, "what's this about Aldon?"

There was no other way so I jumped right into it. "Actually, it's not about Aldon at all, Mrs. Rodman. Oh, I know what's going on between the two of you all right. I saw the episode by the pool this morning and, as a matter of fact, had a hard time tearing myself away. I could tell your husband about it, and I will if you don't cooperate, but that's not what this is about."

"Call me Elise," she said.

"What?"

"Call me Elise. You might as well. I mean if you saw me this morning we're already ah, intimate, so to speak. You might as well call me Elise."

I wasn't sure quite what, but something wasn't going according to plan. I decided to push ahead anyway. "All right, Elise," I said.

"Good," she answered. "Now if it's not about me fucking Aldon, what is it about?"

She used a little more of the Southern accent on the word fucking, drew it out a little, warmed it up, stretched it out. "You watch the news?" I asked, thinking there was a distinct possibility she didn't.

"Almost always, there's an anchorman on one of the stations who fucked me on a pile of laundry at a party last year. I watch him out of loyalty. He fucked me good."

She turned a little toward me as she spoke, drawing one leg up under the other one. I thought I could see the flash of red-gold again. "Was it a theme party?" I asked.

"Pardon?" she raised another eyebrow and stretched her arm along the back of the sofa.

"I mean what was a pile of laundry doing at a party? Was it like a po' folks party or what."

She laughed and rocked back a little, giving me clear visual access to one of the lushest little acres of pubic silk I'd ever seen. I was rapidly losing track of the reason I was there.

"No," she said, becoming serious again. "The party was at his house and it happened in his basement. I'd asked him where the wine cellar was and he asked me if I wouldn't rather see the moan cellar. I thought that was funny. I like funny men. They say humor is cruel. Do you believe that?"

The question put me back on track. "I think death is cruel," I answered. "If you've been watching your friend you must have seen the story of the guy getting his throat cut in Cockeysville and another one about a man named Fredericks getting shot in his driveway, only a few miles from here."

"Death isn't cruel," she said, "it's boring."

"Spoken like someone who's never been shot at."

Her eyes widened. "You've been shot at?"

"Several dozen times, but not lately, and I'd like to keep it that way. How about you?"

I stood up to get away from her scent and the sight of that glowing patch of hair, which for the last few minutes had been curling up over the bottom edge of her robe.

"Elise," I said, "am I getting through, can you hear me? Remember the deaths I was just talking about? In Cockeysville? The other one near here? What I'm telling you is that your husband is involved, in both of them."

She sounded almost pleased when she said, "You're not from the pool company at all."

"Welcome to earth."

"Where's Aldon?"

"I put him out a few miles up Falls Road."

"Maybe I should call the police."

I pulled the Beretta out of my waistband. "Just keep away from the phone and listen to me," I said, showing it to her.

"Is that a real gun?"

"As real as death and taxes."

"Can I touch it? I've never touched a gun before."

Her mouth was drooping again. She thought it was a game and I wasn't going to get anywhere unless I could convince her it wasn't. I was tired. I was hungry. For all I knew I was running out of time and I was for sure running out of patience. Without thinking about it, without wanting to, I took two steps forward and slapped her hard across the face.

She uttered the smallest of cries as her head snapped to the side but didn't attempt to run or scream. She just turned back to look at me, a large red imprint of my fingers forming on her cheek. Somewhere inside I felt something grow very tired. I guess I should have felt more than that, ashamed maybe, but I didn't. I like to think it was because, viscerally, I knew what was going to happen next. She was looking at me levelly, her Scotch-colored eyes heating up to full force.

"Fuck me," she said.

"What?"

"Fuck me. Do me. Do me anyway you want. Anything you want, I'll do it. You want me to blow you?" She sank to her knees in front of me and started to reach for my fly. I took a step back.

"You don't want me to blow you?" she asked from her knees. "Then do me any way you want. You can hurt me, you know. You can do anything you want as long as it doesn't leave scars. Aldon likes to tie me to the pool table across the hall. He makes me hold a cue ball in my mouth, like a pig he says. If I drop it while he's fucking me he makes me stay there like that for an hour while he hits me all over with a yard stick."

Now I didn't feel too bad about making Aldon walk home from Falls Road. She was still on her knees. I noticed for the first time that her nose was a little too pointed and she had tiny lines around the corners of her eyes. Little frown channels were starting to descend from both sides of her nose in the same arc that might be taken by falling tears.

"You must really hate your husband," I said.

"Oh I do," she said from her knees. "I do."

"Why?"

"Why?" she repeated, as she got up from her knees and dropped her robe. She walked naked to a cabinet on the far wall. As she moved away from me the tiny white imprint of her bikini bottom winked at me with each step.

"I'll play," she said. "I always do don't I? Whatever the game is." She seemed to be talking more to the room itself than to me. "You want to know why? Do I have to say why before you fuck me? I have to talk about it? That's good. That's a new one. Make me talk about it first. Here's why." She opened the cabinet to reveal four shelves full of videotapes.

"They're all of me," she said. "Of me being fucked in every way imaginable by everyone from a ten-year-old kid to six midget clowns from a circus in Florida. My husband flew them in especially for the occasion. He likes to watch. He likes to have it on videotape to show his friends. He likes me to be there when he does. You weren't the only one watching this morning. Mrs. Downey was upstairs with a video camera. That's her main function around here you know. She takes the movies. Now can we get on with it?"

She went to the sofa and bent forward over its arm. The towel fell off her head, allowing a rich flow of autumn-colored hair to cascade over the red silk. "Maybe you like to do it from behind," she said. "You can have me that way too. Anyway you want, as long as you want."

Somewhere inside me the monkey man was rattling the bars of his cage and screaming to get out. *Let's go*, he was saying. *Dive in. Do it. Do it. Don't worry about what. I'll think of that. You just follow my instructions.*

She was in front of me, still bent over the sofa, whimpering now, begging in some porno-movie argot. I felt wrapped in a slow fire, as if I'd melt if I didn't do it. I even took a step toward her but then I stopped. I thought of the lines descending from her nose. I thought of Arla, of money, of the guy on the hillside with the automatic rifle. I thought of Mrs. Downey somewhere in the house making a video of the whole thing through a secret peephole and the fire turned to ice. If she was making a video my face was now on it, in a supporting role to be sure, but still on it.

My lust turned to panic. I went to the sofa and straightened her up. "Listen goddamnit," I said, pulling her close enough to escape the sight of her body. "I wasn't sent by your husband. I don't know anything about this shit you're telling me, and I didn't come here to fuck you. Got that?"

She looked incredulous. "You don't want to fuck me?" she said, as though there was something new under the sun after all.

"Yeah, I do want to fuck you. I'm not dead, not yet. But not here, not now. And especially not on videotape."

"Well just who in the hell are you then?" she said as she walked over to get her robe. "If you don't want to fuck me what do you want?" She shrugged easily into the robe and knotted the sash. What a woman! If you didn't want to fuck her you were invading her privacy.

"First I want to know if Mrs. Downey was somewhere making videos of what just went on. I have a reason for asking."

"My husband didn't send you?"

"Believe me, to your husband I'm nothing but a bad dream."

"Well, if the son of a bitch didn't send you there's no movie."

"If you hate him so much why do you go along with it?"

She looked down at her feet and then back up to me, actually down to me since she was close to six feet tall. "Because I like it," she said in a twisted voice. "The bastard's got me so I like it. Like it hell, I love it."

"Sounds like a little case of low self-esteem to me."

"Bullshit," she said. "I'm a slut. It's my role in life. Beside's that, I'm good at it. People should do what they're good at. I just wish, I just wish that . . ." She started to cry but stopped herself.

"Wish what?"

She shook the tears off again with a throw of her auburn hair. "I just wish I'd met a man who appreciated it enough to keep it to himself."

"What do you mean," I asked her, incredulous. "You talk like Rodman was the first man you ever had. What'd he do, pick you off a farm or something?"

A hard little zipper smile played across her lips. "You want to know how old I am?" she asked me. Then, without waiting for an answer she told me. "I'm twenty-two."

I couldn't hide the shock on my face. The body was twenty-two all right, maybe even a ripe eighteen. But the face was that of a woman in her early thirties. She tilted it at me and stepped closer, like she was daring me to believe it. "I was seventeen when I met Peter, training to be a beautician, in Sumter, South Carolina. He was down there on business. We met in the bar of a bowling alley. He turned me on to coke. He had lots of money. My parents thought he was a good catch. Better than being a beautician, you know."

"You mean he . . ."

"No, I was a slut before I met him. It's in the genes I guess. I always liked men, many and mean. But I always thought the guy I married would save me for himself."

I leaned forward and kissed her on the cheek. "I like you," I said. "You don't meet many people in life with as hard a take on themselves as you have. I really like you."

She pulled the robe a little tighter across her breasts. Her drill-bit nipples bored their way into the terry-cloth. "I think I sort of like you too. You're kind of short but you've got nice shoulders and you seem more . . . real than most men I see. But if Peter didn't send you I don't think I can fuck you."

"You can't fuck me unless Peter says to?"

"Ah, no," she said. And then a slow parting of the lips and an unfolding of the arms. The robe loosened a little. I could see she had a few freckles across the tightly-sprung tops of her breasts. I could also see an increase in the rate of their rise and fall. She shrugged and the robe loosened a little more. Now I could see the beginnings of their secret white underside. That twisted little fishhook smile darted across her mouth. "No, I couldn't," she said again. "You'd have to rape me I guess. I'd fight. But not loudly enough for Mrs. Downey to hear."

I was stunned, dumbfounded. What the hell was I going to do? My strategy had been to get into the house and then use the old blackmail routine. Either she told me what I wanted to know or I'd tell her husband what I'd seen by the pool, only now it turned out he'd be watching it himself as prime time entertainment. It was one of those moments that seem to lack a cue. I was standing in a strange house three feet away from a live centerfold who'd just invited me to rape her while a man with an automatic weapon sat around outside waiting to kill someone, quite possibly me.

I didn't say anything. I just stood there looking at her, trying to come up with a new strategy. There was nothing in my experience to tell me what to do. I was considering fucking her just to buy time. I began to feel the heat rise through my body. Her upper lip was sweating. I was sweating all over. The situation was deteriorating. There was no situation. There was no reality. For a moment I considered throwing in the towel, throwing her down and doing it until I couldn't stand up.

Then I looked at her again; a twenty-two-year-old girl with a thirty-two-year-old face. Suddenly I thought of my daughter and what she might look like at twenty-two. The heat in my gut went away, replaced by anger and frustration. I had to break into this creature's world. But her whole world appeared to be sex. Sex and pain, sexual pain and painful sex. Nothing I'd said to her had really registered. She still wasn't sure I was real. Her life was masturbation. The people in it were just flesh and blood vibrators. A new strategy was beginning to form.

I moved quickly toward her and hit her again, harder this time, as hard as I could without closing my fist. The force of the unexpected blow knocked her to the floor. Her eyes went wide with shock. "That's the difference," I said. "That's the difference between sex pain and real pain. Get it? Most of the pain in this world doesn't lead to an orgasm, Elise. Most of it leads to more pain, injury, and death."

I shoved her hard onto the sofa and forced her mouth open. When it opened I stuck the barrel of the Beretta into it. "Feel that?" I asked. "That's what real rape feels like—cold, hard, and bitter. Not much like a dick at all is it?"

Her eyes were as wide as those of a spooked horse. She was afraid now, really afraid. They'd hurt her, abused, and humiliated her, and she'd loved it because they'd hurt her just enough to keep this kind of pain away. "Fright pain's not sweet like the other kind, is it?" I asked. The gun barrel kept her from speaking but her eyes answered. "This is all real Elise, there's a man outside with the machine gun who'd gladly kill us both if his boss told him to." I shook her violently by her robe's collar. "Are you hearing me now; are you?" I asked again.

She mumbled something around the steel in her mouth and shook her head in the affirmative. "Listen," I said. "I'm going to take this gun out of your mouth now so you can talk and because I really do like you. But if you try to call Mrs. Downey I'm going to stick it in there again. Understand? It won't feel good and you won't come." She was starting to cry. The tears were falling onto my wrist where they held her collar. My hands were shaking so I kept them on the robe.

"Stop that," I said, moving as if I were going to hit her again. She flinched and drew away. "Stop crying and listen. Those two murders? The ones on TV? I'm involved too. The man on the hill is very involved. Come over here." I put the gun in my waistband and pulled her off the sofa to the wall beside the plate glass window. I picked up my binoculars and scanned the hillside until I spotted movement. The swarthy guy was taking a leak. "Come here," I said to her. "Look through these binoculars. See across the stream, next to that big tree with the two dead branches? See the mound directly below and to the left of the tree? Look there. See him?" She wasn't used to doing anything which required as much concentration as looking through a pair of binoculars but she wasn't stupid and she wasn't blind. Finally she saw him. She gave a quick intake of breath.

"See the gun?" I asked.

"No."

"Look close to his feet. If he's not holding it he'll have it somewhere close to his feet."

Another little gasp told me she saw it. "Yeah," I said, "that gun's even more real than this one. It'll cut you in half."

She lowered the binoculars and turned to face me. Her lips were trembling for real this time. Her rapid breathing was caused not by lust but incipient panic. "What's going on here?" she asked. Somehow the rank of fear in her face made her look younger, more girlish. It was as though, for the first time in her life, she was asking that question in its broader context. But like they tell you in college; start with the particular and work up to the general.

"What's going on here," I said, "is your basic little war. There's something everybody wants, and they want it bad enough to kill for it. Your husband's probably just a pawn. I don't know much more than that and you don't need to know any more than that. What you need to know is that I want something from you. Once you give it to me I'll go away and so will the man on the hill. It's very simple. Three names. All I want is the names of the three people your husband mentions most in connection with his business."

"He never tells me anything about his business." Her face colored a little, as though she was embarrassed or even angry; at me, at him, at the fact she was living a life she knew nothing about.

"That's good," I said. "That means any name you've heard him mention even once is an important one. Now think."

I was hoping she was so used to taking orders that if I adopted an authoritative air she'd fall right in line but she balked.

"I can't tell you anything without asking Peter."

"You said you hated him."

"Maybe I do but he pays the bills around here. What am I going to do if he gets hurt, or, or something?"

I'd scratched masochism and uncovered greed. She wanted it all. She wanted to be taken care of. She wanted all the decisions to be made by someone else. . . . All right then.

"Listen carefully," I said. "If you don't try to help me there's going to be trouble. I'm getting impatient. If you don't help me I'm going to ask the guy on the hill, and he and I have never been close. There's liable to be shooting, and shooting attracts police, so many police you'll think the president is dropping by for a state visit. But it'll be your anchorman friend and about a hundred of his buddies who drop by. Everyone of them will ask your husband what happened and he'll lie and they might even believe him but the cops won't. He's connected to the same company where the two dead guys worked, and cops believe in coincidence like pimps believe in virginity. From now on they'll be watching both of you, looking for leverage, and you're a walking crowbar. They'll take one look at you and know there's a coke stash around here and while they're using that as an excuse to go through your underwear drawer, they'll find the movies. Believe me those movies are going to get about a hundred thumbs up at police headquarters. Then all those critics will start taking junkets out here to see the star. You're liable to have to fuck the whole police force. That might be exciting at first, but I'm willing to bet you get bored with it a long time before they do."

I was improvising but the part about the cops wanting to fuck her was certainly true. "Now," I said more calmly, "compare that with what I'm asking. You give me the names, I go away. Whatever happens, happens somewhere else. No shooting, no cops, no trouble. Your husband probably never even gets involved. I think he's just being used in this by someone else anyway. See what I'm saying? The percentage of the two of you getting involved goes way down if you help me now."

She was looking at me silently, a frown of concentration creating small dunes in her Sahara-smooth brow. "Why don't you talk to Peter about this?" she asked after about thirty seconds of heavy eye contact.

"Because I might be wrong about him. He might even be the main man. He might want to kill me. If that's true what I said about shooting and the cops is doubled."

"He doesn't tell me anything about his business."

"How about who he works for? Everybody mentions who they work for. They get mad, they say, 'That goddamn so and so. He wants me to be superman?' That kind of thing. I know he's high up but he must work for someone. The way I have it figured he might even work for two companies at once."

"What's that mean?"

"You don't want to know and I haven't got the time to explain. Now make up your mind. I'm starting to get to the point where I don't care anymore which way it happens so do it fast." I pulled the Beretta out for effect and started toward the window.

"Wait," she said, "wait a minute. Look, ah, you'll go away? No trouble?"

"Believe me, the last thing I want to do is cause you any trouble. I told you, I like you. But I've got things at stake here you couldn't know anything about. Help me out, then you can do a few lines and forget the whole thing. If you hear about it again it'll be on the news."

She threw back her hair and ran both hands through it. "I don't know if I want to forget the whole thing," she said, in a choked little growl that was all the more seductive because it was unconscious. It reminded me of what Humphrey Bogart said to Mary Astor in *The Maltese Falcon*. "*Now you're really dangerous.*"

"That's a remark I'd like to explore further," I said. "But we've got business."

"Yes," she said, sticking her hands in the pockets of her robe and starting to pace. "Yes, yes, business." Now she looked, even with her short robe, bare polished feet, and tongue-sculpted legs, businesslike. There was one hell of a real person in there, no matter what her husband thought.

She stopped pacing. "Look, there is a guy who was here once when Peter was showing . . . showing the movies. He mentioned he was from the company but I don't know if he was above or below Peter. His name was Marshall, Eric Marshall. That's the only one I can remember ever having been here. Then there was one time I remember he was doing what you said—cursing a man named Dorn who must have been in the company because Peter was saying how when some deal was done he wanted to find a way to squeeze Dorn's balls the way he was squeezing Peter's. Those were his exact words. Talk like that stays in my head. I can only remember one more. Fred Staniford. I overheard Peter talking to him on the phone one time about the price of resistors? Transistors? Something like that. Those are the only three names I've ever heard him mention connected with business. The people he has over seem more interested in . . . well, they just don't seem like business types."

"Well," I said, "there's all kinds of business." She nodded in agreement and shrugged like she was saying goodbye. "Just one more thing," I said.

"You're a fairly nasty man you know," she said.

"There's all kinds of nasty too."

"Uhhh-huh," she said in a tone that assured me she knew that better than I did.

"I need the phone numbers of those three men. I'm sure your husband must keep an office in the house and I'm sure the numbers will be there. All we have to do is go get them. I'm not gonna break my promise to you. I'm not even gonna talk to them. I just want to call the numbers."

"I'm not that stupid. If you're not going to call them why do you want them?"

"I didn't say I wasn't going to call them, I said I wasn't going to talk to them. All I want to do is see if they're working numbers. If they are, I can find out the addresses."

"It wouldn't be a very good idea for Mrs. Downey to see you in Peter's office. I don't know what I'm going to say to him about you anyway."

"Why say anything?"

"If I don't Mrs. Downey will."

"No problem, I'm the pool company manager and I don't want Aldon spending so much time on your pool. It's shortchanging the other customers. I suspect what's going on but I don't say so. It fits perfectly."

"Yes, I suppose it does. Poor Aldon."

"Yeah, as for the numbers you can get them for me and bring them back here."

"I could, yes. But I'm still not sure it's the right thing."

"Look," I said wearily, "this is important. Do you think for a minute I'd pass up a chance to fuck you if it wasn't? Do you think if I care that much about it I didn't mean what I said. Now get the numbers or bad things are going to start happening."

That seemed to convince her. She turned on her heel and that double-pumping bounce in the back of her robe followed her out the door, out of my list of options. Sigh.

Maybe it was the lingering scent of honeysuckle that changed my mind. I'd been planning to call the three numbers while watching the guy on the hillside to see if he reacted to any of them. That way I'd know who was the next link in the chain. But what was he going to think if Elise started calling important numbers with a pool guy in the house? What could he think? Either the pool guy was waiting around while the lady of the house was conducting business or he was in on the business. Either way it would be bad for Elise. Fredericks was the last person to have a phone conversation about this affair and he was now in an unreachable area code. I didn't give much of a damn what happened to Rodman but I hadn't lied when I said I liked Elise. She had a kind of bizarre innocence. I doubted she'd ever hurt anyone but herself or wanted to. Besides, I'd made her a sincere promise, and sincere promises to strangers are really made to yourself. An idea hit me between the eyes like a diamond. I went to the door, checked for Mrs. Downey, and grabbed the nearest cordless phone.

She was back in five minutes with the numbers scribbled on a sheet of note paper.

"Here," she said. "I don't know what the hell's going on but here. Take 'em, but please, just leave me out of it."

"I promised didn't I?"

"Honey," she said, shaking back her hair. "Any similarity between promises made and ones kept is purely ah . . ."

"Coincidental?"

"No, financial. You're gonna get, you gotta give."

I held up the numbers. "So, you gave."

"And now you're gonna leave?" she said, with what I hoped was a trace of wistfulness.

"Well," I said, "don't think it hasn't been interesting."

"But not tempting?"

"Tempting! If I was Adam I'd have thrown away the apple and eaten you."

She tossed her hair again and smiled; fully this time, her eyes as well as her mouth. "So," she said, cocking a hip. "What kept you from it?"

What had? Nothing? Everything? "History," I answered.

"Whaaat?"

"Yours, mine. They've gotta stay separate. I'm using my history to work off of. If it gets mixed up with yours I'm liable to get confused."

"Jesus," she said, "this is one of the weirdest days I've ever had. And, believe me, that's saying something."

"Oh, I believe you all right."

I put the binoculars in their case, the Beretta back in my waistband and took the phone. "Time to go," I said.

"Yeah, well, like you said don't think it hasn't been . . . interesting."

I felt as if we'd been on a date and now it was time for me to give her a good night kiss. "Yeah," I said, "it's been a privilege, and I mean that."

"I'll walk you to the door."

"There's no need."

"It's either me or Mrs. Downey. It'll look funny to her if you just walk out by yourself."

"In that case it's an easy choice."

She walked me to the side entrance where I'd come in. I looked up on the way and thought I saw Mrs. Downey peeping out of a room along the upstairs hallway but I wasn't sure. When we got to the doorway we were only a few inches apart. "Goodbye," she said. For some reason I stuck out my hand and she took it. We shook. "Goodbye," I said. Then, because it was impossible for me to resist and I didn't want to anyway, I reached around and under her robe and grasped a sheen-soft, bite-firm handful of honeysuckle-scented buttock.

"Mmm," she murmured.

"Mmm," I replied.

We stood like that for what I wanted to be an hour but was only about five seconds. "Maybe some other time," she said.

"Yeah." I doubted it but I meant it. I let my hand slide down and off, turned and headed for the van. I could still feel her on my palm. I drove with the other hand as I wound down the lane to Butler Road.

14

The only risky part was ditching the van. I wasn't too worried because it had only been ninety minutes since I left Aldon. Even if he'd made contact with the cops I had no problem as long as they didn't catch me with the truck. The chances of my ever seeing Aldon again were going to be as slim as I could make them and if we did meet it would be under different circumstances; on the street or in a bar somewhere. We'd pass and he'd have a moment when he was sure, and an hour when he was sure he'd make a fool of himself for accusing an innocent stranger.

I ran the van into a clump of white pines a quarter mile from my rental car, as happy to get rid of it as an escapee losing his leg irons. When I got to the K car I half-expected to see one of those yellow things they put on the windows of abandoned vehicles to make sure the state gets some kind of public storage fee if you break your leg while walking to get gas. To the state of Maryland your car is an instrument for revenue enhancement. Driving isn't a right, it isn't even a privilege, it's a goddamn honor. But my windshield was still virgin. So I was confident that the cops had yet to get the picture. I walked by the car a couple of times to see

if a SWAT team was going to swoop down on me, got in, and
was careful to stay within the speed limit all the way back to Huan
Lo's.

It was five o'clock when I got to my room. I remember because
my face passed close to the clock as I dived toward the pillow. I
don't remember anything else until I was awakened at eight by a
sharp pain as I rolled from my back onto my erection. It disturbed
me to realize I couldn't remember whether I'd been dreaming of
Elise or Arla. Faithful husband that I am, I called Arla to convince
myself it was she who had spiced my sleep. It didn't help. She
sounded narrow, drawn, bureaucratic in her concern for the particular. She talked in amounts. How much was left in the account?
Had I made anything? How much had I spent? What was going
to happen, and when? Her voice was pitched at some strident level
a half octave higher than normal which made me forget what she
felt like in the dark. I answered the questions I could and avoided
the ones I couldn't by asking to speak to the kids. All they wanted
to know was when I was coming home. I couldn't answer that
one either but it made me feel better; as though there was a home,
as though I was only temporarily dislocated from connections I'd
come to think of as immutable.

Arla came back on the line and her tone had been softened a
little by the thrill in the kid's voices but now it had that choirlike
formalism women affect when they're in the process of convincing
themselves they can do without you. I had to hang up before I
started smelling honeysuckle so I made some excuse about needing
to meet Daz. Then I realized that's what I did need.

Li Anh, who answered the phone, said he was on the roof doing
Tai Chi, and put me on hold while she went to get him. Daz had
built a small tower on the back of his university-library sized house
from which a twenty-by-twenty-foot platform jutted like the prow
of a ship. That's where he liked to do his Tai Chi, alone and
under the sky.

Daz got on the phone and said he'd meet me at nine in the
Dong Ha.

Even though I dreaded it, the next thing I had to do was call

Samski. He was my weak link, the one who could burn me at any time. I was afraid he'd forget that he'd also be burning himself. The main thing I had going for me with him was the West Virginia factor. One thing you can count on about people from the Mountain State is their stubbornness. When they tell you they're going to do something they usually do it, even if they don't want to, even if they don't like you, just because they said so.

I thought the Mercedes crowd might be bugging him like they'd bugged Rodman's place so when he came on the line I went into my best West Virginia twang, hoping he'd recognize my voice. "Hey there, buddy," I roared good naturedly. "Willard here, how's it hangin'?" There was a long moment of silence while he tried to remember if he knew anyone named Willard.

"Yeeah," he drawled, still not certain.

"Hey, buddy," I yelled again, "I gotta get outta the house for awhile. The old lady's drivin' me bugs if ya know what I mean, an' I know you do." There was another moment of silence during which I prayed Samski had watched enough TV to be familiar with the double meaning of the term bug.

"Yeeah." This time there was a slight sunrise of understanding in his voice.

"Shit yeah," I said, "it's enough ta make ya take up night work just to get outta the house."

"I know whatcha mean."

I could hear a lightbulb go on over his head. "I thought maybe you could meet me down at Pete's bar on the corner for a few brewskies, that is if you think Doris'll let ya."

"You let me worry about the old lady. I'll be there in half a hour."

There is a neighborhood bar on every corner of working-class Baltimore. They've been converted from the same formstone row houses in which their customers live, and have as regular an attendance as the Catholic churches found on opposite corners. Pete's was only a block away from Samski's house. I got the number from information and called it after waiting a half hour. The bartender answered and put Samski on the line. I could hear ESPN and country music in the background.

"Yeah?" he said when he came on the line.

"It's me, Lowell Ransom."

"I know."

"What's going on?"

"The sumbitches threatened to fire me," he said.

The roots of my hair went cold. "What do you mean?" I asked, looking out my window for swarthy guys carrying automatic weapons.

"What the fuck you think I mean?"

"I mean what do you mean they threatened to fire you, goddamnit?"

"Calm down, boy," he said.

That made me calm down. He was calling me boy. He was calm. How bad could things be? He didn't seem scared at all. They threatened to fire him and he didn't seem nervous. Why the hell didn't he seem nervous. Had he told them? No. He'd be dead. Unless . . . unless what? "I wanta know what the hell happened when they threatened to fire you," I screamed.

"Sumbitches pissed me off," he said. "Called us all in an' gave us some shit about leavin' the door unlocked, asked to see our keys just like you said they would. You ain't a bad detective, you know that? Anyhow, the bastards threatened to fire us."

"Yeah, so what happened? Did your two friends see you leave the door unlocked?"

"Hey, Cochise, I may be ignorant but I ain't stupid. They was both all twenty feet away from me an' one of 'em was blasted on coke. He thought they was calling us in about drugs. Christ, the poor fucker almost had a heart attack, I mean after the news dicks had all that shit on the tube about cocaine. Sheeit, he thought he was gonna be public fuckin' enema number one. Thought he was gonna take it up the ole yin-yang in public, an' then have to run for it."

Samski laughed in a long slow haw-haw-haw that made me think of a talking mule. "What the hell are you so happy about?" I asked him.

" 'Cause I got the doctor with me." He gave me another one of his mule impressions.

"What doctor?"

"Doctor Beam," he said. "Doctor Jim Beam."

So he was drunk. That was fine with me. What I wanted to know was whether it was due to defiance or guilt. I glanced out the window again, reaching for the Beretta every time I saw a beige car. "Listen, goddamnit," I said, with as much authority as I could muster against a man drunk on bourbon. "Did you tell them anything or not? Did anyone tell them anything?"

"I didn't tell 'em shit," he answered. "I tole you the sumbitches pissed me off. I was scared before they called me in there, but goddamn, where the hell do they come off? I been workin' there for years, an' them talkin' like I done somethin wrong. I tole 'em that too."

"You were the one who did it, though."

"Hell yeah, but they don't know that. Where do they come off?"

"Listen man," I said, "you saw the news, didn't you? I don't wanta see Dr. Beam give you such a big balls transplant that you forget what's been happening. I mean act dumb. That's all. Whatever you do don't let 'em think you know what the score is."

"Hell," said Samski. "That's what I been doin' all my life. I been doin' it with you ain't I? I ain't never liked the sumbitches."

"What son of a bitches?"

"The sumbitches," he said. "The sumbitches you work for. The sumbitches call you in an' talk to you like you was late for fuckin' class. The sumbitches think you gotta wear a tie to keep the blood in your brain."

"That's not who we're dealing with here. We're dealing with killers here, not executives."

"Same thing in my book," he said. "One kills you quick, the other does it slow."

"Let's get into politics some other time. Things are heating up. I may need your help soon and I want to know if you're up for it."

"Son, if I could just get a little cash I could tell the whole world to kiss my ass. Armco, Doris, the whole fuckin' world."

"I can't guarantee you anything. I don't know how much is in it yet."

"I ain't had any other offers lately."

"I know you're up for it now but are you gonna be up for it when Dr. Beam isn't around?"

"Fuck Dr. Beam," he said through what sounded like clenched

teeth. "An' fuck you too. You're talkin' to one fed-up mountain boy. If I say I'm up for it then I'm by God up for it."

"All right, all right. I'm gonna give you my number here. If you write it down make sure you do it on something you can eat. I know, it sounds bullshit but we're not playing around here. Call four-seven-five seven-seven-nine-six from a touch-tone phone. It has to be a touch-tone. Press six on the phone and if it's time to do something you'll get a message from me. Got it? The thing is, you tell me you're up for it, I'm gonna count on it. I know I pulled you into this thing and it's getting bad. If you want out go ahead, no hard feelings. But if you say you're in, be in."

"What'd I say before?"

"All right then. Something's gonna happen tomorrow. I don't know what it'll lead to, but call in every few hours and see if there's any message."

"Ten four," he said and laughed.

"Jesus!"

"Don't worry about it."

"I won't if you will."

"Gotcha."

"Later."

I hung up, feeling fairly certain about him because he'd given his word. A guy like Samski, that's pretty much all he has to give. I didn't think he'd do it lightly. Of course he was drinking, but I was willing to bet he'd been drinking like that since he was twelve—out hunting deer in the hills at five on a cold morning. He could probably nail a running buck at a hundred yards after half a fifth. I just hoped he didn't lose the phone number.

Daz showed up at 9:00 A.M. sharp wearing an olive rayon jumpsuit bloused over the tops of alligator combat boots. I told him he looked like he'd just come from rapping old Elvis tunes at a lounge in Vegas.

"Not a bad idea," he said. "If Elvis is alive he better not show himself, it'll ruin his career. What's up?"

"That's why I dressed like this," he said when I told him. "This is what the well-dressed commando is wearing these days."

"It's just an idea. I could probably do it myself."

"Right, what're you gonna do after you snatch the cat, put him up at the Hilton?"

"You got a place?"

He rocked back in the booth where we were devouring Lo Mein and laughed. "Have I got a place? Brother Lowell I have a place that's actually gonna get the dude high." He laughed again like he'd robbed a Brinks' truck with a water pistol and I knew better than to ask what he was talking about.

We decided the next morning was the best time, after Rodman left for work and before Mrs. Downey arrived. The guy on the hill would be glued to his binoculars, waiting for his daily fix of Elise. My best guess was that she'd ignore anything she heard. There was always the chance Mrs. Downey would get there early or even stay over, but what we decided about that was fuck her if she couldn't take a joke. The whole thing should be over before she figured out what to do about it. It would be over, one way or another.

After we finished eating, Daz went to my office with me to pick up my answering machine. I was 90 percent certain no one on the other side had any inkling it was me they were looking for, but I'd seen more than a few people get killed when their 10 percent margin was called in. Daz cruised the front of the building first, and when he saw nothing we went in for the machine, me with my Beretta and him with a sawed-off twelve-gauge shotgun he'd produced from his office in the rear of the Dong Ha. He carried it in one of those leather shoulder bags gay boutique owners use to haul around their invoices and coke.

I went in and got the answering machine while Daz stood in an alcove down the hall covering the door. There was nobody there but us paranoids. We put the machine in Daz's leather bag under the shotgun and left. I hooked the thing up to my phone above Huan Lo's and we talked about turning in early and meeting at four-thirty in the morning, just like two guys making plans to go on a hunting trip; which of course is exactly where we were going.

15

The temperature had dropped into the sixties during the night and there was a low-sifting ground fog coiling out of the alleys below my window. It was four fifteen. I'd had about three hours of fitful sleep since Daz had left. I packed the gym bag with the M-79, four high explosive rounds, one white phosphorus, and two shotgun. I was wearing the same camouflage suit I'd worn the previous night. There'd been no time to wash it and it felt like a touch of the grave when I put it on. A touch of the grave might be just the mojo I needed on this operation.

That's the way I was coming to think of it, as an operation. If I thought of it that way maybe old habits would come back. One of the common complaints among Daz's counselees had been the feeling that, no matter how long we lived, we'd never really get out of Viet Nam. Now here I was, preparing in the same way, at the same hour of the morning, and feeling the same wired blood heat I'd felt twenty years before. And I was doing it by choice. I stood in the middle of the room for a few seconds and wondered why that didn't bother me. Maybe it was what Daz had said about chaos theory; repeating eccentric ellipses. Reality works its will.

Might as well put it to use instead of fighting it. I threw the ludicrous KKK-style pillowcase hood into the gym bag and placed the cordless phone I'd stolen from Rodman's on top of it. Then I went downstairs to wait for Daz.

He showed at four-thirty in a full-sized Ford Bronco. We drove to the fundamentalist church without saying much, something unspoken on each of our minds. It was a little after five when we got there, still about forty minutes until full light. The fog was unwinding out of the empty church parking lot and rising like Dracula's cape over the field beyond. Daz pulled the Bronco into the parking lot and cut the ignition. I could feel him looking at me in the darkness.

"Yeah, what?"

"It's been a while since you did this," he said softly.

"It's only been twenty-four hours."

"Touché. But this is different."

"Yeah?"

"You gotta snatch the cat."

"You agreed with the plan."

"Plans are like politicians' promises."

"Except I'm not depending on a politician."

"Still, you been around enough to know how things got their own plans sometimes."

I knew, but I asked him anyway. "What's your point, Daz?"

"You have to make up your mind now," he said. "If you try to decide later you could be dead by the time you do."

I stared straight ahead into the fog, knowing what he was talking about but wanting to avoid it. If something went wrong, if the plan blew up, if it came down to it, was I willing to kill? Up until now there'd been no direct contact so the possibility was fairly remote but now, did the thing mean that much to me?

"I'm in it with them, Daz. They'll sure kill me if they find out who I am. I don't have a whole lot of choice at this point."

"Still time to get out and hope for the best."

"I'd never feel safe."

"Come on, man, this is the Daz."

"All right, I want it, the money if there is any, but more than that. I want to know what they're doing. I want to know who they are. I don't want to be a drone. I want to know who's got their fingers on the buttons. I want to be a player, not just a consumer unit. That answer your question?"

"So you're willing to get bloody?"

"I've already been bloody, this time at least I've got a reason. What about you? Why would a guy with all you've got going for you want to get mixed up in something like this."

He lit a cigarette and covered the windshield in a wash of blue smoke before he said anything. "Well, I tell you," he said as he watched the smoke curl back into the rear of the Bronco. "I prayed about it. Yeah, yeah, I really did. I prayed to God, and I meditated with the Buddha and what came to me was, and this is no shit, my man, it's some kind of public service. Don't ask me how or what. That's just what came to me."

I thought I knew all the Daslow Gervins there were but this was a new one. For a few seconds I thought he was joking but then I saw him gazing steadily through me with those landing-light eyes and I knew he was sincere.

"I don't know what to say, Daz. Politics seems like it would be a lot safer."

"I been thinking about that," he said. "But this is now. Besides, I'm just a backup. You play it right and it's so easy it's greasy. Now do it."

I'd already been over the ground between the church and Rodman's property a couple times so I ate up the distance in a loping stride, knowing the fog would cover me. When I got to the wooded ridge that marked the beginning of the estate, I dropped to the ground, took the infrared binoculars out of the gym bag and crawled to a spot where I could see down the hill. I scanned until I saw a greenish form hunched against a tree. They must have changed lookouts a couple times during the hours since I'd left, but this one's form looked a lot like the first one. He had the same forlorn stoop and gestured every so often as if he were muttering to himself. Every few seconds he would look nervously over his shoulder. "Man," I said silently to the form, "you are one unlucky son of a bitch. You get to pull the first shift in somebody else's shoes and now this."

There were too many leaves and twigs on the ground for me to make it to my original hole without him hearing something but it didn't matter. He was only about seventy-five yards away, actually a little close for the M-79. It would have to be more of a flat shot than I wanted. An M-79 round should come in nose down.

But that was for later. The first thing I had to do was find a spot along the ridge where I could hide when the sun rose. I dropped down below the ridge and went left about thirty yards to where I could see a loose stand of pines rising through the mist. I eased over the top of the ridge and pushed the gym bag ahead of me. When I saw through the binoculars that the lookout's head was nodding or his attention was fixed to the front, I crawled a few feet to where I had placed the gym bag and then stopped to check him again. Once my rear foot scraped against a fallen limb and he swiveled quickly, the machine pistol at port arms. I flattened against the ground, resisting the urge to look at him. I knew if I lay low and quiet he wouldn't come up the hill. He'd stand looking until his neck muscles started to burn and his eyes started to droop. Then he'd feel the familiar dark close back around him and his tree-stump home. He'd turn back to the front, congratulating himself on how alert he'd been, convincing himself it was nothing but the wind or an animal. Putting myself in his place, I gauged how long that would take. I felt his fear, the hardness of his stare, and his inner conversation. I stayed flat until I felt the darkness start to enfold me in its homey embrace, then put the glasses on him again. He was facing front, the machine pistol close but leaning against the tree. He was taking a drink from what looked like a Thermos bottle, something to ward off the chill, and the ghosts.

I worked my way a little further into the pines and stopped behind a hummock formed by moss growing over a downed spruce tree. I rolled onto my back, took out the 79, broke it down, loaded it with a high-explosive round, and placed it next to my right leg. I put the Beretta outboard of the 79 a few inches and made sure my hand knew where to find them both. I ran the aerial up on the cordless phone and pushed the switch to the talk position. The reassuring hum of the dial tone told me I was close enough to the house. The click would register on the lookout's equipment but he'd think someone in the house just changed their minds about making a call. I switched off the phone, placed it alongside my left leg, and took out a pint of Jack Daniels. I needed it to take away the chill, and perhaps bring back the ghosts of other shrouded mornings. Nothing to do then except wait for sunrise.

By eight-thirty the fog had burned off, only to be replaced by a carbon monoxide-laced haze caused by one of the infamous temperature inversions which hang over summertime Baltimore like dragon's breath. That was good though. It made me feel as mean and poisonous as the air. I rolled carefully onto my stomach and steadied the glasses on the hummock. The guy below was taking off his jacket.

Rodman left at nine. The minute I lost sight of his car I decided to do it. I didn't see Mrs. Downey's car and didn't want to give her time to make it. Elise might not even be up but I was sure Downey had already gulped down two cups of coffee and was, even now, speeding toward us, hands clenched on the wheel, eyes bright with the anticipation of another day of depravity.

I picked up the phone and dialed 844-1212. The well-modu-lated, computerized voice of the time lady came on and the guy below me on the hill picked up his earpiece.

"At the tone, the time will be nine-o-three, and ten seconds," said the time lady.

"Hello," I said. "You with the earpiece and the machine pistol. Look ahead about twenty yards to your left and keep your head down." I dropped the phone, rolled into kneeling position with the M-79, aimed down at the spot where I'd told him to look, felt the hard kick, heard the thunk as I got off a round, then dropped to my stomach. I was gratified to see that, even after twenty years, the hard mean bang blew open a little crater very close to where I wanted it.

The other guy wasn't so gratified. He dropped the machine pistol and covered his head to fight off the evergreen fallout.

"Now listen," I said into the phone as the time lady informed me it was now nine-o-four, exactly. "The next one lands right on top of you unless you do what I say. No bullshit, no second chances. The next one turns you into something they can mail home. Raise your left arm if you understand. You have two seconds." His left arm shot into the air like it was trying to achieve orbital velocity. "All right," I said. "We're going to unload your weapon like this. Stand up, slowly, with the gun pointed at yourself. Now take out the clip and put it in your rear pocket, keep facing front. Now empty the round out of the magazine. Keep it pointed at yourself, be careful now. Just so I'm sure it's empty lock it and pull the trigger on yourself. Do it. You've got another ten seconds." He double-checked the magazine and did as I said.

"Good, good. Now take off your shirt so I can see you don't have anything under it." After I had him bare-chested I put the pillow case over my head and told him to get his book and his bugging equipment. "Now turn around and walk up the hill," I said. "Sling the machine pistol and bring it too. Walk slow. Keep the earpiece on so you can hear my instructions. Now walk."

As he trudged toward me I loaded the 79 with a shotgun round. Then, when he was about twenty-five yards away, I told him to stop and face left. He still hadn't seen me, and before he did, I wanted to show him something. "Have you ever heard of an M-seventy-nine?" I asked him. He shook his head in the negative. I wasn't surprised. It's the age of high-tech weaponry, Uzis and the like, the emphasis on speed. The 79 is very low-tech. It breaks down like a shotgun and only loads one round at a time, but it's your basic pickup truck of a weapon, durable, dependable, versatile, and carrying a very heavy payload. "I want you to see something," I said into the phone. There was a small stand of young clump birch in the direction he was now facing; saplings clustered together in a little thicket of white wands. I fired the shotgun round into them and the tops blew away as if they'd been attacked by a firestorm of rabid locusts. I loaded another round while he was picking himself up off the ground.

"That was the M-seventy-nine," I said, standing up so he could see me in my hood. "It can blow you apart either of two ways. Understand?" This time he nodded vigorously in the affirmative. I threw down the phone and gestured for him to continue up the hill. Below I could see Mrs. Downey's car winding up Rodman's lane. It didn't matter now. In a matter of minutes I'd have the guy over the hill.

When he got to me I had him kneel, hands behind his head while I packed the gym bag. I decided to keep the 79 on him instead of the Beretta because of the terror factor. Most people would rather be killed neatly than watch pieces of themselves sail into the breeze. I packed the gym bag with my belongings, his bugging equipment, his book of phone numbers, and his Uzis. Then I walked him over the hill. When I waved to Daz he launched the Bronco across the field like he was auditioning for a Ford commercial. He lurched to a stop at the bottom of the small rise where I was standing and leapt out of the door wearing his hood and carrying two sections of rope.

"Hi there," he said to the shirtless man kneeling in front of the M-79. "You look like you might be a foreigner so you probably can't appreciate the irony in my wearing this hood. Take my word for it though, there are certain parties who'd be home guarding their sheets if they knew. Now stand up and put your hands behind your back."

We dumped the guy in the back of the Bronco and covered him with a tarpaulin. "I just thought of something," I said as we jolted back across the field toward the church. "What're we gonna do if we get stopped by the cops and the guy starts yelling from under the tarp?"

"Hell," said Daz, "I don't know. I was a lifer. That's the kind of thing never comes up in military operations."

"I don't know either," I yelled over the roar of the low-geared engine. "Maybe we could douse him with whiskey and hit him over the head, you know, we were all out hunting and he got drunk."

"What were we hunting with a goddamn M-seventy-nine? I don't believe there've been any elephants in this area for quite some time?"

"Hiking then, we were hiking."

"You got whiskey?"

"Yeah, Jack Daniels."

"Gimme a drink."

"You're driving."

"Yeah, and I got a tied-up greaser and three illegal weapons in the truck. Gimme a drink."

"Drive carefully," I said, handing him the bottle.

"Sure," he answered, popping a tape into the Bronco's cassette player. He tilted the bottle to his lips as the Stones rolled out of the quad speakers. "Ahh," he said, wiping his lips. " 'Sympathy for the Devil.' Used to hear that over the radio on the choppers when they were flying us in." Daz nodded his head in time to the music. We were at the edge of the church parking lot when he started the bottle toward his lips but stopped in midmotion. "Oh shit," he yelped. "Who's that?"

I looked where he was pointing and saw a big beige Mercedes turning into one end of the U-shaped drive in front of the church.

"Son of a bitch," I yelled at him. "Hit it! Hit it! The bastard must have had the bug running into the walkie-talkie somehow when I was talking to him."

Daz punched the Bronco and we swung out of the opposite end of the U, heading north on Carr's Mill Road. The Mercedes sent up a rooster tail of dust and gravel as it jumped out of the drive to follow us. I could see four figures inside. "We got no chance on these curves," Daz screamed over the Rolling Stones singing "Gimme Shelter." The Bronco was lurching from side to side like a commuter plane in a thunderstorm and the guy in the back was yelling in his language as he banged into alternate sides in the rear. "Fuckin' Mercedes is gonna tear us up," yelled Daz. "No way we can corner with em."

"Get off the road."

"Where goddamnit? There's trees on both sides."

As we flew around a turn on the wrong side of the road I saw a trail of dirt puffs as a burst of automatic weapons fire whipped the side of the road where we should have been. "Christ!" I said. "They're shooting at us."

"I know they're fuckin' shooting at us," Daz shrieked as he took evasive action by snapping the Bronco from one side of the road to another with no regard for possible approaching traffic.

"Do something man," he screamed. "Fuckin' do something."

Both windows were down, bringing in a jet roar of air and screeching tires. The Stones were wailing, the guy in the back rolling, bumping, doing his own wailing, I was screaming some kind of wordless noise with each turn and I kept seeing the dirt puffs rake the road to the side and in front of us. It wouldn't be long before they got lucky and Arla would never know what to tell the kids when they asked her what had happened to Daddy. *Do something.* I had to do something, so I did what I'd done so many times in the past when I was terrified and cold under a hard rain of fire and circumstance; reached for the fat round barrel of the M-79. I dug into the gym bag as Daz made another test pilot turn at the beginning of an uphill grade. He was still making crazy S turns to avoid their fire and I dropped the shotgun round three times before I got it into the breech. I picked out a high explosive and a white phosphorus round, stuck them into the big side pockets of my camouflage pants and rolled into the rear compartment, landing on top of our prisoner who protested with a loud string of foreign curses and an attempt to bite me on the thigh. I kicked him aside, squirmed around so I was facing to the rear and blew out the back window of the Bronco with the shotgun round.

The howl of the wind was even louder now as I groped in my pants pockets for the high explosive round. I dropped it once, loaded it and tried to figure what kind of shot to make. They had to follow Daz's evasive action to keep from slamming into us so they were being held anywhere from fifty to seventy-five yards from us. The two in the rear were doing the shooting; leaning out the windows, hanging on with one hand and firing their Uzis with the other. It was a low-percentage way to shoot but they were getting better with practice. I decided it would be futile to try and actually hit the car so I aimed low into the road in front of it. The blast rocked them to the left and almost sent them out of control. One of the shooters let go of his Uzi as he was forced to use the other hand to keep from being thrown completely out the window. The driver was good, though. He careened like a pinball from berm to berm as he fought for control and we gained ground, but with each swoop he got a little more traction and, finally, as we hit a long straight stretch he evened out and came at us like some kind of crazed jet jockey. "Let him gain, Daz," I yelled into the roar, hoping he could hear me. "Let him gain, goddamnit. We've got to take a chance. This is it, goddamnit. Let him gain."

I could feel us slow slightly and the Mercedes came on with a rush. I loaded the white phosphorus and braced my feet against the tailgate as I aimed. Willie Peter was the slang term for it; a term of respect. It's white hot. It'll burn through anything and when it hits, it spreads, and it sticks. But the shot has to be good. The explosion has to move it onto the target, not by it. They were coming on; now just one guy firing with an Uzi and the guy in the front using a pistol. We were still on the straight stretch but I glanced around to see a curve in the distance. It was time, get them going straight. "Straighten out," I yelled to Daz. "Straighten it out." The guy next to me tried to kick at me, but I had no time so I whacked him lightly on the jaw with the seventy-nine's stock and braced myself again. As we straightened out and the guy with the Uzi took the opportunity to lean forward and aim, I let it go.

A small blue-white sun obscured the Mercedes for a second and then dispersed to reveal what had now become not a car, but a comet. It had been close to a perfect shot. The front half of the Mercedes was being eaten away by the burning phosphorous glue and the windshield was an opaque mass of melting gook. Before we headed into the turn I had time to see it swerve into a steep bank bordering the road. Flaming doors flew open and the men inside dived out like sailors jumping from a burning ship. They hit the ground running. I didn't know whether I was relieved or disappointed that they weren't on fire. As we rounded the bend I heard that solid satisfying whump a Mercedes makes when it explodes.

"I told you it would get the cat high," Daz said later that morning as he took a big toke of the Thai joint.

"I never thought of you as such a literal guy," I answered, as he passed the smoke to me.

"Just a simple man with simple pleasures," he sighed as he gazed lovingly upward at the big balloon with the words Pleasant Acres printed on the side.

The balloon was tethered with two 150-foot hawsers tied to two giant oak trees in a far corner of Daz's seventy-acre spread. I could barely make out the small gondola that contained the sentry we'd brought home in the Bronco.

"I can hardly hear him yelling from that height," I said.

"Hell," said Daz, in a high, pinched voice as he exhaled the Thai smoke. "The man can yell until he learns to sing. I bought this place for its privacy as well as its natural beauty. He'll get hungry in a while and start munching them noodles Li Anh fixed him and drinking that saki. I only hope he doesn't try and fly down."

"What's Pleasant Acres?" I asked, listening lazily to the Arabic cries from above.

"New housing development I got out in Harford County," Daz answered. "This is gonna cost me a few days extra rent on the balloon but what the hell?"

"Thanks. You know those guys know the license number of your Bronco."

"Wrong, they know the license number of a nineteen sixty-five Buick now resting in peace in a junk yard out by the airport."

"You mean we were driving around with expired tags?"

"Nah, I just took the eighty-nine stickers off one of my other cars and put 'em on the Buick's tags."

"Yeah, yeah, the stickers. Saves the state a lot of money in new license plates."

"Don'tcha just love an efficient bureaucracy?" he asked.

We gazed upward. The haze was burning off and it was turning into a clear summer day. A slight breeze rocked the balloon to and fro, bringing us the faint cries of the man in the gondola along with the chirping of the birds. "Kinda reminds you of those exotic movies with Arabs singing their prayers from the tops of mosques, doesn't it?" Daz asked, and then laughed.

I laughed with him. It was late morning. The weather was good. We were stoned on great weed. We were alive. It was a nice day.

16

I was back in Miller Sorenson's office at *Warfield* magazine, wearing my suit and carrying my Naugahyde briefcase. But this time he wasn't buying it. "Come on," he said, "fool me once, shame on you. Fool me twice, shame on me. You're no graduate student."

When I had matched Roger Dorn's number to one in the Arab sentry's book I'd called Sorenson and told him I needed a bit more information to complete my study. He'd agreed. The following morning found me scrubbed and eager and asking for information on Dorn. "I don't know what you mean," I said.

"Well," said Sorenson, again feeding Winstons to his duck ashtray, "I started thinking after the last time you were here that you looked too old. No offense, it's not your face. That could belong to one of those eternal grad students. But I played lacrosse for Hopkins and I notice how people carry themselves. You're, what? . . . a little too, ah, instinctive to be a graduate student. And that plastic briefcase; give me a break. I had my mind on the stock market when you were here before or I'd have noticed it then."

The stock market. He played the stock market. Of course. Business majors play the stock market like coal miners play the football pools. Sorenson was looking especially smug today. He was wearing fairway-green pants, yellow shirt, regimental tie, and a Navy blue blazer. I know, it's an outfit that should only be worn by the referee at a croquet match, but it's summertime *de rigueur* for a certain class of Marylander.

"You're an observant man, Mr. Sorenson," I said. "You'd do well in my business."

"Which is what?" he asked, propping his feet on the desk, his hands clasped behind his head.

I whipped out my new PI license and waved it by his eyes, too fast for him to read my name. "I'm a private investigator," I said. "And now that you know I suppose you've guessed what I'm doing." I tried to sound a little dispirited.

"Uhh, not exactly. But you're not getting any information about Roger Dorn until you tell me."

"You do have the information?"

"Don't even have to look it up on the computer. He's an interesting man, a minor legend around here."

"I'm not from around here."

"I'm not surprised."

"Listen," I said, leaning forward in my chair and lowering my voice. "I'll tell you, but then you have to repay the information. If you don't, what I have to say will do you no good."

Sorenson's feet came down off the desk and he retrieved the Winston from his silver duck. "Shoot," he snapped.

"Like I said, I'm a detective. I hold licenses in four mid-Atlantic states. Remember the last time I was here you told me Armco was a subsidiary of Dynatron, and that controlling interest in Dynatron was held by Pecosa Diversified. Well, I'm doing some discreet, and bear in mind that's the operative word here—discreet—investigations on all Pecosa's companies and executives."

Sorenson stubbed out the cigarette with the flourish of a pianist hitting the final note. "Takeover!" he said. "That's it, isn't it? A takeover. Pecosa's stock will triple. Jesus!"

"I said discreet, remember? If this gets out it's over, understand? And any Pecosa stock you might happen to buy in the next few days will be lucky to stay where it is."

"Sure, sure." Sorenson's fingers started to move involuntarily toward the electronic rolodex where I was sure he kept the number of his broker. "Discreet, that's me. Especially when there's money on the line."

"How about that information on Dorn?"

"Oh yeah, right. I told you, I don't even need the computer. Dorn's a native Baltimorean. He was a fighter pilot in World War Two, shot down some big number of Germans, and got a couple of the major medals, a hero if you will. He came home and majored in aeronautical engineering at Loyola University, put himself through school by being a stunt pilot at airshows and driving a cab. When he got out of school he founded his own company, which was then called Dorn Airfoil. He made wings. Then he made some big advance in flaps or fuel tanks or something like that and hit it big. He expanded the company, went into all kinds of aircraft parts, then diversified into hydraulic pumps, brake shoes, all kinds of parts for cars, trucks, boats, and so forth. That's when he incorporated. But he's always held most of the stock himself. The word on him personally is that he's a genius at design and development. That's the basis for his success, not business acumen per se. He's a tough guy and a straight arrow. Was married to the same woman for thirty years until she died of cancer a couple years ago. Catholic Church, Knights of Columbus. He was part owner of the Colts back in fifty-four until he and the others were bought out by Carroll Rosenbloom, the bastard, who then sold to that scumbag Irsay who moved them to the land of corn dogs."

"Yeah," I said a trifle impatiently. "That was a tough break for Baltimore."

"Tough?" Sorenson whined, "lacrosse on Saturday, the party afterward, then the Colts on Sunday. The best hangover cure in the world was a brace of mimosas with brunch and then the Colt game. But you don't care about that. The funny thing about Dorn, the thing that got people buzzing around here was when he sold controlling interest of Dynatron to Pecosa. He'd always been as jealous as an Italian husband about that company. He'd had countless chances to sell his interest to bigger outfits but he wouldn't even listen to their offers."

At that point I thought I should ask him something that sounded like a takeover-type question. "Why'd he sell then?" I inquired. "Did Pecosa get taken? Was the stock overvalued? Was he gutting the company to get a good quarterly picture for Pecosa? Is he the kind of person who would do that?"

"I told you," Sorenson answered, "he's a straight arrow. A war hero, WW Two. He's from the old school. According to our sources Dynatron is as sound as any company its size on the Eastern Seaboard. The best guess around town as to why he sold out was that he was despondent about his wife and wanted to travel or become a recluse or something, but he hasn't done that either. As I'm sure you know, he stayed on as Dynatron's CEO."

"Yes, yes of course."

"It's a mystery. I'm telling you the guy was as married to the company as he was to his wife. Everyone figured after she died it would be the only thing he had left. You know, like those NRA bumper stickers say—they'd have to pry it out of his cold dead hands. But then, maybe it's as simple as him getting his price. That's what usually matters isn't it?"

"Umm yes, usually." Sorenson's hands were inching toward the phone again at the mention of money. He'd been a big help. I hoped he didn't take too much of a beating when it turned out there was no imminent takeover of Pecosa. But then you can't cheat an honest man. You'd think that would make them more plentiful. "I guess I've taken up enough of your time. Remember now, I'm not authorized by my client to promise that anything you might assume will take place actually will take place." That was true. Doris Samski was my only client and she'd never authorized me to promise any thing.

"Of course not," Sorenson said. "Now if you'll excuse me I have to make a phone call."

17

The first thing I did when I got back to my room at Huan Lo's was to check the answering machine. It had been forty-eight hours since I'd told Samski to check in and I still had nothing for him. Sure enough, he was getting impatient.

"Hey there, buddy," said the recorded voice. "You jerkin' me around or what? Halloween ain't for another two months an' April Fool's Day has done passed, so what the fuck? How long do I have ta keep callin'? Leave me a goddamn message. Otherwise I'm liable to figure you're dead an' I don't wanta start celebratin' unless I'm sure." He gave a couple of haw haws. It sounded as if he'd become a long-term patient of Dr. Beam's.

"It's okay," I said to the machine. "Things are just moving a little slower than I thought. We've got a big piece of information, though. I found out who the big daddy in this deal is and I'm going to make a move on him. So keep calling."

The next thing I did was call information. If Big Daddy was tapping everyone else's phone I had to assume he was tapping his own in the hope that I'd work my way up to him. I couldn't think of a way anyone might tap a car phone, so when I got information I asked the operator for Dorn's car phone number. She told me she was sorry but I'd have to get that from him. Car phone numbers aren't listed. Fine, I would. I hung up and thought about Dorn.

If Armco was. doing the boards for Dynatron, and Dorn was CEO of Dynatron, he figured to be the one behind the circuit board scam. Rodman had told Elise that Dorn was squeezing his balls. It had to be Dorn, but I was less sure than I'd led Samski to believe. Dorn's profile just didn't coincide with the kind of person who ordered wholesale killings. Sorenson had said he was a straight arrow, family man, Catholic, Knights of Columbus, war hero, and general self-made man. I didn't doubt he was capable of killing. Anyone who's killed in a war is capable of doing it again under the right circumstances. I was becoming living proof of that. But Dorn just sounded like a guy who'd have to have a more personal reason than I'd seen demonstrated.

Maybe it was like Sorenson said. Maybe it was just a matter of the right amount of money. Maybe Dorn had turned bitter after his wife died and just didn't give a damn anymore. Or maybe I had a sentimental view of World War II vets. My father flew twenty-five missions over Germany and is also a straight arrow, family man, faithful husband, member of the church, and all-around man of his word. I forced myself to remember that Dorn had sold out. I remembered that an administration of bright-eyed World War II family men had sent me and my generation off to Viet Nam without blinking an eye. They were hard guys. Who knew how hard? I had to count Dorn as armed and dangerous. I also had to talk to him.

The Dynatron complex was south of Baltimore on Dorsey Road, an area of industrial parks and country music joints circling BWI airport. It was twelve-thirty when I pulled into the visitors' parking lot. The fifteen-mile drive from my room in Waverly had taken almost forty minutes in the noon rush of office workers cruising for burgers. Being a detective was beginning to seem a lot like being a trucker. To cover my irritation I played the radio and tried to feel superior to the grazing herd but it was hard. They were all lazing around statues and fountains munching corned beef while

I was dodging traffic on too little sleep. Of course they were only paroled for an hour and I could stay out all day, or until I got killed.

I pulled into the parking lot, stopped, and walked casually toward the headquarters building, a two-story brick rectangle with Dynatron zapped across its front in blue lightning-bolt script. I thought it seemed a little flashy for a guy like Dorn but then I remembered he didn't own it anymore. I didn't see what I was looking for in the front of the building and I didn't think it would be in the employee parking lot, which was to the right rear and guarded by a gatehouse containing a young black guy in a brown uniform. The uniform fit like it had been sewn together by his mother while she was being dragged behind a horse.

I couldn't see the CEO waiting in line with the proles, even if he was a self-made man. Especially if he was a self-made man. What I could see was an executive parking space, probably within a few steps of the building, a space that would be labeled with his name.

I went around the left side of the building and there they were, two Volvos, a Lincoln, and a Mercedes 300 SE two-seat convertible. That one had to be the ex–stunt pilot's. I walked into the lot behind the cars and proudly surveyed the neat black and white signs planted militarily in front of the cars. Samski was right. I was getting pretty good at this. The sign in front of the Mercedes read: Roger J. Dorn CEO. I walked up to the driver's side and peered through the glass. The car phone was planted in a console between the seats. The sun created a glare on the back of the phone, so I had to move my face around on the glass like some kind of algae-eating alien, but I managed to read the number.

"Hey there, my man, you looking for something?" The voice came from over my right shoulder. I looked down and to my right to see an uneven pair of brown pant legs.

"Nah, nah," I mumbled casually as I straightened up and turned. The guard backed off a step and I could see he was holding a police-issue canister of mace loosely by his side. "Damn, these are beautiful," I said. "I just wanted to check out the upholstery, real leather. If I ever get any money this is gonna be one of the first things I buy."

The guard relaxed a little. He looked about twenty-one and bright eyed. I guessed he was a college kid earning money for night school. He was wearing a kind of wary, embarrassed look. I suspected it was because of the uniform. "Yeah, well, that's nice and all but I'm gonna have to ask you to kinda get on about your business. This is the man's car. See the sign?"

I looked at the sign. I was impressed. "Oh yeah, shit. The CEO. Sorry. I guess that's one of the things you gotta do, huh? Keep spectators away from his car. Chief Executive Officer! What a job; come late, leave early. That's the way to do it, get'cher money for nothing and your chicks for free." I sang the last part in a poor imitation of the Dire Straits hit and the guard laughed.

"I don't know," he said. "That's what I thought, but the car's always here when I get here and he doesn't leave till about six most of the time."

"Really, hmm, I guess everything's got it's price."

"Yeah, but ah, like I said, if you've got business . . ."

He nodded his head slightly in the direction of the front parking lot. "Oh yeah, sure, I've gotta be at the personnel department."

"There's an information desk in the lobby," he said as we headed toward the front of the building.

I thanked him, entered the lobby, went to the desk manned by another guy wearing another ill-fitting uniform, asked directions to the Baltimore-Washington Parkway, and listened while he gave me a route that would have sent me on my way to Philadelphia. I exited quickly, hoping the first guard wouldn't notice that my business in personnel had only taken five minutes. Big deal, so they had no openings for vice presidents.

It was about two o'clock when I got back to Huan Lo's. I had a late lunch and went to the library where I thumbed through magazines and tried to figure out the best place to meet Dorn. I decided a mall parking lot would be good; lots of other cars and very little security. Also, I found out from *Time* Magazine that the stock market was up and interest rates were down. There was the problem of that pesky federal deficit but foreign investments were going to take care of that. On the down side, there were thousands of homeless people lying in the streets like trash after the Super Bowl, and a ballet company in Minnesota was doing a production of Swan Lake that contained sections of total nudity. I wondered what the male dancers were going to do about the problem of centrifugal force during those fast turns? It certainly gave new meaning to the term on point.

At three-thirty I went back to my room and talked to the answering machine. "Listen, Samski," I said to it. "At six-fifteen call this number—four-seven-seven eight-eight-nine-five. That's a car phone. If nobody answers wait fifteen minutes and call again. Keep doing that until somebody answers. When the guy answers say this. Say it exactly. We're getting down to money time. Here's your speech—Mr. Dorn, you don't know me but I know something about you. I know about the circuit boards Armco's been altering for you at night. I know you've had two people killed because of them. I also know they were the wrong people. I know because I've got the boards. If you want them back drive immediately to Golden Ring Mall. Park on the upper level lot directly in front of Caldor's. Don't try to call anyone on the way. Don't even hang up your phone. I'll be listening. If I hear you hang up all bets are off and I get what I can for the boards from whatever magazine or papers want the information." I told Samski to make sure he wrote the speech down. Then all he had to do was stay on the line until he heard my voice.

At five I drove back to the Dynatron building and parked in a space where I could see Dorn's convertible. I listened to the radio and wished I'd taken time to buy or rent a car phone of my own. What if he left early? Nothing, that's what. It would just give me another day to get a car phone and the Arab another day to spend in the balloon. Li Anh was the one I felt sorry for; having to feed noodles to a guy in a balloon. It's not something your mother prepares you for.

At six-fifteen, a blocky figure in a gray suit came out the side door with a taller figure in a blue suit. The blocky one removed his suit jacket and got in the Mercedes. It was six-sixteen. His phone should be ringing. He leaned out the window talking to the blue suit. He lighted a cigar. He began talking again. It was six-eighteen. Maybe I'd screwed up the answering machine somehow. Maybe Samski had a previous appointment with Dr. Beam. The blocky guy pulled his head in the car and started the engine.

He leaned over and picked up the phone. He rolled up the window on the guy in the blue suit. Lift off. It was a go. Samski's engines were just a little late kicking in. The blue suit got in his car and Dorn leaned back in his seat, not bothering to smoke his cigar, just staring. He put the phone down, waited a few minutes, and picked it up again. *No, Roger, it's not just a bad dream.*

The trip to Golden Ring took forty-five minutes in the rush-hour traffic. The slow pace made it easy to keep Dorn in sight. I didn't chance getting close enough for him to see my car, so I couldn't tell if he followed Samski's instructions and maintained the connection. Even if he did call someone I didn't think they'd have time to set up at Golden Ring unless they happened to be shopping there. I was more worried about him stopping for some help on the way but he didn't.

When he pulled onto the ramp leading to the upper level of the Golden Ring lot, I took a sharp right into the lower level. I'd have to move fast, find out if Samski was still on the line, and exit smartly stage right if he wasn't. I jumped out of the car, took the Beretta out of the trunk, stuck it under my windbreaker, and took the stairs to the upper level two at a time. When I got to the top I slowed, took three deep breaths, and strolled onto the lot into a gossamer summer twilight that helped me maintain the dreamy air of a casual shopper as I ambled along searching for Arab types. I made a circuit of the airfield-sized expanse of concrete, then headed toward the Mercedes convertible from the rear. I felt stupid when I slipped the pillowcase hood over my head but I did it anyway.

He just looked at me blankly as I dodged into the dark leather upholstery, Beretta pointed at his chest. He was a squat-pulling guard of a man with round wire-rim glasses and black hair going gray. The hair was combed straight back and embalmed in the kind of dab'll-do-ya hair cream I hadn't seen since the last Jerry Lewis telethon. He had a square face with slight jowls and a pair of the most arctic blue eyes I'd ever seen. They stared out from behind the wire rims with the same pale, distant calculation as those of a lead sled dog.

I picked up the phone, careful to keep the gun on Dorn. "You there?"

"Yeeah," came the familiar slide of Samski's voice.

"He break the connection?"

"Nah, I been here the whole time."

"Stay on the line. If you hear anything wrong, or anyone hangs up until I say so, you come on in."

"Come on in where? What the fuck you talkin' about? I'm down here in Towson with people thinkin' I got this phone stuck in my ear. Where the hell are you?"

"I'm right where I said I'd be, get it?" I didn't know whether he got it or not. I just hoped Dorn didn't get the fact that I was solo without a net. I put the phone down and faced him.

"Yeah," Dorn said. "What?"

The war and the years of stunt flying showed in his face. The incipient jowls looked like they'd been poured over concrete and his nose had that bullish spread noses get after they've been broken a few times. Yeah, he could kill you all right, but. . . .

"What?" he said again, seemingly unfazed by the Beretta.

"You know what," I answered.

"You're not gonna look me in the eye when you talk to me?" he said, like that put him one up.

"Every car salesman I ever met looked me square in the eye the whole time he was talking to me." I stared at his belly as I spoke. "Besides, I'm looking at where I'm gonna shoot you if I have to, that may not work in a plane but it's good policy when you're in the infantry, which is where you are now."

"You know I'm a pilot."

"I know a lot of things about you. I know you had Rodman tell Fredericks to tell an engineer named Mosby to design some alterations in some Armco circuit boards. I know the boards were stolen because I'm the one who's got 'em. I know you ordered Mosby and Fredericks killed, and Rodman's phone tapped, because the boards were so important you didn't even care who had 'em. You just wanted anyone who knew what was going on dead. This is your life, Roger Dorn."

Dorn leaned against the door as I talked, clasping his hands comfortably across his belly. They were big hands, with broken nails and the faintest trace lines of grease in the ridges of their skin. They were the hands of a man who liked to put together things other than deals. Somehow they didn't fit the man I was talking about.

"So what do you want?" he asked. His voice had a pinched tension to it. He was staring at the gun now that the eye contact hadn't worked.

"That's simple. I want to know what you're doing to the boards."

"Why?"

"Because then I'll know what to do with them."

He smiled crookedly. "So you don't even know what you've got," he said almost sadly.

"No," I answered. "But I'm in a position to check whatever you tell me with an engineer I know. And you damn sure won't get 'em until I do."

He didn't say anything for a minute, just sighed once and gazed out the rear window. "Who the hell are you anyway?" he asked. "How in the hell did you come to get mixed up in this thing? I mean who the goddamn hell are you working for?"

His voice had risen to a hoarse bark on the last question but it sounded more exasperated than angry . . . like he was frustrated that a new player had entered the game. I decided to answer the question truthfully and see his reaction. "I got into it by sheer coincidence and I'm working for me," I said easily.

His wolf-dog eyes widened and then narrowed as if he were looking at a blackjack dealer who'd just told him the house's down card. He seemed to think he might be getting lucky. "You mean you're actually in this alone, that you just stumbled into it?"

"Well, it was a little more scientific than that, but not to the untrained eye."

"And you're just nosing around trying to see what you can get out of it?"

"Like I said, it's a little more scientific than that, and I'm not completely alone. I have what you might call subcontractors."

"Jesus," Dorn said, "I almost feel sorry for you."

"I'm touched. Why is that?"

"Because I don't think you have any idea what you're dealing with."

"So what am I dealing with?"

He shrugged and spread his hands. "I don't even know, but I'll tell you one thing. If you're some small-time operator my advice is to get out now if you can because this goes high, higher than someone like you is prepared to fly."

Steam was starting to seep out around the edges of my pillow-case. Here was a guy sitting in his own car with a stranger holding a gun on him, a stranger who had something he desperately needed, and he was telling me I was the one who was surrounded.

"Listen, wheezebag," I said, "I've got you, I've got the boards, and I've got a prisoner. I know who you are and I know who the other players are and you haven't got a clue as to who I am or where to find me. And I can find you any time I want so you can skip the fucking State of the Union message, all right? And as far as I can see, you and the rest of the greaseballs in this operation are only good at one thing, and that's blowing people away while they're looking at the sky and counting butterflies. I stalked better men than you people every day for a year in Nam and I'm here to tell you about it. If you think I'm scared you're right, but I'm used to it. It doesn't make me fuck up."

This time he looked at me differently. He was calm, thoughtful. I could see the machinery working. "So you were in Viet Nam huh?" He said it like he was evaluating a stock he was about to buy.

"Yeah."

"And you've killed people?"

"Yeah, when that's what it came down to."

He was staring at me again. "And what is it you hope to get out of these circuit boards you've stolen?"

"That depends on what they're for."

"So, for all you know, you may get nothing."

"Oh I'll get something all right. If nothing else I'll get satisfaction. This is getting to be kind of a personal matter with me and I'm willing to bet heavily that you all aren't going to risk the information getting out. Not after you've already killed two people."

Dorn was getting a little red in the face. A few drops of sweat were beginning to form along the dark slash of his briar-patch eyebrows. He was making silent deals with himself, calculating odds. He kneaded his big fingers into a rootlike tangle. When he spoke it was in a different voice, a raspy whisper that came out hard. He had to almost cough it out. "Suppose," he said, "I could show you a way to make fifty thousand? A sure fifty thousand?"

I thought he was going to play "Let's Make a Deal" with me; give me fifty thousand cash in exchange for the prize behind door number one. I'd have considered it too. Fifty thousand would have put me in solid with Arla. But that's not what he wanted. What he wanted was for me to kill someone. Not just someone, a United States congressman.

"Zale," he said, "First District Congressman Roland Zale. I'll give you twenty-five thousand now just to show good faith and another twenty-five when it's done."

18

"Well," said Dorn, "I can tell you generally what it is but not specifically."

At nine-thirty the following morning the three of us were sitting around a big mahogany table in a meeting room at Dazco, Dorn, myself, and Daz. Dorn was holding one of the circuit boards I'd stolen. He was turning it around and over, holding it by the edges the way careful people handle record albums. He put it down and picked up the other one, turning it the same way.

"Here," he said, "you can see they're making a slight modification in this part of the circuit. I can tell you what kind of circuit it is because I've designed them myself. As a matter of fact, this looks like an extrapolation of one of my designs."

Daz was standing in a corner smoking a Pall Mall and eyeing Dorn's face, "assimilating his aura," like he said he would when I'd phoned him the previous night from the bar where Dorn and I were drinking.

I was busy trying to assimilate my own aura. The sight of Dorn's rocky hands on the circuit boards was putting me into some kind of automatic rewind. I kept remembering the moment in Dorn's car when he'd asked me to kill Congressman Zale. It was one of those moments they say only happens when you're drowning. I'd been grateful for the hood because it kept him from seeing the psychic whiplash in my eyes as my life flashed in front of me. I wasn't who he thought I was. I was Lowell Ransom, a West Virginia boy. I was Lowell, loving, if temporarily estranged husband of Arla. To my daughters I was Daddy, for Christ's sake. I was the poetic kid who used to climb to a tree-ringed circle of grass overlooking the valley where I was born and imagine I could see spring through a hole in the winter clouds. Hell, I thought I could see the rest of my life from that spot. In those days it looked a lot like spring.

I never imagined the day when I'd be sitting with a hood over my head, gun in hand, listening to a man offering me money to kill another man. It couldn't have been me in the car with Dorn. That kid on the hill was me. He'd been looking right over my shoulder but I hadn't been able to touch him.

"Why?" I'd said aloud.

"Why what?" Dorn had growled.

"What the fuck do you think, why?" I said. "Why do you want me to kill the guy?"

"What do you care? You're in it for you, and I'm offering you a chance to come out with substantial cash instead of just fucking around hoping for the best."

"Where the hell are you coming from? You watch too many cop shows on TV or what? All that shit about hit men? You think there're hit men on every corner, idiots who'll kill anyone for money without even knowing why?"

"No, but from what I can see, you're the kind of guy who's doing whatever it takes to make a score."

"I thought we'd already established the fact that you can't see too much."

"You said you'd done it before, in Viet Nam."

"The old crazed Viet vet, huh? I wouldn't think an executive like you would have time to watch that much TV. You were in a war. You were an ace. Maybe I missed something. Maybe you WW Two guys just played touch. Is that the way it was, or did you burn twenty-some men alive on their way to the ground?"

"Yeah," he said in his hoarse bark. "But I ain't running around with a goddamn hood over my head holding a gun on people."

"No, you get someone to do that for you."

He tightened and drew in a breath like he was going to yell, but then he stopped and exhaled slowly, slumping against his door. "Look, aside from all the bullshit, you want the money or not?"

"I don't know that until you tell me why."

"You saying you might?"

"I'm saying give me a reason and I might. I don't do things without a reason unless I'm drunk, and I try not to get drunk as often as I used to."

"You have to promise me you'll think about it."

"I don't have to promise you anything. You want the guy dead, you tell me why, otherwise we go back to plan A. I don't care much either way."

I wasn't about to kill anyone for money, not for fifty thousand or fifty million. But my new occupation was confirming what my cursory study of politics had caused me to suspect: People believe what they want to believe, and you win by letting them.

Dorn was desperate enough to believe I was sent by some malevolent providence to make up for the ill luck he'd been having. He thought I was an instrument to work a fantasy. He thought I was a sign he was getting lucky again. And, as he talked, I began to think he might be right.

"Zale," he said, his lip curling involuntarily into a snarl. "The slimy son of a bitch is a big wheel on the congressional appropriations committee. Some people say he's got more pull than the chairman. Some people think that's because he's got something on the chairman. Anyway he forced me to sell Dynatron out to Pecosa International. That's why I want the fucker dead."

"I need to know more than that. What do you mean, forced you to sell. How could he do that?"

"Sheeeit," said Dorn. "You don't know much about the defense industry do you?"

"It hasn't exactly been my life's work."

"Well let me tell you about it. It's the goddamndest biggest mountain of money the world's ever seen. It's a sea of money, it's a continent of money with Uncle Sam standing at the gates handing out tickets. And those tickets are defense contracts to make everything from megaton bombs to midget squeegees for tank drivers' goggles. A defense contract is a license to print money. Cost overruns are built into the contract, and you can be damn sure there are gonna be cost overruns. They're a perk. That's the way the game is played. The point is, Uncle Sam is represented by appropriations committees that say what projects are gonna get funded and which aren't. They can also cancel any projects that are already under way. You beginning to get the picture?"

"Zale canceled one of your projects?"

"Nah, he threatened to cancel one now and make sure I got none in the future. He threatened to flat ruin me. I built that company with these two hands and this head. My wife and I sweat more blood over that company than we did over our kids. Now she's gone and the company too. That was *my* company."

Dorn hammered what looked like a two-pound fist onto the Mercedes steering wheel so hard that I gained new respect for German workmanship. "What project?" I asked him.

"What?" he said, staring at the quaking wheel to see if it was dead.

"What project? What project was he going to cancel?"

"Too many overruns," Dorn said bitterly. "Too many fucking overruns, and them with their six-hundred-dollar toilet seats. He was gonna cancel *me* because of too many cost overruns."

"Hey," I yelled. "Quit whacking out on me and answer the question. What project was he gonna cancel?"

Dorn snapped his attention toward me with the kind of look you give a short, skinny kid who suddenly dunks the ball. "Right," he said, "right. That's a good question. It was the F-one-eleven presale modification. They're modifying a batch of F-one-elevens to fit the specs of a sale order. We're doing the electronic circuitry."

"Who're they selling them to?"

He rubbed his chin and reached thoughtfully for a cigar. "Uh, let's see," he said, "the air force, for one. They're not *selling* them to the air force of course, they already have them, but we're upgrading some electronic systems. The sales are going to Israel and Saudi Arabia, mostly, a few to Greece." He started to light the cigar.

"Don't light that in here," I said. "The smoke'll get under my hood. I'd hate to get blinded and have to shoot you just as a precaution."

"You're not going to shoot anybody, are you?"

"Oh, if I have to I will. Oh, yeah."

"I mean you're not going to shoot Zale for me."

"Did you have Mosby and Fredericks killed?"

He laughed, snorted actually. "I told you, it's not even my company. Why would I kill anyone for a company I don't even own anymore? Hell, if I was going to have people killed I'd have started with Zale."

I had to agree with him. My whole scenario was crumbling under the weight of Dorn's information and his personality. If he'd been forced into selling the company then he couldn't be the top rung of the ladder. "But you did give orders to Peter Rodman, didn't you?" I asked.

Dorn snorted again. "Yeah, sure. I'm the president, for what it's worth, which isn't a thimble full of boot sweat."

"What'd you tell him?"

Dorn had been in a kind of introverted funk but now his attention came fully back to me. "This isn't 'Nightline,' buddy, and you're not Ted Koppel. If you're not gonna kill Zale then I've got no more reason to talk to you. I don't give a shit what you do with those boards. It's not my company anymore."

"It may not belong to you but you still belong to it, don't you? People you know, friends in the field, they still put the name Dorn together with Dynatron, don't they?"

"There's nothing I can do about that."

"Suppose there is?"

I could feel my monkey sense sharpening the facts into an olfactory picture of the forces out there in the dark. I was beginning to sense their shape and size. I couldn't see them yet but I was beginning to know them. I could feel the facts forming into a vague plan. I was convinced Dorn had been in the chain but that he'd done what he'd done out of a desire to protect a company he thought of as his oldest child.

"Suppose there is what?" he asked.

"Suppose there's a way to get your company back? That'd be even better than shooting Zale, wouldn't it?"

"Hell," he said, "that'd be better than being six years old on Christmas."

"Why don't we go to that bar across the road and talk about it?"

"You gonna take the hood off or do I have to tell people you're the Elephant Man?"

I took the hood off and we went to the bar where we talked. I told him what I was about but not who I was. He told me that Rodman had been sent down from Pecosa to "oversee" the F-111 modifications. Nominally, Rodman was supposed to report to him but they both knew who was giving the orders for the project. Still, Dorn had sweated Rodman as much as possible, refusing to sign invoices unless he was told what they were for, refusing to sign checks unless he got weekly printouts on production schedules and quality control.

"Yeah," I said, "I heard Rodman said you were squeezing his balls."

"Where'd you hear that?" Dorn asked, sucking the ice in his Chivas.

"His wife told me."

Dorn gave a low whistle. "Well," he said, wide eyed. "Well, well, well."

"Yeah, that about says it all."

"Does it?"

"No, but for the time being let's stick to the subject. What did you learn?"

He shrugged and lit his cigar. "Nothing really, everything seemed to be going along fine. Everything was just routine."

"I'll be damned," I said. "You're the reason for this whole thing. You're the reason they had to do it at night. They knew you'd blow everything if you knew."

"Knew what?"

When I told him about Samski's night work the cigar almost fell off his lower lip. "At night," he roared. "They're doing off-spec modifications at night. You're damned right. I'd have blown the whole thing out of the water."

"They'd have killed you too."

"Hell, why didn't they just fire me and put Rodman in charge?"

"I think it was because they needed a fall guy if anything happened. That way Rodman's their man. This way he's your man."

"Son of a bitch."

"That about says it."

Daz had been skeptical when I told him I was bringing Dorn in. He'd asked me how I knew the guy wasn't just bullshitting me to get a look at us and the boards. I'd told him that, aside from the fact that I'd already found out he sold the company, my monkey man told me so.

"All right," he'd said. "I can get with the monkey man thing, but I'm gonna stand aside and assimilate Dorn's aura. And if I don't feel congruent with his inner warps I'm not gonna be responsible for what I might do, dig? I got a lot at stake too. And by the way, Li Anh's gettin tired of havin a dude floating over the house in a balloon. We're having whatcha might call a waste disposal problem. It's like living on a planet with flying cows, if you get what I mean."

I'd almost forgotten about the Arab in the balloon. "Don't worry," I said. "I think I've figured out a way to use him."

"Nothing like working with an experienced professional."

"Hey, I may not be professional but I'm experienced."

"So was Jimi Hendrix, and he's dead."

I knew better than to ask him if he wanted out. It's just that he's still a sergeant at heart, likes to keep everyone from getting overconfident.

So there we were in the Dazco office. Daz lighting another Pall Mall and looking a little less skeptical, Dorn engrossed in the boards, and me drifting away, thinking now of Arla's thighs and how long it had been since I touched them. "So," I said impatiently, "generally but not specifically, what is it?"

Dorn had the board up close to his eye like a jeweler examining a diamond. "That Mosby was good," he said. "Very neat, very economical."

"A hell of a guy," I agreed. "What did he do?"

"Well," said Dorn, placing the board carefully on the table. "All I can tell you is that it's a modification of the radar damping circuit."

"No kidding? Daz, it's a modification of the radar damping circuit."

"Damn!" said Daz, "that was gonna be my next guess."

"A couple of wise guys," Dorn said, pulling a cigar from the inside pocket of his suit. "A couple of pothead wise guys are gonna get my company back for me. You guys are potheads, aren't you? I knew when I saw that one's earring." He gestured toward Daz with his cigar.

Daz blew a long plume of Pall Mall smoke toward the ceiling and then leveled his eyes on Dorn. "Well, my man," he said, "I can afford to take little mental vacations because I haven't lost any of my companies lately."

It was more a gentle prod toward the business at hand than a needle and Dorn was big enough to take it that way. "Yeah," he said, "potheads, why not? Right out of left field. Why not . . . ? Here's the story. Modern radar is sophisticated. You can't just take a plane and fly in by the seat of your pants with your scarf flappin' in the wind. The other side will lock onto you a hundred miles out and stick a missile up your butt as soon as you cross the border. So what you do is, you design an electronic system to confuse their electronic systems—circuits that send out false signals to confuse their radar. The whole thing's a big chess game. They design better radar, you design better radar damping, then they design better radar again. It keeps everyone employed. That's what we're doing with the F-one-elevens. We're upgrading the radar damping. That's what this first board is. It's the design we're using. This second board is a modification of that design which is not specified in the contract."

"But you can't tell us exactly what it's supposed to do?"

"Nah. This circuit board interlocks with a dozen others. If I could look at the overall schematic I'd be able to tell you."

"So," I said hopefully, "is that a problem?"

Dorn chewed on his cigar and rubbed his chin. "I don't know," he said, "it shouldn't be. We bought a new computer system last year and it'll tell you anything about any part of the company. All the schematics of all current designs are filed on it. You're supposed to be able to call 'em up just like that, but with Rodman and his boys running around at night . . . I don't know."

I was fighting down that wave of panicked optimism you get when you think you've run across something too good to be true.

"But why would he put it on the computer? I mean it was dangerous, not to mention illegal."

Dorn looked at me and rubbed his eyebrows. "Jeez," he said, "you think designers nowadays sit around hunched over drafting tables like Bob Cratchett or something? They design right on the computer. Mosby probably hadn't used a drafting table since his sophomore year in college. Besides that, you don't know engineers. They even organize the coins in their pants pockets. Once they're used to something they stay with it."

"He's right," said Daz. "The man had something valuable. Not a thing he'd want to leave in the bedroom closet with his old pocket protectors."

"You're the president," I said to Dorn. "You have access, right? Please tell me you have access."

He said he did. He said he would. He also said he was sure there must be someone in computer operations who would tell Rodman he was rummaging through the files. What we finally decided was that we'd wait until night and access the files with a modem from one of the computers at Dazco realty. All Dorn had to do was get what he called an autocad disc from his office. He said he could put the disc into any of Daz's computers and it would let us read the schematics out of Dynatron. There was a number/letter code you had to have to get into Dynatron's files over the phone, but being even a phony president has privileges. Dorn had the code and we had Dorn. For him, we were the only game in town.

"There is one thing," I said to him before he left for Dynatron. "You know they've been killing people."

"Yeah?"

"It appears they're killing anyone they think knows anything. They don't care who did what. You understand what I'm saying?" Dorn took the big cigar out of his mouth and used it to point at me. "Lemme tell you something," he said. "I'm sixty-four years old. My wife is dead, my kids are grown, and my company's gone. And like you said to me, I fought better men than these guys every day, only I did it for more than a year. You understand what I'm saying?"

"Just so everybody understands."

"They do." He replaced the cigar in the corner of his mouth as he turned toward the door.

When he was gone I asked Daz what he thought.

"Hell," he said, "the man was all the way into those boards. He'd never seen 'em before. Besides that, he's one of your old-timey entrepreneurs. Got rich outta mechanical skill. You check out his hands?"

"Yeah."

"Not soft enough for the kinda sneaky shit we're seeing."

"That brings us back to the original problem."

"Yeah?"

"Yeah, who's the guy with the soft hands?" I asked.

"Rodman's close."

Rodman was close but he was too close. The main man had to be someone further away, someone who was using Rodman as a buffer, someone sending a Mercedes with DC plates north to Baltimore.

"Tell Li Anh she's gonna be getting rid of the guy in the balloon," I said.

"When?"

"After tonight."

"That's great. She'll be talking to me again in no more than a month."

19

Dorn showed up again at the Dazco office at 8:00 P.M. At nine, the three of us were staring at a computer screen with the resigned disbelief of people everywhere who had bet the favorite and lost. Dorn had brought the autocad card. We'd tapped into the Dynatron computer with Dorn's code, and we'd called up the F-111 files. No problem, except that the schematic we were looking for wasn't in them. We'd looked under the project name and we'd looked under Mosby's name but come up with nothing. There were schematics under both names; some of them were even of the F-111 project. One of them was the original spec drawing of the modifications, but there was nothing integrating the board I'd stolen into the overall system.

"Maybe they just deleted it when they found out there were other players in the game," Daz suggested.

I asked Dorn what he thought.

"Maybe," he said, "but it's not all that easy. Any deletions on active projects have to be cleared through the head of computer operations and he sends me a report."

I reminded him that he'd told me Rodman had been the one really giving the orders.

"Still," he said, "the head of computer operations has been there fifteen years. He's one of those guys who keeps his top button buttoned when he's not wearing a tie and pisses cause it's time to. That's why I put him in the job."

"Maybe they just paid him off."

"Possible, sure. But he makes seventy grand a year and still drives a 1978 Dodge. My gut tells me it must be in here somewhere."

We decided to ride with Dorn's gut for a while and keep looking. I asked him if the engineers created their own files or if they had to go through data processing. He told me they worked at individual terminals linked to the mainframe, which automatically created a printout of the new file titles for the data processing department.

"Suppose someone worked at home, just like us?" asked Daz.

"Sure," said Dorn, "they could do that."

I asked him how that person could get around the printout of new file titles.

"Put it in an old file," he said. "But all the old project schematics are purged from current memory and stored on tape in a warehouse. He'd have to physically go there, get it, put it into the machine, add to it, then take it back again. No way he could do all that without attracting attention."

"What about another kind of file?" asked Daz, tapping his forehead with an unlit Pall Mall.

"Huh?" said Dorn.

Daz looked at me. "I mean another kind of file than a project file, some kind of file that nobody would be looking at but that would still be in the active data base?"

"Yeah, yeah," I said. "But which one, where do we look?"

Both of us looked at Dorn. "Don't look at me," he grumbled. "There's all kinds of files like that—personnel, inventory, billing, legal. Shit, I don't know."

None of us knew where so we decided to start with who: Mosby. We pulled up his personnel file, still active pending dispensation of insurance benefits. The thing that hit us in the eye like a jab was that he'd minored in computer science. He had graduated from one of the best engineering schools in the country, Remson University, and he'd been a little more active than your stereo-typical science nerd. He'd spent three years on the staff of the Yellow Lackey, a satirical campus quarterly apparently named as a jab at Remson's athletic teams who played under the name Scarlet Knights. He'd also been president of the campus chess club and finished tenth once in a nationwide masters tournament. There was nothing much else that seemed significant. He was a single middle-class Irishman from New Jersey who was thirty years old when he died going after the big money.

"So," I said when we'd finished looking at the file, "what we've got here is a guy who was computer fluent, probably had a good sense of humor, and was good at chess, good at moves."

"Good at hiding his moves," said Daz.

"Where do we go from here?" asked Dorn as he leaned back in his chair and bit angrily on his cigar.

"You asking me?" I said.

"You're the quarterback of this deal, aren't you?" He chomped the cigar like he hated the idea. He was going to hate what I told him even more.

"Well," I said, "since you put it that way, here's the play. You have to come back here tomorrow and keep going through old files. Start with uh, what? Anybody got any suggestions?" I looked hopefully at Daz who shrugged and said: "Think chess."

"Think humor," I answered.

"You guys think of whatever you want," said Dorn. "I'm starting with personnel because that's where I already am. I'm gonna check the files against payroll to see if he might have stuck it under a phony name."

I told him it sounded right to me.

"What're you gonna be doing while I'm here with my shorts stuck to my balls?" Dorn asked.

"I'm gonna go get a man out of a balloon," I answered.

20

"You sure you don't want me to go?" Daz asked as he pulled on the rope.

"Nah," I said, pulling the one on my side of the balloon. "Stay home and get next to Li Anh. Samski's looking for something to do anyway."

"Man sounds like the kind of person who'd piss on his own foot to me."

"I've got a feeling he's all right as long as you keep him out-doors."

Daz quit pulling on the rope and faced me. A rainless summer mist hovered in the air and the sweat on his bald head caused him to glow silver in the moonlight. "Seriously man," he said, "this Samski sounds like some kinda Southern mutant, might be into gothic shit like marrying his sister."

"You've never seen Doris. If you had, you wouldn't think that's such a bad idea."

"You know what I mean."

"Daz, it's just that high lonesome. Mountain people are born a little closer to the moon. They've all got a few . . . orbital harmonics."

"Yeah," he said, "I noticed."

"You talking about me?"

"Let's just say I always suspected you of being some kinda closet bluegrass freak."

"If it's blue, it's true."

"Yeah, well just remember what they say, the truth sometimes hurts." He gave a final tug on his rope, pulling the balloon to within ten feet of our heads. The Arab was hanging over the side, cursing us and spitting. Daz picked up a clod of dirt and winged it toward the irregular shadow of the guy's head. We heard a satisfying whack and the cursing subsided to a low murmur. The spitting stopped altogether. "How're we gonna handle this?" Daz asked.

"Simple," I said, "we put the hoods on, show him the gun, and he gets in the trunk of my rental."

"What if he doesn't wanta get in?"

I was about to answer when a hurtling shape from above made it all academic. With some kind of horrendous Middle Eastern shriek, the Arab plummeted into the ground between me and Daz. There was a cartoon oofing noise as he hit, then a few seconds of agonized gasping as he tried to will the air back into his lungs. I was about to reach over and help him up when he jumped to his feet and assumed an apelike crouch. His hands dragged the ground as he pivoted like a cheap dashboard ornament to alternately face Daz and me. He was cursing again, practically frothing at the mouth in fact, ready to fight, ready to gouge, kick, bite, and knee. He'd been kept in a balloon eating noodles and excreting over the side for days and he was mightily pissed off. Things would have turned really ugly if Daz hadn't stepped in smartly and delivered a whipping kick to the side of his head. The man went down like he'd been hit by low-flying aircraft. "Emotional type, isn't he?" Daz said, then dropped to one knee and felt the side of the Arab's face. "I don't think it's broken," Daz explained. "I tried to catch him right where the two big bones join so I wouldn't break anything."

I didn't have time to ask Daz if he was kidding because the Arab was starting to make groggy noises as he reentered consciousness. Daz and I each took an end and carried him to the trunk of my car. Daz held him upright as I emptied his pockets of wallet, change, keys, gum, matches, and one Trojan lubricated condom. I was glad to see he was living safely. All I left him was twenty-five cents—one quarter, and only one. We pulled the weather stripping off the trunk so he could breathe and dumped him in along with a canteen of water. It was five after midnight.

I was late. Before I'd left Dorn at the Dazco offices I'd put a message on my answering machine telling Samski to meet me at twelve-thirty. When I'd called the machine at eleven, I'd got a confirming drawl through the noise at Pete's bar. It would take about forty minutes to get from Daz's house in Brooklandville to the Exxon station at the entrance to the Baltimore-Washington Parkway. I hoped Samski would wait. I hoped he was sober enough to know he was waiting.

I didn't ask for completely sober. That was the reason I'd chosen the narrow parkway rather than the six lanes of route 95. I'd never seen a cop on the parkway. Ninety-five was the glamor route. That's where you caught your dope smugglers making the run between New York and Florida. All you might find on the parkway was a rental car with phony license plates driven by an armed man, accompanied by a crazed hillbilly, a high-tech phone tap, and a kidnapped Arab in the trunk. On the way to the Exxon station I took a couple of pulls on a bottle myself.

I was two blocks away when I spotted the gold eagle on the hood of Samski's Trans Am. I was half a block away when I heard Johnny Rivers doing "Ten Days on the Road" on WPOC. Good tune but I preferred the original by Bill Dudley. I'd also have preferred it if Samski hadn't been playing his radio loud enough to ignite the Exxon station's gas pumps. I hoped any cops in the area liked country music.

"How's it hangin', pard?" he screamed out of his window as I pulled in next to him. "You're even later'n I was."

"There's a first time for everything."

"Hey babe, I'm ready fer Freddy. Let's do her. We gonna hunt possum or just bark at the moon?"

"We're gonna do it."

"Okey dokey. What is it we're doin' exactly? You didn't say on your tape."

"We're delivering something to Washington."

He gunned the Trans Am into a roar and popped its clutch a couple of times. "Heeey, the Eagle has landed, babe," he said. "Hop in and let's fly."

"No, we've gotta take my car."

Samski looked at the rental like it was a plate of quiche.

"Hell man," he said, "whyn't we just take a fuckin' bus?"

"Because I don't want to buy a ticket for the guy in my trunk, that's why."

Samski pushed back his John Deere hat and whistled. "Alive or dead?" he asked.

"Alive."

"We gonna run into any of his friends?"

Before I could answer, I watched the evil black eye of his sawed-off twelve gauge appear over the sill of the Trans Am's window. "'Cause if we do. . . ." he said as he patted the barrel. "Six-shot Remington pump action. I toldja, I'm ready fer Freddy."

I told him we wouldn't need it but he insisted on bringing it anyway, said he was afraid someone would steal it if he didn't and besides, he wasn't used to this kind of shit and it made him feel better. Hell, if he felt any better I'd have to dance with him, but I figured I had the Beretta, and one weapons charge is as good as another.

We moved the Trans Am to a parking lot across the street and headed down the parkway toward Washington. It was a little after one on the kind of airless summer night that turns the front steps of Baltimore's row houses into an all-night desert oasis. Black families sit outside in lawn chairs wearing T-shirts, drinking beer, and running numbers on each other as their kids skip between stoops. The white people play cards and eat crabs and watermelon with their beer. It's hard to cool rowhouses with window air conditioners, and if inner-city families had the money for central air-conditioning they'd move out instead. So the party goes on until it cools off or they get tired enough to pull the heat over them like a blanket and sleep. Samski stared out the window as we rolled over the Green Street viaduct on our way out of town.

"Sheeeit," he said, "party time. Let's turn this fuckin' air-conditioning off an' let a little air blow through. How about some music?"

"You act like you love this kind of shit."

"Hell, pard, you know what I'd be doin' right now if I wasn't doin' this? Tryin' to fuck Doris while she recited the rosary and pretended she was bein' crucified."

"You mind if I ask you something?"

"If I do I won't answer it."

"Why'd you marry her if things are that rough?"

"Shit," he said, and pulled the hat down over his eyes. He studied a passing junkyard as he spoke. "Shit," he said again, then leaned out the window and spat. "Same old story. She .was hot stuff before we was married, an' then she got pregnant. Stop me if you done seen this soap opera. Besides that, I love the bitch." He took a pint of Beam from the hip pocket of his jeans and raised it in a toast. "At least I would if she'd lose twenty-five pounds," he said as he took a hit. "Whooeee, pard, how 'bout that music."

I stuck the jump-jive title tune to Little Feat's *Let It Roll* album in the tape deck and took the bottle when he offered it. "Here's to Weight Watchers," I toasted.

"Less watchin' an' more losin'," he said and laughed, stomping the floor in time to Little Feat's Olympic pace. "Let it roll, pard," he yelled into the night.

"Let it roll," I answered.

It takes about forty minutes to get from Baltimore to the outskirts of Washington. The parkway is just that, two lanes each way divided by a wide tree-lined median. Tall oaks and sycamores line both sides of the road, except where they're broken by long stretches of lawn marking industrial parks or government installations like Fort Meade. It used to be the only fast route between the two cities but Interstate 95 made it a backwash, carrying only short-haul commuters and passengers to BWI airport.

I like it though. The interstate keeps the cops busy so you can do pretty much what you like on the parkway. If you had to, you could hide in its thick foliage. You can also take a leak anywhere you like, a treat Samski took full advantage of. After an evening at Pete's bar he had to stop three times in the thirty minutes it took to get to the Capitol Beltway. Each time I wondered why I'd brought him. I could've done it alone or asked Daz, but then Daz didn't sign on to be my daddy. I was supposed to be operating my own business. What I needed was an employee or two. It's tough to get employees to work on speculation, though, so I was stuck with Samski. I considered the night a kind of interview. So far he'd done everything wrong, showed up drunk and obvious, carrying a sawed-off shotgun and a kiss my ass attitude. I was beginning to like him.

When we hit the Capitol Beltway I went east toward Largo. I didn't want to go all the way into Washington because it would give the Arab in the trunk too many choices. What I needed was some desolate area with a roadside phone booth.

Largo is the home of the Washington Bullets basketball team and the NHL's Washington Capitols. The seventeen-thousand-seat Capitol Centre sits out in the middle of a marshy plain like a mothership. I thought if I drove around in the vicinity of it I'd find what I was looking for. There are a few residential sections to the east but they're surrounded like wagon trains by a virus of low-rent shopping malls and liquor emporiums. If you drive west you come to Wild World, a combination zoo and amusement park. Somewhere on that road I knew there had to be a store or gas station closed for the night but featuring an outdoor pay phone.

Five miles past the center I saw a Royal Farms convenience store. I thanked heaven it wasn't a 7-Eleven because Royal Farms closes at midnight and it was almost two. I rolled into the store's lot where two phones were attached to the front wall. Two were too many so, with apologies to C&P Telephone, I got out and jammed a handful of dirt into the coin slot of one of them. I kept pressing the dirt in with the edge of a quarter until it was completely impassable. Then I took the tiny electronic transmitter and stuck it to the side of the other phone with a dab of crazy glue. I'd need to get it inside the phone to be sure of hearing the other end of the conversation but, since I'd need plastic explosive to get the speaker cover off a pay telephone, I had to be satisfied with just a number. It would show up on the LED console just the way I'd seen it in the woods at Rodman's house.

"Where'd you get that thing?" Samski asked nodding at the bugging device, when I got back in the car.

"From the guy in the trunk."

"Hah," he grunted, "poetic fuckin' justice."

I looked at him, amazed. "Where'd you hear that?" I asked.

" 'Wheel of Fortune,' " he answered. "Sometimes I look up the shit on there when I get tired of lookin' at Vanna's tits."

No doubt about it, I was beginning to like him.

"What's the deal?" he asked.

"Okay, I get out here with the bug and hide up there on that little hill behind the dumpster. You take the car down the road far enough that he can just see the store. Make sure he can't see any other place to go. Take that hood in the back seat and put it on so they won't know who to kill later. Then you take the guy out of the trunk and leave him. After that you drive back by here, find a spot close enough for me to get to you within a few minutes and wait for me."

"So what's he supposed to do?"

"What would you do if you were dumped out of a car near a city where you had friends, at two-thirty in the morning, near a pay phone and only a quarter to your name?"

"Uh-huh," said Samski. "He makes the call, we get the number."

"You got it pard."

"What if he don't go to the phone? What if he just takes a hike down the road?"

"Are you kidding me? It's *two-thirty* in the morning and he's just ridden forty miles in an overheated trunk."

"Suppose he lives around here?"

I looked at Samski's long-drawn furrowed face but it was as deadpan as the side of a rocky mountain. "What?" I said, not knowing whether to laugh.

"Well, there is always that chance, ain't there? Be kind of a amateur move ta fuck up 'cause we were too cocky, wouldn't it?"

"Okay, Sherlock, when you let him out point him toward the

store by waving your gun around. If he doesn't move away from the gun he's got a reason. In that case get him in the trunk again and we'll try another place."

"Gotcha," Samski said as he flipped me a salute.

As it turned out we didn't have to worry. From my position behind the dumpster I could see the Arab almost drop to his knees and face the phones like Mecca. He came half running, half stumbling across the parking lot groping in his pockets as he moved. He stopped short and stiffened when he discovered they were almost stone empty. He did a little dance as he clutched the insides of his pockets. Then he went into a distraught mutter and searched again. I was starting to think he'd dropped the quarter in the trunk when he hopped straight into the air, giving a little shout of triumph. There were heavy sighs of relief from both of us as he bolted to the phones. He tried the quarter in the one I'd filled in with dirt, shouted a complaint to the sky, then tried the other one.

He had an infinite number of choices. He could use his quarter to call a cab, to order a pizza, call his mother or, God forbid, get a wrong number. Or he could call his headquarters to tell them he was alive and, for Allah's sake, to come the fuck out here and get him. That's what I would have done in his position and I was hoping anger and frustration was part of the universal language that makes us all, if not brothers, at least sibling rivals.

The cherry-red little LEDs lit up the console in my hand: 777-1256. I had on the earphones and could hear his end of the conversation perfectly. I heard no mention of pizza and I didn't think a nice Arab boy would talk to his mother in that tone. He was still pissed off. Since he was speaking what I assumed to be Arabic I couldn't tell if his anger had a target or he was just describing the shortcomings of balloon living. I couldn't hear the other end but that would have been just a bonus, probably an Arabic bonus at that. I had what I'd come for. I should have gone. I didn't.

I decided to stay and see who showed up. The late hour must have affected my mind because I thought maybe it would be someone other than the boys in the beige Mercedes. But I was wrong. About a half hour later a big 450 SL with the usual doctor's office paint job rolled into the parking lot from the west carrying two olive-skinned types with grease-pencil mustaches. They opened the rear door and my guy collapsed into the back seat. The door closed but nothing happened. They just sat there, the engine running, air-conditioning on. Five minutes. Ten. Every so often one of the windows would roll down and I'd see a set of fingers flip out a cigarette butt. That's all. They just sat there, like they were waiting for someone, me for instance.

An unhealthy sweat broke out on the back of my neck when I realized my Beretta was probably outnumbered about six hundred rounds to fifteen. My stomach was dropping toward the center of the earth with nauseating speed. What the hell were they waiting for. If they knew I was here why didn't they come out and get me? Did they think I was a decoy? Or, Jesus! Maybe they were the decoys. Where was Samski? Where was the car? It was time to leave.

I put the console in my pocket and took out the Beretta. It would be nothing more than a nonviolent protest against their Uzis but it made me feel better. Taking a deep breath, I tried to remember that, just like the mind, the senses like to fool themselves. The senses tend to believe whatever makes them comfortable. Maybe the Arabs really didn't want to see me.

Trying to refrain from any loud thoughts, I glided vertically up the hill to where the dumpster's shadow ended, moved two steps laterally into the shadow of the store, and headed for the top of the hill. When I was over it I dropped to the ground and looked back to see if anyone was following. Seeing nothing, I shoved my gun hand in my jacket pocket and headed overland, trying to keep bush between myself and the road. Moonlight silvered the tall grass as rushes of nightwind combed through it, tossing lateral shadows like dark sparks. That was good. It set up the direction of natural movement. Men often move against that direction and throw graceless blocks of darkness against the prevailing current. Their lack of poetry makes them easy to spot. I kept low and tried to move with the wind. About two hundred yards west I saw my rented car parked in a semicircle of ruts which formed an unofficial turnaround. I cut laterally into the tall grass and scrub pines, and circled the car.

Dropping to the ground, I looked under the chassis for feet on the other side. Nothing. I jumped up and covered the distance to the window in a low rush. No one. No one anywhere. I made a full circle with my eyes, darting them instead of walking them. I still saw nothing. Then I heard a noise, a tiny scrunch of gravel, from the road . . . from behind me. One more fraction of a second and I would have had time to dive to the rear of the car but it was too late. I'd already heard the voice, a voice with a burbling mid-East accent. "Don't move, azzole," it said, "or I cut you in half."

Like any amateur would, the bastard had been waiting by the side of the road for someone to come along. I was too experienced to just walk up the road so he'd caught me with my back turned.

"Don't turn around, fook'ed," he said. I could hear him coming toward me. "You fookin' turn around I kill you now."

Time slowed to a stop. There was no movement, no life, no one anywhere but the two of us. I could almost feel the hair-thin line separating his finger from the trigger. I was looking into a descending funnel whose darkness made the night look like a glare of white sand. I was at that place where death is so close that the fear of it is gone, replaced by a sadness for the ones who'll miss you. I'd been there only a couple times before and I was going to do the same thing I did then. I was going to jump and see where I landed.

I had to make some kind of move because once they got me in the car I was gone. I was as gone as Samski. The man was close behind me. I could hear him breathing. I could smell the dragon odor of garlic. I'd wait until he touched me with the Uzi's barrel. That way I'd know just how far away he was. All I had to do was move fast enough to get my hand between the barrel and my neck, then push it away, hit him in the balls as he fired into the air, and get away before the ones in the Mercedes got there. That's all.

But he never touched me with the gun barrel. I heard a thud like an ax chopping rotten wood, then another voice.

"How's it hangin' pard?" asked Samski as he rolled the Arab onto his back. "I can feel a pulse in his neck, not that I give much of a shit." He looked up at me from where he was kneeling and gave me a long-fanged grin. "Don't look so surprised," he said.

"I may not have been no LRRP but I been on a few ambush patrols in my time."

"Jesus Christ!" I blurted as my knees decided to sit down.

"Nah," said Samski, "the resemblance is strikin' but it's just old Walt."

"Where the fuck were you?"

"Well, I been huntin' enough times to know it's more blessed to see than be seen. So I was over there in back of the car, in that clump of pines when I seen the two of 'em come up the road."

"There were two of them?"

"Yeah, this one went over across the road and the other one come lookin' around the car, a lot like you. He went around to check the trunk and I clomped him. This one just come lookin' fer him, I guess."

"I'll be a son of a bitch."

"Don't feel too bad, pard. You went about it the professional way but you was dealin' with amateurs here, least when it comes to woods walkin'."

"Walt," I said, "have I mentioned that I'm really starting to like you?"

"Hell," he laughed, "everbody likes me. You don't notice at first but I got a sparklin' personality."

We left the Arabs lying in the bushes and pushed the car onto the road so we'd be heading west when the sound of the starter broke the night, then got in and floored it. We were ten miles down the road, taking the exit ramp from Wild World onto the beltway before I relaxed enough to speak again. "You don't have a sister, do you?" I asked.

"No, why?"

"Never mind."

"Ya know," he said, "y'ore kind a weird sometimes."

I looked over at Samski slouched under his John Deere hat and thought that only a short time ago I didn't even know he existed. "Yeah," I agreed, "I must be."

21

Arla and I had come to the party together. It was in a huge old house with rooms built up along a rickety staircase shaped like a character from the Chinese alphabet. I was unsure just who was giving the party but I had the feeling it was an acquaintance of Arla's. That's why I was surprised to find Elise Rodman in a varnish-blistered room furnished only with an unmade bed and a bare lightbulb hanging from a wire. Arla and I seemed to have become separated. I was looking for her when I opened the peeling door and saw Elise. She was naked, her skin as soft and warm as a glove on a cold day. I knew that because I was on the bed with her doing something nasty with my fingers. Then the door opened and Arla looked in and smiled. That was the scary thing, she smiled. She smiled and ran her hand over the back of the guy's neck, the one who had his hands around her breasts. She wasn't naked but was allowing the guy to get her that way. She smiled, shut the door, and disappeared.

I jumped off the bed and ran down the hall, opening doors as I went. Every room had some pink-skinned, rose-nippled set of young thighs and eyes in it who opened her sugary mouth and drooled slightly at the sight of me. I didn't stop, though, because I heard Arla's voice. It was moaning soft and familiar, in a way that shouldn't be heard by anyone but me. I followed the sound and found her in a plush peach room being inhaled by a guy with the proportions and technique of a porno star. She got up and ran but I chased and caught her.

Holding her beneath the sardonic wink of her understated rear, I lifted her to me. I tried to squeeze away Elise and the other guy but it didn't work. Arla wasn't mine any more. I tried to hold her but she gave me nothing but angles. She moved away, always away, but never out of sight. All she said was, "No," blank and factual, not even any anger. "Why?" I pleaded, but got no answer. I felt like gnawing off my hand. I was alone.

I was alone in a sweat-soaked little bed above a Chinese restaurant staring at a ceiling with water stains the color of diseased piss. I'd had the dream about Arla and the house and Elise several times lately. Each time I was left with a painful empty space where Arla should be and a desperate desire to call her. This time was no different. Reaching blindly for the phone, I realized I had no idea what time it was. I rolled over and looked down at the floor, searching for the clock. But I turned to stone as I remembered how I'd fucked up royally last night. If it hadn't been for Samski I'd be dead right now, or wishing I was. Arla would never have known what happened to me. She'd have had to make up something to tell the girls. The thought opened a hole in my center, letting in a weeping giant of longing.

I wanted to be a schmuck. I wanted to be a nine-to-fiver in a cardigan sweater who could take his girls to the mall for ice cream without fear of seeing them chopped into dog chow by automatic weapons. I wanted the perspective of Arla's smile. I wanted the ballast of my family. I wanted the rest of me. I floated above all that in the poignant delirium of an astronaut floating above the God's blue eye of earth. Then I remembered that, like the astronaut, I was there for a reason. Before I could go home I needed something else. I needed to know whose house I'd get when I dialed 777-1256.

I found the clock under the bed and eyed it blearily for a few seconds before the numbers registered. It was almost one. The light outside my window told me I was in the P.M. I threw the clock back onto the pile of socks where I'd found it and lay back on the bed. My mouth was filled with a cottony bile from the four beers I'd had when I got back to the room around four-thirty. I'd needed them to erase the sound of the Arab's voice and the smell of his garlic. He would have killed me all right. He would have loved it. You get numb to facts like that if you're in a war and they're there every day. But this was different. I wasn't used to it anymore. I wasn't twenty anymore.

For a few seconds I was on the verge of losing it, breaking into tears and asking aloud how I got into such a mess. Then I remembered it was precisely because I was indeed, still twenty. He may have been encased in a forty-year-old shell but the twenty-year-old was still there. Arla told me so all the time and I could feel him. He didn't give a fuck. He wasn't going back to nine-to-five. He had his teeth in the prospect of money and he wasn't letting go until it was over. I smiled dimly. The hard little bastard was still there, and he didn't care if I was alone or scared or even if I'd fucked up the night before. Business, all he cared about was taking care of business. I laughed aloud. No more a nine-to-fiver, I was becoming a business man.

After a shower, a Tsing Tao beer, and some peppery Szechuan noodles to burn off the fog behind my eyes, I was ready to think about strategy. Back in my room, I sat looking at the phone. What would work? I was almost sure to get an Arab. What would he be likely to accept? What did Moslem Arabic countries have in common with the United States besides Coca-Cola? Money, that's what. Money equals business, business equals technology, and technology equals computers. Bingo! Every technostate takes computers for granted, and where you have computers you have computer error. Then you get those annoying but necessary human contacts. I took a minute to get into character, then dialed 202/777-1256.

"Ello," said a dry voice out of the desert.

"Hello," I answered, trying for a kind of warm Nazi PR-man tone: *Awfully sorry but we've screwed up your bill, hope you understand. If you don't we'll just have to throw you in a camp, you know how it is.* "Fred Helmsley, sir, C&P Telephone. I'm the customer service supervisor for your prefix code."

"Yesz?"

"I'm sorry to bother you, sir, but we've had a problem with one of our computers. A line surge caused some names to be attached to the wrong numbers. We're having to check each one individually. Some people have received bills for calls they didn't make and the information operators have been giving out some unlisted numbers because they're attached to the wrong names."

"Thisz numbeer isz unleested."

"Well, sir, in that case I'm sure you don't want us giving out your number through general information, or sending an itemized list of your calls to another address." I laughed genially. He didn't.

"That weel not happeen?"

Though it was phrased as a question, his tone made him sound like he was climbing into the line with a knife between his teeth.

"No, no indeed, sir. That's why I'm calling. All we have to do is make sure we have the correct name and address of the person who is billed for this number. I reenter it in the computer right now and the problem is solved before it begins. Now sir, the number is nonpublished, seven-seven-seven one-two-five-six, and I currently have it as being billed to an agent Donald A. Harris, FBI building, Washington DC. Is that correct, sir?"

"No, no, no, no." He said it four times instead of screaming. "No, that isz certainnnly not correct. You understand? Not correct."

"Yes sir, I understand. No problem at all. If you'll just give me the correct name and address I'll enter it and that will be that."

There was a moment of silence on the other end during which I had a horrible flash of some arcane reverse radio detector tracking down the source of the call. "Let me speak to your supervizeer," he said.

"I am the supervisor, sir. I thought I mentioned that."

"I meean," he answered with understated relish, "yooour supeerior."

I tried to put a little peacock in my voice: "I'm senior man for your prefix code sir."

"You meean you oowen the telephone company?" he asked sarcastically.

"Of course not, but you can only contact my superior in writing."

"I weel do that."

"Fine sir, uh, I take it then that you want us to go and send your bill to agent Harris?"

His urbane manner cracked, letting through a thin stream of red-hot lava. "Stop the fooking beel then, you imbeceel. Just stop the fooking beel." I could picture him staring beseechingly at the ceiling, wondering what malignant fate had sent him to an infidel country where the phones didn't even work.

"Bills with names and addresses go out, sir, even if they're not correct."

"Well then," he said, regaining his calm. "Just wipe out any address for theese bill and it weel not go out."

"Uh, I'm sorry sir, but the computer program won't let me do that. I can substitute an address but I can't simply wipe one out."

"And why ese thett?" He was getting that dull, emotionless tone people get when they realize once again that the public utilities have very private rules.

"For your own protection, sir. If some dissatisfied employee could just wipe out all the addresses then the company wouldn't be able to bill for them and it would lose hundreds of thousands of dollars. And then your rates would have to be raised to compensate for the loss."

"My rates?"

Welcome to the wacky world of public corporations I thought. "Yes sir. Public utilities can't operate at a loss. It's the law."

The lava was now pouring through the crack in his demeanor in a river of enmity. I could hear it rushing through the phone lines at me. "I weel not tell you the addrresss," he said. "I weel not make it thett eeasy for you fools because I know thett you must have hard copy zomeplace thett you do not want to bother looking up. So I weel tell you the name and theen you can gett yoore fooking asz into the hard files and match eet. The name ease Gottus. G-O-T-T-U-S, John R. And if these beel goes anywheere but heere we sue. We sue. Now fook you and goodbye." A little explosion went off in my ear as he slammed the phone into its cradle.

"But I don't have any hard copy," I said to the dead phone in my hand.

I sat looking at the name I'd scrawled on a note pad and suddenly my head started to feel hot and swollen. I felt as though I was levitating, floating out over the years to 1973: I was in college on the GI bill, cutting class to watch the Watergate hearings on TV. What had started as a possible cover-up had exploded into an *Alice in Wonderland* of paranoia and greed. There were enemies lists, daisy chains of payoffs, and interlocking bribes. I sat before my tube day after day, wasted on good Colombian, watching the whole executive branch being exposed as wolves in a pork chop factory.

I couldn't quite remember what John Gottus's job had been in the Nixon administration, some kind of high subrepresentative on the vice president's staff I thought. His actual alleged job had been as an alleged fixer who arranged alleged bribes from favor seekers to Spiro Agnew. None of that was ever proven of course. The vice president resigned to plead *nolo contendere* and Gottus went down with the Good Ship Agnew.

I remembered him though, he looked like a shorter, thinner version of the vice president. His hair was the same graying Vitalis rake job. His face had the same sort of Beefeater puff to it, and he had the same small eyes staring out from under foliage eyebrows like separate ferrets from their holes. Unlike Agnew though, he scared me. The difference in the voices is what did it.

Agnew's voice was thick, phlegm filled, a purulent pastry, topped with a sugary little twang of self-mockery. Gottus's speech was an unwavering series of metallic hyphens. Delivered at seemingly electronic speed, they almost skipped the language centers on their way to the response nerves. The man was a human electrode trying to attach himself to the collective brain. I never remembered what he said, only that he was completely sure of it. It was impossible for him to lie because he was the one who defined the truth. He impressed me as a man who thought the only things between Hitler and greatness were a shave, a haircut, and a Valium.

In the intervening years I'd wondered about Gottus from time to time. I was dead-solid sure he'd lasered out some prime cuts of any payoffs he might have arranged and must be doing just fine. Sometimes that worried me. In 1973 I experienced the government as a real presence. I'd only been out of Viet Nam for three years and still took the whole affair personally. I felt the American and North Vietnamese governments had conspired to kill me. It was the only logical explanation for the war. Gottus was the guy my subconscious chose as suspect number one. Seeing him on TV had been an emotional moment for me, and emotional marijuana moments tend to become permanent psychic tattoos.

Sixteen years ago I'd looked at the gleaming Gottus in his perfect suit and listened to his computer-chip voice and I'd known he'd do fine. Sure, "mistakes were made," and "bad judgment was used," but he'd do just fine. And I wouldn't. I'd decided then that the only way for me to avoid murder or insanity was to avoid certain types of people.

The cost had been heavy: years working for social services with other losers and even there, ducking people with a trace of the Gottus digital luster. He'd ceased to be an individual presence but he'd stalked me just the same. Still stunned, I sat looking at the name. It was nothing personal. That was the amazing thing. It was as impersonal as planetary conjunctions or beach erosion. I wondered if it was as inevitable. Was fate just another word for noticeable chance? I thought of what Daz had said about chaos theory, that it was the search for a pattern in the seemingly random. Sixteen years ago I'd seen what I thought was the face of a malignant future on television. Now I was holding the name and phone number of that face in my hand. I'd been frightened by him. Now maybe it was his turn to be frightened.

On the other hand maybe it wasn't even the same person. I had to see him, and to do that I had to find out where he lived. How to do that? That was the one constant I'd discovered during a week in my chosen field, an unending stream of how-tos. So far, I'd answered them by using the resources at hand, foraging off the communications landscape. I was beginning to warm up to the idea that we're all part of someone's data base. I was even beginning to feel affectionate toward the phone company. They'd been so helpful. I'd asked and received so I decided to ask again.

I went down to the restaurant and got a dog-eared old copy of the DC phone book I'd seen in Daz's back office. In it I looked up the number and address of a Herbert R. Jones. Then I went back to my room and called DC customer service. I told the well-modulated woman on the other end that I was John R. Gottus of 202/777-1256. On the off chance he'd called before, but more to get myself in the mood, I tried to imitate the electronic pulse tone I remembered hearing in Gottus' voice. I told the customer service woman my number was unlisted but that I'd lately been getting a lot of calls for a man named Jones, Herbert Jones . . . people wanting to talk to him, pizza places confirming take-out orders, once even an escort service wanting to confirm an appointment. I told her I was tired of it. I told her I didn't like pizza, that I was a married man and couldn't have prostitution services calling my house. I told her I was paying extra not to be bothered by unwanted calls. I was working up a pretty good case of urbane outrage.

She said she didn't see how that could have happened unless I'd inadvertently given out my number.

"I got his bill," I said.

"What?" she asked, in as close to a squawk as a customer service rep will ever get.

I repeated that I'd got Jones's bill and that I bet he'd got mine. When she said she didn't see how that could happen, I asked if she'd heard of line surges scrambling computer data bases. I explained that part of my legal practice was for a computer firm and the people there told me it happened a lot. She said she never remembered anything like that happening.

"Remember if Jones has my number he can charge long-distance calls to me. If he does that," I said, "I'll sue the phone company!"

She said she was sure nothing like that would happen. I said something like that was happening. When I gave her the name and cited an amount, she thwocked her computer keyboard a few times and told me that was not the correct amount of Herbert Jones's bill. "See," I said triumphantly, "everything is out of synch. I've got the wrong bill with what might be the right amount and I'll bet he has the same."

She told me that the amount I'd named was considerably less

than my bill. I asked her what exactly was my bill. She told me. I asked her how I could be sure that was correct in view of the fact that another man apparently had my nonpublished number.

"Give me the address," I said. "Give me the address to which you're sending my bill."

"All right, sir," she answered with stiletto politeness. "If you'll just give me your address I'll check it."

"Oh, no!" I said, trying for the maximum amount of Gottus's subliminal authority. "No, no. Let's face the facts here, miss. What you are, essentially, is a secretary, an executive secretary to be more accurate. I have secretaries too, and they get rid of troublesome callers by telling them what they want to hear. I know. I train them that way and I refuse to believe the telephone company is more warm and fuzzy than I am. I tell you my address, you parrot it back to me, the whole thing's on tape so when I sue your lawyers cut me off at the knees. I'm sorry but we do it this way. You tell me where you're sending my bill and I tell you if it's correct. If you refuse it's *meas rea absentia*, presumptive absence of truth. Nothing personal, I'm just protecting myself legally."

She assured me there was no absence of truth on anyone's part and thwocked her keyboard again. With just the merest sheen of gloat surrounding her sculptured voice she informed me that my bill was being sent to 1975 Vermont Place NW just as it always had been, and that I should have received it by now. I tried gamely to mask embarrassment with executive bluster as I asked her how, if that were true, I was holding Jones's bill and had not yet received mine.

"I suggest you contact the post office," she said. "We're not responsible for the disposition of our mail once it's in their hands. Of course I'm sure someone as well versed in the law as you are knows that already."

"Well what do I do with Jones's bill?"

"Well sir," she said with a sweet poison, "I'm not as well qualified as the post office but, if you like, I can suggest a place."

22

My first impulse was to run down the Baltimore-Washington Parkway to 1975 Vermont Place as fast as my rented K car could carry me. I didn't though, for three reasons. First, I had no idea where it was. Second, it was already two-thirty in the afternoon. I had to assume that if John Gottus had an address and phone number he must be more than a transient resident. If that were the case he probably didn't transact business at home. He wouldn't be there. He'd be at the office, busily ordering killings or beige paint for his fleet of Mercedes.

The third reason was logistical. If I left immediately I'd get to Washington just in time for the Roman circus of rush hour traffic. They say in the civics books that Washington was laid out in an imitation of Paris and I believe it. After all, Paris is the home of surrealism. Washington's streets lead outward from the Capitol like spokes from the hub of a wheel, which might explain why it's easier to get to Virginia from Fourteenth Street than it is to get to Twelfth Street. The only way to go crosstown is by a series of circles which at rush hour are like Dante's circles of hell.

To get to a cross street you have to enter a circle at fifty miles an hour, move outward through three lanes of traffic, and exit on the correct street like Eric Dickerson cutting back against the grain. If you pause for a second to consider the tons of rushing metal bearing in on you, you're likely to end up the cause of a screeching whirl of mixed paint and exploding glass.

If I hit Washington at quitting time I stood a better chance of seeing Mount Vernon than John Gottus. The thing to do was hang around town for the rest of the day, then head to Washington early tomorrow morning. I'd get to Gottus's house at about 6:00 A.M. and wait for him to leave for his office.

I decided to use the rest of the day taking care of a little housekeeping. I straightened up my Gulag of a room as well as I could. Then I went to several gas stations in search of a map of Washington. After I located Vermont Place I cruised by my office to see if anything looked suspicious. I parked in a lot across the street and sat for half an hour staring up at my one window to see if there were any shadows moving through the light.

The fact that I was using Miles's binoculars brought home the unpleasant realization that I owed him over a thousand dollars for the Beretta and the other equipment I'd borrowed. He wouldn't mention it for a while, but if I didn't pay him it would put a definite crimp in our friendship. He wouldn't get angry. As far as I knew, Miles didn't get angry. He'd lose respect for me though, be a little less quick to do me a favor, a little slower to laugh at a joke, a little more personal in his kidding. That would bother me, largely I had to admit, because if I stayed in the business I'd need some favors of the kind only he could deliver. If I didn't stay in the business maybe I'd ask him for a job.

Miles wasn't the only one I was going to owe. There was Daz, and Samski, and most of all Arla. If I came out of this with nothing but a shrug and a sheepish smile I was going to be everybody's idiot cousin.

When I was satisfied there was no movement in my office and no one else sitting around in their car like me, waiting, I went in to get my mail. I spent a few minutes just standing on the plush carpet looking out the window at the street below, feeling full and proprietary, a man in the saddle. The feeling contrasted painfully with the smell of soy sauce and the sound of screaming cooks in my room above Huan Lo's. When was my life going to get off probation and acquire tenure? *Jesus!* I thought. *Get the hell out of here before you call and apply for an Amway franchise.*

Back in the car I leafed through the mail and found it was made up largely of telegramlike notifications that I was on the list for the five-inch TV or the ten-inch microwave. All I had to do was go to a swamp in Virginia or Florida and listen to a ninety-minute sales pitch for a trailer pad.

I winced when I looked at the new balance on my Master Card bill, then went into a kind of monetary daze, wishing I could somehow get into their files and mark it paid every month. That way their computer wouldn't even bother to read my transactions. Of course the merchants would eventually complain when they didn't get paid but . . . but . . . to hell with the merchants. The computer wouldn't read the transactions because the bill was marked paid. . . . Damn! Finally! I thought I knew where Mosby had hidden the circuit board schematics.

I spent the rest of the day in a mating heat waiting for Dorn to get to the Dazco offices. When I called him at eight he said he was going to cross-check the last of the payroll and personnel names. I tried not to sound too dramatic when I told him to forget about that, I thought I already knew where to find what we were looking for. He caught on immediately when I asked him what would happen if Mosby had created a file in billing and then marked it paid every month in advance of the due date.

"Goddamn," he said, "the program would skip right over it. The computer would just issue a receipt and move on."

"Check on it will you," I said. "I know who we have to talk to and I'd like to know what we're talking about."

At seven the following morning I was in Washington slowly trolling around Vermont Place, a four-mile loop that looked like a theme park for homesick Colombian drug dealers. The houses were villalike white stucco affairs with archways to courtyards to circular drives, all connected by spiderwebs of tile walkways. Surrounding and overhanging everything were giant ferns and magnolias. I caught myself wishing for a white suit.

Gottus' place was about halfway around the loop. A low stucco wall surrounded it interrupted by a high archway, which led into a parking area the size of a basketball court. My heart pump-faked a couple times when I saw the lot was filled with six beige Mercedes 450s and one black stretch limo. A dark-skinned guy in a tan suit stood idly on a portico. He was leaning against a stucco column with one hand inside his coat, adjusting his shoulder holster the way a hitter adjusts his jock before he steps to the plate.

If I tried to park a K car near that house I'd stick out like one of the homeless at a charity fundraiser. A guy with as much on his mind as Gottus had to be an early riser who'd be on his way downtown by seven-thirty at the latest. I had a half hour to find an inconspicuous spot. I checked my DC map and noticed that Vermont Place bordered a big patch of green called Rock Creek Park, and parks mean public parking.

Once inside the green, I swung onto one of the blacktop capillaries and stopped. I thought the spot was roughly parallel to the Casa de Gottus but couldn't tell because I was facing a wide green lawn that merged gradually into a forest of beech and maple. I knew the park police would be curious about anyone roasting hot dogs at 7:00 A.M. so I wrote them a note saying my car had broken down and I'd be back to pick it up in the morning. Then I took Miles's binoculars and loped down the lawn to a hiking trail where strategically placed Snickers wrappers marked the way for future pioneers. Sweating greasily in the early morning heat, I crossed the trail and headed uphill into the forest.

Slowing down as the grade began to flatten, I hunched close to the ground looking for a fence or a no trespassing sign to mark the beginning of private property. I hadn't brought any kind of weapon because I assumed I'd be sitting in my car on a public street when Gottus came out of his house. I'd been to Washington plenty of times and it always seemed like your typical urban tic-tac-toe. I never imagined Gottus would live in what looked like a Casablanca Mercedes dealership surrounded by sets from *Lawrence of Arabia*.

My joints started to melt when I remembered the way they had put a lookout in the woods around Rodman's house. I flattened against the ground and tried to breathe by osmosis. I could hear engines starting on Vermont Place so I knew I must be close. Why wasn't there a goddamned fence? I heard another engine start. It was six forty-five. I had to find out where I was. To low-crawl or not to low-crawl, that was the question. If they saw me crawling toward the house they'd know I knew they knew . . . etcetera. On the other hand, if I got up and walked they'd probably think I was just a nosy hiker. But it was six-fifty in the morning and there was no one else around. Would they even care who I was? These guys weren't known for discrimination when it came to killing. I almost decided to do nothing and come back another day when I was armed, but we were getting close to the crunch. They had to know by now that some outside party was in their business. There was nothing to stop Gottus from changing houses, or even cities.

I decided to compromise. I'd stand up and walk, but I'd walk low. If someone saw me I'd be just a nature lover trying to sneak up on a family of ground-dwelling finches. The Arabs still couldn't identify me and I hoped I hadn't made them nervous enough to shoot someone in their own backyard without a reason.

I got up and walked forward in a hunch until the trees began to thin out and I was almost lifted off my feet by a breeze of fresh perfume. I stood nose to the wind, mesmerized by the porous sweetness in the air. It wrapped me in half memories of West Virginia, my grandmother's porch framed by rows of the same scent: magnolias. Gottus' house had to be right in front of me. I straightened up and walked toward the smell, just a dreamy nerd out for a morning with the bees. As I left the trees I saw the magnolias in front of me. A solid wall of them surrounded the rear of the property. I looked for an opening in the magnolias but didn't see one. No opening meant no guard. A guard would either have to pole-vault back and forth or walk through a neighbor's property carrying his Uzi.

It was seven o'clock. I looked around until I found a small tree branch about three inches in diameter. Sighting down its length, I pushed it carefully through the magnolia thicket. I pried the small limbs until some of them broke, leaving me a knothole-sized viewing port. I was to the left of the Mercedes parking area.

I could see the entire length of the limo but it was parked at an acute angle to my sightline, leaving me a very small window of light through which to identify Gottus.

Moving left about twenty-five feet and repeating my tree branch incursion, I got a straight-on look at the area between the portico door and the limo's side. The guard I'd seen when I drove past was no longer visible. I checked my back and looked down the line of magnolias. They were planted in a gentle arc which swept around the rear of the property and disappeared on the other side of the house. There was no way anyone could get to me without walking around the perimeter or boring through the foliage. Either way I'd have time to run to a public spot and hope the guard had orders to avoid displays of bad taste in the neighborhood.

At seven-fifteen an Arab type wearing a gray suit and a chauffeur's cap came out the door and started the limo. He went around and stood by the passenger door. I pried left with my tree branch, trying to enlarge the picture. When the chauffeur opened the door, I turned the binoculars on end and sighted one lens through the opening I'd made in the magnolias. The door opened and there he was, moving through the little round circle of light just like he'd moved through the TV lights. His hair was a little grayer, his face a little more puffed by fifteen years of martinis, but it was him. He finished a cup of coffee, handed it to a man on his left, gave a final instruction to another on his right, smoothed his hair, tucked his tie, ducked his head, and entered the limo door. He was as sharp and crisp as a new thousand-dollar bill, with just as much soul. The chauffeur closed the door, then went around to the driver's side. The limo wheeled out of the parking lot with the low-end rumble of a fine pipe organ.

I lowered the binoculars but kept staring at the house. I'd expected it to be the same Gottus, would have been surprised if it hadn't been, but it was still a shock. A short time ago I'd been separated from him by sixteen years and a thousand small decisions which had made us as different as two contrasting species. Now I was only a few yards from his house and our lives were on an intersecting path. I wondered if he'd felt my presence all these years in the same way I'd felt his. What if he'd felt the hate of people like me coming through the television cameras at him?

Maybe everything he'd done since was to insulate himself from contact with someone like me. I wondered if he ever thought, like I did, that any encounter with a certain type of person would result in violence as surely as the fusion of atoms in a hydrogen bomb. I wondered if we were really as different as I'd thought.

I don't know how long I stood thinking. It couldn't have been more than a minute but it was long enough. I didn't hear the soft thud of footsteps coming down the line of magnolias and by the time the sound registered it was at a point almost opposite me. It had to be the missing guard. He must have seen movement when I enlarged the hole. I felt the same jolt of death juice as the night Samski saved me. But Samski wasn't there and the footsteps were.

It was too late to run. He could simply stick the barrel of his Uzi through the hedge and hose me. Maybe he wouldn't. What would I do if he wanted to take me inside? Maybe I could bluff it out. Maybe I could just say fuck you and leave. He didn't know who I was. But no one knew I was there and he could kill me. I was alone and he could kill me. That was the only thing that counted.

I picked up the tree branch just as I saw an eye appear. It looked through the hole I'd made. I could see the pupil, the iris, and the whitelike concentric rings, like a target. Before either of us had a chance to think about it I shoved the end of the branch into the eye as hard as I could. It felt like mashing an oyster. The eye's owner shrieked like a gelded calf and I ran into the woods and down toward the hiking trail.

I didn't look back. I didn't stop when I fell on the downhill grade, just somersaulted back onto my feet and kept running. I ran up the other side into the woods, out onto the flat lawn and down the blacktop. I glanced over my shoulder and saw nothing but kept running even though my lungs were shrieking with the same voice as the guard's. They felt like they were going to rupture and send a fountain of blood out my mouth but I told myself to keep running until I died on my feet like a used-up horse.

When I got to the car I leaned against its side to hold me upright as I searched my pockets for the keys. I was seized by the terror of knowing I wasn't going to be able to drive until I caught my breath. Resting my head on the roof, I tried to breathe without making my eyeballs bulge. After two breaths I looked over the roof and saw a figure emerging from the trees. Instead of running toward me though, it turned and ran back up the hill toward the house. I realized with new horror that he must be heading for his car.

"The hell with breathing," I thought, "stay alive, worry about breathing later." I got in the car and tore open the map. The way I'd come led right to them. The only way out was to take Military Road west to where it intersected with Connecticut Avenue, then go north and get lost in Chevy Chase. I whipped the car around, knocking over a trash barrel, and headed for Military Road, my foot braced against the accelerator and my back against the seat. I fishtailed onto the road and screamed toward Connecticut Avenue. Checking my mirror, I expected to see the drab beige death machine behind me but there was still nothing. Maybe there was an argument as to whether to follow me. Maybe they were waiting for orders from Gottus. Wherever they were I could feel them on my shoulder. Connecticut Avenue looked like the promised land.

As I pushed the car to its modest limits I realized that lately I'd been assuming too much benevolence on the part of civilization. I decided that when you got near the money things weren't any different than in Viet Nam. Some drill sergeant had even told me that once. So, since I'd drafted myself into this little war I decided I wasn't going anywhere unarmed or unwilling to fire until it was over.

I screamed into the mall/town of Chevy Chase and stuck the car into a rear space of the first parking lot I saw. Then I went into a Bob's Big Boy, grabbed a paper, and sat in the back with it in front of my face until a sixteen-year-old waitress with a nice smile and a run in her panty hose asked me what was going on.

"What do you mean?" I asked, thinking she'd noticed my incipient panic.

She backed away a step and I realized I sounded like an airline hijacker who's just been asked if he'd like the stewardess to take his bag. "I, uh, just meant the paper," she said, crossing her arms defensively.

I tried to smile congenially. "Oh nothing much," I said, shrugging.

"You sure seemed interested in the news," she answered, regaining her Big Boy smile.

"Nah, nothing going on but the usual—war, mayhem, murder, Meryl Streep getting nominated for an Oscar."

"I just love her," said the waitress. "I'd like to be an actress just to get out of here. Nothing ever happens around here but politics, and you know how dull that is."

"I used to," I said, "I used to."

23

There's a Zen concept I read about somewhere that says if you stop actively looking for a thing it will come to you. Sometimes it works. We used to marvel in Nam about the way things turned up when you really needed them. You'd be hungering for something sweet and one of your friends would remember a can of peaches he'd saved. You'd be out of dope and out in the boondocks when an ancient mama-san would come bumping over a mountain trail on a bicycle with a kilo of weed to sell.

The trick is to not want it until you absolutely need it. Then you just have confidence and it appears. That's the idea as I understand it and I've seen it work. It worked for me when I got back from spotting Gottus.

I was beat. I was wiped out by the hours I'd been keeping, the tension, and the genuinely weird turn my life seemed to be taking. I realized I'd become obsessed by the whole affair. I couldn't even call it a case because no one had asked me to do it. I didn't have a name to give it but I'd convinced myself it was going to solve my marital and financial problems. So far all it had done was prove that anyone who ever said I was maladjusted was right. I was sneaking around poking people in the eye with a stick, for Christ's sake! And paying a lot of money I didn't have to do it. All in the hope of somehow making money from a scheme that was still unknown to me. As aircraft controllers say, when the blips start to be nothing more than blips, I was losing the picture.

So I said the hell with it for a few hours. I drove out to Bellman and went to the Basics Grocery Store. That's where Arla did her shopping and it was the day she usually did it. I saw her in the pasta aisle, moving by the rigatoni in her dancer's quick-step, her firm little butt winking at me as she went. The kids were the first to see me and they came running down the aisle with a chorus of Daadeees. They created an embarrassing little scene as they jumped me like a couple of chimps and knocked over several cans in a tomato paste display. I didn't mind, though, because I was too busy gathering them to me like rafts to a drowning man. Arla didn't run. She walked tall, her head cocked, a little sun showing through her partly cloudy smile. She didn't kiss me, just laid a hand on my shoulder while she checked my face.

"Very nice," she said, "if you like the tortured-artist look. You look like you could use some lunch."

At the word lunch both girls started crowing for happy meals so we went to McDonald's. It was taking a chance but I knew no one had followed me out of Chevy Chase and I hadn't been back to the office or my room since.

I'd always hated fast food restaurants but Bob's Big Boy had felt awfully good that morning and McDonald's felt better. The kids gurgled and argued and smashed their fries into ketchup-laced starch paste while they attempted to connect the dots on their happy meal boxes. Arla and I talked, a little too politely for my taste, but I hadn't expected more. She tried lightly to find out what I was doing and I tried to sound logical when I told her I didn't quite know. I said it was going well, though. She didn't buy that so I changed the subject to a hotel room. She could drop the kids at her mother's and we could get a room. She didn't buy that either.

"Why?" I asked. "You always loved that kind of thing before we were married. Hell, even after, especially after." She just looked at me, an eyebrow arching away from her half smile. I tried again. "We're in love, right? At least I am."

"We don't seem quite able to get together on that point do we?" she said, staring out the window.

That was Arla at her most irritating, her acting classes coming into play. I felt like whacking her alongside the head but instead, I told her that together was what I was trying to arrange. She said I was missing the point. The kids started to get interested so we changed the subject. I said we'd have a long talk after the thing was over and I'd tell her everything. She said maybe we could have it in the lobby of a hotel.

"You mean and go upstairs if it turns out to your satisfaction," I answered. "Excuse me, but that's a little bit like asking for money, Arla."

She just turned slightly in her seat and stuck out her chest. "As I recall you've always liked a little whorelike behavior."

"The question is how little."

"No, the question is how much."

"You know what I mean."

"But you don't know what I mean. You have to take the whole package, Lowell, or nothing."

I knew what that meant. If I didn't come out of this thing with some sign of success I'd be looking at either divorce or a management trainee position at Tire World. I told her not to worry, that soon I'd be home with my own business and everything would be fine. Then Katherine put her happy meal box over her head and started talking like a robot and we all laughed. Things went better after that. We laughed some more and had dessert we didn't want, just to prolong the meeting. It was two o'clock before we left McDonald's. Shana asked me when I was coming home and demanded an answer. When I told her next week, Arla raised an eyebrow to ask if that was true. I told her it probably was but Shana made me promise and Katherine told me I was a "stupid daddy" for staying away.

"Don't call your daddy stupid," Arla said to Kate, then mumbled, "perceptive little devil," under her breath. She told me to be careful, leaning up to kiss me, lightly but longer than goodbye requires. I told her again that everything was going to be fine. On the way back to the city, I actually started to believe it.

*   *   *

At eight o'clock that night I was in the Dazco offices listening to
Dorn hold court. Daz was there too, smoking a Pall Mall while
gazing at the ceiling. I'd checked the machine when I got back
from my lunch with Arla and Dorn's voice, heavy with suppressed
excitement, announced that he'd found a way into Mosby's schematics.

Now he was brandishing a cigar like a maestro's baton and
barking happily about how easy everything was going to be. He'd
followed my suggestion about billing files but found nothing, then
he remembered the IRS. If the plans were in current billing they'd
be discovered at tax time. But to be found in accounts closed
they'd have to be the object of a specific search.

I verged on game-show glee until Dorn told me that the accounts
closed file went back five years and that the entries were by name
and not year. Daz began edging toward the door when he realized
what that meant; we might have to pull up over three hundred
files looking for the phony one. "Tedius maximus," he said. "I'm
receiving heavy warning signals from my brain's early boredom
system."

I began to consider the therapeutic value of a screaming rage
but then I noticed Dorn's little bet-collecting smile. "Coupla dope
fiends," he said, shaking his head. "So hopped up they can't wait
until I finish." His smile got broader when he told us that his
loyal computer operations chief had installed a clock card on the
mainframe which would give us the exact date and time of entry
for any file in memory.

That was better but we'd still have to pull up everything after a
date to be decided upon. Daz and I had just about settled on six
months as the cutoff date and were moaning about the amount
of work that represented when Dorn began to laugh; a basso ro-
tundo hah-hah expanded merrily out of his chest like a steel bubble. "Three months," he said, "he could have done it in three
months, easy. And we don't have to pull the files, all we have to
do is check 'em." Then he reached into a drawer and whipped
out a sheet of printout paper. "Twenty-five names, gentlemen,"

he crowed. "Only twenty-five names. The rest of them I remember as being legit."

"Mr. Dorn," Daz said, pointing an unlit Pall Mall. "You're living proof that form equals function."

"Dope fiends," answered Dorn. "I'm mixed up with a couple dope fiends." Then he boomed out another steel hah-hah.

Twenty minutes later no one was laughing. Each file contained nothing but a list of invoice numbers. Every bill had an invoice number and in some of the files there were more than a hundred numbers. We'd have to either guess the right file or pull up all the invoice numbers. I started swearing under my breath like a curbside psycho who's just seen Satan on the number six bus.

Daz drummed his fingers in time to my swearing for a few minutes and then said, "Wait a minute, you're a detective . . . got a license, office, everything. Why don't you think awhile and see if you can detect something?"

I thought maybe he was joking but his space-alien eyes were staring at me levelly. "Go on," he urged, "give it a shot. You been doing all right so far."

I realized suddenly that he was right. Dorn passed me the print-out and I stared at it, wondering what I was looking for.

"Now what do we need to know to find the right file?" I asked rhetorically.

"Doesn't matter much what we need to know," Daz said, "it's what we do know we have to work with."

He was right, but what did we know? We knew Mosby. Who was he? A smart guy who liked games with moves and wrote for a college humor magazine—a humorous smart guy, smart-alecky maybe. He knew he was the one who really made the plan work, knew they needed him. Only they didn't. Smart, but maybe not as smart as he thought. So what kind of name would he choose for his file? Something humorous, a private joke, yet chosen by a smart aleck who couldn't resist letting you in on the joke. Something punlike maybe, but what?

Daz had been staring silently through the wall and into the night. Now he turned and looked at me. "Haiku," he said:

Many paths before me
The tree in Winter
Ah, the Spring.

Dorn asked if we were taking a poetry break and Daz rose to answer him. Waving his window-glass glasses professorially, he explained that the key was in the double meaning of spring. It meant that the source causes all paths to blossom. "Consider the source of the paths, dig?" he said, speaking to Dorn but looking at me.

He was right. Who was the source? Who sent Mosby on whatever path he took? A man named Gottus with an Arab chauffeur and Arab bodyguards. A man who less than a year after Watergate was reportedly buying American real estate for unnamed Arab investors. I decided to check the list of names for any cute Arab connection. The best of the bunch seemed to be Barkley-Hearns. I told Dorn it was a fight; Iran Barkley vs Tommy Hearns. He replied that the government wouldn't allow you to deal with Iran. I asked him if there was really no way.

"No way Iran can come to you," he said. "You gotta go to them if you want to sell them anything, find some front outfit from Germany or somewhere and build a plant in Iran under their name."

Barkley-Hearns turned out to be a plumbing outfit but we'd started thinking Arabic and one thing led to another. As it was, I skipped over it twice. I was working the list from the bottom to the top, wishing my Iran Barkley idea had been right. It was so clever, so apt, and it would have been so quick. But Dorn was right. Iran didn't figure. Whoever was doing the deal was doing it here. They'd come here. No one had gone there. They had come here, used Gottus as a point man, and moved a sizeable operation here.

"Quick!" I said to both of them. "What's the most famous saying in the English language that involves an Arabic name? Besides fuck Iran, that is. It shouldn't take you long. There aren't many. In fact there's only one. No? I'll tell you—if the mountain won't go to Mohammed, then Mohammed must go to the mountain. Right? Now I refer you to number fifteen on our list of names—Mountain Enterprises."

24

Two and a half hours later, the three of us were sitting around staring at each other, unwilling to grasp what we'd learned. I'd been right. Every invoice number in the Mountain Enterprises' file had represented one portion of the overall schematic. We printed each one, then turned Dorn loose on them. It took him two hours. Daz and I went into the conference room to smoke a little Thai stick while we waited.

We began with some serious conjecture about what Dorn would discover but weed is a discursive medium. We ended with Daz swearing the rewiring would make the plane invisible to the pilot and me saying it would drive him insane by tuning the radio to any station that was playing a Barry Manilow record.

By the time Dorn came into the room Daz and I were playing badminton with two small electric fans and a feather we'd found on the floor. Daz was ahead nineteen to eight but his cord was longer. The concrete look on Dorn's face stopped the game at that point. There were no more games of any kind for some time.

So we sat at the conference table, Daz's fingers drumming a

dirge on the mahogany, Dorn looking at the sheets of papers in his hand. I watched Dorn, knowing what he would say.

"We've got to go to the newspapers with this," he muttered.

"No way in the world," I answered.

He jabbed a coin-roll-sized finger onto the plans in front of him. "If these boards get into those planes every pilot who flies one might just as well shoot himself in the head before he takes off."

"You're sure?"

Dorn hissed through his teeth. "I've been in this business a long time," he said. "I know a transponder when I see one."

"Let me get this right," I asked. "The commercial airlines all have to use them. They produce a little blip on a radar screen that tells the controller your altitude?"

"And in this case, your speed," he said.

"So what it's doing is making the plane easier for ground radar to find and track?"

He made the hissing sound again. "Not easier, easy! As easy as finding the moon over Miami. The pilot will think he's engaging his radar jamming when what he's actually doing is saying here I am, kill me. And that's not even the worst part. Today it's all missiles. The other guy locks on you with his radar and sends a missile up your tail pipe. To counter that, your own radar gives you a tone telling you someone's got a lock on you and you take evasive action. It would be possible to bypass that system altogether but then nobody would ever get a lock warning. Someone would start looking into the reason. What they've done is put in a delay. It's easier and twice as smart. The pilot will get the warning tone but by the time he does it'll be too late to do anything but wave bye-bye. The pilots will get blamed instead of the aircraft."

"But doesn't the radar have to be set up to receive a transponder signal? I mean, it's like a radio or something, isn't it? You've gotta know the frequency or whatever it is?"

Dorn took off his glasses to massage his eyes for a few seconds. "So what's the problem?" he asked when he looked up. "The people with the radar are the people who're making the goddamn planes. Don't you see it? They might as well be throwing a dinner plate up in the air and blasting it with a shotgun."

"Yeah," I said, "I see it. Who'd you tell me is getting the planes?"

"Israel, Saudi Arabia, a few to Greece."

"Gee, is there anyone in the Middle East who might want to shoot down Israeli planes?"

"Only everyone. Only every single one, except maybe Saudi Arabia, who's too rich to care."

"And they're getting the rest of them."

Dorn looked at me wide eyed. "Don't forget the air force is getting some," he said. "The United States Air Force."

"God almighty, they're picking our pockets."

"No they're not," said Dorn. "They're buying the suit."

Daz hadn't said a word as Dorn and I talked. He just sat there tapping his fingers on the table, the speed of the tapping increasing steadily. When he finally spoke it was with the high-pitched frustration I'd heard in his voice when the Orioles used to drop fly balls. "It's happening again," he wailed. "It's been happening for twenty years. Uncle Samuel's getting his ass kicked by a little country with big ideas."

"It's not the ideas," answered Dorn. "It's the goddamn money."

"Sheeeit," said Daz, "you can't buy what's not for sale. It's the motivation. They got it. We don't."

"Sonsabitches," Dorn agreed, thumping the table. "We've got to go to the papers. Once the story gets out these bastards will be out of business."

"Don't forget their business is your business," I said.

For a second he looked as if he'd been tapped lightly between the eyes with a hammer. "I don't care," he roared, recovering quickly. "This involves the country. It's bigger than just me."

"That's what the country would like you to think."

"Goddamn, man, did you ever hear the word patriotism?" he said, staring at me as if I'd made a sexual reference to his mamma.

"Patriotism is what TV uses to sell beer during the Olympics."

Dorn rose and stood over me, his Stonehenge shoulders blocking my view of Daz's amused smile, his glasses reflecting daggers of light. I thought maybe he was going to get violent.

"This is your country we're talking about," he yelled as he punched the air with his unlit cigar.

"I know."

"It's where you live, it's how you live."

"I know."

I liked Dorn. Men his age had saved me from being born into a German deathocracy or Japanese ant farm. But just because his generation was father to mine didn't mean he could get me to believe they sang the "Star-Spangled Banner" every time one of them went down in flames. All the anthem singing came later, when they were kidding themselves into torching sixty thousand of their sons. I made up my mind that if he did try to hit me I'd just get out of the way. I was younger, faster. He'd be out of wind before he could get hold of me. I edged my chair away from the table in case I had to bail out.

He came a step closer as he spoke: "You haven't learned the value of anything."

"And you haven't learned to pay attention," I told him. "There's the country, and then there's the government. You're not going to be doing the government any favors by blasting this all over the papers. They're going to look like fools. What's left of their credibility in the Middle East will be shot. Politically it will be a disaster for them. Any paper that prints this had better have drop-dead proof because the government will be all over them."

Dorn snatched up the papers and held them in front of my face. "What do you call these?" he asked. "Any engineer in the field will verify what I'm saying."

"Sure he will. Then there'll be an investigation that'll take a year. Meanwhile all the circuit boards but mine will disappear; the computer files will be purged; your loyal operations guy will be gunned down on the street; Dynatron's lawyers will say you fabricated both the circuit boards and the schematics; then they'll sue you for your liver. The investigation will turn up some mild-mannered, nonplussed group of peacenik Arabs who are undoubtedly political refugees from their evil regime and who only came to our friendly shores because they believed in the American dream of freedom, justice, and an equal opportunity to get disgustingly wealthy. Even if the majority of the citizenry doesn't buy that and votes the present government out for being airheads, the peaceful boys at Pecosa will be all right because you won't have any proof, and one of the great things about our country is that the laws protect scumbags as well as the innocent. You and I will end up with nothing but our patriotism and maybe a warm place over a steam grate on cold nights . . . Trust me. I've had experience at this kind of thing."

He pointed the cigar at me and bellowed: "Experience! What experience? Viet Nam . . . ? You lost. You lost the whole damn country."

"What country?" I asked. "South Viet Nam never existed. They should have called the place Oz. It was invented in Washington by people who wanted to prove they had a brain and a heart."

Dorn sat down in his chair with an exasperated sigh. He lit a cigar and watched its train of blue smoke disappear into the past. "Jesus," he said, "you guys . . . There was a time when we believed in things. Know what I mean? None of this figuring that all the answers are bad. We believed in things. How do you think I built my business? I believed. When I was young we thought if you believed in something that could make it happen. We believed that believing could make it so."

"I believe you were right," Daz said quietly, no sarcasm, no humor, like he'd just realized it. Then he turned to me and said in the same voice, "You know, I liked the army. We had a way to live, rules, customs, loyalty, something bigger than its parts. It made you a bigger man. That was the whole trip for me. But I saw it all leaving in Nam, our people dying, their little generals getting rich. I'd already made up my mind to quit before I found the money."

I'd known Daz for years but the subjects he was sincere about had always been obscured by movement, touched upon lightly like rocks he was using to cross a stream. Now he was wading right in. "Yeah, so what're you saying?" I asked him.

He stopped to light a cigarette, gazing blissfully at the ceiling. Then he looked at me, eyes as full of the possible as the galaxy. "I guess what I'm telling you is that there's a more ah . . . poetic side to this."

"Not if we go to the papers," I answered. "I don't want to get distracted by the big picture, it changes too fast. I want to keep this strictly personal, them against us. I want my family back and Dorn wants his business back."

He'd been staring at Daz, surprised by my fellow pothead's feeling for the army. Now he snapped his attention to me. "I could sue," he said, "after it all comes out."

"If it all comes out you'll be ten years even proving there's something to sue about, another ten suing. And they'll countersue, if they don't decide to kill you. You can see that can't you? Suits are for legal disputes. This one's illegal. Think about it."

I convinced Dorn. Daz was already convinced that going to the papers would be futile. It was just that he lived in strict accordance to a Judeo-Christian-Oriental religion he'd made up himself. As nearly as I could glean from his oblique references, the core of his theology centered around the proposition that Jesus was able to endure the crucifixion because he understood Zen well enough to find God in the wood of the cross. If he hadn't, he'd have ripped the nails out of his hands, come down and kicked ass with the karate he learned on his out-of-body trip to China.

Daz just wanted to be sure I wasn't becoming a yuppie with a gun. The trouble was, I'd told Dorn I could get his business back, but didn't have the slightest idea how to do it. I was just warbling the same happy tune as the two of them, hoping that believing could make it so. They, on the other hand, were waiting for me to come up with an idea.

The one I'd been considering was a kind of sting involving only me and an undecided amount of cash. The key would be to convince Congressman Roland Zale of something I didn't believe myself, that I was just as ready to go to the media with the story as Dorn. Why not try to fold in Dorn's business? Why not two stings? Why not two in one?

"Daz," I asked, "can you get me some video equipment by tomorrow?"

"I can walk down a floor and get it right now. Whaddya need, maestro?"

"A camcorder to start, maybe a portable television, and two

VCRs." I looked at Dorn. "Can you have papers drawn up transferring controlling interest in your company back to you so that all that's needed is signature of a Pecosa representative?"

"Sure."

"By tomorrow. I'm afraid they're going to get nervous and move. I want to do it tomorrow."

Dorn was already reaching for the phone. "I'll call my lawyer and get him out of bed," he said. "What're you going to do?"

"Right now," I said, "I'm going to load the video equipment into my car. And tomorrow I'm going to send a man named Samski to pick up those papers."

"Samski . . . where will you be?"

"Oz. This time I'm going stay on the yellow brick road until I find the wizard."

25

When I got to Ace Sporting Goods the following morning, Miles was in the back racking spear guns. The Temptations were doing "Get Ready" on an oldies station attached to the store's speakers. I could see Miles's head of frizzed curls bobbing along in and out of time making me a little dizzy. He was wearing an open safari jacket over a white shirt, tan corduroy pants, and a pair of Clark desert boots. When he saw me he threw out his arms like a circus barker. "What's happenin' my *main* man? Where you been buddy? Tell me somethin' good."

"Is that the Richard Chamberlain in Africa look?" I asked.

"Hollywood," he said as he put on a pair of pink-tinted prescription glasses. "This is the shopping safari look." He pointed at my jeans and T-shirt. "My man's still in his Brando outfit. Next time you send those out don't forget to take 'em off."

I nodded toward his office. When we were inside I told him what I wanted.

"The M-sixteens are easy," he told me. "Banks are giving those away with new accounts, but the M-seventy-nine ammo . . . no way I can get that by tomorrow. I can get it, but it takes a few connections. You telling me you, ah, used what I gave you be-fore?"

"You want me to tell you?"

Putting his feet on his desk, he tilted back in his swivel chair. He was chewing a wad of gum so hard it was about to send out sparks. "Look," he said, eyes level on mine, "I'm starting to get a little worried. I mean if you're using the shit you must be in deep. I have to ask myself if I wanta get you in any deeper. I mean I do a little business for my friends but I'm not the war department."

"It's not the money?"

He leaned back further and threw out his arms again. "Hey, did I say anything about money? Did I say anything about money?"

"I was just wondering if. . . ."

"Did I say anything about money? One word?"

"No."

"When I get worried about the money I'll tell ya. Until then I'll let you worry about the money. I'm worried about what you're doin' with the shit. I mean are you robbing banks? You invading an island? What?"

He thumped his chair into an upright position and pointed at me. "I mean are you going to jail, and am I going with you?"

"I don't think so."

"You don't think so!"

"I know you're not. I don't think anybody is."

"I'm not?"

"No."

"You're sure, then what's going on? Tell me something good."

"I think I'm about to make some real money. If everything goes right in the next few days I'm gonna be in fat city."

Miles blew a huge bubble and pointed around it at me. "Uh-huh," he said, then popped the bubble. "You make sure it goes all right."

"That's why I'm here. Things always go right after I come to see you. Now tell *me* something good."

"You want the M-sixteens to do full automatic I guess?" he said, sighing the way my father used to when he gave me the keys to the car.

"That's why I came here instead of K Mart."

"Right, rock and roll it is. How many rounds?"

"Two hundred and fifty . . . each."

He looked at me for a long second through the pink glasses. "You're legitimate, right? I mean you're not running coke? I just wanta know whether to stand clear of you when I hear a car coming around the corner."

"I'm defending the interests of the US of A. No shit. And about to make some money doing it, I think."

"About time someone made some money doing that," Miles said. "When do you want the stuff?"

"By one today. I've got to be in Washington. I'll send a tall hillbilly kind of guy around for them. His name's Samski."

"Today," he said, throwing in the afterburners on his gum. "It's a lucky thing you got your Uncle Miles."

When I started down the parkway to Washington it was eleven-thirty, the morning simmering toward an afternoon boil. Already the pavement was softening into tar, the sun drawing off an oily mist which hung fender high in front of me like a storm at sea. No neighborhood party this time. The morning sweat of the highway misted the roadside neighborhoods with a visible stink. I could see the beer cans lying crushed on the storm drains and the drunken lumps balled into doorways, dying of heat stroke inside their winter coats while not-in-school kids hopscotched over their vomit.

It was all very colorful. Dried-blood brick turning brown over the teeth-yellow steps. Faded-blue Busch signs boarding up the smashed windows of stores done into expedient plaid with swatches of leftover paint. The kids were wearing reds and seal-sheen blues. Gold chains around their necks thudded flatly against their chests. Crushed glass sawtoothed the streets like diamond-studded graters for the banana peels and lettuce leaves strewn down the gutters; third world salad, midnight's carnival ripeness warping the heat waves with fruit rot. Headaches and hangovers, minimum wage, the daytime nothing but the night's excrement. The city should hire hyenas instead of garbage men.

I shoved a Lou Reed tape into the deck, mean mud-chord guitar, sincerely snide talking vocals about the country purity of city depravity. Lou was forty-five now. The old rock and roll animal, married and living in the pines of New Jersey. Angrier than ever, breaking out on guitar in sarcastic solos like Eric Clapton talking out of the side of his mouth. Forty-five and better than ever. Not like Dylan, who now wrote notes to leave on his woman's pillow because love was the only thing he could remember about being ordinary. Hell, Lou had just discovered what ordinary meant. He was new to himself again and mightily pissed off about the same old shit he saw going on around him. Not a very cheery guy it seemed, but he was righteous enough in his own mind to get righteously angry.

That's what I was looking for when I put on his tape, an injection of righteous anger. I needed it because I was nervous. No, not nervous, afraid. Until I'd started for the congressman's office I'd been sure of myself, or at least acting it. By now I knew it could work and that scared me. If it did work things were going to get nastily delicate. I was going to need everything I used to have, timing, judgment, will, most of all instinct. So far I'd had surprise on my side but now I was going to be operating in the open. I was going to have to face down a congressman and a man who'd been doing just that for at least fifteen years. It was going to be moment-to-moment and hand-to-hand.

The greasy summer glare of the city's outlying reef of junkyard industrial parks gave me a headache. The bloodless cool of the car's air conditioning turned the sweat cold against the back of my neck and my stomach kept trying to slink away until the day was over. I wondered how much I'd lost in the years beneath the fluorescent lights of the state office building. How much my senses had been deadened by all that blinkless glow, all that unending phony daylight.

Zale was a member of the Congress of the United States. Since college, I had had no respect for politicians; sure they were all degenerate phonies who liked little boys or women dressed up like Nazis. Worse yet, they didn't really like either and got aroused only by missiles and game-show grins. They were the people who were so disliked in high school that they spent the rest of their lives begging for love in the form of votes; geeks who'd harangued you at college parties about commies in Central America and then thrown up on your shoes; voids who'd sent you to Nam to stall for time while Generals Nimh, Binh, Khanh, and all their kin got rich in the heroin trade. I had no respect for politicians.

But now that I was actually going to be sitting in Zale's office surrounded by the scent of his power and perks, I suddenly found myself thinking of him not as a politician but a congressman. He was someone consistently referred to on the news. Not a star yet, but a person who was in file footage, network file footage. His life was bigger than mine. He was Congressman Zale and I was . . . what? The well-known crazed Viet vet is what I was. That's how they'd refer to me: *Viet Vet threatens Congressman*. No, *Unemployed Viet Vet Accuses Congressman . . . self-styled "detective" Lowell Ransom today claimed Congressman Roland Zale . . . Ransom is a veteran who once sought counseling by black Baltimore businessman Daslow Gervin. Gervin is a self-styled counselor of . . .*

Jesus! Everyone on my side was self-styled except Dorn. They wouldn't refer to him as World War II vet Walter Dorn though. I wondered when the statute of limitations ran out on being a vet.

I'd seen Zale's picture. He was a smooth article. All planes and angles, expensive suits, deep-set eyes. He was a congressman and I was a . . . yeah, a vet, but also a constituent.

I was a goddamn constituent. He hadn't represented me properly and I was going to seek redress, just like the founding fathers had planned. I had history on my side. That saying again—history is made at night. I'd been good at night. Hell, once I'd owned the night. I'd been able to stand on a ridge in the falling blue of a full Asian moon and feel the shape of the wind with my fingertips. I could feel when its normal outline was bent by the presence of other men, even if they were more than a mile away. I could fall into the ground shadow like a leaf. I could lie there and let the temperature change in the soil tell me the direction of hostile body heat. The night is controlled by stillness. It obeys only those who let it. The day is a big noisy drunk who wants to arm-wrestle. You can either fight the day or avoid it.

It came to me that it was only the day that was making me nervous. It had been the literal-minded obviousness of daywork that had forced me out of social services. What I had to do was get inside the falling blue of the moon and stay there. I had to carry it inside me so I'd always be operating at night. Lou's tape ended. I put on a pair of mirrored sunglasses, then replaced the tape with some snake-in-a-silk-scarf blues by Robert Cray. You want blue, listen to the blues. It seemed logical. I punched the accelerator. The night had dawned.

Zale's office would have made a nice little restaurant. It was paneled all around and halfway up in mahogany veneer. The walls were painted a comforting money green in contrast to the coin-silver carpet. Paintings of happy Marylanders doing happy Maryland things like riding to the hounds covered the walls.

The secretary, a tall suburban blonde, sat behind something that looked more like a polished mahogany parking space than a desk. I figured Zale must be sleeping with her to keep her so isolated. She wasn't much though, feathery blond hair and a face that didn't come up to code. The bones were in nice places but too thin and her large pores made her face look like someone forgot to sand it. She just missed.

Not that she cared what I thought. I was just a salesman, Hank Shurrow of Omega Office Supply. On the phone from Baltimore I'd begged, pleaded, cajoled. I thought I was going to have to bring up the words Dorn or Gottus prematurely but she finally agreed to let me stop in long enough to leave some literature concerning our new line of letterheads. When I told her I wanted to deliver them in person to the congressman she looked at me as if I'd asked to deliver a pizza to the Pope. Then she told me that the congressman didn't get involved in things like office supplies. I told her he'd been personally involved with our company in the past and I was sure if she'd just ask him he wouldn't mind doing it again. I said he knew the owners of Omega Office Supply personally. When she asked me their names I told her they were Messrs. Gottus and Dorn. She repeated that to Zale in a kind of cling-peach voice, then said he had someone with him and would be with me as soon as possible. I replied that Gottus and Dorn were writing their memoirs and, even as we spoke, were talking with their publishers. They wanted to know if it was okay to mention him. She said he'd squeeze me in next.

Zale was taller than I expected. Maybe six-foot-one, and he had a Palm Springs tan which I'd always assumed was makeup. His face was a perfectly formed masculine triangle, rock-carved brows sheltering gray eyes the color of his carpet, wide cheekbones tapering evenly to a strong jaw. His black hair was brushed straight back but it was too thick to lay flat to his head. It rose up slightly forming a perfect frame for his perfectly shaped face. His lips were absolutely parallel to his chin and had the same thick, yet tasteful, moistness as those of a television evangelist. His nose divided all this symmetry with the clean efficiency of the crease in a pair of hundred dollar slacks.

He held out his hand but didn't smile. "I'm Roland Zale," he said. "And you are . . . ?"

The voice was the kind of soothing baritone that gives you a little nap every time you hear it, but his underlip pouted a bit, begged a bit too sincerely for your confidence.

"Never mind my name," I said, "let's get down to business."

Withdrawing his hand, he remained standing. "And just what business is that?" There was a small angry echo in his voice but his lower lip was still sincere.

"Just what your secretary told you—Gottus and Dorn."

He swept an arm toward a leather wingback in front of his desk. "Have a seat for a minute Mr., ah, that's right, you don't want to tell me your name." Going behind the desk, he plopped into a high-backed leather swivel chair. I liked the chair but I loved the big Zenith console television to its left more. That made one less thing for Samski and me to carry.

"No," I said, "I'm afraid if I tell you my name I'll be killed like Mosby and Fredericks."

He was a politician so he had no trouble pretending he couldn't remember the names. We sparred around for a few minutes, him smoking handmade Nat Sherman cigarettes while admitting he knew Gottus, but only as a big-time lobbyist, me telling him that if he didn't take me seriously he stood to lose his career, maybe more. There was some talk of security throwing me out. He said he'd give me five minutes to tell him why they shouldn't.

"Well, in the first place," I answered, "Roger Dorn offered me fifty thousand dollars to kill you."

That's when Zale got foolish. He asked me what I'd say if he told me there was a taping system in his office recording my threat. I told him that since Watergate, only the pure in heart installed taping systems and I didn't think he qualified.

Sherman cigarettes will go out if you don't keep puffing them because they contain no additives to keep them burning. His had gone out, and I mentioned it, with some banter about him being too nervous to keep it going. He parried by saying crazy people always made him nervous. I responded that he was the one who was crazy if he didn't take me seriously. Roger Dorn was a tough guy and he was very pissed off at Zale for making him sell Dynatron.

Like most liars who're trying to find out how much you know before admitting anything, he asked me why he would do a thing like that. I confessed truthfully that I didn't know but I was willing to bet it would look like he'd been bribed when the story hit the media.

Since Zale persisted in raising his eyebrows and smiling sardonically in the upscale version of surprise, I ran it down for him. "Look, I know you told him if he didn't sell you'd be sure the project he was working on would be canceled and you'd do your best to see he never got another one. He sold. When Pecosa got hold of Dynatron they put one of their own, a man named Rodman, in effective charge and he paid the comptroller of a company called Armco to induce an engineer named Mosby to do a little redesign work on the F-one-eleven project. One of those redesigned circuit boards was stolen by an unknown party and people started getting murdered. First Mosby, then Fredericks, because they knew what the boards were all about."

Zale undid the strangle button on his collar and loosened his tie. Then he reminded me that television had said all the murders were over some drug business at Armco. He mispronounced the word Armco, substituting an n for the m, a smooth touch but somewhere down in the calm darkness of his baritone a frog croaked.

It occurred to me that he probably had no idea what Gottus was doing with Armco. That was good. When he started imagining his name linked to sabotaged airplanes he'd know all the spin doctors in the world weren't going to make him believable. I told him the drug story was just a literary touch by Gottus. The murders had actually been committed by a bunch of Arabs in beige Mercedes because they didn't want anyone alive who knew what the missing circuit boards were about.

His cigarette had gone out again. He gave me some more ironic eyebrow while he relit it, then told me all Shermans go out because they don't have any chemicals to keep them burning.

"Yeah," I said, "but it's hard to keep puffing when you're wetting your pants."

He responded to that witticism by blowing a big cloud of expensive smoke at me and saying I was wasting his time. He didn't believe me. I was just a small-time shyster who thought I knew enough to blackmail him with a story made up of "whole cloth."

I could tell the whole cloth reference was just a rehearsal for a sound bit he was putting together in his head. He was proving a tough sell. If he kept stonewalling me for much longer I was afraid I was going to either give up and panic or leap over the desk to show him some physical sincerity. Settling on a course somewhere between those two poles, I got up from my chair and placed my fingertips on his desktop. Leaning forward slightly, I held his eyes with my own as I told him I was the one who had stolen the circuit boards, that I still had them, and I knew their purpose was to change every plane they were installed in to a perfect target. I assured him I'd verified that with an expert, that I'd found the complete schematic. I informed him that one of the recipients of this large practical joke was the U.S. Air Force, as were Israel and Saudi Arabia. Then I threw down what I hoped was the convincer—that I knew Pecosa holding company was just a front for one or more hostile Arab countries, maybe Iraq, maybe Iran . . . Libya. I didn't know which, but I knew Gottus was their man and he was Gottus's man.

Zale couldn't have acted more outraged if we were on "Meet

the Press." He jumped up from his desk and started whating and whooping about my imagination, saying it couldn't be true, that he'd have heard something, that I didn't have any proof. Where was my proof?

"Hell," I said, "it was all over the news after Watergate, Gottus representing Arab real estate interests. What were you, a poet in those days? Never watched TV or read a paper? Then you decided you could serve mankind better by going into politics and all of a sudden . . . boom. Here comes this Gottus character you've never even heard of? I don't think the public's going to buy that. I know the networks won't. *The Washington Post* won't. They'll Woodward and Bernstein you until you start to bleed from the ears. It's going to be feeding time at the zoo. Even the guys in prison will hate you and you might be seeing some of them close-up. I have the boards and the boards are the proof. Oh yeah, and it's not you I want to blackmail."

I thought the last part would interest him and it did. Very carefully, trying to maintain an even tone, he asked me just who I planned to blackmail. When I told him it was Gottus he sucked in a little too much smoke and asked me how I planned to do it. When I explained that I planned to videotape Gottus offering him a bribe, he coughed once and gave up trying to smoke for a while.

26

Samski complained that we were doing all the work while Zale just sat at his desk smoking those skinny brown cigarettes. But I told him not to spook the congressman because he could still back out.

"Besides," I said, "he's not making any money on the deal."

Samski squinted at Zale from beneath his newly spattered painter's hat. "Yeeah?" he drawled, "why's he doin' it then?"

"Just doing his sworn duty, upholding the Constitution of the United States."

"Wull he kin uphold it all he wants, I ain't gonna vote for him."

"Why not?"

"Well, it's like the man said, I never vote cause it only encourages 'em."

"Maybe a little encouragement once in a while would do them good."

As we talked we were carrying the secretary's desk into Zale's office. Samski put down his end and pushed back his cap. "That how you talked him into doin' this for nothin'?" he asked. "Encouragement?"

"To make a long story short."

"If we live, I'd like to hear the long story."

"Now what would give you doubts about our living?"

He pulled the cap back down over his eyes and mouthed a Marlboro. "This goddamn desk for one thing," he said, preparing to heft. "I'm strugglin' like a one-legged pallbearer at a fat woman's funeral."

"How's Doris' diet going?"

"Just great. We done got to the part where she's cut out between meal snacks. Now if she'd just quit eatin' those six meals a day we'd be makin' some real progress."

We were moving Zale's furniture around because, after an afternoon of persuasion, he'd seen the light. For a while his vision was fogged by bravado, then he'd tried self-justification. That did him no good either, but in the course of it he'd told me a few things I hadn't known.

Zale had explained that jobs were product number one in the political industry. If what Zale called "the six-pack guys" lose jobs, their congressman will soon be losing his. I knew that part. The part I didn't know was that those overachieving newcomers to our shores, Pecosa Diversified, had been featured guests at the eight-year takeover party thrown by Wall Street. In addition to Dynatron they now owned Jersey Southern Tires, Chattler Brothers Soap, Cola King, and Rembert Homes. If Zale hadn't helped Gottus acquire Dynatron they were prepared to shut all those businesses down or move them to another state, promptly making unemployment Maryland's biggest industry.

"You'd better think about that before you pull anything on Gottus," Zale said.

He was right. I didn't mind taking a calculated risk for a big reward but I wasn't about to be the guy who put a third of Maryland out of work. Aside from the ethical problems, I lived in the suburbs and my property value would go through the floor. But I wasn't quitting. I'd already planned to lock Gottus into a bad position with the videotape. I was going to sell him the boards for cash, then give him the tape of him bribing Zale in exchange for Dorn's company. All I had to do was secretly duplicate the tape, trade him the original, then keep the second as a hammer. Trading the first one was going to be the tough part.

Zale delivered a short testimonial to the ruthlessness of John Gottus, which I rebutted by pointing out that Gottus was just an employee. His employers were interested in power and wealth, not his personality quirks. The congressman accepted that argument in principle, as we say in Washington. What he didn't accept was the idea of him being offered a bribe on tape. He wanted to know how his career would survive a tape of him discussing the forced sale of Dynatron. When I explained that the tape wasn't even going to mention Dynatron, he rolled his eyes toward the ceiling and asked me how I planned to blackmail Gottus with the circuit boards if he was talking to him about something else.

"Would it seem suspicious to call Gottus and make an appointment to discuss another project?" I asked.

"After the way he bullied me on the Dynatron deal?" he said. "The bastard expects me to make the appointments."

Gottus' current hot project was something called the Slingshot missile, made by Ergotronics in Delaware. It was a wire-guided antitank missile, which was supposed to be carried in a kind of quiver on an infantryman's back so he could fire it while in the prone position.

"A piece of shit is what it is," Zale said offhandedly. "It blew the heads off six test dummies the last time they tried it."

"And they're still trying to sell it?"

"Of course."

"What happens when it blows the head off a real infantryman?"

"We pay them a lot of money to fix it."

"Of course."

Zale shrugged. "Look, this stuff was going on long before I got here." He explained the way it worked. Gottus would want to know what his recommendation on Slingshot would be. Ordinarily, Zale said, he'd tell Gottus what a piece of shit he was selling and Gottus would try to convince him otherwise. But since the Dynatron deal their relationship had changed. Gottus was more fatherly now—if you thought of that term in its child-abuser mode.

Instead of persuasion Gottus would issue a vague threat, tell Zale how many jobs the project represented and how losing the contract would force Ergotronics' parent company to take a look at restructuring some of their holdings in other states. Zale used his fingers to make quotation marks in the air as he said the word restructuring. Naturally, that would grieve Pecosa deeply, and of course it would be only a coincidence that the holdings that got restructured were in Maryland.

I held up a hand to stop him. "Wait a minute. You're sure he'll mention Maryland?"

What I was looking for was a place in the conversation where it would be logical for Gottus to hand Zale a briefcase full of money. I needed a spot where Zale could make what might be interpreted by Gottus as a subtle request yet be well short of so-licitation. Zale nodded and reiterated that jobs were product number one in the political industry.

"Well, that's it then," I said, "it's simple. No matter when he says that, you stop him, gently, but stop him. Here's the way it should go—he comes in, you talk about the Slingshot project. When he mentions how many jobs it'll supply, you say you need some consideration for Maryland. That gives us an appropriate place to stop the tape. You end the conversation as soon as possible after that point. After he leaves we call him. We tell him the deal about the boards on the phone. We tell him he has to come back with the money. We give him hours, not days. For this to work he has to be wearing the same clothes he had on during the first visit. We start the tape again as he's about to hand you the money. The tape shows you talking about Slingshot and him offering you money to give it a favorable recommen-dation. That's it."

Then Zale started to waffle; Gottus would know something was up. We weren't experts with the camera. The timing was too difficult. He didn't actually have an appointment with Gottus in the near future. . . .

I could see we weren't having a rational argument. Something was blinding him to the fact that my plan was a lot safer politically. It was fear. Plain physical fear. He'd rather be back in his district looking for a job than in the land of permanent silence with Mosby and Fredericks. If I was going to get him to see it my way I had to close the fear gap a little.

"You're forgetting something," I said.

"What's that?"

"The fifty thousand dollars Dorn offered me to kill you."

His eyes widened but he still said nothing. I had the feeling he was trying to remember what profession his mother had wanted him to pursue and why he hadn't taken her advice.

"I don't believe you," he said hopefully. "You're no killer."

"Oh, but I am. Once I spent a whole year killing people."

"You're referring to Viet Nam, aren't you?"

"Yeah, I was good at it. And I haven't forgotten how."

"It's not the same thing."

"You're right. I didn't make fifty thousand dollars, and I liked them more than I like you."

His face turned a lighter shade of tan but he stayed skeptical. "I still say it's not your line of work."

He was right. I wasn't about to murder anyone, but I was getting mightily pissed off. "How the hell do you know what my line of work is?" I said through clenched teeth. "I've got three unregistered weapons, no visible motive, and family problems that fifty thousand dollars would solve. I love my wife. I dislike you. I could kill you anytime I wanted. Hell, I'd be home before they found the body."

The whites of Zale's eyes began to show but he tried to stay tough. "You're bluffing," he said. "The idea scares you as much as it does me."

I jumped out of my chair and went around to his side of the desk. "Suppose you're right," I said, leaning into his face. "What if I can't go through with it? What if I have to go public and make what I can from a book and the talk show circuit? Suppose that isn't enough? Then suppose you land on your feet with some nice consultant's job working for Gottus? I'm going to feel like a sucker. Then I might start thinking about you and the fifty thousand, and how easy it would be, how quick, how neat. You're going to think about it too, every time it gets dark."

My face was no more than two feet from his. I could smell his syrupy after-shave. I could smell the odor of cleaning fluid wafting faintly off his suit like a hint of the morgue. I could smell the musk of worried sweat seeping around the corners of his vest like the scent of oily meat being charred over a fire. I knew he was on the verge of transferring that smell to me through his stubbornness and I hated him for it—hated with sizzling electric volts that went from the soles of my feet to the palms of my hands. He sat still as a lizard and just as poker eyed; waiting, watching, his body frying in fear but his politician's deceit convincing him he was cool. It was that penchant for grooming the moment that had led him to cut the deal with Gottus, and it was that I had to kill.

I reached out with my left hand and raked his hair from back to front so it stood out from his head like a landing crow. Looking like a fourth member of the Three Stooges, he rose from the chair to answer me, but the motion crossed my wires and I hit him with a left-hand body shot to the liver. It was a good one, corkscrewed up from underneath using the thighs as a power source. It dropped him to his knees, sending his tan back to Palm Springs and me back to my chair so he couldn't see the surprise on my face.

He stayed on his knees trying to breathe normally and failing. Drawing in great whoops of air, he looked at me like he'd awakened from a bad dream only to find he hadn't been sleeping. I was empty and shaking, astounded at the predatory nature of what I'd done. He'd needed convincing. I tried to convince him. I was a salesman. It was business. As I watched Zale groping to his feet I realized with a receding sadness that, at forty, I was beginning to learn what goal-directed behavior was all about.

I was a little dizzy and disoriented, sensations which escalated to outright nausea when I happened to look up at the ceiling. I saw it for the first time. Really saw it. I'd counted on Zale's office having a drop ceiling, a gridwork of metal rails supporting an expanse of hole-punched white ceiling tiles. For some reason, I'd assumed his office would have the same kind of ceiling as the one I'd spent days staring at when I worked for the department of social services. My whole plan depended on getting a man and a camera into the space above that ceiling, but there was no space. Zale's ceiling was ten feet high and made of ornamental plaster. I hadn't noticed it in the outer office because I'd been so intent on getting to the inner office. Then I'd directed all my attention to being enough of a bastard that Zale would see things my way.

"You son of . . . son of . . ." He didn't have quite enough air yet to finish the phrase but I was glad to see he was feeling better.

"I'm sorry," I said, and meant it. In light of the ceiling snafu what I'd done felt more like gratuitous cruelty than salesmanship. I was in a very bad karmic position and saw no way to salvage it except to press on and have faith that I'd think of a way to make things work. So despite the existential problems, I kept on with my bad self. Trying not to let my knees buckle, I got up from the chair, took a step toward the desk, picked up a sheaf of papers, and smacked him across the face with them.

"Think about it, Zale," I said. "Your career gets saved. . . . I know you'll certainly get my vote from now on . . . You help a constituent get his business back, and you avoid the chance that I'll kill you if you don't do it." With that said I sat down before I fell down.

The next few minutes were spent in silence. Zale puffed a couple cigarettes while looking anywhere but at me.

"I can't appear culpable in any way," he said finally.

It made me feel better to think it was the irrefutable logic of my position that convinced him and not the body punch. Then I remembered I had to think of a way to place a video camera in a room with two people without it being noticed.

As if he were reading my mind he asked where I planned to put the camera. But I said it was time to go meet my associate, that we'd reconvene at eight to set it all up. That was inconvenient, he had an important dinner at six.

"Leave early," I said patiently. "Say it's a matter of national security and all. Maybe Bermuda's serving bad Pina Colada mix and we were getting ready to invade."

Clenching his teeth, Zale agreed to cut the dinner short, and we adjourned the meeting. As I left he was putting in a call to Gottus.

It was two o'clock. I had only a few hours to come up with a workable idea for the placement of the camera. My stomach began to feel as if I were the one who'd been punched.

*   *   *

I went to the mall and sat beneath the Washington Monument to mull over the camera problem. As I sat staring at some workmen on a scaffold that framed a side of the main Smithsonian building, the answer hit me like one of the bricks they were dropping into a dumpster. I hauled out my credit card and went to a paint store on upper New York Avenue where I bought paint, rollers, brushes, drop cloths, white jumpsuits, painter's hats, and a low cart with a high handle on which to push it all. Then I traveled north to meet Samski where the Baltimore-Washington Parkway becomes New York Avenue. Twenty years in Baltimore and he'd never been to Washington. He wasn't nearly as dumb as I'd originally believed.

Zale finished his business day at about six. He went to his dinner somewhere uptown while Samski and I ate at Popeye's on Fourteenth Street. He was probably having an after-dinner brandy while the two of us spent the better part of an hour splashing paint on our jumpsuits and dropcloths. Then we all met across from Zale's office building. Not only was he on time but he'd made an appointment with Gottus for eight the following morning. Zale used his key card to get both cars into the underground parking garage where we unloaded the painting equipment onto the push cart. After Samski moved his Trans Am outside we were ready to go.

As I'd instructed him, Zale explained to the security man that he'd decided to have us start painting his office at night in order to keep things running as smoothly as possible during the day. The video camera, VCRs, and weaponry were on the cart under the dropcloths. Zale asked the guard if he'd like to help. But he declined with a laugh, saying he was scared of heights. I allowed as how we weren't likely to be getting very high in the congressman's office. He said he didn't know about that, what with smelling all those paint fumes. Everyone was chuckling a little as we headed toward Zale's office.

27

It took us over two hours to get it right. We used the big desk Samski and I were carrying as a base, then piled the rest of the stuff from the outer office on and around it until we'd made a kind of high barricade. It filled a quarter of Zale's office but it wasn't enough, so we borrowed a few chairs and a filing cabinet from an aide's adjoining office. The pile then filled almost half the room. By the time we spread our drop cloths and painting supplies around the outer office it was almost eight-thirty in the evening.

We had to rearrange the pile of furniture in Zale's office four times. We'd find a good camera angle, one that covered both Zale and the person sitting in front of his desk, and then discover the lens was visible. So we'd move the camera only to find that the field of view was too narrow. At that point we'd have to take the pile apart and put it back together in a different way. The work was physically demanding and also had the disadvantage of being completely maddening. I thought Zale and Samski were going to get into a punchup when Walt heaved a standing brass ashtray through the door and into the outer office.

"What the hell do you think you're doing?" Zale howled. "That's a three-hundred-dollar ashtray."

"What?" Samski asked, shocked.

"You heard me, goddamnit, three hundred dollars."

Samski looked at me with raised eyebrows, then turned back to Zale, eyeing him with the disgusted pity of a farmer studying ruined wheat. "Anyone," he said carefully, "who would pay three hunnert dollars for an ashtray would pay a whore for a handshake."

"What's that supposed to mean?" Zale asked, taking a step forward.

"Chee-rist," said Samski, slapping a hand on his thigh, "if you need both hands to find your butt then you oughtta spend your life standin' up."

"Well you're just full of fucking folk wisdom, aren't you?" Zale answered, then turned toward me. "Why don't you tell your hill-billy friend that he's in Washington, not on the Grand Old Opry."

When Samski heard the word hillbilly he dropped the Marlboro and started toward Zale, and the congressman had endured just enough to oblige.

I stepped between them and held up my hands. "Wait a minute now," I said to Zale. "Walt just has a little poetic streak he likes to exercise. Isn't that right, Walt?"

Samski stopped and beamed, so pleased that someone had finally recognized his unexpected depth that he forgot about fighting. "Poetry," he said, warming to the concept. "Poet-fucking-tree. That's me."

Zale backed off a step, almost getting caught in a smile. "Just treat things with a little respect, that's all," he said.

"Right, Walt," I agreed. "You probably helped pay for them."

What we finally ended up doing was setting the camera on its tripod exactly where we wanted it and then building the pile of furniture around it. We hung a drop cloth over the interlocking structure so that a kind of loose teepee was created with the camera in its center pointing out an opening we made by folding the cloth back on two sides. It was dark in the center and, after we taped the blinking LED, the only way to see the lens was to peer steadily into the interior. We ran a couple sample tapes and played them back using the VCR and Zale's television. They were too dark for a positive identification so we took three lamps from the aide's office and placed them around the room in what we hoped was a subtle pattern. Finally, we threw a drop cloth over half the television to add a raffish note to the ensemble and it was almost showtime.

All that was left was to run the remote wire from the video camera under the rug, into the hall, then under the door to the aide's office. I took one of the small transmitters I'd kidnapped along with the Arab at Rodman's and stuck it under the flange of Zale's desk. Then I went into the adjoining office with the receiver. I could hear Samski and Zale perfectly.

"Am I supposed to yell cut if Gottus says the wrong thing?" Zale asked.

I'd been working all night and the tone of cocktail party sarcasm got on my nerves. "Look," I said, "I could make a deal for the boards and forget the rest. The film is your protection so you'd better get committed to it."

"Oh, I'm as committed as a victim of extortion can be," he said. "I just don't see how we can guarantee a logical place to stop."

I told him that was up to him. All he had to do was be smooth, remember it was a real conversation. He wanted some consideration for Maryland, nothing hard about it.

"What about starting again?" he asked.

I hadn't thought of that. "It's simple," I answered, "We'll do it the easiest way." What was the easiest way? "I'll just direct him. I'll tell him when to hand the money to you. When Walt hears me say that he turns on the camera." I looked at both Zale and Samski for confirmation.

Zale nodded his head slowly but he wanted to know how I was going to get that much control of the situation. I shrugged and showed Zale the Beretta.

"He's not stupid," Zale harumphed. "He'll know you can't shoot him in here."

"Maybe, but I could sure fracture his skull. For all he knows I'm crazy enough to do it."

Zale gave a crooked smile of acknowledgment. "It's no crazier than anything else you've done."

Samski was silent but I could tell something was worrying him by the way he was chewing the filter of his Marlboro.

"What're you gonna say when you tell him to hand over the money?" he asked.

"Ah, let's see . . . how about go? No, go ahead. I'll just say go ahead. When you hear me say that you start."

I was getting to know Samski pretty well because when he looked at me I knew what he was going to say.

"What if somebody else says that?" he asked. "Before you do, or at the same time?"

Zale groaned and swiveled his chair to look out the window. I told Samski it was okay, that you could distinguish between voices on the earphones. He went into the aide's office and listened while Zale and I go-aheaded ourselves to the point of hoarseness.

"It's a take," he said when he finally emerged. "Don't change a thing, babe. I love ya." He winked at Zale and gave him the thumbs-up sign.

"Six-pack guys," Zale muttered.

"Good thought," I said. "That's just what my associate and I are going to go have. If Gottus is due in the morning at eight, we'd better meet here at seven to run through it." Zale gave an acquiescent grunt and waved us toward the door. We left the M-16s and the Beretta rolled up in the drop cloth but I took the Dynatron transfer papers and the boards. I was married to them. Only death or a big divorce settlement could put us asunder.

28

Samski and I were in our room at the Holiday Inn on New York Avenue. The TV was tuned to CNN where an oil tanker was gushing its contents into the after-shave blue of some pristine bay. I didn't notice which one because we were arguing about how much money we should demand. He said a million. I said that was too much, if only because of the logistical problems. It was going to have to be cash and I wasn't sure Gottus would be able to get his hands on that much in the few hours we were going to allow him.

Plus, neither one of us had any idea how big a package a million dollars would make. I knew from Daz's experience in Nam that it could be carried in something the size of an infantry pack, but fully loaded those packs weighed sixty pounds. I thought I might have to do some running and didn't want to end up with nothing because I had to choose between my money or my life.

Samski's share was only 35 percent, so he held out for a million. He got a little sulky when I pointed out to him that he really had no vote. "Seems to me there wouldn't be nothin' to vote about if I hadn't clouted that A-rab on the head a few nights ago."

He had me there so we argued some more. Gottus had already had two men killed just because they knew of the existence of something I'd stolen. Even if he came across with the money he was going to try and get it back. Preferably off my dead body. The problem from his side was that he had no idea what I looked like. No doubt he'd get a description of me from Zale but there was still a chance he'd never learn who fit that description. He had to balance the possibility of losing the money against the trouble it would cause him to refuse the whole deal. I thought asking for a million might tilt the balance too far toward refusal.

Realistically, all I had was high-grade nuisance value. I couldn't stand up in front of a congressional committee with the boards without giving away my name and address. All I could do was slip them anonymously to some party who would pay for them. Who would I go to in that case? The newspapers . . . or the Israelis.

Israel would be better, much better. The American government would go rattling into a preannounced investigation with the same clanking subtlety it had used in Asia, and with the same results. The infiltrators would disappear. By the time anyone actually got down to the Armco plant to look at the circuit boards, Gottus would have the place inhabited by virgins manufacturing rosaries.

But Israel. Once my story was quietly verified by the appropriate Mossad agent Gottus would be number twenty with a bullet on the Tel Aviv hit list. I couldn't be sure they'd actually kill him but they always do something, and they have long memories. Very high-grade nuisance value. I had to be sure to mention Israel to Gottus.

Even so, I had to remember it wasn't his money. Whoever he was working for might care less about Gottus' health and Pecosa's position than the precedent of giving a million bucks to an extortionist.

What I needed was a figure Gottus could take out of petty cash without asking for authorization, something he could just write off as part of the cost of doing business. True, a million dollars probably wasn't much to his employers but they might ask about it when they checked his expense account.

"It's gotta be less than a million," I told Samski. "We want to make sure the trouble of giving us the money is less than the trouble of not giving it to us."

He stared morosely into his beer bottle. "A million ain't nothin' these days," he griped. "Hell, they prolly spend that much just flyin' whores out to their boats. I read about that shit in the *Enquirer*. They got them big yachts tied up all over the world and they fly in these clothing store managers who're really madams with white women they kidnap outta the changin' rooms. Miami an' San Pedro. That's where they get most of 'em. Get 'em hooked on coke and money and turn 'em into whores. Prolly costs 'em more than a million ever six weeks."

"Maybe," I said, "but we're not nearly as much fun as coke and whores, and besides that . . . San Pedro?"

"Yeah, them A-rabs ain't dumb. Lotta your as-piring actresses live in San Pedro. An' they gotta buy a lotta clothes."

"I thought San Pedro was in the north, around San Francisco."

"Nah, it's in the south, around San Diego. Besides that, there's as-piring actresses all over California. That's where we oughta go when we get this money—California. Buy a boat, get some young actresses to come out for a party."

Samski was reciting into the bottom of his Budweiser bottle, as if he'd had this dream many times. "Walt," I said, "Walt, forget the coke and actresses a minute will you? Worry about staying alive and getting Doris into a weight-loss program. Gottus has to answer to the guys with the boats. What they consider all right for them might not be all right for him."

"Nine hunnerd thousand then. Get a boat for three, then . . ."

"Nine's too much. I want something he's comfortable with."

"This guy your brother-in-law or somethin'? What about somethin' we're comfortable with?"

"Okay. What could you be comfortable with?"

"A actress in San Pedro."

"Forget that. Why don't you just take Doris on a trip to Op-ryland?"

"Five."

"Two."

"Don't be such a pussy. He's gonna try an kill you no matter what ya get."

"Three."

"Four."

"Three-fifty."

"Sheeit, my share of three-fifty would only be, ah . . ."

"One hundred twenty-two five."

"That's less than it'd take for a boat and San Pedro both."

"Yeah, but it's tax free."

He pushed back his John Deere hat and lit up a Marlboro. "One twenty-two-five," he said, trying it out.

"You could buy a nice thirty-five-foot Chris-craft for half that. Keep it down at Ocean City. Not many actresses there but plenty of bodies in bikinis, plenty of parties."

"Awright," he said, "awright. Three-fifty an' Ocean City. Maybe get into some parties with that country music crowd from Glen Burnie."

Three-fifty it was. My share would be $227,500. Enough to go to San Pedro in search of actresses if I wanted. But I decided I'd give Arla the first shot. If she didn't like the private investigation business at those rates she was just being intentionally difficult.

29

"Why the hell did I run around like a fool to pick up them legal papers if we ain't even goin' to need 'em till tomorrow?" Samski asked.

At seven in the morning, the shadeless August sun was already fading the blue sky to the color of old denim. It torched its way between the venetian blinds of Zale's office creating slats of light across the cool early air: the perfect setting for a second cup of coffee and a leisurely read of the morning paper. I imagined myself on the deck of my house in the suburbs, under the umbrella shading the glass-topped table, listening to Arla go on about the dance company she was in at the local community college. The big concert was in early September. I hoped I'd be there to see it. I wanted everything to be over so I'd be there for sure, watching her and the other trim women, their leotards cleaving their earnest butts into an encyclopedic spangle of firm half-moons. The big concert was always great, especially since I knew that one of the better half-moons in the bunch would be resting in my hand after the show. Marriage too has its guilty pleasures. . . .

"Hey pard, ya havin' a little stroke there or what?" Samski asked.

I'd drifted so far into the slats of light that I'd forgotten him. We'd been on the third run-through of the John Gottus show. Since I'd be operating the camera during the first session, Samski was sitting across from Zale playing the part of Gottus when he'd stopped to ask the question about the papers. I'd explained it to him before but his mind was still looking for the shortest distance between two points.

"How can you have spent a year in Nam without learning to think in circles?" I asked him.

"Practice," he said.

Zale came around from behind the desk and stopped in front of Samski. "Let me explain it to you," he said. "You're not going to give him the papers to sign until tomorrow because you need time to duplicate the tape. Understand? You can't dupe the tape at the same time you're making it because that's the first thing he's going to suspect. You're going to show him that you've only been running one VCR."

Samski's jawline tightened enough to force Zale back a step. "Sure, pard," he said amiably, "it's just that us who ain't politicians have a hard time keepin' track of how many lies we're tellin'."

"It's your friend's plan," Zale said, nodding at me.

"Took you to explain it to me though, didn't it?"

Zale shrugged and went back to his seat. "See there," I said, "we're becoming a real team."

At seven forty-five Samski slipped into his painter's coveralls and went outside to see who'd show up with Gottus and what they'd be doing while he was inside. I went into the aide's office where I locked and loaded an M-16 just to feel I had a friend. Zale's staff had been told to come in late.

I heard Gottus as he and Zale said their hellos. It was the same electronic whip of a voice, his words frying little patches of air and disposing cleanly of the charred remains.

Fifteen years had worked a difference in my reaction. There was less fear now and more hate. Then I'd been sure he was going to prosper while I chased my tail. Now I was chasing his. I pressed the start button on the camcorder's remote switch.

After the opening apology and explanation for the state of Zale's office the conversation moved right into Slingshot. It worried me that Zale was doing all the talking. I wanted Gottus to seem more insistent. As I listened though I gained more respect for my elected representative. To frustrate Gottus he was purposely overtalking his position, giving out a barge load of garbage about how much he appreciated Ergotronics' past contributions to the country's defense and Gottus' frankness in past dealings and how this project had a lot of potential but that he was having certain "cognitive" problems with the statistical profile of the field tests.

Wisely, he didn't mention the decapitation problems. If I went public with the tape, he didn't want anyone wondering why he was considering a weapon which was more suicidal than homicidal.

Zale went on shoveling until he forced Gottus to dig his way out by slipping into the pattern we'd anticipated.

"I want to know your position, Roland," he said, lasering one of Zale's sentences in midflight. "Did you call me in here to tell me you're going to recommend against Slingshot?"

The question was delivered deadpan but there was an undertone that suggested a Mafia don asking one of his shooters how the autobiography was coming. Zale told him that any such action would, of course, be premature but there were certain problems. He simply wanted Gottus' response. He toadied a little, whined like he was sorry he had to bother the don about a few heads on a few test dummies. Gottus' answer cracked out before Zale even finished what he was saying.

"Oh no, no, no, no, no. That's not going to happen! Never! What you want is my imprimatur on your decision. You want me to, ah, what . . . acquiesce?"

I was sweating so much that the earphones kept slipping off my head. The tape was no good unless Gottus believed Zale could use it and the word acquiescence made it sound too much like he owned Zale. But I needn't have worried. Zale was a practiced broken-field runner. He combined the political sidestep with the stiff-arm stroke in a bubbly sentence which used the word acquiescence enough times to strip it of any connotations.

"No one expects you to acquiesce to anything John," he said.

"We both know that's not your line of work. Acquiescence would be both unprofessional and out of character. I'm not asking you to give way, just to explain, to justify."

Gottus let go a little burst of laughter which was as cheerful as a burst from one of his employees' Uzis. "Explain," he said, "justify." He ripped off another blast of muzzle-velocity laughter. I could feel him coiling his whip. He was a slave master whose houseboy had just asked him to justify the latest welt and he was about to issue the only justification possible, another welt. The word whipsnaked out with a crack. "Jobs. How about jobs? The number of jobs assigned to this project, including collateral tradesmen is five thousand! Five! You'd be well advised to consider this project not only in light of its considerable intrinsic merits but its region-wide economic, demographic, and political fallout."

Every hair on my body pointed to magnetic north. My fingers tensed, almost stopping the tape. Zale however was as cool as a captain steering his ship through familiar waters. "Region-wide?" he asked in a worried tone.

"Yes, yes of course," Gottus fired. "There are many factors in any economic equation, as you know. Ergotronics is an important piece of a large financial puzzle, if you will. Take away one piece and the whole puzzle might have to be reconstructed. I want to avoid that."

Zale responded with a lot of ass-covering blather that made me sweat even more. He went on about statesmanship sometimes superceding normal priorities and how any problems would have to be corrected. I was afraid Gottus would get the feeling someone was looking over his shoulder as well as Zale's. If that happened I'd have to barge into the room and proceed right to the bottom line. I'd get just as much money that way but the odds against living to spend it would go up dramatically. The tape was my hidden ace. Without it this would all turn into a simple cash transaction, the circuit boards for the money. Afterward it would be devil take the hindmost, and my hind would be the most vulnerable. But Zale knew just when to quit the verse for the chorus in time to save the song.

"That said," he murmured in a more confidential tone, "I have to remind both of us that I was elected to be a representative as well as a statesman. I work for the people of Maryland and I need some assurance that if Slingshot is perfected and approved, the puzzle won't be reconstructed anyway." Gottus started to say something but Zale interrupted him. "Understand me clearly, John. I want priority consideration in the distribution of any collateral benefits which may flow from the Slingshot project."

I pressed the stop button and kissed it. The son of a bitch was brilliant! Collateral benefits which may flow from . . . anyone who'd believe Gottus didn't see that as a bribe opportunity was dumb enough to think Ronnie Reagan was a real cowpoke.

Part one had gone down. I was happy, as happy as Gottus but not as smug.

I heard what I thought was static in the earphones but it was Gottus laughing. "All you wanted was for us to leave Maryland intact?" he was saying. "I thought at first you were going to try to hold us to the contract specs." His laughter crackled through the phones again. "Yes, Roland, yes of course. You were very cooperative regarding the Dynatron deal and we appreciate that. Maryland's in a safe harbor. Of course this is business, and business is always a contingent enterprise. But rest assured, as long as Maryland, and its representatives, maintain a harmonious relationship with Pecosa there's no reason for us to look for a more user-friendly environment."

It was worse than listening to him in 1973. In front of a congressional committee Gottus had been forced to modify his tone to a poor semblance of respect. But now it was obvious he considered the congressman to be appearing before him. Not that there was any emotion in his tone other than a vague amusement. He wasn't unsure enough to feel triumphant or grateful enough to feel condescending. He was just completely, finally, faultlessly certain he was on the winning side because the side that wins is the side which cares about nothing but winning.

Gottus was, above all, an orderly person. His clothes, his cars, his house, and his business were orderly. If a thing threatened that order he had it killed. Democracy was a little too messy for him so he'd gone to work for some sons of the desert who thought that businesses were no different than camels or countries or women, you used one to buy the other. Gottus had been working for other countries so long that he'd forgotten the most important thing about America. We were founded by visionaries and misfits. Our trade was in dreams and nightmares. Blood and belief. Stubbornness and perversity.

My generation had invaded Viet Nam and lost. We outgunned and overmanned them but we lost, and some of us had paid attention. We learned what it takes to win—stubbornness and perversity. Now it was time.

I looked at the M-16 in the corner, its toy plastic stock, its inner-city blackness, its little varmint bullets with their avalanche velocity. "C'mon," I thought to Gottus, "bring it on, sheik. Bring on your power. Bring that big smile a little closer. My monkey man is waiting. He likes those electric smiles. They shine in the twilight. They sit up bright on his sights."

30

Samski, Zale, and I were sitting in front of the big Zenith staring
at the face of John Gottus. He looked like a plump lizard sunning
on a hot rock, as unlined and puffed at the jaw hinge as an adder.
The olive-oiled furrows of his hair had thinned and receded to an
arrowhead of gray. His eyes were hooded and dull. They seemed
to blink only when he willed it. Once he looked straight into the
camera, his mouth sewn into a seamless Iguana smile, wondering
about the pile of junk he was seeing.

"You arrogant son of a bitch," Zale was saying to the screen.

"Boy's pretty sure of himself, ain't he," Samski said to Zale.
"Seems like you'd enjoy what we're about to tell him."

Gottus had left at 8:20. I'd given him ten minutes, then took
out the tape. It was crisscrossed with shadows, and when he faced
left you could only see the back of his head but the rest of the
time there was no doubt it was him. Ten minutes to get out of
the building and into his car, ten more to get into traffic . . . time
to make the call.

Walt's suggestion wasn't too bad. Why not let Zale get a

little emotional payback? I asked him if he'd like to make the call.

"I don't know," he said.

"Go on, just tell him there's someone here who wants to talk to him about circuits. I bet you can hear him start to sweat. Besides, it'll prove I'm not just some crank who got hold of his car phone number." He hesitated a few seconds but then he started to like the idea of being the first to inform Gottus that his little universe was about to experience a big bang.

"Why not," Zale decided. "As long as it doesn't involve me any more than I already am. You put the actual proposition to him."

"I wouldn't have it any other way."

Zale had the slightest trace of a smile on his face when he informed Gottus that there was a man in his office who wanted to speak to him. No, he didn't know the man's name actually, but it was something to do with circuit boards. There was a long pause during which Zale's slight smile broadened a little. "Yes, John. Circuit boards. Something to do with the F-one-eleven. Yes, he's right here. Just a second."

"You were right," Zale whispered as he extended the phone toward me. "He's tight as a bow string."

I'd decided to play it courteous and businesslike rather than tough or insolent. I was tweaking a powerful man, no percentage in making him any angrier than necessary.

"Mr. Gottus?" I began tentatively.

"You already know that, what is it?"

His voice disoriented me for a second. It was so perfectly in tune with the telephone that I had the feeling he was a recording calling to tell me I was facing disconnection. He was the audible sound of a printed final notice.

"Do you have something to say to me or has Zale started to indulge in pranks?"

"No," I said, "it's no prank. It's a straightforward business proposition. I have the two F-one-eleven circuit boards missing from the Armco plant. I'm willing to sell them back to you."

He said he wasn't interested and I began to think the polite businesslike approach might have to be modified. I told him he was interested enough to have Mosby and Fredericks killed. He said he'd heard they were killed because they were involved with a drug ring, that it was a dangerous business, and added that I sounded like I might be on drugs. I should have known he'd mistake politeness for weakness.

"You're one of the reasons there's a dearth of good manners in this country," I told him.

The pitch of his voice went up slightly but without emotion. I'd pressed a different button on a touchtone phone.

"What?"

"I come to you politely with a simple business proposition and all I get is a ton of attitude. That's the reason Ervin was so hard on you during Watergate, he didn't like your attitude."

"Mr. Ervin's dead. I'm alive and prospering. Take a lesson."

So much for polite and businesslike. "Listen," I said, "I took the boards. I found out what they do to the F-one-eleven's radar. I found out you had Mosby and Fredericks killed. I kidnapped your man at Rodman's and gave him back to you when I was ready. I know about Zale and the Dynatron deal, and that you were the one behind it. At this point I'm not impressed with how slick you are. Let's do business and skip the bullshit."

There was a slight pause. I remembered him taking a drink of water during the Watergate hearings. "How much?" he asked.

"My first and last offer, no bargaining. Three hundred and fifty thousand dollars. Cash."

"That's completely ridiculous. I'll give you a hundred."

"Fine, I'll give the boards and the whole Pecosa story to *The Washington Post, People, Life,* the *Enquirer,* anyone who'll pay me a buck. I'll make an easy hundred thousand that way."

He said he'd look forward to seeing my face on the talk shows, possibly he'd drop me a fan letter at my home.

"Possibly you won't be in any condition to write," I told him. "Because before I do any of that, I'll give the story and a verified schematic of the boards to the Israeli embassy. I'll mention your name prominently." I paused but there was nothing but silence on the other end. I thought I could hear him breathing, a little faster it seemed. "Does the Mossad interest you?" I asked. "Eichmann had twenty years to hide and they found him. It took them fifteen to get everyone involved in the Olympic massacre of seventy-two but they got them. I don't think they're going to like paying for sabotaged fighter planes. I think they'll consider it a bad precedent. I wouldn't be surprised if they considered it necessary to make an example of someone. If that sounds good to you just keep kidding around. Three-fifty. Cash."

"All right. I'll concede you a certain nuisance value."

"Concede me three hundred and fifty thousand dollars and we can both get on with our business."

There was another, longer, pause during which I heard him say something nasty to his chauffeur. When he came back on the line, his mellow tone told me he'd decided to draw me out with the money and then kill me. He said to meet him in a parking garage on upper Thirteenth Street the following evening at 5:00 P.M. I said that was very neat. Five o'clock, the middle of the rush hour, crowds of Yalie lawyers rushing to happy hour. He could kill me and it wouldn't even be mentioned until the second drink. "Today," I told him. "Zale's office at six P.M."

He said that was impossible, then started to give me a princely monologue concerning high finance, something about how you don't just go in and take out that much like it was a Christmas Club account, how certain things have to be capitalized. That's when I lost my temper.

"Who the hell do you think you're talking to?" I bellowed into the phone. "When you were on TV getting your ass chewed by Sam Ervin I was in college getting an A in money and banking. The people you work for keep this kind of cash around just to bet on changes in wind direction. And they have so much invested in this country that you could get the bank manager out of bed at two in the morning to change a ten. Now get the money and have it in Zale's office by three today. Today, with no more than one engineer to verify the boards, or I'll go to the Israelis and capitalize your high-financial ass for you. And tell me now. In ten minutes, I'll already be on my way."

This time there was no pause before he spoke. "I'll be there," he said. "I'll look forward to seeing you. I'll look forward to—"

I hung up before he could tell me what else he looked forward to. It wasn't hard to imagine.

"I hope you're aware of what you've done," said Zale. "I've never heard anyone speak to John Gottus that way."

Samski gave a low awed whistle. "I'll be goddamned," he said. "That money and bankin' musta been a hell of a tough class."

31

"What do you think?" I asked Samski as I pulled a pair of panty hose over my head.

"Ya didn't get the support kind, did ya?" he said. "They'd likely suffocate ya."

"No, these are regular. Persimmon. I thought a little color might help confuse him."

"Well, it's true I can't see ya too good. Can you see out, that's the question."

Actually I could see pretty well. Things were a little dark but I had good peripheral vision and they were cooler than the rubber Nixon masks I'd bought at first. That would have been funny but impractical.

"One thing," he said, "cut them legs off. Havin' 'em hang down the sides of your face like that makes ya look like the Easter Bunny with a hangover."

At two-forty-five Walt was stationed at a pay phone downstairs. At three he rang Zale's office to tell me Gottus was on his way up. He had only one man with him but parked outside were two Mercedes full of black hair and beards.

I ducked into the adjacent office where I stood holding the boards in one hand and the Beretta in the other. When I heard the door to Zale's office open and close I stepped into the hall where I could listen. Gottus didn't raise his voice but it sounded far away, as if there were a ventriloquist waiting in his head with a sniper's rifle.

"It's three. I'm here," he said to Zale. "Produce your man."

Zale started to explain that I wasn't his man but before he could finish I moved through the hall door and nudged Gottus's back with the pistol barrel. "Don't turn around," I said. "If you try to turn around I'll lay this up the side of your head and we can start again. If you come to."

I told Gottus to sit in the leather chair. As he did I noticed he kept his hand on the cordovan attaché case he was carrying. The engineer with him was an older man wearing a brown worsted suit with two pens and a pencil in the breast pocket. The suit bagged here and there, as if he might be carrying his lunch in it, but he wore an expression of bemused arrogance. He had frameless glasses and a cumulus cloud of gray hair exploding from his head that probably hadn't been combed since he was in the Hitler youth. I told him to take off his suit coat.

"What," he asked with the slightest trace of a German V at the beginning of the word.

"Take off your coat so I'll be sure you're not carrying your old SS Luger underneath."

"SS?" He was shocked but he removed the coat. Nothing more threatening underneath than sweat stains. I handed him the boards and asked how long it would take him to verify them.

"Not long," he said.

"How long?"

He looked down at me, trying to see through the panty hose, twisting his head one way and then the other. It made me nervous. I told him I hadn't done this kind of thing much, that if I thought he was anything but an engineer I might get scared and shoot him.

"Chust thinking," he answered. "No more than five minutes."

"It took my expert two hours."

He told me condescendingly that if you knew what you were looking for it was simply a matter of locating a few key points in the circuitry. Also, there were serial numbers on each board. He smiled slightly, twisting his head again as if he were amused that I bore no serial number. Or maybe it was just the cutoff panty hose on my head.

The old guy sat down in a chair next to the wall and hunched over the boards. I reached over Gottus' shoulder to hand Zale a sheet of paper on which I'd typed my instructions. He read the sheet as though he'd never seen it. Then he pushed the paper across the desk to Gottus who didn't take his eyes off Zale as he reached for it. When Gottus leaned back with the paper I stepped up and tapped him very lightly with the gun barrel just to emphasize the sincerity of my instructions. I could read them over his shoulder:

1. You're a dangerous man. To keep my contact with you at a minimum you will deal with Zale. DON'T turn around. If you attempt to look at me I will fracture your skull. Then I'll cart you out in a bag and dump you in an alley.

2. When your man verifies the boards he leaves with them. Then, when I tell you to, you hand the money to Zale. DO NOT attempt to get up from your chair until I tell you to hand him the money. After you have given him the money sit back down. Do not get up until you hear me leave the room. For the results of ANY deviation from this plan see item one.

3. Now, open the case and count the money, out loud. When you have finished, close the case and put it in its original position.

The back of Gottus' neck was turning Valentine red but he was careful not to turn his head when he spoke to me. "You should realize it's impossible for you to carry me out in a bag or any other way. There are two carloads of men outside who would all be gratified to see you."

I didn't want to undercut the fiction that I was staying silent because I was afraid of him so I confined myself to a minimal answer. I stepped up and tapped him with the gun, a little harder this time, and told him I wasn't kidding.

"Yes, you are," he shot back. "You're kidding yourself. You're a digit, a unit masquerading as a prototype. Give me the boards, forget the extortion, and we'll be less inclined to look for you among the rest of the units."

The red on the back of his neck drained to normal color as he spoke and his tone was a little less like an echo. His hands were interlaced across his moderate paunch with the two index fingers pointing together toward the front. According to an article in *Psychology Today*, it's a gesture characteristic of people accustomed to command. That was him all right. Command. He enjoyed it so much I suspected he'd forgotten it wasn't innate, but came down from the Mideast on wings of money. He probably thought of himself as some kind of postliberal Napoleon, imbued by the great personnel director in the sky with the power to cut checks or terminate us units as he saw fit.

Gottus made no move to count the money. I had the feeling he was trying to draw me into conversation because the situation seemed a little too surreal and he was testing the truth of it. That made me a little sad. It was beginning to seem that no one responded to anything but violence or the threat of it.

With more anger than I felt I reached up, grabbed the back of Gottus' head, and shoved the gun barrel hard into his ear. He stiffened, and I shoved his face toward the sheet of instructions, I took the gun out of his ear and pointed with it at number three. Then I stepped back as Gottus put the case on his lap to open it. I noticed his fingers were shaking. Maybe it wasn't violence at all. Maybe these guys just hated getting their hair mussed. Gottus counted out loud as I watched. When he got to 350,000 he closed the case and put it back on the floor as instructed.

"Verified," chirped the old guy on my left.

"You're sure?" asked Gottus.

The old German raised an eyebrow as though no one had ever questioned him before. "Absolutely," he said, a little thicker with the accent this time. I motioned for him to get up, which he did.

He tightened the knot on his tie before swimming gawkily into his suit coat. When he was dressed I pointed toward the boards in his hand, then the door. He obeyed, but as he passed me he stopped and winked. "Very efficient," he whispered. "So far."

Wonderful, I thought. The old Nazi's impressed. I resolved to do something inefficient as soon as possible.

After the engineer had gone I took a deep breath and said the magic words: "Give him the money. Go ahead."

Gottus leaned forward to slap the attaché case on Zale's desk. "There," he said. "Is that—"

Before he could say any more his staccato was overwhelmed by Zale's voice in its television baritone mode. As soon as the case hit his desk the congressman rolled easily into sync with the previous conversation. He spoke as he flipped open the latches. "Now let me stop you right there, John," he boomed with rising indignation. "By collateral benefits I meant jobs for Marylanders, not this. You know very well I can't accept this."

In the few seconds it took Gottus to realize he was being scammed Zale had tilted the case toward the camera, snapped it shut, and tossed it disdainfully back to Gottus who swatted it to the floor like it was a mosquito. He leaned forward to sweep a pen and pencil set off the desk.

"You weasel sonofabitch," he hissed. "I don't know what game you have in mind but you know me well enough to know I can't be held up for—" He stopped in midsentence, realizing in a flash of pain that what he'd heard from Zale was a denial. He had the instincts of a reptile and struck back like one. If Zale was trying to distance himself from the transaction Gottus knew the best tactic was to include him again. "You asked me here," he said pointing at Zale. "This was your idea, your meeting, your proposition."

"Yes," Zale said deferentially. "Yes John, it was. Look over your shoulder and you'll see why."

Gottus snapped a look to the cloth-covered pile of furniture just as I leaned down to where the remote wire emerged from the carpet and yanked it out of the camcorder. The force of my pull caused the tripod to topple with a metallic clatter inside the canvas tepee. Gottus threw the drop cloth aside, and kicked over the base of a swivel chair that had obscured the tripod's legs. Afraid he'd try to crush the now exposed camera, I stepped in front of him waving the pistol and told him to sit down. He just stood there, his sleek lizard's face turning chameleon pink. His eyes were a wintry charcoal gray, the color of dirty ice on a city street. A concrete tundra seemed to stretch far back into his head, and one of the eyes jerked spasmodically. I almost shot him. The impulse ran all the way down my arm to the end of my finger and vibrated. He must have felt it somehow because he backed away a step, feeling for his chair.

"I'm afraid you've been caught, John," Zale said with true empathy.

32

To call Gottus angry would be like calling the atomic bomb an explosion. He wasn't just mad, he was approaching critical mass. After we'd played the tape for him he started to turn sunset shades of red and purple. He was beyond yelling. What he was into was a high-speed recitation of all the rules of illegal behavior we'd broken and what happened to people in Washington who broke the rules. He reminded Zale what would happen when word got around that he was the kind of scum who'd blackmail a partner, and further reminded him who he'd been partners with, and me that I was partners with nobody.

When Gottus stepped close, I caught a slight smell of used gin coming off him, deathlike as embalming fluid. "You may not know it but you're twisting in the wind, right now. You're all alone against enough money to buy this whole country and shake it out looking for you. You will be found, and by people without Western family values who enjoy their work."

That was only the beginning. He paced, gestured, pointed, hissed, and generally acted like he was a Viking and I was a primitive beet farmer.

"You haven't even heard what I want for the tape," I said. Gottus stopped and stared at me, trying to will his vision through the panty hose covering my face. "What?" he said stupidly. "Did you think this was some kind of prank? You think this is a fraternity and you're being hazed. I want something else."

I could see his mind working, trying to think what else he stood to lose. A lone streak of sweat oozed down the side of his neck but he didn't speak.

Since he wasn't going to give me the satisfaction of asking, I told him: "Dynatron. Signed, sealed, and delivered back to its original owner. This is nonnegotiable."

The anger disappeared. He stepped back, sat down, and looked at me as coolly as a surgeon at a patient. "You know this goes beyond inconvenience or embarrassment," he said. "What in the world ever made you want to get yourself into a position like this? Don't you have a life? Anything you care about?"

I was beginning to feel the way I had when I watched him on TV in 1973: that he was right, that there was no way I could win. Then I remembered that we were playing my game instead of his. What I'd told Dorn was the truth. I had won. Every time I came out of the bush I was a winner. I reminded myself that Gottus was just a soldier in a three-piece suit. He had his idea of what constituted the bush and I had mine. It was too late to quit anyway so we'd have to see who was right.

Since there was no point in being mannerly anymore, I decided to go in the other direction. Maybe if he was functioning out of blind rage he'd get like a boxer who loses control and starts swinging wild instead of punching.

I walked up to where he was sitting and put the barrel of the pistol under his chin. I told him to get up. He wasn't inclined to do it but when I started to lift he noticed my finger was on the trigger. As he stepped away from the chair, I stuck out my foot and tripped him. He went down clumsily, landing on his elbow.

"You're getting fat," I said, looking down at him. "I'd say sex is the only physical thing you do . . . and this ain't that."

When he got up I had him sit back down in the chair and watch the tape for a second time. When it was over I pointed out that if it was released he'd be out of a job. No more unlimited expense accounts. No more influence. He'd be just one more schmuck who got caught doing what everybody suspected but nobody expected. He might as well trade in his telephone for a one-way transmitter since it would be the turn of the century before anyone returned his calls. The Arabs would say they thought he was just doing charity work for starving kids in the Sudan and drop him like he was radioactive.

When I told him he had twenty-four hours to get authorization, he said he already had power of attorney from Pecosa and could sign if he felt like it. Then I said he could have twenty-four hours to think it over.

"Where are the papers?" he asked, ready to do anything, sign anything, that would get him out of the office and back into his limo where he was in control.

First though, he wanted to be sure he was buying the only copy. He wanted to see what I had in the other rooms. If he saw more than one VCR there would be no deal. We'd just "get on with what's to come."

When we walked into the next room, Samski had pulled a pair of pantyhose over his head. He was standing jauntily near a desk smoking a Marlboro through a hole over his mouth. "Step into my office," he said, covering the room with an arm sweep.

After a close look around Zale's suite, Gottus was ready to sign, but I needed those extra twenty-four hours. If we didn't duplicate the tape we had nothing to keep him from killing Zale, Dorn, me, or Arla. Jesus! Arla. I had to put him off without letting him know that's what I was doing. If he knew I needed the night the whole balance of power would shift.

I sat on the edge of Zale's desk and tried to look insolent. Zale didn't mind. He'd been in some kind of catatonic state since I'd tripped Gottus. His face was frozen into a kind of hopeless dreaminess, as if he were trying to decide what to order for his last meal. I shifted to place myself between him and Gottus.

"Listen," I said to Gottus, "the truth is, I didn't expect you to be such a used-up old fart. I thought it would take at least a day for you to cave in. The papers are still being drawn up in Baltimore. We're going to have to meet back here tomorrow morning."

He looked at me without blinking, a still snake waiting for his mouse to hop in the wrong direction. I looked back, pretending to chew gum even though I had none. I wanted to appear as much the rube as possible, an overconfident swaggering rube who thought this economic general was an old fart. Hell, it was true. I was a rube. I was just a stubborn West Virginia mountain boy with a college education. It was the education that fooled everyone, even Samski. I laughed out loud, a high, keening sound.

Gottus tilted his head the way people do when they think someone else is crazy. Then he asked if 9:00 A.M. the following morning was okay. When I said it was, he agreed to sign. But to make sure the one and only copy of the tape stayed just that, he was going to leave two of his men with me. I said he could only leave one man, since he was using professional killers, and I was only an amateur. I needed the odds on my side. It was nonnegotiable. He could agree or take his chances with various higher authorities. He agreed, with the stipulation that the tape wasn't to leave his man's sight. He had me pull the tape from the VCR and lay it on Zale's desk. Then he smiled his airless iguana smile and called one of his cars to send up Safir.

"Boy, you sure do get the shit details, don't you," I said when Safir walked into the office.

"Fook you," he said emphatically. I didn't blame him. If someone had kept me prisoner in a balloon and then made me ride forty miles in the trunk of a car I'd say the same thing. Gottus must have thought that since Safir had a personal reason to hate me he'd be the soul of vigilance. But I knew he was as soulless as Detroit without Motown.

It was a long, boring night. Safir's English left a lot to the imagination. If he'd wanted to say anything but fook you we might have had a hard time communicating. I knew he'd like to kill me so I brought Samski in just to show he was outnumbered. Zale thought it was the kind of night that might rain bullets so he decided not to go outdoors. Instead, he went to spend the night in the lounge, a place on the top floor with leather couches where congressmen could have gin and tonics while they discussed the empire.

That left Safir, Samski, and myself. Samski and I watched TV while Safir sat in a corner staring at the tape lying on Zale's desk. He was probably already in Gottus's dog house and intended to follow instructions literally. Samski was taking little hits off a pint of Jim Beam and was starting to feel aggressively friendly. He kept asking Safir if he wanted a drink. Safir ignored him for a while, but when Samski kept insisting, he tried to explain that Moslems didn't drink.

"Hell, pard," Samski said, "I wouldn't wanta insult anyone's religion. Course if I said you looked like you could use your nose for a bottle opener that wouldn't be insultin' your religion any, would it? I mean ugly comes in any religion."

Safir's response was a predictable, "Fook you."

After a few hours of snappy repartee with Safir, Samski and I decided to play the tape. We played it a number of times, laughing and sharing the whiskey to dull the discomfort of the ski masks we were now wearing. They were less claustrophobic than the pantyhose, but hotter. At first the tape aggravated Safir. Then we thought we noticed a few flickers of amusement when he saw the raped look on his boss's face. We tried to get him to laugh but he wouldn't so we played the tape some more. We played it so many times that Safir got bored. We kept on playing it. We played it, taking hits of Jim Beam and whooping like we were at a tractor pull, until he was beyond bored. He was numb. He sat in a corner and stared at the end of his cigarette, blowing on it occasionally for excitement. He must have felt like he was back in Daz's balloon. Finally, I said I was going to the car for some beer.

Safir jumped to his feet and vibrated. "No!" he said, "no beer. No car. Tape stays here." He gestured toward his eyes. "Here or no deal!"

I told him to relax, the beer was in a cooler in the trunk of my car. We didn't have to leave the premises. I wasn't pulling anything. We'd go together and take the tape with us. He didn't want to go but I picked up the tape and started toward the door. "What're you gonna say to Gottus if you don't go with me?" I asked him. "He'll ask you if it's the same tape and you'll have to tell him you don't really know. I'd hate to have to tell him that if I were you."

I let him carry the tape. That way he could be sure I didn't have another one in my car. I also showed him the pistol and told him everybody would be happy as long as he didn't try to run away. He sneered, but he took the tape out of the VCR. I called Zale to clear us with security and we were on our way.

It was a fairly long walk to the garage beneath the building and the fact I had to take off my ski mask made it seem longer. I tried to stay behind Safir but several times I caught him staring fook yous at me.

"You know," I said to him, "you're a really beat character. They give you all the lousy jobs and you're lousy at them. You oughta get a job more suited to you. Does your mother know you do this kind of work, staying up all night. Jeez, you look terrible."

"Fook you," he said. "We kee-al you, soon."

"That's good," I told him, "get in touch with your feelings."

It was good. He hated me. He hated the job. He was bored and scared of screwing up again, but he was confident enough to threaten me. He had the tape in his hand and his eye on me. If it hadn't been such a long walk, he might have been having fun.

The walk took twelve minutes, plenty of time for Samski to run a connecting wire out of the back of Zale's VCR, under the rug, and into a storage closet down the hall where we'd hidden the second VCR. All he had to do then was set its automatic record timer for ten-thirty. When Safir and I got back Samski was happily drinking Jim Beam and making wise-ass remarks to the ten o'clock news on channel five.

"Hell," he said, "you two been gone so long I thought you got mistook for a congressman and run off ta jail. Where's that tape? I gotta see Gottus get got just one more time."

At ten-thirty we played the tape again. We drank Beam chased with beer and goofed on it until Safir wanted to puke, and we were sure the tape had dubbed itself onto the machine in the other room. Then, so it would all be a blur to Safir, we watched it again. By that time we were drunk enough that it was also a blur to us. We gave up the ghost about eleven-thirty. Safir held the tape while Samski and I slept in shifts. He tried to stay awake but dozed off regularly, clutching the tape like a teddy bear. I wished him sweet dreams. He got all the shit details.

33

I awoke to the plinking sound of Samski shooting paper clips at beer bottles with a rubber band. A cottony shriek of white noise blasted out of Zale's TV set. Budweiser bottles were scattered around the room and an ashtray haze of dead smoke changed planes aimlessly in the hung-over air. It was the kind of stinking shipwrecked scene that Death avoids because he thinks he can always come back for it later. It was a carcass of a morning but I loved it. I had that eagle eye you get when you stay up all night getting not quite drunk. Your nerves are just irritated enough to feel every atom of the morning like it was rough tweed and you were a tailor.

It was a bush morning. I'd awakened with the same feeling half the mornings I was in Nam; the spongy cold of sandy dirt leaching into my back, every earthen lump a dent in my body, the beginnings of moss on my eyelids, but feeling as snakily powerful as a wraith.

Death would miss you on a day like that because you were so much a part of the ground that you were your own camouflage. You were so down and dank that you were subhuman, and death liked to eat humans the best. They were plump and juicy. Become a beast and you're a force of nature.

"Mornin' there, pard," Samski said, plinking a beer bottle by my foot. "Have some breakfast." He reached into the cooler and threw me a Bud. It tasted good. I like beer for breakfast. It's as fizzy as mouthwash but more fun. I took two more long swallows, then put the half bottle aside. Samski said he'd been on the phone to Zale who was going to bring some food down from the lounge as soon as he'd showered and shaved.

"Think we should shower and shave?" Samski asked me.

I decided to have one more big swallow of the beer. "Nah," I said, slamming it onto Zale's desk and belching soulfully. "This ain't no date we're going on, is it, pard?" I walked over to Samski and punched him so hard on the arm he fell off his chair. His John Deere hat came off and I noticed he was beginning to go bald on top. I reached out to help him up.

"Goddamn," he said as he rose above me. "You're right. It sure as hell ain't no date an' if you punch me like that again I might have ta tell everyone you're a hillbilly just like me."

I had just started to laugh when he whacked me on the arm, tall skinny leverage. It hurt.

"Hurts, don't it?" he asked as he leaned over to pick up his hat. "You fuckin' hillbilly."

"Take the high ground bro," he said. He pulled the hat down and nodded like he knew he should have been Gary Cooper.

I nodded. Safir stood up from the corner where he had been pretending not to sleep. He checked his arms for the tape and when he found it was still there, lowered his thatched eyebrows like awnings over unlit windows. "We kee-al you soon," he said.

Samski and I looked at each other then at Safir. "Fook you," we said in unison.

At eight breakfast came down from the lounge but without Zale. He phoned to say he'd called a meeting of his staff for nine o'clock. He was holding it in a conference room on the floor above but it would be over by ten. If Gottus and I weren't finished by then we'd be overrun by wing tips and prep ties. He wanted to know who was going to move all the stuff in his office back where it belonged. I said I'd leave a campaign contribution of five thousand dollars under the blotter of his desk. It was the best I could do. Once the deal was done, having me around could be dangerous. He agreed and asked me to leave the dubbed tape with him. I told him I'd rather trust a junkie with my credit card. He'd leak it to someone in return for a favor and Gottus's strategy would change to scorched earth. He was offended, but I never thought we'd be close friends anyway.

Samski went out to make it look like he was meeting someone to get the Dynatron papers. While he was gone Safir tried to be annoying by tapping the tape against his knee and glaring at me. "Soon," he said, "soon." He tried an evil smile, but one of his upper canine teeth was missing. He looked like a bus station wino getting ready to bum a quarter.

"Get a job Safir," I said.

When Samski returned, he made a small show of handing me the papers, then we slipped into the hall for a private conference. The plan was for him to take his share of the money and leave. I'd stay for the final meeting with Gottus then work my way out alone. Gottus still didn't know what I looked like. All I had to do was get back into the suit I'd worn when I first met with Zale, go down to the parking lot, and drive away.

"Ain't you forgettin' somethin', pard?" he asked. "Our buddy Safir seen your car when you went for the beer last night. He's dumb as ripe melon but you're dumber if you don't think he noticed what kinda car you're drivin'."

He was right. That was why Safir was so sure they were going to kee-al me soon. All they had to do was wait by the entrance to the lot and follow me. Samski could go down and switch his Trans Am for my rental before the meeting with Gottus, but they were probably already watching every entrance. A guy in a Trans Am goes into a parking lot, then drives out in a K car. They wouldn't think he'd suddenly started worrying about fuel economy. Of course they might not see his face, might not notice it if they did.

But if we counted on that and were wrong we'd be the settlers and they'd be the Indians.

It was a quarter of nine and I was starting to sweat. Samski was staring at me, waiting for an idea. When he saw I didn't have one he came up with one of his own.

"Whyn't I just stay until the end an' we walk out together. We go to my car an' leave. They don't know what we look like."

Not bad, but they did know something about what we looked like together. One tall lanky guy, one short ropy guy. Together, carrying something which could hold a lot of money.

"Hell then, we split up," he said. "We go out alone and meet at my car."

"What do you have to wear?" I asked him. "Either painter's clothes, which they'll be looking for, or jeans and a work shirt." I noticed the logo on his chest, "A fucking work shirt with Armco over the pocket for Christ sake! Are you nuts, Walt? You wore a shirt with Armco on the pocket?"

"Damn," he said, embarrassed. "I always wear these. The company cleans 'em. Saves Doris havin' to do the wash. I'll just take it off, that's all."

"Right, you walk out of a congressional office building wearing a T-shirt and a John Deere hat. They'll never guess you're not just another lawyer."

"Well goddamnit, I'm sorry." He was looking at his shirt like a hound dog at his pile on the rug.

"It's no big deal," I told him. "None of this was your idea anyway. I kind of forced you into it. It's no big deal. I just wear my suit out of the building and catch a cab. I'll fit in better alone. They'll be sitting around waiting for a guy in a K car while I'm on my way to the train station. It's good."

It was too, except I'd be on foot and Safir had seen my face. I told Samski to take my share of the money with him. I said I was sure nothing bad was going to happen but I wanted Samski to give the money to Arla in case it did.

He insisted that he was going to stay. He'd never run out on a buddy in trouble and this was no different.

"Look at it objectively," I said, "if you were betting on the two of us together or me alone in a suit, where would you put your money? Besides, I did all this for Arla and me. If by some stroke of bad luck something happens I want her to have it. She'll need it. It's the least I can do if I'm irresponsible enough to get killed in a deal like this.

"Think about it. Even with your trouble with Doris, would you want to take a chance on leaving her and the kids with nothing but bills?"

"Damnit all," he answered, shaking his head. "Ya think you got steak an' potatoes an' find out it's a stew."

I almost asked him what he meant just to see if he knew, but there wasn't time. "I think I know what you mean," I said.

"That's cause you got a poetic streak, just like me."

"I work good alone, Walt. It's the way I was trained."

"Hell, pard, it's prolly the way you was born."

"Walt, you gotta get control of that poetic streak."

I gave him my home phone number, told him he probably wouldn't need it, and asked him to wait a couple days before he got in touch with Arla. After I took out Zale's five thousand and a couple hundred for pocket money, Samski left. It suddenly occurred to me that I was trusting him with enough money to tempt a saint. But that didn't worry me at all. What did money mean to poets?

Gottus showed up at nine. Like most people who confuse work with fun, he was always on time. There wasn't much to it really. He didn't need a lawyer to tell him what he was signing. Basically, it was the same agreement Dorn had been forced to sign except for less money, one dollar to be exact. Dorn's people had pre-witnessed and notarized the contract. All Gottus had to do was read it and sign, which he did with a minimum of conversation.

He was wearing an ink-blue suit so soft and rich that a poor family could have eaten it for Thanksgiving dinner. His tie was blue silk, his white shirt so crisp he could have tied a string to it and flown it like a kite. No sweat. No tension. He was as brisk and businesslike as a certified letter, but inside I could read controlled tension. He moved only in straight lines and had to force himself against the back of his chair while he read the contract.

"There," he said as he slashed his signature across the bottom. I was sitting behind Zale's desk and he sailed the contract over it and into my lap. He'd already taken the tape from Safir and played it once to satisfy himself it was the same one he'd seen the day before. He stuck it in his attaché case and snapped the locks with an air of finality. He said with a poisoned smile that our business was concluded, for now.

"No," I said, and handed him a dollar bill. I explained that since I was just an innocent in the business world, I'd like a signed receipt for it. "Just in case some legal mumbo jumbo arises about the contract being faithfully and herewith completely executed on and about the time stipulated," I said. "I think I heard something like that on 'LA Law' once."

He took the dollar and sailed me a receipt, looking as superior as a rich father buying off his daughter's low-life boyfriend. I'd actually begun to feel a little guilty about what I was going to do next but that look changed my mind. Now I felt nothing but warm as I opened another drawer and took out the dubbed tape.

"One more thing," I said, as I walked from behind Zale's desk carrying the tape in my left hand and the pistol in my right. I motioned for him to back away from the TV. Keeping the gun pointed at both him and Safir, I shoved the tape into the VCR and turned it on.

Gottus went fish-belly white and his mouth pulled itself into a kind of palsied grimace. Then he turned and gave Safir a look that surely must have turned his testicles into raisins.

"You smirking nickel-and-dime little pimple son of a bitch whore," he said to me. Safir started forward, but I leveled the gun at Gottus's chest and he stopped Safir in midmotion with an Arabic phrase.

"You really thought I was going to take my chances along with the money, didn't you?" I asked. "Don't be too hard on Safir. We wore him down with hillbilly behavior."

Gottus stared at me for a long time but that taking the measure stuff is for athletics, and when he saw I wasn't going to play he spoke: "This isn't going to make any difference for you."

"I can arrange for it to get into the right hands if I go down," I said.

"I'll take my chances."

"Not with Maryland industry you won't, not with Zale."

"No," he said with another bacterial grin. "But you're different. Them I'll leave alone in the interest of business judgment. But you . . . I'll take the gamble."

There wasn't much to say after that. He and Safir left. I got into my suit. Then I broke down an M-16 and stuffed it into the large camera bag along with three hundred rounds. As the eminent philosopher Yogi Berra said, déja-vu, all over again.

34

It was going to rain, hard. I could see an iron-gray bomber formation of clouds moving in low over the tidal basin to the southeast. I could also see two Arabs in a Mercedes parked across the street. Herds of haircuts wearing suits like mine and mooing legalspeak trailed by the window where I was standing. I could see their reflections in the glass. Several of them glanced furtively at me like I'd lost my corner office or missed the scheduled maintenance on my BMW. I wondered what was wrong then realized I was the only one standing still. Their looks reminded me that I was carrying two weapons and enough ammunition for a squad of infantry. I had to move before some retired cop on the security team recognized the weight in my camera bag.

The problem was I seemed to be rooted to the floor. Why couldn't I move? I had the suit, the guns, the money was in safe hands and none of the Arabs knew who I was. No one except Safir. He had had almost a half hour to memorize my face. That might be enough, even for him.

Once I walked out of the building there was no way back. I couldn't get through the metal detectors with the guns and I wasn't about to leave the guns. How would Safir have described me? Medium short, boxerly build, sandy hair, blue eyes and a mustache. I looked around the hallway and saw two or three people who fit that description but they weren't leaving the building.

I had to make maybe the biggest choice since I'd decided to volunteer for the LRRPs. I could either walk out of the building and hope I caught a cab before the Arabs caught me, or I could be sneaky and attack first. Sneaky had worked well so far. I decided to stick with it and attack.

It was 9:50. I had ten minutes to get back to Zale's office before he adjourned his meeting. When I got there I retrieved the bug from under his desk and its other half from the adjoining office. I also took one of the Nixon masks. It was one of those latex molded ones you see people wearing at ballgames when they think they're on TV. Nixon is a perennial, besides as he's said so often, he's a survivor. I hoped some of his mojo would transfer to me.

When I got back to the door the Arabs were still there. They were drinking coffee. People who don't drink alcohol consume more coffee than soap opera doctors. Like most speed freaks, the guys in the Mercedes would be alert but have the psychotically short attention span of birds. I suspected that after several hours in the Mercedes their eyes would be doing the eagle jerk in time to whatever was on the radio. I hoped they'd do two or three takes before they realized that one of the people exiting the building was Richard Nixon.

Actually, I hoped they'd never heard of Richard Nixon and think I was just one more rubber-faced politician with a big nose. But it really didn't matter what they thought. All I needed was a few seconds of indecision, and something to cover my head. A hat would be perfect but no one wears hats anymore. Hats went wherever romance went. Umbrellas though are forever. I roamed the halls for a few minutes, glad for the threat of rain. Then I saw a young blond guy with a recent haircut, loafers, and a tan poplin suit, a summer intern; junior year in college, small salary, could use a little cash. I walked up to him and offered fifty dollars for the black umbrella he was carrying. When he held out for a hundred I knew why he'd gotten his internship. I paid it gladly and told him he was a credit to the free enterprise system.

Back at the window I checked the Arabs drinking their coffee. There's one bit of common wisdom that applies to both coffee and alcohol; you don't buy it, you rent it. I knew that soon nature would be calling to them louder than duty. Down the street, I spotted a bar and grill. That had to be the place they were getting the coffee and the place they'd have to go to return it. They couldn't both go at once. Someone had to stay behind to watch for me. That's when tricky Dick would try for just one more comeback.

In ten minutes the one on the passenger side got out and headed for the bar. After he'd gone a block I went to the door. Patting the Beretta in the pocket of my suit jacket, I waited a few seconds until a cluster of people were leaving and put on the mask. As I stepped outside, I popped open the umbrella. Ignoring people's subtly incredulous looks, I slanted down the steps toward the rear of the Mercedes. I had the umbrella angled toward the driver so what he saw was mostly umbrella and nose. It wasn't raining, so I kept looking up and hunching my shoulders as if I'd felt the first few drops. When I got to the curb I sprinted in front of an approaching limo, stopped to let a truck go by, then ran to a spot about thirty feet past the Mercedes.

I don't know how I made it without breathing. I was trying, but I couldn't get my chest to move. I hadn't been able to even shoot a glance at the driver of the car. For all I knew he was following me over the sights of a silenced Uzi and wondering why I wanted to die in a Halloween costume. I'd never made a parachute jump but knew without a doubt that I was in free-fall; just stepped off into space, trusting the fold of my chute, no more safety checks, no last looks, just faith against space.

The first few drops of rain were coming in on mean little wind shears, hints of a nasty beyond that caused everyone to look skyward. I raised the umbrella enough to peek through the back window of the Mercedes. The driver checked the sky like everyone else then resumed his swivel scan of the opposite sidewalk. He must have seen me cross but when you're looking for the particular you overlook the general.

The wind was gusting harder now, the rain flying horizontally. I covered the thirty feet to the car in five steps, threw the umbrella away, took out the pistol and opened the passenger door. He was holding an Uzi in his lap but before he had a chance to move I ducked and shoved my arm into the car so the pistol was an inch from the side of his head.

"Not one move," I screamed above the truck-rumble thunder rolling up from the river. "One and you're dead." I picked the Uzi off his lap and tossed it into the back seat, then swung my camera bag onto the floor of the passenger side. Keeping the gun next to his ear, I eased in beside him and closed the door to a sudden quiet. The wind and thunder were now just noises from a neighbor's television. His eyes widened when he saw the Nixon mask, but he knew who it was.

"Boy!" I said. "You do get all the shit details, don't you?"

"Fook you, sonabeetch," he said, with a little overtone of hysteria.

"Drive, Safir," I said.

He just looked at me blankly. I thought maybe the Nixon mask was disorienting him so I whipped it off and whacked him on the jaw with a quick left jab. He started across the seat but stopped when his forehead ran into the barrel of the pistol.

"I've got no time," I warned him. "Drive or I'll kill you and drive myself." He gritted his teeth and turned back to the wheel.

I made sure he didn't drive past the other Mercedes I knew would be parked around the corner. After we'd gone six blocks, I had Safir turn into the parking lot of a Sheraton. The lot was full of limos and Lincolns, which might cover us long enough for a phone call. Telling Safir to put his hands on the wheel and keep them there, or I'd shoot him, I took the bug out of the camera bag and stuck it onto the phone attached to the car's console. Safir had been grooving on a little music while waiting to kill me. I took the tape that was sticking out of the deck and stuck it in the phone tap's recorder. Then I told Safir to call Gottus.

"I know he's somewhere waiting for the good news," I said. "Call and give it to him. Tell him you've got me. Ask him what to do next."

Safir didn't want to do it. In fact he refused to do it. I looked around the parking lot. We were forty yards from the motel and the storm was spooling up like a 747, the wind winding into a howl, lightning cracking level with the horizon, taking flash pictures of the black wings exploding toward us in thunder bursts.

"Call," I told him.

"Fook you, no!" he sneered.

"You'll call."

"No, you need." He pointed toward himself.

I covered my ears with the bug's headphones. "You need," I said, placing the muzzle of the gun against his knee. I lowered the muzzle a fraction and fired. The bullet scorched the underside of his knee but the only damage it did was to his resolve.

"I call," he screamed, "I call." I told him to be sure he used Gottus's name. When he reached for the phone his hand was shaking. He was sweating like an Alabama well digger, filling the car with a bearish stink of armpits, fear, and hate. He was wired as tight as he could get but he made the call. I pressed record on the bug and Gottus' voice crackled through my headphones. He barely had time to say hello before Safir was screaming in his ear.

"Meester Gottus, Meester Gottus. We have him. Yes we have him. What do we do? Instructions please."

Gottus turned away from the phone and said something I couldn't hear. Then he said, "Kill him of course, as per my instructions, in whatever slow ways your ancient culture may have invented over the years. Just make sure it's unpleasant. I want a full report."

That's when Safir snapped. He shrieked a long stream in his native language. The only words I was able to pick out were Nixon and Rodman. He mentioned Rodman three times and Nixon once. He was looking at me as defiantly as a saint at the stake, expecting to be shot at any second. But I already had what I wanted. When he wound down I took the phone out of his hand and told Gottus it was all true. "You're quite a sucker for these tapes, aren't you?" I asked him, and hung up.

Now that I had Gottus on tape ordering my death I didn't need Safir. I told him to get out but he began blubbering about what Gottus would do to him for screwing up so royally.

"Can't go back," he wailed. "Can't go back. You fook me up too bad with Gottus. I'm dead man I go back, you peeg focker!"

There was no reason for me to feel sorry for Safir, but I gave him some advice anyway. "Go to the American Embassy and ask for asylum," I told him. "Make a deal for what you know about Gottus." Then I fired another shot under his leg and told him to get out.

"No more warning shots. No more time," I said and he believed me. I saw him slouching through the rain toward the Sheraton as I wheeled the Mercedes in a circle and headed for the exit.

I figured Gottus' first move after my phone call would be to contact the other cars. I now had him on two forms of tape committing two forms of crime. If he wanted to keep on being Lawrence of Arabia's evil twin he had to get me before I left town. By now his boys would be cruising the area looking for beige. I didn't see a sign on the Sheraton advertising car rentals and probably didn't have the time anyway. I was stuck with the car I had until I could get north of the Capitol Beltway.

My plan was to double back onto Constitution Avenue, cross the Roosevelt Bridge, and head north on the Washington parkway until I hit the beltway. Then it would be easy to jog east until I got to Route 95. A half hour later I'd be back in Baltimore, anonymous and wealthy. First though, I had to get to the bridge. I pulled over long enough to assemble the M-16. After it was locked and loaded I cruised west, obeying all the traffic laws I could remember.

The storm was now fully rabid. It was dark as dusk outside the car and so much water was flogging the windshield that I felt like I was driving a submarine. White comets of ball lightning turned the Potomac into liquid neon as the bridge came into view. Just as I was congratulating myself on how hard it would be to spot me in this kind of weather, I noticed that mine was one of a very few cars on the move. Everyone was pulled to the side waiting it out except for me, a slow-crawling bus, and a big beige Mercedes coming toward me from the opposite direction. I tried to stare straight ahead as we passed but I could tell by the bustle in the car and the extended middle fingers that they saw me.

The street we were on had a median strip and I knew they

couldn't take a chance on attracting the cops by crossing it. They had to speed on a few blocks before they could turn around, enough time for me to gun the car onto the approach to the bridge. I crossed it doing sixty-five into the rain, barely able to see the hood of my car, guided only by the center line, but knowing I'd rather die by my hand than theirs.

There was still nothing in my rear view mirror as I surfed the car off the bridge and onto the Washington parkway. I punched it up to eighty-five, heading north along the Potomac, Georgetown on the other side, safety ahead. I was grateful for the lightning striking the river because it allowed me an intermittent look at the road. I pulled the car onto the center line and stayed there. The big Mercedes would have glided up to a hundred in a whisper but at that speed I'd have sailed it out over the side and into the ozone haze of the water. I was even considering throttling back to seventy when I saw the lights in my rearview mirror, two stalking cat eyes blinking in and out of the rain and the curves, and gaining. It had to be either them or the cops. No one else would push ninety through a vertical flood.

The thing that makes a parkway a parkway is the median strip of grass or shrubs. This one was no different. I saw a good curve through a flash of lightning and swung into the left lane. When I was out of sight around the curve I picked the most level spot I could see and fishtailed across the grass and into the southbound lanes. My headlights picked out a blue painted trash barrel a half mile ahead. It was sitting off the road in what had to be a rest area. When I came even with it I whipped the car into the gravel turnaround and jammed on the brakes, slamming a picnic table into the trash barrel like it had been whipped by the tail of a giant alligator. I grabbed the M-16, got out of the car and knelt behind the fender, sighting on the road.

The car was only a flash of beige blurring the darkness for a second but I knew it was them, only one car, maybe four men. If they drove into the picnic area I'd go on full automatic and maybe get them all in a bunch. If they came on foot it would be tough. They'd spread out. I hoped I could hold them off until the storm lessened and the parkway got too busy to hold a war.

I waited. The rain in my eyes made it hard to see. My clothes had already turned into wet slime against my skin. The wind had to be gusting to forty. It iced me each time, leaving me shivering too much to be sure of an accurate shot. I flipped the switch on the rifle's grip to automatic and waited, then waited some more. Nothing. I saw a lot of movement in the trees on the bank above my head but held fire because it was rhythmic, in time with the wind. Men can't quite move with the wind unless they practice and I didn't think these guys spent much time with nature. I waited twenty minutes before I made a darting run to a picnic table and looked from behind it around the curve. Still nothing. I'd seen enough of their work to know they weren't this subtle. They were gone. They'd been pushing ninety in the rain and had missed me.

I must have had a near-death experience then, because I seemed to see myself from above, standing there alone, a half-drowned swamp creature slumped along the parkway holding an assault rifle. I laughed out loud. If there'd been any food I'd have had a picnic in the rain.

35

I was slapped out of my interlude of goofy euphoria by the realization that I was driving a stolen car. If his men couldn't find
me, Gottus could call on the help of the DC cops. Once I was
in custody he could send someone downtown to wait until I made
bail, follow me, and presto, it would be carving time at the meat
market. Of course I could tell the whole story to the police, but
they prefered a felon in hand to a complicated story any day.

I had to separate myself from the car, but how? Start walking
along the road carrying a bag full of weapons? Sure . . . why not
just wear a sign saying arrest me? Call Daz? Then wait by the car
for two and a half hours? Take the chance that a passing cop
wouldn't spot my license number? Or I could drive the car back
into town, ditch it, and call Daz from the safety of a motel room.
No contest. The Mercedes was a target and it's harder to hit a
moving target. I'd go back to town, but which way?

As an arrow of lightning cracked along the river, I was struck
just as suddenly by a bolt of genius. If Gottus and the cops were
hunting me where was the last place they'd look? I was directly
across the river from Potomac Palisades. If I drove about three

miles back toward DC, crossed the Key Bridge and went up Wisconsin Avenue, I'd come to Rock Creek Park, and Gottus' house. It couldn't be more than ten miles through what was still a blinding rain. No traffic and most of the cops would be looking for the shelter of the nearest 7-Eleven. I wouldn't even chance a motel. I'd just phone Daz before leaving the car somewhere near Gottus', then head into the park until he got there. I liked it. It was sneaky.

Most of the lightning was moving north toward Baltimore as I slipped the Mercedes in along the curb and cut the lights. It was still raining though and the light was more like dawn than noon. I was about two blocks south of the entrance to Gottus' cul-de-sac.

Daz wasn't in his office so I dialed his home number and left a message on the machine. He had promised to access it by beeper every two hours so I knew it wouldn't be long before he was screaming down the parkway in the fastest thing he owned. I gave the time and a location, then stepped out into a rain that was now more aerosol than waterfall. A smoky fog powdered up as I worked my way through the dripping trees toward the place I'd parked during my first visit to Gottus'. I was carrying the camera bag in one hand and the M-16 in the other, stopping every thirty yards to listen for sounds between the raindrops.

When I reached the spot where I'd gouged the guard's eye I stopped to gloat a little but something dropped me like a stone. I stared at the house, sniffing the damp like a dog, scenting a flaw. I was standing in a vacuum. Gottus' black limo stood alone in a corner of the parking lot. One light burned in a front corner room of the house. Except for that, nothing. Sure, most of Gottus' Arabs would still be out looking for me but when you're being hunted you can feel it. Maybe it's a slight pressure on your heart from the hunter's step. Maybe hate travels through space like sound waves. Whatever it is, once you're used to it you can feel it. It's something the monkey man knows. I wasn't being hunted, not from that house. I'd overlooked something and if I went further without knowing what, someone was going to get hurt, maybe someone who shouldn't.

I stood in the wet leaf rot and leaned against a tree, going back over the last few hours. I stopped when I recalled Safir's Arabic harangue to Gottus. He'd mentioned Rodman three times in connection with Nixon/me. Maybe logical connections had followed conversational ones. Gottus must have asked himself how I could grab Safir, even know he was there, know all the other things I knew, without some inside help, without Rodman's help.

I jumped to my feet, sure as death that Gottus had sent his men to Rodman's. The men would ask who I was. The Rodmans wouldn't know. They'd be asked again, painfully . . . Rodman . . . and Elise. Before I finished the thought I was running up the hill toward the car, the M-16 feeling more familiar with each step.

36

I ran sweating and clanking . . . wet lungs and burning thighs, gun in hand, toward something I wanted to escape. The faster I ran the less I wanted to get there. When I reached the car I was going to have to make a decision. I had the money. I had the business. I was going to have Arla. I was going to be the King Hell Kingfish, sitting late into the night on my back porch and laughing at the morning. Arla at my side, money in the bank. I didn't have to go.

Rodman knew what he was getting into, but they'd torture Elise too and she didn't. She thought it was about sex. Wait till she found out it was about money and what a difference that made. I chilled as I pictured her sliced and diced, that wondrous body turned to meat. But it was her eyes I knew I'd see on my porch, turning soulless as glass under the pain and thinking of me. At the last she'd know I was the one who'd brought on the hell— me on my porch with my money. She'd grab for me like she was drowning and take part of me down with her.

By the time I got to the car there was no decision left to be made. Stolen car or not, I was going. The first thing to do was call Daz and tell him to meet me at Rodman's instead of Gottus'. As I reached for the phone, a pair of headlight beams hit the dash ahead of my hands. Nothing to do but hold the phone and pretend I was talking. The beams were still on me. Only the cops do that. I couldn't look around, couldn't think of a story, almost reached for the gun.

"Goddamn, pard, if you ain't a hard man to catch." I heard a familiar drawl outside my window. "What'samatter there, ya look like you're havin' a little heart attack or somethin'."

"What the hell are you doing here?" I asked when I was able to unclench my jaw.

"Well," said Samski, taking an unlit Marlboro from behind his ear. "I seen all them Mercedes and started thinkin' what a godawful chore it'd be deliverin' that money to your wife. Christ, I never was no good at shit like that. So I put the money in a locker at the bus station an' come back. I was cruisin' by when I seen you gettin' in with that A-rab. I was goin' the wrong way so I lost you. Picked you up again when you was headin' back down Consti- tution. Lost you again cause I went the wrong way at the end of the damned bridge, seen them A-rabs bustin' down the parkway so I followed 'em until they pulled over an' stopped. Figured they lost you so I turned around. Passed you as you was goin' over that other bridge, got on the bridge, lost you in the park, found you here. I don't think I'd be wantin' ta drive that car much more if I was you."

"You got any whiskey on you?" I asked.

"Dr. Beam," he said, pulling a pint from his pocket. I took a long hit and he did the same. Then I said all he had to do was get me to Rodman's. The rest was my problem.

"How do you know they went to Rodman's?" he asked.

"Hell," I said, "think back. Didn't you ever just know?"

"Maybe, but I wasn't never sure enough ta say nothin'."

I insisted that he didn't have to go.

"What the hell you talkin' about?" he said. "I'm takin' one twenty-two five of the money ain't I? You think you're the only one believes in ghosts?" He took another long hit of the Beam and offered it to me. "Last chance," he said. "The old Trans Am is gonna be punchin' a hunnert an' we don't want no whiskey on board if the cops stop us."

"You sure?" I asked.

"Pard," he said, battening down his John Deere hat. "I'm ready fer Freddy."

When we'd driven hard enough to catch up with the rain we got to the Rodmans'. I was moving through a solid wall of it as I hunched my way along the muddy bank of the creek bed. The water was thigh high from all the rain and I was having trouble keeping my balance. I squatted to chest level and went into a slow duck walk, holding the M-16 just above the surface. I'd taped two clips together bottom to bottom so I could just drop one out and flip it over to reload. I had two more in the chest pockets of the hunting vest Daz had brought for me. Ninety-six rounds in all, more than enough if I remembered the technique, short bursts of three and six, don't just hope, aim.

When I phoned Daz to change the message, I asked him to bring bush clothes, the M-79, and what was left of its ammo. But when we pulled into the church lot in back of Rodman's property, Daz got out of his Bronco wearing camouflage fatigues, a black leather beret, and carrying a banana-clipped AK-47.

"What are you gonna do with that?" I asked him.

"Make a fuckin' lamp out of it," he said. "What do you think I'm gonna do with it?"

I told him he wasn't making any money on the deal. He'd already done enough.

"The deal was I'm backup," he said. "And that's all I am. You're on the point."

When I told him again I didn't expect it from him, he locked home an AK round and said, "Just think of me as a branch of the small business administration helping a poor white boy get his piece of the American dream. Now let's cut the sentiment and get on with it, bro."

So we did. Samski took the M-79 and the sawed-off shotgun he had in the trunk. The seventy-nine had one shotgun round and one white phosphorus left. He put those in his jacket pocket and slung the M-79 over his back. If Gottus had his men there they'd be watching the back of the property since that's where I had surprised Safir. We'd have to flank them, so we climbed in the Bronco and drove up Butler Road to where it intersected the left side of Rodman's property. They dropped me off low so I could go down the creek bed, closest to the house. They were coming in higher up, Samski in the middle, Daz at the top. The idea was for me to go for the house while they cleaned out the area to my rear.

The creek formed the border between house and woods. To my right, above the bank, was the spot where Safir had been stationed when I grabbed him. Through some clump birch to my left was the house. I was almost directly in line with the pool where I'd spotted Elise and the pool boy. French doors faced a patio by the pool. Above the doors was a terrace off an upstairs room. That's where the guard was posted. I slipped neck deep into the water. The rain was coming from behind me, toward the house, into his eyes. He hunched his shoulders as a blast of firehose wind off the creek hit him in the face. He turned away and I flattened against the bank, easing an eye over the edge to check the woods to my right. Nothing. Where were they? Probably on the leeward side of the trees, maybe with their backs to the wind and me. I could wait until I spotted them but Elise couldn't. I thought of her and what a strange kind of innocence it must take to bend over for strangers, a certain kindness too. Other things yes, but kindness. Maybe the other things should go but I wanted the kindness to stay.

Sometimes you don't know you've burned your bridges until you feel the flames on your back. Then there's no way out but forward. In the house were several proven killers and the presence of the guard erased any doubts I had about what they were doing. Elise had become my responsibility. Now there was no way but the old way. We were outnumbered and outpositioned. Unless we went for the throat they'd turn her into a human husk and then kill us when we knocked to politely ask why. The last bridge was burning.

I ducked below the bank and estimated the range to the top of the terrace . . . about seventy-five yards. An easy shot but a long run afterward. I eased over to a spot that put me at an acute angle to the corner of the terrace, checked the woods again, then crawled out and flattened myself into the scrub brush growing between the trees. I crawled forward with each gust of wind, its movement covering mine. The guard had an Uzi. With its stubby shape it was good for close-in spray jobs but about as accurate as a handful of gravel. I felt a familiar spot start to burn in the back of my head. The guard was out of luck. The ones in the woods were another story. I had to move away from them as fast as possible.

I moved forward another twenty-five yards to the edge of the birch, and decided on full automatic, a three-shot burst. The wind was gusting to about thirty and I didn't trust a single shot to stay true. Miles had told me the M-16 was zeroed at a hundred yards. At fifty the round would be rising fast, so drop the sight to the crotch, aim a little to the left to allow for the up-right movement of full auto, and let the blue moon fall. . . . For me, it had always taken place in a spot of blue moonlight. The moon would fall on me and the ones in my sights like we'd all taken a drug that joined us together; slow blue junkies in a floating alley where we were all dead but only certain of us would be gone. It's a love from hell. You have to empathize with the target, anticipate his still points, then . . .

Two of the shots hit him dead chest, whipping him back against the stucco wall in a shower of red. As I ran for the wall adjacent to the French doors, my mind a scream, I hoped the wind and what they were doing inside had distracted them. I hit the wall beside the doors and flattened myself against it, looking briefly toward the woods. When I didn't see anything I looked through the doors, then stepped inside. I was alone in the room where I'd talked to Elise. In two jumps I was in the broad center hall.

There was no one there. They hadn't heard the shots, probably because of her screams. No, not screams, gut-launched moans out of a body so deep in pain it was eating itself alive, biting its tongue so it could strangle on the blood and escape, hating itself for staying alive. I could see the end of the pool table through the door, Elise's feet had cords tied around each ankle, a sweating Arab held each cord, pulling. I could see a wire trailing between the ankles to a transformer like the one on a kid's electric train. Another one of them was working the transformer, twisting a switch, programming the moans.

I stepped across the hall and got the three of them with two bursts of three. Leaping through their flying bone into the room, I saw one look up from Elise's head and cut him in half with a six burst. Rodman was in the far corner, blond and slim. The only reason I hadn't shot him was that he was crouched and still. But he wasn't bound. His tie wasn't even loose. His mouth moved but nothing came out.

Through the French doors I could see two men coming from about fifty yards away. I couldn't use the pool table as cover because Elise was on it, naked, with a copper prod shoved farther up in her than any man could go. The prod was attached to the transformer wire. She was babbling wildly but didn't seem able to move. I picked up one of the Uzis, locked a round, and gave it to Rodman. "They're coming," I told him. "Use this just like a hose."

The French doors crashed open and I sprayed six shots into the living room, sending one diving for a corner and the other one back out the doors. It was a standoff. Him behind his wall, me behind mine. I poked the rifle around my corner and let go the rest of my clip at the living room floor, hoping to catch him with a ricochet. No luck. I was loading a new clip when I noticed Rodman aiming the Uzi—at me. Jesus, his tie hadn't even been loose.

"You son of a bitch," he said. "Mrs. Downey told me about you." That was it. I was dead. My last thoughts were of my daughters. Shana was frail, Kathleen stubborn. They both needed me. That was just before Rodman's tie came loose at last—along with his head. The window behind him blew out as he turned into a floor lamp with no shade.

"Good Christ," Samski said as he stepped through the window with the M-79. "Don't this thing just clean house?"

Samski grimaced when he saw Elise and pumped a shell into his Remington. "Sorry," he said. "We was just movin' on 'em when they heard your shots and ran down the hill. We had ta chase 'em. The black dude got one at a hunnert yards, started in back of the bastard an' just climbed that clip right up his back."

The one across the hall heard Samski and was out the French doors before Daz stepped through, almost catching a gale of automatic fire. Daz hit the floor along with Samski and me, as a repeat blast slammed into the wall above the pool table. "Stay down," I screamed to Elise, hoping she could understand me.

"Down the front drive," yelled Daz from the other room. I saw his legs move as he scuttled to a spot below his window. He chanced a look and then ducked again as another volley exploded a chandelier above his head.

"See anything?" I asked.

"Yeah, they're behind some kinda goddamn drainage culvert, about seventy-five yards away." He shouted the last through a dust storm caused by bullets plowing the old plaster walls above our heads.

"Cheerist," said Samski, "they got us up a tree."

I heard Daz crack off a burst from his AK-47 and then agree with Samski. "He's right. If they don't get us they'll take off when the neighbors call the cops, and we'll hit the papers as a goddamn drug cartel."

Like the ex-sergeant he was Daz had identified our situation in seconds. We were pinned down in a constant shower of plaster, glass, and screaming metal. By now someone had surely heard the noise and called the police. Soon the whirling blue lights would be there to take us away. There was no way to explain to the cops or anyone else. By morning Arla and the girls would be seeing me shoved into some courtroom with a coat over my head.

"Shit fire," wailed Samski as a rack of pool cues shattered into splinters over his head. "If this was Nam we could at least call in the fuckin' artillery."

"Walt," I said to him, "slide me over the M-seventy-nine."

I took the seventy-nine from Samski, loaded the last white phosphorus round, crawled to the front door, reached up, and opened it a crack. I could just make out the two of them, firing at their convenience, rifles propped on top of a concrete pipe imbedded in one of the lawn's rolling swales. Daz was right about the distance. I shut the door and motioned for Samski to crawl over. When he got there we waited for a break in their fire and when it came he swung open the door. I rose to one knee in the doorway, arched the 79 just slightly, and let go.

"Son of a mule-fuckin donkey bitch," said Samski as the two men disappeared in a molten white ball. "You ain't forgot much, have ya?"

"Let's take her and disappear," Daz said, gently removing the prod from Elise. We wrapped her in a blanket and carried her easy, as easy as we had others, in other times. But this time it felt good. This one we brought back alive.

37

The next time I saw Gottus was in his house and he was sweating.
We'd taken Elise to Daz's place where Li Anh put her in a silk-
screened flowered bedroom and told us to get out. We were swamp
things covered with a mortar of mud and blood. Elise was in no
shape to tell the good guys from the bad. Li Anh gave her a sponge
bath, brushed her hair, burned incense, and did some chanting.
I took a shower and headed for Gottus' with only the Beretta for
company. We'd killed the men he'd sent to Rodman's, and Safir
was probably in the basement of the state department being questioned by guys in identical suits. How many shooters could Gottus
have left?

Only one as it turned out. Cruising by in Daz's Lincoln, I saw
him standing by the door. I suspected he might be the only one
but didn't know for sure so I went to the nearest Domino's Pizza
and bought a large plain. While I was waiting I looked through
the yellow pages for a costume place. Then I stole one of the
Domino's signs from a car outside and stuck it on my roof. At the
costume place I rented a clown suit, some balloons, and a clown
mask.

When I got out of my car wearing the clown suit and mask the bodyguard looked at me like I was a fool. At the door he sneeringly explained that there were no children at that address and no one had ordered the special birthday pizza. I told him it was a very special pizza and opened the box to prove it. He was experienced enough to know that the cheese sticking to the Beretta's grip wouldn't affect its operation. So after we checked the house for any friends of his, he took me to Gottus, who was pacing the floor of a library big enough to be an oil company's board room. A fax machine was parked in the far corner. Gottus had his shirtsleeves rolled to the elbow and there were half moons of sweat visible under the arms.

"Nice place," I said.

When he saw who was inside the clown suit his back stiffened like he'd been shot with an arrow. I showed him the gun, but he took a deep breath and did his best to stare me into a heart attack. "Great look," I told him. "I wouldn't try it in job interviews though. Maybe sort of a controlled eager beaverness kind of thing. If that doesn't work you can always try a little groveling."

Gottus' suave smile was like lipstick on a corpse. "Oh, there will be some groveling done," he said. "I can promise you that." He gave me the hard stare again.

"I guess you haven't heard the bad news."

"Oh, that." He waved his hand airily. "Employees are easy to find. My guess is that a new batch will be arriving any day, and a new batch after that, for as long as is needed."

"That's not the bad news I'm talking about."

He kept staring but he knew what I meant. His face started to sweat, big oily drops oozing down the sleek jowls onto his shirt collar. "Sit down," I said to the bodyguard, pointing him toward a conference table in the middle of the room. "There's something your boss hasn't told you." The guard did what I said.

"You look a little flushed," I said to Gottus. "Why don't you have a seat too? Why don't we all have a seat?"

He loosened his rep tie and clasped his hands on the table. Then he unclasped them and spread the palms, clenched them again when he noticed they were moist. "Is there some point to this?" he asked. "Or are you just trying to get arrested for assault and unlawful imprisonment?"

"Yes, I'd like to ask you a question. I think I already know the answer but I want to make sure your man knows it too." I nodded toward the Arab. "See, the thing is, I started wondering why you went so berserk over a videotape that wasn't going to be released, not to mention that audio tape of you telling Safir to kill me." A light began to come on in the bodyguard's eyes as one began to go out in Gottus'.

"Let me give you the answer to the question," I said. "Then we can decide if I'm going to shoot anyone." The Arab remained motionless, waiting. I spoke to him but looked at Gottus. "See, I don't think you all were supposed to kill anyone. I think your job was to get Pecosa into the defense industry so you could play around with certain projects. When a leak developed, your boss here knew his bosses would make him into the bad guy if anything went public. That is when Gottus lost it and started burning down the house because the fireplace didn't work."

The light in the Arab's eyes came all the way on and he turned toward Gottus, who got quickly to his feet and backed away. Taking out a handkerchief, he wiped his face, twisted the cloth into a rope, untwisted, wiped his face again, pointed at me. "Call the police," he said to the bodyguard. "I told you to call the police. This man is the cause of all our problems. I've been in charge, I am in charge, and I will remain in charge. We now have a chance to eliminate him legally. I'm telling you he won't shoot anyone in this house."

It was the same brass balls in velvet attitude Gottus had used against the Watergate committee years before. It slowed the guard's already snaillike brain to a stop and he sank back in his chair, thick brows converging into a single skid mark across the blankness of his forehead.

"I've got an idea," I said. "Why don't we just fax a message to your home office and ask them? Any objection to that?" Gottus cast a panicky glance toward the fax machine. A vein in his neck began to pump like it was trying to strangle him. He ran a hand through his hair and wiped the oil on his shirt, puffing it out over his belt. He was changing from a titan to a waiter in a greasy spoon. I pointed the guard toward the fax but before he could get there it began to roll out a page. I pulled it out of the machine and laughed my way through the entire message.

Safir had taken my advice. He'd gone to the state department and traded asylum for everything he knew. The Arabs had good sources. They'd heard what Safir confessed almost as soon as the people at state. Now they were covering their asses. The gist of the message was that Gottus was fired. They'd already canceled his access to their accounts and he had one hour to vacate the house, taking nothing he hadn't brought with him. I handed the message to the bodyguard and laughed some more when I realized it would be Gottus and not me who wound up getting his mail at the bus station. The guard was smiling like a convict who gets to fire the warden. I took the clip out of his gun and gave it back to him. Then I left for the bus station to retrieve my money. I felt so good I let them keep the pizza.

Arla moaned from the center of her chest and snaked an arm over my shoulder and around my neck. In the past forty minutes we'd been bed to floor to bed. Lick to suck to bite. We'd taken every emotion of our time apart and detonated it in an explosion that helixed us into a growling strand of DNA about to discover again that place where God meets science. I rose high with her legs propped on my shoulders and watched myself disappear into a place where the backs of my eyes saw as much as the front. Arla raked me with her nails and lapped my chest with a milk-soft tongue.

It was going to happen better than ever. I'd felt it building since I walked in the door and slapped the briefcase on the table. "Two hundred twenty-seven thousand five hundred dollars," I'd said. "Sixty-five percent of what I made on my case. My new employee, Walter Samski, got a hundred and twenty-two, five."

Arla is one of the last puritans. She thinks you have to earn happiness. That's why she has such good orgasms. It's also why she can be such a pain in the ass.

"Is this honest, Lowell?" she asked me, looking at the money like it might be looking back. "What'd you do, hijack a plane?

Should we run out and hide the parachute? What is this?" She was sputtering but I could see a lustful look coming from behind her eyes. That's when I whipped out the copy of the receipt I'd given Roger Dorn. To cover me with the IRS I'd billed him for services rendered in the amount of $350,000. As a bonus he'd even given me 5 percent of Dynatron. At thirty-two dollars a share that came to $162,000 in stock: $387,500 combined.

"As honest as any other business deal," I said. "Enjoy!"

Oh, she felt compelled to give me some static about how unstable it all was. Where was I going to get my next client? I told her that with $387,500 I only had about five years to find one. She had some more objections about the danger but I said I thought money was always dangerous. That was probably why it felt so good to have it.

Assuring her that this was a once in a lifetime thing, I predicted I'd probably spend the rest of my time following cheating husbands from Dundalk.

"Have confidence in me, other people do," I said, and changed the subject. "Let's argue about whether we're going to the Bahamas or Tahiti on vacation." "Bahamas," she said, and her smile was so bright it gave her a tan.

It was happening now, Arla's third . . . that last tooth-bearing grind of crucified pleasure that goes with the end of her ability to come. She bit me hard on the shoulder as I gave back her three and one of mine in a rush of poetic fluid and brutal growls. We were done but not finished. As we lay latticed together, I thought about Elise.

Daz's doctor had informed us that although there was some trauma there was no lasting damage. We were going to tell the cops she was an old friend of Li Anh's. They'd been out shopping. She'd had a few too many drinks and decided to stay over, had no idea what happened at her house. When I confessed that we'd killed her husband, she told me he'd helped put her on the table.

Elise opened the silk robe, showing me the swell of her breast-top tan. She lifted the ends of her hard nipples and touched my arm with them as if with fingertips. "I don't want what I wanted before," she said. "I want someone to make it better. I want someone who looks at me when we do it, who talks to me when we do it. Like me. Smooth me. You're the only one who ever would have come for me."

She was still in the bedroom wearing a silk robe borrowed from Li Anh, white, with amber brocade that matched her Chivas eyes. She was sitting on the edge of the bed, robe up. I couldn't help but see the birth-white smoothness where her lower lips kissed her thighs. I looked away. She was kind. "I knew who you were," she said. "When you came through the door and shot those . . . men. I knew who you were. I tried to move but I couldn't." Her voice was steady, but two tears rolled down her cheeks. She touched herself delicately on the cheeks with both fingertips, finding unexpected value. "And you'd never even . . . done more than touch me."

I took her breasts and kissed them, then let go. "I'm not your hero," I said. "I want to do it to you until you sweat blood, if you want to know the truth."

"Maybe sometime, but not now."

"Don't look for someone who talks to you when he's fucking you," I said. "Look for someone who talks to you before he fucks you. Then you can be as rough as you want because you know it's just a game." She traced a soft S on my cheek with her palm. Then we both laughed, the first time I'd seen her do that. Two little apostrophes at the corners of her eyes, almost lines.

"How'd you like a job," I asked. She said she'd think about it.

Arla's foot touched the back of my leg. "What's the matter honey?" she said. I ran the length of her inner thigh with my hand . . . remembering it all: Elise, Samski, Daz, bodies, Laos, the killer gleam in my eyes.

"You remember the beginning of the movie *2001*?" I asked her. "When the apes see the monolith and learn to think?"

She rolled onto an elbow and leaned over my face. "Sure," she said. "Why?"

"Remember the look in the eye of the first one with an idea, that look he gets when he knows he can make a weapon out of a bone?"

"Yeah?"

"I've always identified with that monkey. Sometimes I feel just like him, like all the differences are a disguise."

"And?"

"I don't know. It's a little . . . uh . . ."

"Depressing?"

I looked carefully into her sea-green eyes, the eyes that would match the evening color of Bahamian waters, then thought how glad I was that I was going to see that match. "Nah," I said, "it doesn't depress me at all. And that's what depresses me."

She backed away a little then leaned forward again and kissed me. "Lowell," she said, "if I recall correctly that tribe was being attacked by a bunch that was bigger and stronger. Maybe what you ought to do is just be sure which monkey you are."

"Can I take that as an approval of the detective business?"

She didn't answer, only jigsawed her body into mine, blood to bone, curve to curve like river to bank. She began placing small kisses along my neck like raindrops as she spoke. "You're my man," she said, "my main monkey."

She continued to kiss, then I started to kiss back. I didn't ask the question again. I know when to leave well enough alone. And things were well enough, well enough to let the fire die down, well enough to let the tribe make love in the dark.